# A
# JACK
# STEEL
## THRILLER

# STEEL
# ASSASSIN
## BOOK TWO

## GEOFFREY SAIGN

# Books by Geoffrey Saign

## Jack Steel Thrillers

*Steel Trust*

*Steel Force*

*Steel Assassin*

*Steel Justice*

## Alex Sight Thrillers

*Kill Sight*

Interior design by Lazar Kackarovski

Printed in the United States of America
ISBN: 978-1-703411-62-1 (pbk.)

*For Stan...*

> *"An eye for an eye will only make the whole world blind."*

~ Mahatma Gandhi ~
(1869-1948)

# PART 1

OP: AFIA AMEEN

# CHAPTER 1

J ACK STEEL STOOD AT the back of the stage, watching for any movement in the crowd. The lighting over the audience was subdued. However his view was unobstructed.

He wore black jeans and a black collared shirt, invisible to anyone in the auditorium because the floor lights in front of him were aimed forward at the speaker—Afia Ameen.

A petite woman with black hair and delicate features, Afia was dressed in western clothing; a long colorful dress and long-sleeved blouse.

Steel admired her. She was courageous to give public talks. A cleric of the Muslim Brotherhood had issued a fatwa calling for her execution after she had begun talking about how Islamic extremists use Sharia law to brutalize Muslim women and limit their rights.

Afia's own story was one of rape and torture—she had survived acid thrown in her face—and she eventually fled a forced marriage in Iraq. She was a symbol for women oppressed everywhere and had gained a large following.

Since she started speaking publicly there had been several attempts on her life. Tonight her usual security agency had a commitment elsewhere. They had asked Steel months ago to cover today's event with his own protection agency, Greensave.

Afia had been in hiding for a year but decided to risk coming out for this interview. It had been well-publicized. The Muslim cleric that had issued the fatwa said Afia was going to die tonight if she spoke publicly again.

Steel took the threat seriously. He felt proud that his agency was protecting someone like Afia from violent men. Protecting the innocent had always been a cornerstone of his previous military career.

The interviewer was a local female news anchor. She was asking Afia about her views on Islam, and if she believed Sharia law ever honored women as equals.

Steel half-listened as he scanned the crowd.

They had searched the auditorium earlier. And attendees had been forced to pass through metal detectors as they entered. Yet someone could have hidden a weapon inside beforehand with a plan to charge the stage.

The Macky Auditorium at the University of Colorado in Boulder seated two thousand and every seat was filled. Several hundred people were standing. The Thursday night interview was also being broadcast live to millions.

In the middle of Afia's response, a young man in the audience stood up and began shouting, "You are a disgrace to Muslim women and a traitor to Islam! You deserve the fatwa made against you!"

The man kept shouting, amid boos from the crowd.

Steel ignored the gangly-looking student. He worried the young man was a decoy to occupy his security people, while the real attack would come from elsewhere.

Two of his security detail rose from their seats in front of the stage and hurried to the man. They dragged him into the aisle and forced him toward the doors. The man kept shouting. More people in the crowd booed the student on his way out.

Steel whispered into his throat mike, "Stay alert, everyone. A few angry people in here. Harry, check the immediate area."

"Roger that," said Harry.

"On it," said Christie.

Christie and her brother, Harry, were outside with the exit vehicle. It was Christie's first field assignment with Greensave, but Steel was confident of her skill set. And Harry was an ex-Marine and thus capable of handling tough situations.

Steel had personally trained them both to ensure their expertise, using his state-of-the-art military virtual reality program to refine their techniques to the nth degree.

"That was horrible," said the news anchor. "No one deserves such threats for speaking out. Are you alright, Afia?"

Afia spoke calmly. "I have heard this many times before. It is an example of how radical Islam is converting people to their cause. They wish to spread their version of Sharia law everywhere, as they have done in the UK, Germany, France, Sweden, and Austria. The men threaten violence if anyone criticizes them.

"And their women are not free as they are in U.S. Not free to get jobs on their own. And not free to divorce men as easily as men can divorce them. Women face the ongoing threat of violence for disobedience. Beatings, forced marital sex, and child abuse is common."

Stepping to his right, Steel thought he saw movement in the far aisle. He moved closer to the lights for a better vantage point.

Just someone leaving.

As the interview continued Steel looked at his watch. And smiled. He did that often. Random smiling. Christie said it was because he loved her and had everything anyone could want. She was right. He loved his life, loved her, and loved his daughter, Rachel.

When Carol had asked him for a divorce, he didn't think he would ever find someone to love again. But he and Christie had been together for over a year now. She gave his life more meaning, depth, and beauty. They were a better fit than he and Carol had ever been and he couldn't imagine his life without her.

The last year had erased a year of hell before it, as if it had never existed. Sometimes a few faces from the past still haunted his dreams, but he could live with them for now.

He was also hungry. Christie's other two brothers, Dale and Clay, had flown in from Montana to eat dinner with them tonight. Friday and Saturday they all planned to do some hiking together.

As small as Boulder was, Steel couldn't wait to get out of the city and into the mountains. It made him realize how lucky he and Christie were to have a home surrounded by forest. Though Virginia was his home, his heritage was from Louisiana and Cajun creole—Spanish, French, Native American, and Caribbean—which gave him a light olive color skin.

On Sunday Christie's three brothers were leaving. Then he and Christie were taking their first road trip together. Hikes, lounging, sightseeing. He smiled again.

The interview ended and the audience stood, cheering and applauding.

He talked quietly. "Interview is over."

"Exit area secure," said Harry.

"The car's running," said Christie.

Steel scanned the crowd again. "Be ready. Here she comes."

Afia crossed the stage toward the side door to the left.

Walking behind the lights, Steel quickly crossed the back of the stage. Afia didn't want to give anyone the image of her being guarded or scared, and thus didn't want Steel or his crew visible. He understood.

Afia exited the door ahead of him.

Seeing movement, he paused, remaining at the rear of the stage.

A bearded man in his mid-twenties was climbing onto the stage to the right. The man was swift and solid looking , matching Steel's six-two height and one-ninety weight. Security tried to grab his leg and he lashed out. The security man went down.

Steel stiffened when he saw something black in the man's hand. A knife. Maybe a graphite utility knife or hard plastic.

Running across the stage, the man slashed at the news anchor. Crying out, the woman stepped back, her forearm bleeding.

The attacker continued toward the door Afia had exited. The crowd erupted with shouts and yells.

Steel strode past the lights, his Glock 19 up and aimed.

The man didn't notice Steel until he was reaching for the door knob, and then whirled with his knife up.

Steel shot him in the head and the man collapsed.

Swinging open the door, Steel glimpsed another man climbing the stage closer to him. He couldn't take a shot with the crowd as a backdrop. "Two attackers in here, one down," he said.

"Ready here," said Harry.

Intuiting that the main attack would be outside, Steel ran down the hallway. In seconds he burst through the exit door. The warm mid-September air hit his face as he scanned the immediate area.

Their exit SUV was parked twenty feet to his right, parallel to the sidewalk in the curved lot reserved for performers and speakers. Afia was hurrying down the wheelchair ramp alongside the building. The sun was going down. Shadows filled the area past the SUV.

Harry stood beside the open SUV rear door, Glock in hand. Wearing jeans, boots, and a western shirt, he was built like a thirty-year-old linebacker. Six-three, broad-shouldered, and lean.

Steel stopped on the stoop. Footsteps. He whirled.

The second man. Running down the hallway toward him. Black knife again. No gun. Steel raised the Glock but glanced once more at Afia and Harry.

Beyond Harry, a man slipped from the cover of one of the large pine trees on a small section of ground five feet higher than the sidewalk that bordered the lot. Steel tensed as the man ran toward Afia, arm extended, a gun visible in his hand. Harry and a few trees blocked Steel's shot.

"Harry!" yelled Steel. "Get down, Afia!"

Afia gasped and crouched on the ramp. Bullets bit the wall above her head.

Whirling, Harry shot the shooter in the chest and head.

The attacker stumbled forward and fell off the raised ground, landing hard on the pavement bordering the lot. He didn't move.

"Afia!" Harry waved her to the SUV.

Running bent over, Afia ducked into the back seat of the SUV.

Steel slammed the door into the attacker who was almost upon him. Half-dazed, the man still managed to push open the door and step out, swinging his knife backward at Steel.

Sliding behind the door, Steel shot the man in the side of the head, sending him to the pavement.

Three muted rifle shots hit the back window of the SUV, putting divots into the bulletproof glass. That sent chills down Steel's back. Silenced guns. Pros. They had to get out.

"Go, Christie!" he yelled into his mike. "Meet at rendezvous A."

The SUV roared toward the exit.

Turning, Steel aimed his Glock across the street. Fifty feet away a man holding a rifle stood in the middle of a dozen trees. He was already disappearing into the shadows as Steel fired two shots. What puzzled Steel was that the man could have shot Afia earlier if he wanted to. But maybe the ramp door had blocked his line of sight.

He turned and watched the SUV rocket toward the lot exit. No shooter visible in the street. He glanced back across the street. The man with the rifle was gone.

A jarring crash of metal and glass filled his ears. The SUV had been broadsided in the middle of the road by a small, white pickup truck with a cargo bed cover.

Steel jumped off the stoop and ran across the lot.

Tinted windows hid the pickup driver. The truck had a metal pole on its roof, bent lower by a tie-down attached to the front bumper. The pole had shattered the SUV's rear passenger window.

Steel swore. "Harry?"

"We're okay." Harry's voice sounded stressed.

More rifle shots came from the shadows across the street, hitting the front driver's side window of the SUV. Steel's chest tightened over the possibility of Christie dying here.

"Christie!" Stopping, he aimed his Glock at the trees across the street, not seeing a target. The man with the rifle had to be hiding in the shadows. He hesitated to fire blindly in case there were pedestrians beyond the trees. "Christie!"

"I'm good." She sounded calm.

"Stay in the vehicle! Get out of here!" Keeping his gun up and watching the trees, Steel stepped sideways toward the SUV, and froze.

The white pickup had backed up five feet. But a short man wearing a black hood was standing next to Harry's smashed-in window, holding something inside the SUV.

Steel swung around to fire but checked his trigger finger upon hearing the man's voice on their coms; "I have a bomb. If my finger comes off the trigger, we all die. Coms, phones, and guns on the back seat."

Harry's voice burst through Steel's earpiece. "Don't shoot, Jack! Don't come any closer!"

Steel gripped the Glock, glancing back across the street. No shooter. He heard the man with the bomb say, "Get into the back of the pickup, Harry. Now!"

The rear passenger door opened and Harry got out. He walked past the hooded man to the rear of the pickup, where he climbed into the truck's cargo bed. Someone shut the tailgate. In moments the truck took off down the street.

The man at Harry's door had already entered the back seat of the SUV and shut the door.

"Harry!" Panicked that he had been too passive, Steel expected the SUV to take off. He sprinted for the vehicle, while the pickup sped away with Harry.

The white pickup took a right at the far corner, heading north. Expecting the SUV to take off too, Steel was surprised when it didn't move.

Reaching the rear door, he shoved his Glock inside the corner of the broken window, relieved to see Christie and Afia alive. Christie's face was pale as she stared at the back seat. Afia sat rigidly. They both eyed the same thing.

On the seat next to Afia sat the short man, wearing jeans, a black hoodie, and a black face mask. The front of the man's hoodie was unzipped, revealing a vest with two C-4 blocks fitted with detonators. Wires led from the detonators to a hand switch.

The man's thumb kept the switch depressed.

If the man's thumb released the switch, the bomb would go off.

# CHAPTER 2

A PHONE RANG.

Beside the man a burner phone lay among Harry's and Christie's guns, smartphones, earpieces, and throat mikes.

"It's for you." The man with the bomb had a Latino accent and sounded young. The mask hid everything except his eyes and mouth.

Steel reached in and picked it up, answering it. "What do you want?"

"Put the phone on speaker and keep it on speaker."

Steel complied. The caller had a Colombian accent, but he didn't recognize the voice.

"Drop your gun, personal phone, and coms in the back seat, and get in the front. Tell Christie to drive away. If the police stop you before you leave Boulder, my friend detonates the explosives and we kill Harry. Take highway ninety-three south to six west, into the mountains. We're all ready to die if you don't obey."

The caller hung up. The man's accent seemed at odds with Muslim radicals trying to kill Afia. Steel guessed the caller was in his fifties. Possibly the man with the rifle he had spotted across the street.

Wary, Steel set his gun, earpiece, throat mike, and phone on the back seat, and got into the front.

Christie quickly drove away. She glanced at Steel, her hair in disarray like her black pant suit and white blouse. Her green eyes were steady though.

Steel saw the bullet divots in her window. A powerful rifle would have punched through. The shooter had just wanted to scare Christie, keep her attention focused on the window. He wiped sweat from his brow.

Christie brushed back strands of her brown-and-blond streaked hair and lifted her chin to him. He gave her a slight nod.

Sirens could be heard in the distance. Christie stepped on the gas.

Steel twisted to study Afia.

"I'm all right," said Afia. She appeared calm.

"No talking!" said the man in the back seat.

Steel searched for answers but couldn't find any. Too many things didn't fit. The man Harry had shot tried to kill Afia. If these men wanted to kill her, why go to all this bother? Were they handing Afia off to someone for torture or to videotape her beheading? Maybe Harry was collateral to force their cooperation.

Their kidnappers wanted something, otherwise they would have blown up the SUV already. Maybe they wanted to torture him, Christie, and Harry too—to make an example of anyone protecting someone with a fatwa on their head.

Or maybe they just wanted Harry out of the way. The more he thought about it, he began to suspect that these men might not be connected to Afia and the fatwa.

He twisted to face the man in the back seat. "What do you want?"

"Shut up. Speak one more time and I release it!" The man held the switch in his hand a few inches higher.

Few people had the ability to become suicide bombers, but the young man fit the profile. Steel guessed he was in his twenties. Easy to brainwash. And the man's tone held an edge of vehemence

Steel had heard before in people willing to die for causes. He turned around and kept his mouth shut.

He glanced at Christie, regretting bringing her—he had to shove that aside and focus. He was missing something, but when he ran through possible enemies he couldn't find a fit. Trying to think of a way to deal with the man in the backseat proved fruitless too. He had to wait for an opportunity.

Christie dropped her right hand onto the divider between the bucket seats. Steel grasped and squeezed it. She squeezed back several times before releasing him.

While she drove, he ran through every possible scenario he could think of to get free of their situation. There was always a way out of seemingly impossible situations—Kobayashi Maru didn't exist for him. All of his virtual reality training centered on placing himself in impossible situations until he found a solution.

His own personal motto, *Stay calm, assess options, wait for a solution,* guided him when things got ugly.

In a half hour they were on highway six, headed west into the mountains. It was dark and the traffic was light. Christie flicked her gaze to the rearview mirror several times. Steel understood. They were being followed.

The phone rang and he answered.

"Phone on speaker." The Colombian.

Steel complied.

"Park at the next scenic overlook and turn off your headlights. Stay on the phone and roll down all your windows."

Christie powered down all the windows, letting in the cooler air. In a few minutes she rounded a curve and pulled off the road into a scenic overlook.

The small parking area was empty except for two sedans parked at the far end. When Christie cut the headlights, darkness surrounded them. The full moon gave them some light.

A small pickup pulled off behind them.

Steel readied himself. Slowly he worked his right hand to the horizontal belt-sheath built into the back of his belt. It held a Benchmade 3300BK Infidel auto OTF blade. He pulled it out. Transferring it to his left hand, he placed his right hand close to the door handle to be able to open it fast.

He still had to account for the man with the bomb. He didn't have a solution to him. But if the kidnappers planned to kill them here, he resolved to do something.

A man appeared in his side-view mirror, wearing a black hood and holding a sawed-off shotgun aimed at his head. Through the driver's side passenger window he glimpsed another man on Christie's side. Identically dressed and also holding a sawed-off aimed at her.

Both men stood five feet back from the front doors to minimize any chance of attack. Professionals.

"Jack Steel."

Steel glanced over his shoulder at the speaker, whose voice fit the man on the phone. The man's height and general build also fit the rifle shooter in the trees.

"Face forward," the man said roughly.

He did—and considered opening the door and ducking low.

"If the door so much as cracks open, I step back and shoot you."

Steel swallowed. He believed the man.

"Here's the good news, Steel. You're all going to live. All three of you are going to get into the closest sedan parked at the far end. When you reach Idaho Springs, pull off the highway at the first gas station you see. Then open the trunk. There's a phone inside. Have someone pick up Miss Afia. She isn't part of this. I admire her courage. I'll call with instructions. Do as you're told or your brother dies. You do want to see Harry again, don't you, Christie?"

Christie glanced over her shoulder at him, biting her lip as she faced forward. "Yes."

"Call in the police or any law enforcement, and Harry's dead. We're monitoring everything. We so much as see a police car or roadblock on the road and Harry's finished."

Both men backed up from the doors. The man on Steel's side said, "Get out. Leave the burner phone on the car seat. Go to the sedan. Hurry or I won't be so nice."

Steel exited the SUV along with Christie and Afia, keeping his knife hidden behind his leg as he faced the man with the shotgun.

The shotgun had a pistol grip, and the Latino held it stiffly to absorb recoil, sighting on him, both arms up, left leg and arm forward. He knew what he was doing. Maybe ex-military.

Afia and Christie hurried around the rear of the SUV and joined him. Christie carried her small purse.

The younger man with the bomb got out on the other side of the SUV, still holding the switch. He didn't look experienced like the other two men—who were also huskier and taller.

Steel turned to go, but the older man's voice made him pause.

"Steel, one last reminder. You and Christie are on your own. Call in anyone else to help—outside of picking up Miss Afia— and you can say goodbye to Harry and everyone you both love. When we talk, I'll explain that last point in detail. And if you and Christie split up, same result. You'll be watched."

Steel tensed over the threats but said nothing. Wanting to get Afia and Christie away from the men as fast as possible, he strode across the dirt to the sedan. He glanced at the second car parked a little farther away. Empty.

Christie took the driver's seat, he the front passenger seat, while Afia ducked into the back. The keys were in the ignition. In seconds Christie pulled the car onto the highway. They rapidly pulled away from the SUV and armed men.

Steel put his knife away. After a few miles he concluded the sedan didn't have a bomb hidden in it.

"That was strange." Afia sat up and fanned her face with her hand. "But I give thanks that we're all still alive!"

Steel agreed on both counts. "I'm sorry you had to go through that, Afia."

She sat back. "Thank you for protecting me at the auditorium, Jack and Christy. I hope Harry will be all right."

"Glad we were there to help," said Steel.

"Why Harry?" Christie sounded shaken. "Do you know any of those men, Jack?"

"I didn't recognize their voices." Once more he ran through all the contacts and people he knew. The Colombian's accent reminded him of the Serpent Op in Colombia last year.

A Colombian cartel leader had threatened him with retribution. But these men and their orders didn't strike him as originating from a cartel. Other connections to the Serpent Op didn't fit either.

He checked his sideview mirror, but in the dark it would be hard to see if any of the three men were following them. He assumed at least one was.

They drove to I-70 and arrived at Idaho Springs in twenty minutes. Christie pulled into the first gas station. Steel asked her to back the car into the shadowed rear corner of the large lot.

They exited the car, and he told the two women to move away before he checked the undercarriage and engine compartment for any sign of a bomb. Nothing.

After pulling the trunk release, he crouched and carefully opened the trunk. No explosion.

There was a large zippered duffel bag inside, which he opened. He gaped. It was full of weapons. Two Glock 19s, two Sig Sauer P320s, and three SIG MCX Rattlers—rifle-caliber machine guns with optical sights and carry straps. Along with silencers, ammo clips, knives, zip ties, duct tape, two night-vision goggles, binoculars, gloves, and two black face masks.

Ten thousand dollars in weapons and accessories. The Rattlers had folding stocks and were easy to conceal. The guns also told him the Latino had experience with weapons, supporting his earlier guess of ex-military. It made his mouth dry. His first thought was that he had to get Christie out of here.

A phone lay next to the bag. He grabbed it, zipped up the duffel bag, and shut the trunk. Apprehensive, he rejoined Christie and Afia.

"What's in the trunk?" asked Christie.

He gave a slight shake of his head. "The phone and a few other things. I'll show you later."

Christie nodded. "I'll call Clay and Dale. They'll take care of Afia."

He handed the phone to her. "Alright. And maybe your brothers can search for Harry."

"Agreed." She hesitated, staring at the phone.

He understood and took it back. Taking off the back, he examined the interior, then put it back together. "I don't think it's bugged."

"Thanks." She walked away to make the call.

He didn't want to call the police or FBI. Not with Harry in play. And not until he understood the kidnapper's threat to his family. At least Afia would be safe. All of Christie's brothers had military backgrounds.

He turned to Afia. "Can I ask a favor?"

"Anything." She looked up at him, her brown eyes serious.

"I would appreciate it if you just told the police that your head was down the whole time so you don't know where we are. Tell them we're worried and still checking on other concerns so we dropped you off with Christie's brothers. I don't want them chasing us, since that man threatened to kill Harry if the police are brought in."

He shrugged. "It's a lot to ask."

"Hah. You just saved my life! I am happy to do that." She stepped closer. "I worry for you, Jack. Take care."

"Thank you, Afia. I admire your strength."

Her voice lowered. "Violence never solves anything, and revenge only makes things worse. I hope these men can see that soon."

"So do I." He doubted that would happen.

"The mountains are so beautiful, Jack, but this is ugly."

He grimaced. The weapons in the trunk promised things were going to get a lot uglier.

# CHAPTER 3

CHRISTIE RETURNED. "THEY'LL BE here in twenty minutes. I told Clay that Harry was kidnapped and we needed their help to get Afia out of here. I left out the rest of the details. Otherwise Clay would have questioned me for a half hour."

"Good." Steel remembered the first conversation he had with Clay, her oldest brother, nearly a year ago. A week after he and Christie had survived a harrowing Op in Hawaii, Clay had asked him if he could keep his sister safe.

At that time Christie wasn't going with him on Greensave field assignments. She was just doing the planning. He had answered Clay by saying whatever Christie did, it was her choice. But Clay's words had always nagged at him.

It was a half hour before a blue rental car pulled up alongside their car.

Dale and Clay appeared as solidly built as Harry. Dale was in his late twenties and shorter, Clay in his late forties with a moustache. Both had short hair and wore jeans, denim jackets, and boots. Clay wore a cowboy hat.

Steel liked both of them. Ex-Army. Dependable. Solid. He had visited their homes in Montana and watched some of the winter Korean Olympics with them. They had been welcoming to him, but now they looked serious as they gave Christie a big hug and shook his hand firmly.

"Let's go, Afia." Clay motioned to their car.

Afia hugged Christie, whispering, "I hope you get your brother back."

"Thank you, Afia." Christie held her tightly.

Afia grabbed Steel next. "Thank you for protecting me."

He pulled back. "Anytime."

Once Afia was in the car, Clay shut the door and stepped up to them. His voice was terse, his face drawn. "Who has Harry?"

"Yeah, what gives?" asked Dale.

"We don't know," said Christie. "Harry is in the back bed of a small white pickup truck with a cargo bed cover. Most likely Latinos are driving it."

"Hell, who would do something like that?" Dale frowned.

Clay was silent, staring at Steel.

Steel looked each of them in the eye. "The man in charge is Colombian. I recognized his accent, but I don't know who he is. We're being watched. If we call in the police or any law enforcement they said they'll kill Harry."

Clay stuck his hands in his pockets. "Do you believe them?"

"One of their men held a bomb in our SUV and was ready to die if we didn't do what we were told." Steel waited, concerned Clay wouldn't go along with it.

"I disagree." Clay grimaced. "We need to call in the FBI. They're trained to handle this kind of stuff."

Steel nodded. "The Colombian has something else over me, because he said all our loved ones will die if we don't do as he says. He's going to call me and explain that to me so I think we have to wait to hear what it is before we call anyone in."

He paused. "The way they took us was very carefully planned. They knew where we would be, how to make it succeed, and pulled it off without a mistake. The Colombian is a pro and we have to take him seriously."

"Hell." Clay bit off his words. "I always felt something like this would happen with your background, Steel."

"That doesn't help us, Clay," snapped Christie.

Clay stared at them. "All right. We see what the Colombian has to say and then we revisit this decision, agreed?"

"Agreed." Steel nodded.

"How can we help our brother?" Dale frowned. "We gotta do something."

Steel said, "After you drop off Afia, get a different color rental car and head north on highway six, past Boulder. I think that's a decent bet for where they took Harry, but it's still a long shot." His voice hardened. "I won't let anything happen to your brother."

"Why the different color car?" asked Dale.

"I think they're watching us so they'll pass along the color of the car you have now to whoever is driving the white pickup." Steel assumed Clay and Dale wouldn't be followed. "We have to be cautious."

Clay motioned to their car. "We'll drop Afia off at the Boulder police station. Then we'll swap cars and drive north. We'll wait for your update."

Steel gestured to him. "Thanks. I'm sorry about all this."

"We'll sort it out," said Dale.

"Can I talk to you alone for a moment, Jack?" Clay stared at him steadily.

"Whatever you have to say, say it in front of both of us, Clay." Christie's voice was firm.

Clay frowned. "All right. I might lose a brother over something I don't understand. I don't want to lose a sister too." He looked at her. "I think you should come with us."

Christie stared at him. "If we split up, the Colombian said he'll kill Harry and our families."

Clay's forehead wrinkled. "Why is he making you stay with Jack?"

Christie shrugged. "We don't know."

Clay shook his head, looking frustrated. "Damn."

"Let's see what develops," said Dale. "If we get moving, maybe we can find Harry quick and end all this."

Clay regarded Christie and Steel for a few moments. "Okay. We'll do it your way for now."

"Be careful." Christie hugged her brothers once more.

Clay returned to the passenger seat of the rental car. Dale climbed in behind the wheel.

Steel tapped on Clay's window. When he powered it down, Steel said, "Hang on." He motioned to Christie. "Come on."

He opened the trunk of their car, unzipped the duffel bag, and looked at Christie. "I want to give two guns to your brothers. Do you want a SIG or Glock? There's two of each." She preferred the SIG's steady trigger pull and ergonomics, but she practiced with both.

She gaped at the weapons. "SIG."

"Alright." He preferred the grip of a Glock anyway. He took out one SIG and one Glock, and an extra mag for both. Hesitating, he said, "Let's check them quick."

He handed her the SIG, he took the Glock. They ejected the full magazines, checked the chambers, took off the slides, recoil springs, and barrels.

"Clean." Christie reassembled it.

"Mine too." He put the Glock back together, took the SIG from her, and said, "Walk in front of me to Clay's window so no one can see the guns."

She did. Remaining close behind her, he unobtrusively handed the guns to Clay. "You might need these. We just checked them. Clean and ready."

Clay raised his eyebrows, but he took the guns. "I expect you to take care of my sister, Steel."

"Nothing will happen to her, Clay. You have my word."

Clay and Dale drove away.

Steel stared after them, vowing silently to live up to his promise.

# CHAPTER 4

CHRISTIE NUDGED STEEL'S ARM. "Ignore Clay. Big brother crap. He's always been protective of me."

Steel kept silent, knowing his own concerns for her wouldn't allow him to dismiss Clay's comments so easily.

She walked back to view the weapons in the trunk. "They're arming us. For what?"

"We're going to find out. Let's check the other guns quick."

They both examined a pistol and Rattler, field-stripping them and examining magazines again. Everything was functional. They were finished in minutes and he shut the trunk.

Christie walked into his arms, whispering, "I'll die if anything happens to Harry."

He held her close, his stomach wound tight. "We'll make sure nothing does."

The phone rang and he answered, putting it on speaker.

The Colombian's voice was matter-of-fact. "Here it is, Steel. Op Retribution. Remember Marita? You abandoned our compatriot, refusing to give her asylum, and thus allowed her to be raped, tortured, and killed by Gustavo Alvarez's men in the Choco jungle on your last Op."

He remembered. The DEA informant, Marita, had died on the Serpent Op. He had considered the possibility that the Colombian kidnapper was somehow connected to Marita but had rejected it as too unlikely. A sinking feeling hit him. He had caused all of this. The past wouldn't let go.

Christie's brow furrowed and he saw worry in her eyes. He felt it too but controlled his features.

The man kept talking. "We're holding you responsible for what happened to Marita. You're going to kill the men who participated in her death. We know everything about you, gringo, and if you do anything we don't like, Harry dies. Your first target is in Vail. Garcia Rincón. He's vacationing with his wife and two children, using the alias of Rodrigo Garcia."

A photo of Garcia arrived on Steel's phone. Moustache, dark hair, mid-forties. He showed it to Christie.

The Colombian continued. "He's a cousin of Gustavo Alvarez, the drug lord you killed. He's also one of the men who ruined and killed our beloved Marita. He has four guards. Three are men living in the U.S. but connected to the cartel. The fourth is his most trusted guard, Hernando. Hernando also participated in Marita's death.

"Kill Garcia and Hernando tonight or Harry dies. If you let the other guards live, the cartel will have an easier time finding you. It's up to you. Garcia has rented a house. I'll text you the address. We'll know if you succeed."

Anger and panic rose in Steel's throat. "I won't do anything until I talk to Harry to make sure he's alive."

"Take the phone off speaker and walk away from Christie."

Christie's eyebrows raised, but he did as requested, holding the phone up to his ear.

"I'm texting you a photo of our compatriot."

The photo arrived. It was a shot of Marita's face and shoulders post-mortem. The torture wounds were obvious and horrible. It made him sick to his stomach, and remorseful again that he had allowed it to happen. Hers was one of the faces that still sometimes haunted his dreams at night.

"Now ask yourself if you want this to happen to Christie. To your daughter, Rachel. To your ex-wife, Carol. To Harry. I'll release Christie's photo and photos of everyone in both of your families to the cartel if you fail or if you call in the police or law enforcement."

He felt his world caving in, and he wanted this man dead. "I tried to save Marita."

"Go to hell, gringo."

"This is between me and you. Let's meet."

"I could have put a bullet in you or Christie long ago, but then your deaths would be too easy. I want you to suffer like Marita did."

"Why now?" He glanced around the station, knowing the Columbian wasn't far away.

"Opportunity. I had to act when Marita's killers came north."

"How do you know me?" Steel searched for a way out.

"Information is always available for a price."

He had been sold out on the Serpent Op, his name given to the target—the drug lord Gustavo Alvarez. It wasn't a surprise that the Colombian had traced his name. Gustavo Alvarez had also threatened revenge from the cartel. It hadn't happened, but it had kept Steel on edge over the last year.

He casually strolled farther away from Christie. "Christie had nothing to do with Marita's death. Leave her out of this."

"I want you to worry about losing someone you love dearly, all the while knowing that it's your fault if she dies."

Steel's free hand bunched into a fist, but he kept his voice calm. "If you want revenge, I'll be more effective if I operate alone. Christie will just get in the way."

"That's part of the fun, amigo."

# PART 2

## OP: GARCIA

# CHAPTER 5

STEEL POCKETED THE PHONE. He kept his expression neutral as he walked back to Christie, but her taut face mirrored his tension. "More instructions."

She kissed his cheek. "You're not a great liar, honey. That's one of the many reasons I love you. Let's drive and talk."

"You drive."

They soon were on the I-70 again, headed west, and she said, "You need to ask for help."

"I don't want to involve anyone else in this mess. They could end up dead or tortured, or have their whole family executed if the cartel gets involved."

"There's one person you can call." She gripped his arm. "You have to. For Carol and Rachel."

He hesitated.

"If we don't get help, Steel, people we love are going to die."

"Yeah." He dialed Wyatt's number from memory. Wyatt answered on the fourth ring, and Steel said, "I have two people that need protection—my ex-wife and my daughter."

There was no hesitation on the other end. "Send them."

"Thanks."

The line went dead. He trusted Wyatt. His security-conscious home in Virginia had been designed and built by Wyatt—the wealthy and eccentric survivalist who had sold it to him.

He and Wyatt had bonded in the short time they had known each other back then. Both had military histories. And Wyatt had extended an invitation to help Steel if he ever needed it. Steel was relieved Wyatt was taking Carol and Rachel, because the man was even more obsessive and paranoid than he was about security.

Next he called his ex-wife, Carol. A lawyer working in Virginia, she lived close to his home. She had their daughter Rachel for the week.

He dreaded this call. It had taken Carol a long time to recover from last year's hell and he hated dragging her into his mess again. He had told her about Gustavo Alvarez's threats last year, and they had planned for something like this. They both wanted to protect Rachel. But it was still going to be hard on her.

"This is Carol."

She sounded happy and it made him frown over his next words.

"I'm sorry, Carol." He hesitated. "We're in trouble, and you and Rachel could be at risk. I want you to go somewhere immediately. Going to the police won't help."

"What kind of trouble, Jack? You're scaring me."

"It's related to the threats we talked about last year. I wouldn't be asking this if I thought you two were safe. If you go to Wyatt, he can protect you."

"For how long?"

He paused. "Days, maybe a week. I'm not sure yet."

It was Carol's turn to remain silent for a few moments. "Where?"

Her voice was steady so that was good. "Billings, Montana. I'll text you his phone number. When you're an hour out, call him. No calls to anyone else, no one else can know. Drive, don't fly. After you leave, see if you're followed. If you think you are, don't call me on this number. I'll check in. Wyatt is expecting you. He's solid."

"You're sure there's no alternative?"

"Not right now."

She sighed. "All right, Jack. I'll do it. We'll pack and leave within the hour. I'll take the dogs to the neighbors. I moved all my work around this week to spend time with Rachel anyway. I'll tell her we're going on a road trip and you're going to try to meet us at the end, okay?"

"Thank you." He heaved a breath. "Carol, I'm sorry about this."

"I trust you, Jack. Be careful."

He got off the phone and texted her Wyatt's phone number. Finished, he leaned back in his seat, thinking of his daughter. A year ago Rachel had escaped a two-year-long kidnapping. It had taken nearly a year of therapy for her nightmares to end. She was still strong, but that was in part due to the fact that she had returned to two stable parents. Losing her father now would be a blow that might damage her spirit for a lifetime. He resolved he wouldn't fail her.

"That was crappy," he said.

Christie gripped his hand. "At least they'll be safe."

"Damn him to hell!" His chest heaved.

"You took the words right out of my mouth." She stroked his forearm. "I know the Colombian threatened you. What did he do? Show you Marita's morgue photo?"

"Yes." Steel couldn't meet her eyes. "He threatened to show our family photographs to the cartel if we fail."

She paused. "He's putting pressure on you."

"It's working," he said quietly. "I can't let him ruin our lives."

"You won't." Her voice turned hard. "We'll get through this, Jack. We have to. This is the best time of my life too. The happiest. I love you and our life together too much to let anyone screw it up. And we're not losing Harry either."

He sighed. "Damn straight."

She squeezed his hand. "I want to see the photo of Marita."

"No, you don't."

"Look, Jack, we're being asked to kill these men. I need to see what they're capable of."

He pulled up the photo and handed the phone to her. Her lips pursed and her eyes narrowed as she looked at it. She gave him the phone and he put it away. Both of them remained silent for a few minutes.

Reaching over, Christie took his hand in hers again. "What happened to Marita was horrible, but you didn't do it. Now you have to let it go."

She was right. He had to let it go. He'd been trying for over a year. "Thanks."

"What about our military? Wouldn't they want to protect a threatened past Blackhood Op asset with lots of information?"

"I thought about that. But they'll want to secure me, take me out of this mess. They won't give a damn about Harry. At best he'll be collateral damage. And the Colombian would still release our photos to the cartel."

"Other options?" she asked.

"The police would give us the same results. Harry dead. Our photos sent to the cartel. For now we play along."

"I can live with that." Christie glanced at him. "But if the cartel finds out who we are, we'll be running forever. And my family and yours will be at risk."

"Maybe that's the plan." He looked at her. "To punish me, ruin my life. Even if the cartel is unable to find out that we killed their people, the Colombian could give our identity to them out of revenge once this is over."

His gaze traced the curves of her heart-shaped face. He was glad she loved him. "I couldn't live with myself if Rachel and Carol had to hide for the rest of their lives."

"I couldn't either."

"You need to call Clay and fill him in so he doesn't decide to call the police."

She took the phone and dialed her brother. Quickly she told him about the Colombian's threats to release their photos to the cartel, and that they were being directed to Vail where they were going to get some rest. She talked for several minutes before she hung up.

Steel noted she didn't tell Clay about the Colombian's demands to kill Garcia Rincón and his bodyguard, Hernando.

Christie's voice was calm. "Clay's not happy."

"I wouldn't be either." He glanced at her. "You didn't tell him about the Garcia hit."

"I didn't want to worry him." Her lips pursed. "I also don't know if I can kill Garcia and his bodyguards in cold blood."

He understood. It was one of the reasons he had left Blackhood Ops. Killing terrorists had felt justified. He was protecting the innocent. But after an Op had been taken over by outside interests, he decided blind obedience to orders was something he couldn't live with anymore. His jaw clenched over the fact that he was being forced into the same situation again.

He dredged up a memory. "Garcia is connected to the cartels. I saw intel on him a year ago when I was in Blackhood."

She spoke softly. "Can we go to anyone else for help?"

"We have no proof Garcia killed Marita, just this guy's word. No authority is going to act on that." He rolled down the window a little to let in some fresh air. "I'll go after Garcia and his men, while you think about how we can find Harry."

"I'm coming with you, Jack."

"This is my fault. I—"

"End of discussion, Steel."

He noted her clipped tone. "You're very stubborn once your mind is made up."

"You finally noticed?" She smiled and batted her eyelashes at him.

Normally he would have laughed, but now he couldn't even smile.

# CHAPTER 6

HARRY LISTENED FOR ANY sounds that might tell him where he was, but nothing distinct caught his attention. The young man with the C-4 vest was Latino. He wondered if the rest were too.

The cargo bed was lined with carpet. Including the underside of the bed cover above him—probably to reduce any noise he made. The cover was just above the truck sidewalls, too low to even crawl under.

He swung his arms across the carpet in the dark. Empty. There was nothing available that might serve as a weapon. Still they hadn't bound his feet and hands. Amateurs. Wanting to gauge travel time, he checked his watch. He also considered options, something Steel had drilled into him repeatedly in the virtual reality training. There was always a solution.

Choosing the most likely scenario for success, he rolled onto his side. He positioned his boots so that when the tailgate was unlocked he could kick it hard into the person opening it

After an hour and a half the truck finally stopped.

In a minute he heard a key in the tailgate lock. He waited for it to open, but it didn't. Counting to five, he pulled his boots back and kicked hard. The tailgate slammed open with a jarring thud. He had a clear view out the back.

A man wearing a black face mask and holding a sawed-off shotgun stood five feet from the back of the pickup. Not so dumb after all. Harry believed it was the same man that had been standing near the tailgate when he had climbed into the bed. What little he saw wouldn't help a police description.

"Try that again, gringo, and I will cut off one of your fingers." The man motioned with the shotgun. "Now turn around so your head is a foot from the tailgate."

Disappointed, Harry had to wiggle around to squeeze his legs past the wheel wells. When he did, all he could see was a dark landscape outside. No lights. They could be anywhere in Colorado. However he saw the moon. He figured it rose in the southeast and if he could see it, they were traveling north.

"Lie on your stomach and put your hands beneath your waist."

He did as he was told, resting his head on its side. His captor had only a slight Latino accent and sounded educated. If this was related to the fatwa on Afia Ameen, why kidnap him?

The man pushed the shotgun barrel into the back of his neck, while someone else held a phone against his ear. He couldn't see the second person, but there had been two people in the truck cab. The driver had been smaller and wore a hoodie, but the tinted windows had hidden the person's face.

The man with the shotgun spoke. "Ask to talk to your sister. Tell her you have only a few hours to live if they don't succeed."

Steel answered, his voice coming through the phone's speaker. "Hello?"

Harry swallowed. "This is Harry, Jack."

"Are you all right?" Steel's voice was matter-of-fact.

"Sweet as the moon. How's Afia?"

"She's safe, Harry. They didn't hurt her."

That made him feel better. He had felt responsible for allowing the attacker to take shots at Afia at the auditorium. She could have died there. The shotgun pressed harder into his neck, and he added, "They want me to talk to Christie."

There was a short pause before she came on the line.

"Harry?"

He heard the same concern in his sister's voice. Hating what he had to say, he hesitated. But the shotgun provided motivation to follow orders. "They want me to tell you I might only have a few hours to live if you don't succeed, but—"

The phone was pulled away and he couldn't finish. The tailgate was slammed shut and he heard the lock click.

Happy that Afia was all right, he was also puzzled by it. It meant none of this had anything to do with her or the fatwa. Then what? Most likely something Steel had been involved with in the past.

He doubted the police had been called in, since Jack and Christie were under some kind of pressure to cooperate with the kidnappers. Dale and Clay would be searching for him. They would move mountains to rescue him, but it might not be possible for anyone to find him.

Steel's motto, *Stay calm, assess options, look for a solution*— inspired him. Two people, no matter how good, weren't going to hold him for long.

As he lay there, he wondered if his job in Greensave was worth his life. His wife had died four years ago from pancreatic cancer. While she was sick he had quit his construction job to take care of her, doing small carpentry jobs on the side.

After her death he had quit working. His heart wasn't in it anymore. He and his wife had been saving money to build a house and buy enough land to do beekeeping and grow organic herbs. That plan had faded away.

Steel's new company had seemed like a salvation. Get paid to travel while helping others. Christie had called him about the job. He hadn't seen much of her over the last decade so spending time with her also made it an offer he couldn't refuse.

Considering all of that, he had no regrets. And he didn't plan on dying on the job.

His military background was more basic than Steel's, but the training in Steel's VR sims gave him confidence that he could handle almost anything. Whoever these people were, they would regret holding him.

In less than an hour the truck stopped again. Maybe they were going to let him talk to Christie and Jack once more. He tried to think of a message. Better yet, maybe now he could escape.

He readied himself by lying on his side and resting his fists by his head, which was still close to the tailgate. One punch and the guy would be down. At six-three, two–hundred–fifty pounds, people recognized that he was strong, but they still underestimated his strength.

The tailgate opened.

Before he could lift his head, a soft woman's voice surprised him from the side of the truck. She was out of sight and must have been the person he had seen wearing the hoodie in the truck cab, and the one who had held the phone.

"Lie on your stomach and put your head on its side, por favor, Señor Harry. Hands beneath your stomach and hold still. I don't want to hurt you."

She sounded gentle so he decided to play along. He turned onto his stomach and shoved his hands beneath his torso. Where was the man? Probably five feet from the tailgate again. The woman also sounded educated, her accent barely noticeable, like the man's.

"What do you want?" he asked. "I don't even know you. What's your name?"

The woman didn't answer, but the shotgun was pressed into the back of his neck. It gave him another reason not to try anything.

"Hold still," the woman repeated.

He couldn't see either of them but was curious why the woman had said she didn't want to hurt him.

There was a soft prick on his upper right arm. That startled him, but there was little he could do. Abruptly he felt drowsy and began to fade.

Before he lost consciousness, he heard the man say, "I'm ready to kill the stupid gringo."

# CHAPTER 7

CHRISTIE'S FEATURES TIGHTENED AND her eyes misted as she listened to her brother, Harry. Empathizing with her pain, Steel couldn't think of any way to ease it.

Afterward he asked, "Did you hear anything in the background?"

"No."

"Neither did I." He thought about the call. "Harry can see the moon so it's likely he's headed north. Let your brothers know. The Colombian complied with my request to talk to Harry so he's willing to make small compromises to keep us cooperating with his vendetta."

Christie bit her lip. "How can that help us?"

"Right now I don't know, but it might give us leverage with him at some point." What he kept to himself was that he also sensed the Colombian's deep anger. The man talked calmly and sounded logical, but Steel intuited the man's hatred for him and the cartel. This man wouldn't hesitate to kill. The Colombian also knew how to be professional with his emotions, which meant he was dangerous.

Christie called Clay to tell him about Harry's call. She still didn't mention the upcoming hit on Garcia, instead just repeating that they were being directed to Vail and would rest there for the night. It was between Christie and her brother so Steel didn't comment.

When she finished the call, the phone beeped. A text.

"Garcia 's address." Christie looked at it and handed him the phone. "What if the guys holding Harry are just Garcia's drug competition and this has nothing to do with Marita?"

He leaned back. "I thought the same thing, but this is a risky way to get rid of your competition."

His intuition always guided him, and it said their situation was over Marita. "They're making me pay for Marita's death, while keeping themselves out of the spotlight. Which means they fear cartel retribution as much as we do. Maybe they're related to Marita and they're calling her a compatriot to hide that fact."

"She was their daughter or sister?"

"Something like that, yeah."

Christie shook her head. "If my daughter or sister went through the torture Marita had, I'd probably want revenge too. Wouldn't you?"

"Yes." He thought about what he would do if someone raped and tortured Christie. It would be ugly.

While Christie drove, he tried to think of ways to find Harry and get out from under the kidnapper's control. Nothing seemed viable. Still he clung to his motto for emergencies and seemingly impossible situations. It had always served him in the past and he had to believe it would this time too.

They made Vail in an hour and a half. Mountains surrounded them, forming darker shadows against the starry sky.

When they stopped for gas, Steel bought a tourist map. He paid cash so his credit card wasn't tracked. They studied the map in the car. Garcia's house was south of the main city and somewhat isolated.

Steel folded up the map. "We need to ask Garcia for a list of names of those who killed Marita. I want to see if it matches the kidnapper's list. Then we'll be sure the Colombian is telling the truth about Garcia and the others."

"How many men could have been involved with killing one woman?"

He didn't answer, fearful of what was ahead of them.

Christie glanced at him, her lips pursed. Starting the car, she drove out of the lot, using side roads until they were a half mile from the address.

He rechecked the map. "Pull past the driveway and find a good place to park a hundred yards east of it if you can."

When they drove past the long driveway, he noted it was mostly hidden by trees. The forest hid the house too. Private. What someone like Garcia would prefer. Better for them too.

Christie found a small turnaround and pulled deep off the road onto grass. She killed the lights.

The air carried the scent of the pine trees that bordered the road. Steel found it refreshing, but tension filled his limbs.

Christie pulled the trunk release and he got out and opened the lid. She threw her purse inside, and he tossed in his billfold. She gave him the car keys to carry.

He opened the duffel bag and stared at its contents. For a moment he didn't move. What they were about to do would bring him back into a life that he had walked away from. Killing. Murder. Ops. He didn't want to go back. But it was either this or say goodbye to everything he had.

He put a silencer on a Glock, noticing the serial numbers had been filed off, and stuck it beneath his shirt. Christie shoved the silenced SIG into her waistband.

"Keep the jacket buttoned. It hides your white blouse."

"Good idea." She complied.

He stuffed zip ties in his pockets. The moon was out, but they might need the night vision goggles in the house. Grabbing a pair, he left them hanging around his neck. He gave a pair to Christie too. She slipped them over her head to try them on, and then let them hang down her back.

Picking up a small, sheathed knife, he handed it to her. She stuffed it into her waistband too. He had the OTF knife in his belt-sheath so he opted for not taking another blade. The duct tape might be useful, but he had no convenient way to carry it.

He attached silencers to two Rattlers and handed one to her, along with a spare mag which she shoved into a jacket pocket. He rammed an extra mag into a pocket. Grabbing the face masks, he shut the trunk and led her into the woods far enough to be out of sight from cars on the road.

They stopped, staring at each other.

"Strategy?" asked Christie.

He didn't like her taking such a risk, and he still didn't know how they were going to get through the next hour. All of it ramped up his concerns. "If Garcia participated in Marita's torture and murder, then he's a killer who will kill again. If that's the case, I have less of a problem killing him."

"What about the guards?" she asked.

"If we can avoid killing the three from North America, we'll do it." He had already considered a number of strategies that would minimize Christie's risk, but he was unsure what she would accept. "You wait here thirty minutes. Then come up the side of the driveway."

Her brows hunched. "Really? If you think I'm waiting here while you try to take everyone, you're crazy."

"You don't have field Op experience."

"I'm coming."

He gave it one more shot. "The cartel will have an easier time finding us if Garcia's wife and kids report a couple instead of a lone gunman."

"Nice try. With four guards, plus keeping the kids and wife out of it, it will be a lot easier to question Garcia if I'm there."

He couldn't argue with her logic. "If you hesitate to shoot someone, you'll end up dead."

"I can take care of myself. What if Garcia calls the police?"

"He won't. If he's using an alias it means he doesn't want anyone examining him too closely." He stood there, thinking.

She eyed him. "What do you want me to do, Steel?"

His ability to select optimal strategies in the field always gave him an advantage over the enemy and an edge of safety. But Christie didn't have his experience.

He cleared his throat. "Wait here ten minutes to give me time to reach the back, and then work your way to the driveway. Spot the guards. I'll secure the back of the house. My guess is there might be one guard there, most likely two in the front. That leaves Hernando and Garcia inside.

"After I take care of the rear guard, I'll work my way to the front from the west. In a quarter hour you begin working your way along the east side of the driveway. Stay in the trees. When you see the front guards respond to me, come up fast. We'll use zip ties on them if they're still alive."

"I could come up sooner." She sounded annoyed.

"I have decades of experience in Op work."

"I have experience too."

He nodded. "You're good with a gun, self-defense, and analyzing situations—"

"Not good. Excellent. And you know it."

"Yes, excellent." She had been a counter-terrorism ops analyst when he first met her, with great shooting skills and adequate fighting skills. Over the last year she had honed her physical skills by working hard with him and his virtual reality program—something he had insisted on if she wanted to join him on field assignments.

The VR system had been developed by the Army for Blackhood senior operative training. He had convinced them years ago to allow him to use it in his barn.

After Blackhood fell apart a year ago, he had hung onto the VR program for Greensave operative training. He still used it obsessively to maintain his razor-sharp skills, but he regretted opening up that door to Christie.

"Providing protection for someone is different than trying to take out targets," he added.

"I might surprise you."

He let it go, and whispered, "No risks. Quiet as a mouse."

"Easy."

They pulled on the black hoods. Christie tucked her long hair beneath the mask.

He gave her one more glance, then turned and strode deeper into the woods.

# CHAPTER 8

CHRISTIE DIDN'T WAIT TEN minutes. As soon as Steel faded into the trees she made her way toward the driveway. Keeping the winding road in sight, she remained deep enough in the forest to stay out of view.

Steel wanted her to be out of the action, but she wanted to make sure she could back him up. He was too protective of her. Just like Clay. If she proved to him that she was competent, then he would trust her more and worry less.

More importantly, she had never loved anyone seriously her whole life and now she was head-over-heels in love with a man she respected and admired. No one was going to take him from her.

There was no traffic and the quiet of the woods calmed her racing thoughts, which kept returning to Harry. Were they torturing him? Planning to kill him anyway?

When Harry said that he might have only a few hours to live, it had shaken her. His big smile and calm face always made her feel bright inside. And she had talked him into the job at Greensave. She felt responsible for him.

She wondered how far she was willing to go to keep her brother alive. Whatever it took. She could never face Clay, Dale, or her parents if she didn't. She wouldn't be able to face herself either.

An owl hooted in the distance. Steel loved birds. For a moment she was overtaken by fury at the men trying to ruin their lives.

She took a deep breath. Steel had also taught her to keep emotion out of field work or it could get you killed.

The ground was soft, easy to move over quietly. She had on a decent pair of lace-up work shoes that she could run in if she had to. A hundred feet later, through a break in the trees, she saw the paved driveway—a lighter surface shining in the moonlight.

She stopped twenty yards from it behind a large pine tree. Scanning the area, she didn't see any guards near the road or the driveway. Fifteen minutes seemed too long to wait here. What if Steel ran into trouble? He always had a hard time asking for help.

She began walking parallel to the driveway, wanting to be closer to the front of the house when Steel reached it. Far ahead, lanterns lit up the sides of a two-car detached garage. A sidewalk and steps to the left led farther back to the front porch of the house.

She glimpsed a man standing in the shadows of the porch.

Stopping immediately, she pulled on the night vision goggles. When she looked again, the guard was gone. Had he seen her? It seemed doubtful with the trees between them.

She left the goggles on. Steel had it backward. There must be two guards in back and only one in front. If she took out the front guard, then she could warn him.

Rounding a big pine, she paused, the Rattler level in her hands.

Something pressed hard against the middle of her back. She stiffened. A gun barrel.

"Not a word, señorita, or you die here."

Her hair was pulled back along with the back of her mask, arching her neck. A number of self-defense responses occurred to her, but she didn't see herself surviving any of them. She had to work to keep her panic at bay.

"Drop the gun."

She let the Rattler slip from her hands.

"Kick it away."

She gave it a half-hearted kick, not able to do more with her head tilted back.

"Now slowly. Hands behind your head. Interlock your fingers. Then drop to your knees."

She carefully complied, the gun following her down to her knees, her hair still pulled back hard, making it awkward to lower herself. Not knowing what he was going to do, fear stampeded her thoughts.

He shoved her down hard onto the ground on her belly, jamming a knee into her back. She grunted with the weight of his body as he pressed the gun into her right cheek and patted down her jacket. After finding her knife and the spare mag, he tossed both to the side.

His gun and knee were removed and she heard him step away.

"Turn over."

She felt vulnerable but complied. Where was he? He had to be standing behind her head.

"Lift up the front of your blouse."

Was he going to rape her? She pulled her blouse up a few inches, revealing the SIG.

"Take the pistol and toss it. Two fingers only."

She did, and then quickly pulled her blouse back down.

"Now on your stomach again."

In relief she rolled over, hearing him talk softly.

"We have visitors, stay alert."

She berated herself for getting caught so easily. Stupid. Steel had been right about the guards and her lack of field experience. Her carelessness would get them both killed.

Stopping her racing thoughts, she focused on her VR training with Steel. *Everyone gets into bad situations,* he had told her. *Getting out of them is the key. Stay calm, assess options, look for a solution.*

The guard put a knee into her back again, which made it hard to breathe. He ground the gun barrel into her cheek a second time. "Why are you here?"

Her voice was muffled by his body weight and the soil. "Call the police. Let them figure it out. We're in Vail. You can't hide a body here and expect to get away with it."

The man chuckled. "We'll take you out in a car trunk and have some fun with you later. We'll take turns. My friends will be very happy. It's nice you dressed up for us."

Ignoring his threats, she concentrated on her body and his weight, tensing her arms and torso. Speed and surprise. She had worked on this scenario a hundred times in the virtual reality sims, and in person with Steel. However it wasn't quite the same on dirt with an actual killer on top of her.

"Let's see what you look like." With his knee still pressed into her back, he pulled off her night vision goggles. Next he removed the gun from her cheek and grabbed the top of her head mask.

Without thinking she put everything she had into a violent rolling twist, away from his center of gravity. His knee slid off her back to the side of her so that he straddled her torso, but her right arm blocked his gun enough so the muffled gunshot missed her head.

Her mask was pulled sideways and out of position. She could only see out of half of one eye slit. His jaw appeared. Frantic, she rose up as far as she could, estimating where his eyes would be, and jammed her left fingers at them.

He gasped. She had connected with at least one eye, which gave her a chance to ram her stiff fingers into his throat.

The man was choking, but he back-handed her hard with the pistol. Her head snapped sideways. She ignored the pain and blocked his gun away with her left arm, striking out at the other eye as hard as she could with her right fingers.

This time he cried out.

She hit him again in the throat and heard something crunch. Gasping for air, he leaned sideways and she pushed him off her.

Through the slit in the mask she glimpsed him sliding the gun over the ground toward her.

She rolled on top of him, palming him as hard as she could in the nose. His gun hand fell to the ground, but his other hand came up, jabbing a knife at her.

She twisted to avoid it but felt a burning sensation in her lower back. Groaning, she hammered at his throat repeatedly with both fists until his knife hand dropped to the ground and he lay still.

Her lungs heaved. Adjusting her head mask so she could see, she took some deep breaths. The man appeared dead. She checked his neck for a pulse. Nothing.

She sized him up, something she was good at. Latino, five-foot-ten, one-seventy pounds, mid-thirties. Creep.

Not wanting to sit atop a dead man, she crawled off him and pulled up the back of her torn blouse. She had a cut three inches long on her lower back, shallow and bleeding. Better than dead. She had lost a few buttons on the jacket too.

She crawled to gather the SIG, spare mag, and knife, returning them to her pocket and waistband. Lastly she put on the night vision goggles.

Needles and dirt clung to her clothing and knees, her thoughts in disarray. Wanting time to recover, she was suddenly flooded with images of Steel walking into a trap. The guard's gun was silenced, but the guard on the porch would have heard it.

She grabbed the Rattler, stood, and ran east through the woods, intending to take a wide half-circle route back to the east side of the front porch. The cut on her back burned.

Surprisingly she felt no remorse over killing the man. From the way he had talked about abusing her, this wasn't the first time he had used and killed women. He deserved to die, probably many times over.

She had been wrong. If need be, she could kill all of them.

# CHAPTER 9

S TEEL HEARD THE *ooh ooh ooh* cry of a Mexican spotted owl. It began softly and escalated rapidly to a louder pitch. Wishing he could just stand still and enjoy it, he kept moving. He had a deep, abiding love for nature—which always grounded him.

As he made his way south, he also wished he had taken a firmer stand with Christie and refused her help. It probably wouldn't have mattered. She would have come anyway. But the fact that she was in a dangerous Op, with little field experience, gave his steps more urgency.

A deeper fear lurked beneath that idea. When the Colombian had threatened to send Christie's photo to the cartel, he had intuited that it wasn't just a threat, but a plan. The Colombian would have to die before that happened.

The trees formed dark shadows under the moon. He ran from trunk to trunk until he was far enough south that he could approach the side of the house directly from the east.

Decades of exploring caves had made moving in darkness second nature to him.

As he got closer, the house lights guided him in. He stopped fifty feet out behind a tree. No one was visible in the windows. It triggered an alarm in his head to be more cautious.

He quietly backed up fifty feet, and then worked his way a hundred yards farther south. Using the moon for a bearing, he headed west again and then north.

This was taking more time than he had anticipated. He worried about Christie reaching the front of the house before he did.

A faint noise. Silenced gunshot.

He froze, listening. Nothing followed. Not wanting to think about what had happened, he moved faster.

A hundred feet ahead was a small illuminated patio at ground level. The second floor had a balcony running along the back of the house, empty except for furniture. Lights lit up a large room adjacent to the balcony, but no people were visible. Why leave lights on in empty rooms? Of course, many people didn't care about wasting energy. Still it made him cautious.

He studied the windows. Everyone could be in other rooms, but maybe the Colombian had already tipped off Garcia and Hernando, trying to get revenge on both parties at the same time.

Worse, Christie might have been captured and the guards alerted. The fact that no guards were visible made him wary. Worst case scenario, Christie was dead and Garcia was planning to leave. He would kill all of them then.

He calmed himself. Maybe there were no guards in back, but he didn't buy it. He tried to imagine where a guard would hide to ambush an intruder. If it were him, he wouldn't pick either side of the patio, in case someone came up behind him.

That left the area between him and the patio. From there you could see any entrance onto the patio. The man would be kneeling or lying down to reduce his visibility.

He put on the night vision goggles and studied the area in front of him. Nothing.

Slowly and quietly he walked toward a different tree to get another angle. As careful as he was, he stepped on a twig on the soft soil, giving the faintest of sounds. There was movement ahead of him—in a pile of leaves. By the time he slid behind the tree, two silenced bullets hit the trunk.

Keeping the tree between him and the camouflaged guard, he backed away from it. He hoped the guard would call for reinforcements from the front of the house, leaving Christie safer.

He reached another tree big enough to hide behind and stopped. To his right a shadow moved. The guard was trying to work around to his last location. Dropping to one knee, his gun leveled, Steel watched as the man slowly advanced in front of him.

The guard figured it out and whirled toward him.

Steel shot him in the chest and head. The man went down and stayed down.

Steel rose and ran, circling wide of the west side of the house. Images of Christie captured or hurt made him run faster.

He stopped even with the front of the house, fifty yards west of it. A guard on the porch stared in his direction with night vision goggles. A barrage of bullets struck the trees around him from a silenced machine gun as he dove to the ground.

The shooting stopped.

Quiet.

Two soft shots.

Quiet.

He glanced up. The man had fallen, his body half off the front porch.

He scanned the far side of the house. Christie. Standing on the other side of the porch, just beyond the front steps. She wore the night vision goggles and held her SIG in both hands, the Rattler slung over her shoulder. Relief swept over him.

She gave him a thumbs-up.

The front porch had no railings and was two feet off the ground. A large window overlooked it.

He didn't want to cross in front of the window, nor try to gain entry through the front door. He stood, held up his palm to Christie, and pushed toward her several times until she backed up into the shadows. Next he pointed at her, and then north. She gave him another thumbs-up.

She disappeared along the east side of the house.

Retracing his steps on the west side, he passed by the man he had killed in back of the house, quickly ending up on the east side of the patio. Christie was waiting, holding the Rattler, her night vision goggles hanging down her back.

He wrapped his arms around her and she held him loosely. The relief that washed over him made him want to leave or get her out. Both were impossible.

He pulled back. A small cut on her face and missing jacket buttons made him grimace. She had been in close quarters combat. She could have died. And it was his fault she was here.

Anger and worry collided in his throat. He had to wait a few moments before he spoke. "You're alright?"

She nodded. "You?"

"Yes."

He drew her farther into the woods. "What happened?"

"I killed another guard by the driveway," she whispered.

He frowned over hearing that, but there was no time to discuss it. "I killed one. If the intel was correct, that leaves Hernando and Garcia inside. Hernando will know his guards are down, and Garcia will be armed. That makes the front and back doors too obvious and dangerous. Can you climb the balcony?"

She nodded. "Of course."

"I'll climb up first, secure the room, and signal if it's clear. If you don't see me, get out of here."

She shook her head. "We both go up on opposites sides. I know how to clear a room, Steel. Two of us up there stand a better chance."

For a moment he wanted to argue with her, but again he couldn't fault her logic. And her tone said there would be no discussion.

He hesitated. What would he do if she got shot? Damn the Colombian. "All right. I'll go around to the west side. When I signal, start climbing."

# CHAPTER 10

CHRISTIE WATCHED STEEL FADE back into the woods, overjoyed that he was all right. She had felt certain that he would be shot or trapped due to her mistake. Thus when she had seen him in front of the house she had wanted to shout in celebration.

He had outmatched the alerted rear guard. Impressive. Everyone had always told her that he was the best in Blackhood Ops. But to witness it firsthand gave her confidence in him—and in the two of them as a team.

They had a chance to succeed at whatever the Colombian threw at them. She couldn't wait to put a bullet in the man's head.

Steel hadn't seen her injury. She had used her arm and jacket to hide it. He would never have agreed to her climbing up with the cut and would be upset with her for hiding it. But he needed her.

She made her way to the east side of the balcony. It was a wrap-around, with no windows on her side. To climb up she would have to start at the corner of the house. There was uneven brick from ground level to ten feet up. Woodwork above that would provide handholds.

She remembered watching Steel climb up ropes in his barn with ease. He would get up before her, but not by much. Slinging the Rattler over her back, she waited until he appeared at the west corner. He signaled and she began climbing.

Gripping the edges of bricks about six feet up, she positioned her feet on either side of the corner on narrow edges and began climbing. Her cut ached, but she didn't make a sound.

It was harder than she thought and took all her strength to reach the top of the brick. From there she could barely reach the wood struts beneath the balcony. Stretching her arms made the cut burn. With her shoes balanced on the edges of bricks, she gripped a strut.

The balcony door slid open, and then closed. She pulled herself in close to the wall and quieted her breathing.

Soft footsteps approached her along the balcony. Worried that the person might have night vision goggles, she didn't move. Above her the balcony had tiny cracks between the boards. She hoped the cracks weren't wide enough for someone to see her.

The footsteps continued to the end of the wrap-around, and then slowly returned, the sounds receding to the other side. If Jack was already up he would kill the person.

In a few moments the sliding door opened and closed again. She was glad she had waited.

Moving along the struts, she edged her way to the end of the wrap-around, where a strut allowed her to pull herself up to the balcony railing. She slipped over the side and unslung the Rattler. Her back ached fiercely, forcing her to pause.

Walking to the corner of the balcony, she peered around it.

A row of waist-high windows lined the wall, ending a foot before the sliding door at her corner. A table and three chairs were in the center of the balcony. Whoever had come out onto the balcony had turned off the lights in the interior room.

Steel appeared at the other corner. He held up a palm so she didn't move. Crouching, he scrambled below the windows, stopping and straightening just before the sliding door.

She raised her gun, and he motioned for her to get down. Slipping on her goggles, she dropped to one knee.

Slowly he reached over and pulled the sliding door open.

Peering around the corner, she didn't see anyone inside. Furniture and a wall TV suggested a large family room. Quietly she stood and entered, going right, her gun up. Steel was on her heels, going left.

They skirted the room to the far door, which was open. Steel went through first. She followed him into an open hallway with a railing overlooking the room below.

The hallway ended in a closed door to the far right, and a wooden stairway that led down to the first floor. Dim lighting revealed only furniture in the living room below. They both slipped off their night vision goggles.

Steel led her down the hallway. Halfway along it, the wood creaked beneath their feet. Arms outstretched, Steel flattened himself against the wall. Christie did the same as machine gun fire exploded from below, creating holes along the hallway floor.

Two lines of bullets tore through the wood, coming from both ends of the hallway and meeting in the middle. The firing stopped.

Steel touched her shoulder, then pointed to her feet and left to the end of the hallway. He aimed his gun at the floor and pointed right. She nodded.

They began firing simultaneously into the wood, following the same lines of bullet holes already there.

Steel ran down the hallway chasing his line of bullets. She kept up with him, running sideways while still firing into the floor, but in the opposite direction. Steel reached the door and shouldered it open. Hastily following him, Christie stopped just inside the room. She closed it until only an inch-wide crack remained.

The room was half-lit. A Latino woman in her thirties sat rigidly on the floor next to the bed, wearing a short white negligee, her long dark hair trailing down to her chest. Two young children, a boy and a girl—one tucked under each arm— sat beside her. She whispered to them in Spanish.

"Watch them," murmured Steel. He put a fresh mag into his Rattler.

Christie did the same, and moved farther into the room, seeing terror on the faces of the woman and children. It didn't make her feel good. She wanted to tell them they would be alright, but they wouldn't believe anything she had to say.

***

Steel called out from inside the doorway, "If you want your wife and children to live, Garcia, come up the stairs, hands in the air. Tell your man, Hernando, to do the same."

"I'm unarmed." The voice came from the first floor.

From the edge of the doorway, Steel watched Garcia slowly approach the bottom of the stairs, his hands in the air. Hernando wasn't visible in the room below.

Garcia stopped at the bottom of the stairs. "I am coming up. What do you want? Did Antonio send you? If so, I believe we can work something out."

Steel guessed Antonio was Garcia's competition. The man was stalling.

He backed away from the door. Adjacent to the bed was a master bathroom with a tiled floor. The bathroom door was near the bed, and a wall separated the bathroom from the bedroom door. It would provide some safety for the woman and her two children.

He motioned with his gun. "Lie down on the bathroom floor."

The woman stared at him, then crawled with her children into the bathroom, lying on her stomach with a child on either side of her.

Steel knelt down near the bed, facing the door, gun raised. A sliver of the stairway was visible. Christie knelt beside him, her Rattler ready.

"I am coming up. Is it safe to do so?" called Garcia.

Holes exploded at the edge of the doorframe and along three feet of the wall as machine gun rounds blew through it and into the opposing bathroom wall.

The woman and children cried out.

Steel dropped to his belly, his gun held up with propped elbows, still facing the door. Christie followed suit, using the corner of the bathroom wall for protection.

The gunfire stopped. The bullet holes were four feet above the floor. Garcia was trying to ensure he wasn't shooting his wife and children.

Still Steel wondered how badly Garcia wanted to save his family. He called out, "Last chance, Garcia. Then we'll kill them."

"We're both unarmed and coming up. Please do not hurt my wife and children."

In seconds Steel caught glimpses of the two men almost at the top of the stairs, their arms in the air. But they moved out of sight when they reached the top.

"What do you want us to do now?" asked Garcia. "We're here."

Steel whispered to Christie, "Shoot him in the ankle when he comes through. Don't hesitate. He'll have a gun."

Her face tightened, but she nodded.

Hastily he belly-crawled around to the other side of the bed and faced the wall that adjoined the family room they had entered from the balcony.

Machine gun rounds burst through the wall at the foot of the bed, cutting holes at chest level into the opposite wall at the head of the bed. Simultaneously Garcia burst through the bedroom door, holding a pistol and firing it.

Christie returned fire.

Steel shot at the wall in a waist-high sweeping arc.

The gunshots from the other side of the wall ended.

He crawled around the bed and saw Garcia lying on his side on the floor, groaning and still holding his gun. The drug lord tried to lift his pistol and Christie shot him in the shoulder. He gasped and dropped his weapon.

The kids were crying and the woman exclaimed fearfully.

"Stay here," Steel whispered to Christie.

He crawled to the door, checked the hallway, and then rose and ran to the family room doorway. Carefully he edged into the room. Hernando lay crumpled on the floor on his back. The man had wounds in the chest and neck, his eyes open in death.

Steel ran back to the bedroom. Christie was standing, her gun aimed at Garcia.

Steel drew his blade and knelt on Garcia's wounded shoulder, bending over him and pressing his knife against the man's cheek. "Name everyone who killed the DEA informant, Marita, last year," he whispered.

"Go to hell."

He pushed the edge of the knife into Garcia's face until a drop of blood rolled down the side of his cheek. "Do you want your children to see you cut up like her?" He put more weight on Garcia's shoulder. "Or have your children hear their father screaming for mercy?"

Garcia gasped in pain. "I'll tell you if you let me live."

Removing his knee, Steel pressed the tip of the knife against the bottom of Garcia's lower eyelid. "You get once chance, then you lose an eye."

"Vincente and Diego Alvarez and their men," he whispered.

"How are Vincente and Diego related to the cartel?"

"They're brothers and run the Alvarez cartel. Gustavo was their nephew."

"Where are they now?"

"In the U.S. somewhere. They're going to contact me."

Steel didn't detect a lie in his voice, face, or eyes. "Anyone else take part in Marita's death?"

"No."

"You forgot to name yourself and Hernando."

"I have money. Whatever you want."

Steel recalled the sickening photo of Marita that the Colombian had sent him. He was aware of Christie watching him from the corner as she kept an eye on Garcia's family. The children were sobbing as the mother tried to comfort them with soft words.

He didn't want the children here, but he had no choice. Rising to his feet, he put the knife away and drew the Glock.

"There's no need." Garcia gaped up at him.

Steel put two bullets into him. He glanced at Christie. "We have to get out of here."

She nodded, her face taut.

They went down the steps as fast as they could, and then through the living room toward the back door. In case any neighbors had reported shots fired, Steel didn't want to run into police in the driveway.

The moment he stepped outside, guns were pointed at him from the corners of the house and from behind trees surrounding the patio.

# CHAPTER 11

S TEEL KEPT HIS GUN lowered and didn't move. All the individuals facing him and Christie wore black hoods, black fatigues, and held silenced machine guns. They didn't look related to the cartel. Maybe military, but he couldn't see the connection. Again he wondered if the Colombian had sold them out somehow.

"Face the wall, hands behind your back."

Steel let the Rattler hang from the carry strap, turned around with Christie, and did as requested. Their guns were taken, along with their knives and goggles, and their wrists were bound with zip ties. They found his OTF knife, and someone dug the car keys out of his pocket.

Then they were pushed into the woods, heading east, one man ahead of them, four following. Before they left the patio, Steel saw two women and a man go into the house.

No sirens. No one had called the police. But five trained armed men made an escape attempt too risky.

The moon made the walk easy. And the Mexican spotted owl was still calling. Steel found it odd to hear a small gentle bird call after they had just participated in violence. Nature had always cleansed him after Blackhood missions, but that quality eluded him now as they walked captive toward another unknown threat.

He would have to wait for a better opportunity. As he walked he considered what had happened in the house. They had killed five men to save Harry. The killing gave him an empty feeling.

He had no regrets, especially for what these men had done to Marita—and probably other women along the way. But he didn't want to keep killing. No matter what the reason. This was far from over and he desperately wanted out of the mess.

Part of him felt tainted, dirty, going back to this kind of life. He wouldn't be surprised if it hit Christie just as hard. Glancing back at her, he felt shame that he had allowed this to happen to the woman he loved.

He glanced up at the shining moon. Oddly it gave him hope. Maybe they were walking toward a way out of all this.

They walked about a mile before they reached a different section of the road. A white cargo van was waiting, along with a black SUV. Both vehicles had drivers in the front seats. They were motioned inside the van. Bench seats lined both walls, and he sat by Christie on one side.

Four hooded men sat on the opposite bench, their guns aimed at them. The fifth took the passenger seat in the SUV. Steel guessed the SUV would scout for anyone following them. They were being careful. No one spoke. Christie pressed her shoulder into his. Her presence grounded him.

A half hour later the van stopped. They all piled out and walked into the front door of a house. Led across a living room to a study, they were motioned into two wooden chairs positioned in front of a desk. A stocky, six-foot-tall man dressed in black fatigues and wearing a black hood stood behind the desk.

Steel guessed the man behind the desk was an officer. While the four men stood at attention behind them, Steel sat down with Christie.

The man behind the desk took a phone call, saying, "Understood, proceed as planned." He then turned his attention to them. "Take off their hoods."

Their hoods were pulled off by the soldiers and the officer regarded them intently. "Names."

Steel sat back. "Who's asking?"

The man leaned on the desk with his hands. "I was just informed that you killed five men, which means prison time if I release you to the police. Don't waste my time."

Steel thought about it. The man wanted something and didn't want to kill them. At least not yet. "Jack Steel."

"Christie Thorton."

"Why did you kill Garcia?" The man's tone was matter-of-fact.

"We're being blackmailed," said Steel. "A Colombian man kidnapped Christie's brother, Harry. He said he'll kill Harry if we don't follow through on a hit list of Colombian cartel men that killed his compatriot."

The officer's eyes widened. "What's the blackmailer's name?"

"I don't know."

"The compatriot's name?"

Steel didn't answer.

"Why you?" persisted the officer.

Steel sat back. "I'm not answering any more questions until I know who you are and what you want."

"U.S. Army."

His shoulders relaxed. "Then get General Morris on the line and he'll vouch for me."

"I'm sure he will. Give me what you know or I'm turning you over to the police."

Steel didn't believe him. "It's above your pay grade."

"Let's find out." The man pulled out his phone and punched a number. "Sir, Jack Steel doesn't believe I have clearance to hear why he killed our target." He put the phone on speaker and set it on the desk. "You're on speaker, sir."

Steel recognized General Morris' voice. Morris had supervised the last Blackhood Op that he had participated in, the one which had resulted in Marita's death.

"Major Steel, please cooperate and tell Colonel Jeffries whatever he wants to know. He has clearance. And Colonel Jeffries, Jack Steel is the best operative we ever had in Blackhood

Ops, so trust him and help him." There was a slight pause. "Major Steel, this call never happened. Nor did your conversation with Colonel Jeffries."

"Understood, sir." Colonel Jeffries took off his hood. Black, half bald, about forty. A no-nonsense air about him. He gestured to his soldiers. "Remove their zip ties and leave us alone."

The soldiers cut their zip ties, left the room, and shut the door.

Colonel Jeffries focused on Steel. "I repeat, why are you being blackmailed?"

"Harry's kidnappers consider me responsible for a woman's death during a Blackhood Op over a year ago." Steel paused. "Her name was Marita Lopez. She was a DEA informant. General Morris supervised the Op. What is the Army doing here?"

Jeffries sat down. "Two of my men doing surveillance on Garcia alerted me that you were attacking him, so we came. Too late to save Garcia though. You just screwed up six months of research and planning on Rodrigo Garcia aka Garcia Rincón. Now we've got a problem. You're going to help solve it for me."

"Maybe," said Steel.

Jeffries gave him a hard stare. "After you killed Gustavo Alvarez last year, his cartel kept key cartel members out of the news and off the grid. They didn't want the U.S. government to target any more of their senior personnel or even know who to target. We believe the current cartel leadership continued Gustavo's plan for retribution against the U.S. by supporting a splinter ISIS terrorist cell.

"We believe the ISIS cell is already in the U.S. And we believe Garcia knew who they were and was going to contact them. You killed him before he made contact. He was the only high-ranking member of the Alvarez cartel that we've been able to identify."

Steel was glad to hear Jeffries verify that Garcia was part of the Alvarez cartel. Christie's expression betrayed relief too.

"We have two more names," said Steel. "Garcia gave them up. Vincente and Diego Alvarez. Brothers. They helped kill Marita, and Garcia said they're also running the cartel now. He said they're in the U.S. so they'll have aliases."

Jeffries' eyes shone. "Excellent. We'll see if DEA can track down their photographs."

"Can you help us find my brother Harry?" asked Christie.

Jeffries shook his head. "We can't do a military search for him in Colorado."

"Keep it low key." Steel looked at him. "You need our help, we need yours."

"And what are you going to do for me?" Jeffries eyebrows hunched.

Steel thought on that. "If the Colombian sends us after Vincente and Diego, we'll give you their location."

Jeffries waved a hand. "I need more than that. I need you to get the ISIS information from the cartel leadership."

"There's no guarantee the Colombian will send us after Vincente or Diego," said Steel.

Jeffries nodded. "No, but it's highly likely, and highly likely they are also part of the ISIS plan."

"If we find Vincente and Diego, why can't you deal with them?" asked Christie.

"Blackhood Ops haven't been run for over a year." Jeffries grimaced. "The president revoked covert Blackhood Op missions targeting terrorists because of the mess in Hawaii last year. Thus we can't kill these men on U.S. soil without a trial. Any other organization we bring in will have protocols about arrest and legalities.

"We just want them dead. And we don't want to wait for them to carry out terrorist actions to do it. If they're meeting with ISIS operatives, that's all the proof we need. You two are sanctioned to kill the involved cartel people and any ISIS operatives on sight."

Steel frowned. "How can you sanction us?"

Jeffries gave a grim smile. "You're not U.S. Army. We'll sanction you and not turn you over to the police. In exchange we'll help find Harry."

"An illegal Blackhood Op." Steel didn't like it but found it ironic that the Colombian had called the Op Retribution.

"You're blackmailing us too." Christie glared at Jeffries.

Jeffries shrugged. "You stepped into someplace you didn't belong."

"We had no choice!" Christie said bitterly.

Jeffries crossed his arms. "And you still don't."

"What if the police catch us?" asked Steel.

"You're on your own. We can provide resources, but that's it."

Steel watched Jeffries carefully, wondering if he was withholding information. "Do you know what the ISIS cell is planning?"

"No, but we expect acts of violence mirroring what they've done in Europe and Great Britain. They want to prove they can hit us just as easily as Europe."

Christie leaned forward. "We want you to find Harry before his kidnappers hurt him."

Jeffries shrugged. "We'll try. No guarantees."

"He's in the cargo bed of a white pickup with a bed cover, we think headed north of Boulder." She added, "Marita might be the kidnapper's daughter or sister."

Jeffries stood and sat on the edge of his desk. "We'll contact DEA and see what they can find out about her family."

"What's going to happen to Garcia's wife and kids?" asked Christie.

Jeffries tapped the desk. "Witness protection. The wife was told that if she chooses to go back to the cartel, word would be leaked that she sold out her husband. I've already received confirmation that she's accepted our offer."

Steel felt relieved over that, but another idea bothered him. "What if we can't get the cartel people to talk?"

Jeffries didn't hesitate. "You're sanctioned for whatever it takes."

"Torture." He didn't like it. "If we get the ISIS information from the next target on the list, we'll trade it for Harry's return."

Jeffries' voice was sharp. "You're not in any position to barter."

Steel ignored Jeffries' glare. "The kidnapper might have seen you take us and might ask about you."

Jeffries straightened. "Tell him you don't know who we are, but that we're blackmailing you to kill the cartel leadership too. Let him come up with his own answers."

Christie lifted her chin. "If the cartel finds out about us, we want witness protection for us, Steel's daughter and ex-wife, and my brothers and parents."

Steel didn't want to lose his house or hide the rest of his life. However the desire to protect Rachel, Carol, and Christie evaporated those concerns.

"Done." Jeffries returned to his chair. "Anything else?"

Steel thought about it. "Get rid of the guns we used and give us two more silenced Rattlers, two silenced Glocks and SIG Sauers, and a silenced Heckler & Koch G28 sniper rifle, with extra mags for everything. No serial numbers. We could also use a soft-sided backpack to carry the G28 and other gear." The G28 was light, short, and very accurate, and would give them an edge in long-distance situations.

"Waterproof ponchos with hoods," added Christie. "Dark colors."

Jeffries lifted a hand to her. "Do you want our medic to examine you?"

Christie blushed. "It's nothing."

Steel leaned forward, and then stood up to inspect her. He had to walk to her other side to pull her jacket back enough to see that her blouse was bloodied near her lower back. His eyes widened. She had kept the wound hidden from him. Its location suggested she could have died.

"Yes," he said curtly. "We want a medic."

Jeffries strode to the door and gave orders for a medic and the weapons.

Christie looked up at Steel. "I'm fine."

"Let's see it."

She lifted her blouse.

A knife wound. Steel was shaken and sat down. She should be out hiking with her brothers, enjoying life, not caught up in a life or death blackmail ordeal.

"It's nothing, Jack."

He couldn't respond. He could just as easily be staring at her corpse in the woods now.

A female medic arrived to clean and bandage Christie's wound. Jeffries watched from his chair.

Finished, the medic said, "I put antibiotics and butterfly bandages on it, but if the cut was any deeper you would have needed stitches. If you strain it open, you might end up needing stitches anyway."

The medic handed over a few small packets. "Painkillers."

"Thank you," said Christie.

"My pleasure, miss." The medic left.

Jeffries stood. "Your car is outside, along with your weapons and gear. I suggest you get on the road and wait for the kidnapper to contact you. We'll be in touch."

"The Colombian said we're on our own," said Steel. "If anyone is seen contacting us, he'll kill Harry."

Jeffries handed him a card with a solitary phone number on it. "Memorize it and hand it back."

Steel saw the number, handed the card to Christie, and she glanced at it before returning it to Jeffries.

"What phone is he contacting you on?" asked Jeffries.

Steel recited the number and Jeffries wrote it down.

"Good luck." Jeffries straightened. "Your country is counting on you."

Steel wanted to swear at the colonel, but let it go. All he could envision was Christie lying dead in the woods. There had to be a way to get her out. At least they had help searching for Harry, but he didn't like it that the help entailed more threats.

He stood. "Do you have any timetable for the expected ISIS terrorist activity?"

"Forty-eight hours."

# CHAPTER 12

CARLOS HAD NO IDEA who the men were that took Steel and Christie away. They were organized and moved with military precision. U.S. Army or some other undercover group.

His own government had branches that operated in secret. Maybe they had been watching Garcia. But why? It could complicate things. His oldest son, Mario, was on the road, watching Steel's car, but he wouldn't send him to follow. Mario had military experience, but it was still too risky.

When the three soldiers exited the back door of the house with Garcia's wife and children, he put away the night glasses and climbed down the tree. His boots had simple tree climbing spurs attached to them to make it easier, and he had a waist lanyard wrapped around the tree for support.

By the time he got down he was tired. He took off the spurs and lanyard and put both into his small backpack.

Pedro had already climbed down his own tree and hurried to Carlos' side. At twenty-two, Carlos' youngest son was short and wiry, his long black hair tied back in a ponytail, a baseball cap on his head. He wore dark clothing too. Carlos had chosen to keep Pedro with him since his son had no experience and his temper made him unpredictable.

"When are we going to kill Steel, Papá?"

"Patience. Steel has a lot of work to do for us before he dies."

"We should be the ones killing Marita's murderers." Pedro sounded disgusted.

Carlos put a hand on his son's shoulder. "And then we would all die, Mijo. Follow me. Quietly now."

When they passed the dead guard, Carlos pulled a silenced Glock from his waist belt. He would have preferred his Córdova pistol, but that would tie him too easily to Colombia since it was manufactured there and few were in the United States.

Decades in the Colombian military, along with his instructor position at the internationally famous military School of Lanceros, had given him superb tactical skills at all levels. But he needed few of those now. As a businessman in Mexico he needed fewer still.

Ironically he had moved his family out of Colombia to get away from the cartel, but the cartel had followed him north. Mexico was now more dangerous than Colombia. He wanted the Alvarez cartel to pay for that too.

Quietly he approached the back door, entered, and was led up the stairs by the bullet trail in the ground floor and second floor hallway. He found Garcia's body first. Staring at him, he saw the ankle, shoulder, and chest wounds. And the small cut on the man's face.

"He didn't suffer enough." Pedro used the toe of his boot to shove the man's face.

"Sí." Carlos wanted to unload his gun into the filth, but reason prevailed. The bullets in the wall at the foot of the bed led him to Hernando. He had died quickly too. Too quickly.

They hurried back to ground level and looked out the front door. Another dead guard was hanging half off the porch. It was easy to assume the fourth guard was dead too. Steel and Christie had performed well, as expected.

Retracing their steps out of the house, Carlos paused outside, staring at the tracks leading east.

"Do we follow them, Papá?"

"Too dangerous and too many unknowns." He would press Steel later for details. He walked east, to rejoin the road and their pickup truck.

Pedro walked beside him. "We need to make Marita's murderers suffer more, Papá."

"I agree, Pedro." It still pained his heart to think of Marita raped, tortured, and then thrown on the street like trash. Dead and disfigured.

Pedro spoke earnestly. "Why not have Steel cut up their faces like they cut up Marita? It would make them all pay a higher price."

"Good idea, Mijo." He was playing a very dangerous game in forcing Steel to take out senior cartel members. The one thing he could not do was place his own children in danger.

His wife had died and his three boys and daughter were grown. He originally wanted to do this alone. This was his vendetta. But his children loved Marita like a sister, and when they had seen her disfigured body in the morgue they had been outraged. They wanted Steel and the Alvarez cartel to suffer, along with the U.S. military that had betrayed Marita.

"I worry about Juan and Isabella," said Pedro.

"So do I." His daughter and second eldest son tended to argue. And Isabella had a temper. Neither of them had training for this type of thing, but Juan had experience with guns.

He had instructed them on how to proceed with Harry—the easiest task he could give them—and he talked to them on the phone often. Still a risk.

When Carlos thought about Marita, how much pain she had endured all her life, anger filled his throat. First the Alvarez cartel had killed Marita's lawyer parents—his sister and brother-in-law. Then Marita had sacrificed her life by becoming a DEA informant. She had allowed that pig Alvarez to touch her and use her. Lastly she had been betrayed by the very people she had served—the U.S. government. Left behind by Steel to suffer and die. He hoped she was at peace now.

As her uncle, he had taken her in like a daughter after her parents were murdered. Thus it was his responsibility to bring justice to her family by making all those responsible pay for the crimes against her and her parents.

He had taken risks to find the names of Marita's killers, and Steel's name, buying off DEA agents and cartel lackeys. It had cost a lot of money, but everyone had a price.

He had used third-party intermediaries so nothing could be traced back to him. A few times when he believed his sources would put him or his family at risk, he had killed them. They were scum anyway, rotten men that helped the cartel murder and control others by giving them information. He had also killed Marita's DEA handler for not helping her escape the cartel.

Then he had waited for Marita's killers to travel north. The killers' presence in the United States gave him the ability to force Steel to kill them. It also ensured his family would not be traced as easily as they would have been had he murdered the killers in Mexico or Colombia.

"I won't feel good until all of the Alvarez barbarians are dead, Papá."

"We'll destroy the cartel," said Carlos. "And then we'll kill Christie and Harry Thorton. Steel will know the pain of losing someone you love."

Pedro grabbed his arm, and Carlos stopped to face his son.

"Promise me, Papá. I want to put a bullet into Steel's head at the end."

He rested a hand on his son's shoulder. "We all will, Mijo."

They continued walking and Carlos heard an owl hooting. Mexican spotted owl. Beautiful. *What are you doing this far north, mi amigo?*

# CHAPTER 13

DIEGO ALVAREZ GAZED ACROSS the hotel room at Antonio Perez, knowing what was coming. He was tired, but Antonio had invited him to his room after they had gambled late in the night together. Music was on in the background.

Diego didn't like Antonio. However it would have been rude to have refused. Like himself, they all wore suits: Antonio, Antonio's two bodyguards at the door, and even Angel, who sat stoically in an armchair, not saying a word.

Angel's name had always amused Diego. At six feet, one-hundred-eighty pounds, his head of security was lean and tough for his forty-five years. But his face appeared friendly. His smile easily disarmed people. Only his eyes held a glint of menace. Diego wondered if Antonio saw it.

"Diego." Antonio turned to him, holding a glass of brandy.

A little portly, Antonio had been an old friend of Gustavo Alvarez, but he was not family. He was a competitor to the Alvarez cartel. The two cartels were the largest operating in Mexico, and this was a neutral meeting in Las Vegas. And a warning. Diego waited for it.

"When your nephew Gustavo died, Diego, I wondered who would replace him." Antonio nodded to him. "You have erased all doubts. As leader of the Alvarez cartel you have shown wisdom and intelligence." he smiled. "You have much of both. More than I do, I believe."

"Gracias, Antonio." Diego gave a perfunctory nod.

"I'm glad you wanted my advice on your planned vengeance." Antonio's expression turned serious. "I have given it much thought."

"And?"

"You cannot put time and resources into vengeance." Antonio stepped closer. "The Americans will punish all of us if you do."

Diego kept his voice calm. "I want Gustavo's killer and the U.S. military to pay, and the U.S. citizens to pay for the crimes of their leaders."

Antonio wagged his finger. "It's not wise, nor profitable. I'm asking you, as a favor, to step away from all of this. Give up this alliance with ISIS. Pull the plug on it while you still can."

"And if I don't want to?" Diego said softly, already knowing the answer.

"I hope it won't come to that." Antonio frowned. "We have Mexico now. Colombia. All of Central America. We are successful, powerful, and we don't need to create enemies. The Americans don't want to fight us in the streets of Mexico, but they might if they find out you attacked them here through ISIS."

"They will never know it was me."

"You asked for my advice and I have given it." Anger finally showed in Antonio's eyes. "Please, stop this madness. Now!"

Diego said earnestly, "We have always punished our enemies. Tell me why this is different."

Antonio's eyes softened. "In our countries we can bribe justice, even destroy it. We can't do that in America. Some individuals, yes, but not the system itself."

"You're right. In America the corporations and politicians are doing all of that. They are as ruthless as the cartels." Diego smiled.

Antonio said quietly, "I will go to the other cartels if you can't let this go, Diego. Walk away from ISIS."

Diego lifted a hand. "All right, Antonio. I think you are right. Ending this is a good idea."

Antonio's smile returned. "Perfect!"

Diego turned and nodded to Angel.

Angel got up, fluidly turning and facing Antonio's bodyguards at the door, his silenced Glocks in hand, but pointed down. His reputation was well-deserved and the two guards paled and kept their hands at their sides.

Diego drew his silenced gun from beneath his suit.

"What's the meaning of this?" Antonio backed up. "You know my son will come after you."

"I'm not worried about that fool." Diego fired two shots into Antonio's heart.

Before the man hit the floor, Diego turned away and stepped up beside Angel. He eyed Antonio's guards and put his gun away. "You two, do you want to work for me?"

The two guards looked at each other, and then nodded to him.

Diego gestured to Antonio. "Then take out that piece of trash."

The two guards walked past them.

Angel turned and shot them both simultaneously in the back of the head, using one gun for each. They collapsed to the floor next to Antonio.

From his coat pocket, Diego pulled out an envelope. "We both loved Gustavo. Me as his uncle, you as his longtime friend. Avenge him, Angel. Here are photographs, names, and addresses of Steel's family, his girlfriend Christie, and her brothers and family. Kill everyone in their families first. Make them suffer before they die. Then Steel's girlfriend. Lastly kill the murderer Jack Steel."

Diego grimaced. Before she had died, Marita had described the cowardly way in which Steel had killed his nephew, Gustavo. He wanted Steel to suffer the most.

Angel put away his guns and took the envelope. "It will be a pleasure."

"This vendetta stays between me and you, Angel, so it can never be traced back to us. Antonio was right about one thing, we don't want the Americans to fight us in Mexico."

A slight smile creased Angel's face. "I might enjoy that fight."

"Start with Garcia. He should have checked in by now. Something is wrong. He was in Vail and hasn't answered my calls. It seems too much of a coincidence that Steel and Garcia are both in Colorado."

Angel nodded and left quietly.

Diego felt satisfaction seeing him go. Steel and his family were as good as dead. Angel's other nickname was El Lobo. The Wolf. Once he had the scent of a target, he never stopped until he found it. Diego had often asked himself if the man had an angel helping him, because he never failed. His skills were legendary. However Diego felt he could match Angel in a fight with knives.

As he viewed the bodies, excitement rose in his chest. He had planned to kill Antonio on this trip and had used the ISIS meeting as a reason to coax Antonio to meet him here. Now the Alvarez cartel could take control of Mexico. Antonio's only heir was his son, a fool who would run their business into the ground.

He had also planned on killing Garcia on this trip. Thus if Steel had managed to do it for him, all the better. Now only he and his brother Vincente would rule the Alvarez cartel. The trip north was already a success.

He walked out, eagerly anticipating his meeting with Vincente tomorrow, and then ISIS the following day. Once the ISIS operatives carried out their assignments, he planned on killing any that survived. Any links to him would disappear.

Finally he would have his vengeance against the U.S. government and the citizens of the United States. He would make them all pay for murdering his nephew.

# PART 3

## OP: VINCENTE

# CHAPTER 14

STEEL LET CHRISTIE DRIVE. Despite her wound, she insisted. They planned to travel west to Glenwood Springs and get a hotel. He didn't want to stay in Vail, and they both needed rest.

He was too tired to talk but needed to anyway. "What happened with the first guard at Garcia's place? And please don't leave anything out."

She glanced at him, her eyes betraying concern. "I got sloppy and was grabbed by the guard. He alerted the others so after I escaped I moved up to help you."

He frowned. "Tell me everything from the moment I left you."

After she finished he looked at her for a few seconds. It had been worse than he thought. He couldn't keep the gruffness out of his voice. "You didn't wait like I asked."

She glanced at him again, her eyes calm. "It wouldn't have mattered. He was hidden in the woods halfway up the driveway."

"He could have killed you." His voice was sharper.

"Your training ensured he didn't."

"If I can't trust you to listen to me, then I can't let you help me."

"Then don't treat me like a child, Steel. I'm your partner and you needed my help. I have great analytical skills, and I'm applying those to field work now. Strategy. I get it. Remember Hawaii? Who saved who there?"

"Good point." Despite his concerns, he was impressed. She had escaped a very bad situation, and then climbed up to the balcony with an injury. She was tough. And she was right. He had to adjust and not only trust her but trust his training of her.

He cleared his throat. "Okay. Partners. But next time you're injured, tell me."

"Agreed."

There can't be a next time, he told himself. She was right, he needed her help, but not for the price of her risking further injuries or death. He studied her heart-shaped face, her green eyes, and her hair trailing over her shoulders. "I can't afford to lose you."

"I know. Lesson learned." She reached over and squeezed his hand. "How did you know Garcia would come through the door with a gun?"

"Experience, and his voice and words. He also seemed to believe that this Antonio had sent us and probably figured he was as good as dead if he gave himself up."

"You're good enough for both of us." She flashed a quick smile, but then became somber. "I've never killed anyone premeditated before, Jack."

He winced, instantly feeling guilty. "I'm sorry. I—"

"No, you don't understand. The first guy that grabbed me talked about having fun with me, killing me..." His eyes narrowed and she hastily continued. "Anyway, it didn't bother me at all to kill those men. They deserved it for what they did to Marita."

Steel considered that for a few moments.

"Were you going to cut Garcia's face if he didn't answer?" she asked.

"Yes." He paused. "If what we did today bothers you later on, we can talk."

"I feel better killing these men now that we're sanctioned by Jeffries and we're stopping terrorists."

"I agree."

"I'm starved." She smiled. "You know, I just thought of something. This is our first road trip together. Not very romantic though."

He returned her smile briefly.

The phone rang and she lost her smile.

He answered on speaker, waiting.

"Good job on Garcia," said the Colombian. "I have your next assignment."

Steel kept his voice calm. "I want to hear Harry's voice."

"You'll have to wait."

Steel hung up.

Christie's voice was strained. "Jack?"

"If he can't put Harry on that means either Harry is dead or he isn't with Harry. Either way, we need to find out."

The phone rang.

Steel answered.

"Do that again, gringo, and you get Harry back in bits and pieces, one at a time."

Steel kept his voice neutral. "I want to talk to him or we don't do anything else for you."

"You're not in a position to barter."

"Otherwise we'll assume you killed him." He avoided Christie's eyes.

"We haven't."

"Prove it," he said.

Christie's knuckles tightened on the steering wheel.

"I can end this anytime I wish, gringo, and send your photos to the cartel, and you both will have very short lives."

Steel remained calm. "You might do that anyway. And as a return favor we'll make sure to tell them that someone who loved Marita was Harry's kidnapper, who blackmailed us to kill senior cartel members. Do you have children? People you love? People you don't want the cartel to know about?"

"Be very careful in threatening me. I am not joking when I say I am prepared to die if you do not deliver." There was a pause on the other end of the phone. "You will talk to Harry before you reach the target."

Steel lifted his chin to Christie. "How many more targets are there?"

"One more destination, then we are finished. Now I've made some concessions. I expect something in return. Tell me about your new friends. And if you lie, Harry is dead."

Steel had expected this. He ignored Christie's sharp glance. Perhaps the Colombian or one of his associates had watched the house and seen the military. Even if they had followed the soldiers to Jeffries, they wouldn't know anything more than what they saw from outside the house.

He decided to give the Columbian most of the truth. "I don't know who they were. They're professionals, and they want the Alvarez cartel leaders dead. If we don't cooperate with you, they threatened to hand us over to the police. I had to tell them about you to give them a reason for killing Garcia."

There was a pause on the other end of the phone. "Your military?"

"Maybe." Steel kept his voice even.

"Why would your military be tracking Garcia? That's DEA territory."

"I don't know. They wanted to follow us. I told them no. Any chance another cartel is trying to get rid of Alvarez's people?"

"Did they have Hispanic accents?" The Colombian sounded doubtful.

Steel paused, wanting to give the Colombian an alternative to the military. "No, but they could be hired mercenaries."

"All right. Drive west. You don't have time to get a hotel. I'll be in touch."

The call ended.

Christie eyed him. "Isn't it risky to lie to him?"

"If he learns for certain the U.S. military is involved, he might get nervous and run."

"And kill Harry," she said.

He massaged the back of her neck. "He might be ex-military too, which means he would guess it was U.S. Army. I think he'll be more careful, but he wants his vengeance more than any concerns he has of being caught."

# CHAPTER 15

AT GLENWOOD SPRINGS, STEEL said, "Stop at a gas station."

Christie frowned. "The tank is three-quarters full."

"I want to examine the car without being too obvious." He looked at her. "The Colombian or Colonel Jeffries could have put a tracker on it."

"Is it a bad thing if Jeffries is tracking us?"

He shrugged. "I'd rather have control over any appearances he makes. Saving Harry's life won't be at the top of his list of priorities."

"Right." She adjusted the rearview mirror. "We haven't been followed."

"Good."

She pulled up to a gas pump and filled the tank, while Steel pulled up the hood and inspected the engine for a tracker. Slowly he went around the car and checked the frame.

He found it close to the rear passenger axle. Small and round. Sophisticated. He slipped it into his pocket. Going around the car, he winked at Christie. She winked back and he smiled. He was glad he could still do that, even if he wasn't smiling inside.

When an SUV driver opposite their pump went into the station, Steel drew one of the hand towels from the center island and dropped it. While picking it up he attached the tracker to the undercarriage of the man's vehicle.

They got into their car and left.

"Who do you think it was?" she asked.

"Jeffries. High tech."

She raised an eyebrow. "He might be upset."

"Tough."

"Food?" she asked.

"Something gourmet."

"Mexican it is." She smiled.

He stared at her, wondering how she could be playful when she had almost died.

She found a fast food drive-through and they ordered burritos and quesadillas to go. After getting their food, they drove to the empty parking lot of a store, parked, and ate. Christie took two of the painkillers.

Finished, Steel leaned his head against the headrest. "I'm tired. Can you drive first? When you're tired, wake me and we'll switch seats."

"I aim to please. Take forty, Jack. I'm wide awake."

The phone rang.

He answered on speaker. It was the Colombian.

"There's a truck stop just outside of Grand Junction. Stop there, park on the far east side of the parking lot, and wait for my call."

The phone went dead.

Christie eyed Steel. "What do you think that's about?"

"I don't know. Nighty night." Steel closed his eyes and was out instantly.

***

He woke to Christie gently shaking his shoulder. The nightmare ended, Marita's disfigured face the last image in his mind.

Rubbing his eyes, he watched Christie get out of the car and stretch. He did the same, trying to shake off the disquiet he felt over the dream. Watching Christie, fury at the Colombian swept him for a few moments. He looked around. Christie had parked on the east side of the truck stop, as the kidnapper had requested.

The phone rang.

Christie walked around the front end of the car to stand beside him as he answered it.

"Your second target is Victor Sanchez, also an alias. He is in California, tasting wine and visiting Sequoia National Forest. He has six men, as well as his girlfriend. Kill all of them except the girlfriend. He'll be there no more than twenty-four hours, and it's a fourteen-hour drive for you. I'll text his address soon and send a photo."

"Vincente Alvarez." Steel wanted to be sure. "Garcia confirmed it."

There was a short silence on the other end of the phone. "Garcia gave you his name. Good. Now listen very carefully if you ever want to talk to Harry again."

"We're listening." He was glad the Colombian had affirmed Garcia's information.

"When I say *throw it*, I want you to toss the phone and car keys into the weeds adjacent to the lot. I'll be watching you. Then I want you to get your duffel bag and run to the back of the truck stop. There's a blue sedan, older model. Get in. Keys are under the driver seat. You have two minutes to reach the car or you won't be speaking to Harry. Now throw it!"

The call ended.

Steel threw the phone, while Christie ran to the driver's side to get the keys and her purse. She popped the trunk for him and threw the keys into the grass. Grabbing the duffel bag, he ran toward the back of the lot. Christie was already a dozen steps ahead of him.

Semis and trucks filled the parking spaces. They ran past them looking for the car.

"Here it is!" said Christie.

The sedan was parked between two semis. As they ran a phone rang from inside the car—audible since the driver's window was down.

Christie jumped behind the steering wheel and picked up the phone, putting it to her ear while pulling the trunk release. After throwing the duffel bag in the trunk, Steel hustled into the front seat.

Still listening, Christie found the keys and started the car. Putting down the phone, she put on her low beams and drove straight off the lot into the grass, talking as she drove.

"He said to drive straight ahead. We'll see tire tracks. Go slow, use low beams, follow the tracks to a side road, and drive back to the highway and take it west. He wanted to make sure we weren't followed and the car wasn't being tracked. We'll talk to Harry within two hours."

Steel leaned back. "He's smart and that makes him dangerous. And that also confirms that Jeffries ordered the tracker."

"Garcia gave us two names, Vincente and Diego, so how did you guess the next hit was Vincente?"

He studied her. "I figured it was more likely that the man had chosen the same first letter for an alias instead of Diego."

"You didn't mention Diego."

"Maybe the Colombian doesn't know about Diego. I don't want to add another target to our list." The dirt road was a little bumpy and Steel settled in. "How are you doing?"

She grimaced. "I'm tired of playing this guy's game. I want to know if Harry is safe."

"I'm with you on both counts." He picked up the phone and dialed Carol's number. She answered. His ex–wife and daughter were on the road and hadn't been followed. Carol put Rachel on the phone, and he smiled at hearing his daughter's voice.

"Hey, Dad, we're on a road trip."

"Are you enjoying it?"

"Yeah. Mom said you're going to join us if you can."

"I will, honey, if I can make it. I want to."

"Mom said we can go through South Dakota and see buffalo and reptiles."

"Wish I was there with you, Rach." He meant it—and resented the Colombian even more. He had spent many years hiking, caving, and birding with Rachel, and now he had brought an element of chaos and danger into her life. If they made it through this, he told himself it would never happen again. "Do you want to talk to Christie?"

Rachel didn't hesitate. "Sure."

He handed the phone to Christie, who said, "Hey Rachel. We heard a cool owl in the forest." They chatted a little longer before Christie hung up.

Steel eyed her. "You're good with her."

Christie smiled. "She's easy to talk to."

It had taken Rachel a while to adjust to the fact that he and Carol had divorced while she had been held by a kidnapper for two years. At first Rachel had resented Christie, but in the last few months things had been better. He was thankful for that.

"Never wanted kids of your own?" he asked.

Christie shook her head. "My career mattered more, and I'm fine with playing the cool aunt to Clay's two boys." She glanced at him. "Or a friend to Rachel."

"That makes me happy." He cleared his throat. "You need to call Clay."

"What do I say? Killed five men, Harry might die soon, gotta kill seven more, nothing else new? He'll be angry." Her voice softened. "They might want to join us and that can't happen either."

He understood. "You want me to do it?"

"Might be best."

He punched in the number she gave him and put it on speaker. Clay answered, and Steel filled him in briefly about the Garcia hit. Continuing, he said the Colombian was directing them to another location in California to go after another cartel leader. He quickly added that Colonel Jeffries' men were joining the search for Harry, and that he and Christie were sanctioned on the cartel murders.

Silence.

"You didn't tell me about the Garcia hit in the last call, Christie." Clay's voice had an edge. "Did you both decide that?"

Christie heaved a sigh. "My decision, Clay. Jack asked me why I didn't tell you. I'm sorry. I didn't want you to worry and there was nothing you could do."

Another pause, then, "Neither of you got hurt?"

"Scratches." Christie frowned. "We're fine."

"No more secrets, agreed?" Clay's voice was gruff.

"Alright," said Christie. "Agreed."

Clay continued. "A gas station attendant saw a white pickup headed north. We're taking side roads that look promising for hiding a truck." He paused. "Be careful."

"Thanks, Clay. Any news, let us know and we'll do the same." Steel hung up, wondering how many white pickups there were in Colorado.

"That's something." Christie's wooden expression echoed his own disappointment.

The dirt road ended at a curbed street. Christie gently took the car down the curb and onto the pavement. Taking side roads out of the housing area, they were quickly back on the highway, headed west.

While Christie drove, Steel studied a text from the Colombian. Vincente's photo and a hotel address. Vincente was clean cut, in his forties, with black hair. Buff.

Steel showed it to Christie. California was going to be harder than Vail in every respect. He sent Vincente's photo to Jeffries to forward to the DEA.

Christie yawned. "I'll drive another three or four hours, then you get to take over."

"Great." Curling up, he closed his eyes. His last image was that of Christie's taut face. It angered him that she had to suffer and worry. And he didn't want to think about killing seven men.

# CHAPTER 16

HARRY WOKE UP DROWSY. They had drugged him and he had no idea how long he'd been out. He wanted to rub his eyes, but his hands were tied behind his back and his ankles were tied together. No longer amateurs.

He fingered the wrist binding. Zip tie. Easy to break if he could slip his hands beneath his butt and feet. His watch was missing from his wrist.

His head was still near the tailgate and the gag over his mouth snug. At least he could breathe. He wasn't lying on carpet anymore, just the hard truck bed.

The other thing that had changed was that the truck bed had a different odor. He had a keen sense of smell and it seemed as if someone had transported dirt in the bed recently. They must have changed trucks. The guy with the woman had to be strong for those two to lift him.

He had color blindness, making dark colors in dim light hard to identify. Still he stared at the truck's color. Blue or black or dark green. He couldn't be sure. Not white though.

The truck stopped.

He waited, remembering the last comment by the man about killing him. He felt certain they planned to do it. Escape was mandatory. His mouth was dry and his stomach growled. And his legs were restless from too little movement.

Someone unlocked and opened the tailgate. He couldn't see the moon, but the faint night light suggested it was still out there. New blacktop. He could smell it.

The woman appeared in his field of vision this time. Long dark hair. A black stocking mask hid her face. Dressed in jeans, boots, and a white blouse. The hoodie was gone. Simple, but tasteful. Slender, but not skinny.

Without seeing her face, he couldn't guess her age. Her voice suggested someone around his age. His musings ended as the shotgun was pressed into the back of his neck.

The woman came closer and said, "You get to say hi to your sister." She undid his gag, punched a number on a phone, and held it up to his face.

"Harry?"

It was Christie. Her voice sounded gentle and worried. It brought a flood of emotion to his chest. He hated what he had to say, but he would never hesitate to sacrifice himself to help her.

Gathering his breath, he spoke fast and with force. "I love you, sis. Always remember that. I miss you like I miss the moon and driving with you in Dad's new pickup on fresh blacktop. Don't trust them—"

The woman was pulling the phone away from his mouth before he was finished, but he raised his head and shouted the last words, "—they plan to kill me!"

A dull thump on the side of his head dropped him back to the trailer, leaving him dazed. The woman yelled at the man in Spanish, and then they were both yelling at each other. They were speaking so fast it was hard to understand what they were saying.

But Harry did hear *Papá*. Brother and sister. Maybe their father was orchestrating everything. Must be a crazy family.

He interrupted their yelling with, "Water, please."

"Screw you, gringo!" said the man.

"We can give him some water." The woman's voice was firm.

She reminded him of Christie when she made up her mind. The product of growing up with tough brothers.

The man spoke angrily in Spanish and shoved the shotgun back into Harry's neck.

"We want to keep him alive and well for now, right?" The woman gently raised Harry's head and poured water into the side of his mouth with a spout from a bottle.

Harry took eager gulps.

In moments the woman pulled the spout out of his mouth and lowered his head onto the trailer bed. The man said something else in a harsh tone to her, and she spoke back just as harshly.

Harry listened while they argued further, and then said, "You're never the same once you kill someone. Especially if it's not self-defense. Murder will ruin you, señorita. You and your brother."

The woman blurted, "Shut up with your lies, stupid gringo! Your friend Steel seems happy, doesn't he? And he's killed many! He killed Marita!"

Harry swallowed when he heard that name. "He tried to save her. She ran—"

The gag was positioned over his mouth again by the man, who was swearing in Spanish. At least it sounded that way—ending with, "...estúpido temperamento."

"Shut up!" yelled the woman.

Harry figured he had been right about this being a family affair, and the woman hadn't contradicted his assumption. The argument was brotherly love for a sister. He would have smiled if his life wasn't on the line.

The tailgate slammed shut, leaving him in darkness. The threat of death made him realize that if he survived, he should pursue his dream of building a house, keeping bees, and growing herbs. It was time. He didn't need to wait until he met someone again. Life was too short. He hoped he had the chance to follow those dreams.

He licked his lips. The water had tasted good. *You done good, Harry.* He smiled. Water, giving Christie more clues, creating a fight between his captors, and planting a seed of doubt in the woman's mind was a great start. And he had more information about his captors. They weren't just whackos.

When the woman had mentioned the name *Marita*, he recalled the story Christie had told him late one night about the Gustavo Alvarez Op. Christie had told him what the cartel had done to the DEA informant, Marita, and why it still haunted Steel.

In a sense he understood his captors better. If the cartel had raped and tortured Christie, he would have hunted them all down too, or died trying.

The anger in the woman's voice indicated vengeance. It was obvious they needed to keep him alive long enough for whatever they were demanding from Jack and Christie. Steel would have insisted on the calls. He wondered what he should say next time. Christie would be going nuts. And her situation with Steel might be as dangerous as his.

Steel would feel guilty that they had all been dragged into his past problems. The guy was responsible to a fault.

The side of his head hurt and something wet trickled past his ear. That sobered him up. If they were going to kill him, he couldn't wait for a rescue. He had to break the zip ties and be ready to try something when they opened the tailgate again. He had nothing to lose.

*Let's see how strong you are, amigo.* Scrunching himself up, he tried to slip his hands over his butt. It would take a while, but he figured he had hours.

# CHAPTER 17

STEEL SENSED CHRISTIE'S STRESS as soon as he woke up. They were still on the freeway and she was on the phone, talking to her brothers. She hung up and talked without looking at him, her voice shaky.

"I talked to Harry while you were sleeping. He said they're going to kill him." She wiped an eye. "Harry gave clues about a different truck, new pavement, and the moon. I told Dale and Clay to search any recently paved roads for a dark pickup. Harry was talking about us driving Dad's old pickup, which was blue."

She heaved a breath. "I updated Colonel Jeffries but didn't tell him where we're going or the target. He wasn't happy about the missing tracker and didn't seem to know about our car switch. DEA told him Marita had no family. She's an only child and her parents were killed by the cartel. They're checking on relatives." Her eyes revealed sadness.

He straightened. "Tell me word for word what Harry said."

She did, and he said, "Harry's smart, like his sister."

She didn't smile.

He saw how tired she was. "Did you tell Dale and Clay that it's likely a man and woman are driving the truck?"

"Yes. Clay said they were going to drive back south and look more closely at the side roads to see if they can spot new blacktop."

"Great. Pull over. I'll drive."

They got out, but before they switched seats Steel held her, careful of her wound. "Harry will be okay," he whispered. "He must have heard them talking about killing him. We can confront the Colombian with it and maybe win more concessions."

She gripped him, the side of her face resting on his shoulder. "Are you just trying to make me feel better?"

"No. The Colombian promised Harry will live if we do the Op. But now we know he's lying. We can push for more now."

She pulled her head off his shoulder. "I love you."

"I'm both sorry and glad you're here." He kissed her under the moonlight and squeezed her lightly. "Things will feel better after you get some rest."

They got back into the car and he drove while she curled up on the seat. He was starting to feel this was all going to end badly. There were too many uncertainties. He wanted more control of the situation. The only way to do that was to put pressure on the Colombian. It was the one variable they could influence.

In twenty minutes the phone rang. He answered right away. Christie still slept.

The Colombian said, "You're not on speaker."

"She's sleeping."

"It's good she's resting. She's going to have to be alert soon."

Steel didn't reply, thinking about what he wanted to say.

The Colombian continued. "I want Vincente and his men to suffer. You remember the photo of Marita's face? That's what I want to happen to all of them before you kill them. Do it, or Harry will have that done to his face."

Steel thought about it. The young man who held the dynamite might be able to do something like that to Harry, disfigure him with a knife. He didn't want to do that to anyone.

"Don't think about it, gringo. You have no choice."

"I'll do it if Christie is out of this."

"If she doesn't participate, we kill Harry."

He heard no room for bargaining in the Colombian's voice. "Harry said you're planning to kill him anyway so I don't trust you."

"I gave you my word."

Steel glanced at Christie. "You're going to have to do more than that, because your word doesn't mean anything to me."

"You're playing a dangerous game, Steel. Are you sure you want to go down this road?"

"I want a hand-off with Harry to Christie's brothers right after this job. It has to be set up so they see him and know they can get to him safely when we're finished. Otherwise it's a no, now, to going after Vincente."

The phone went dead.

His fingers tightened on the wheel. What would Christie think of him if Harry ended up dead? Odds were against Harry surviving anyway, but he didn't have the courage to tell her that. And some part of him wanted to believe they could still save her brother.

He resisted calling the Colombian back and drove for a half hour before the phone rang again. Waiting until the third ring, he finally answered it. He was glad Christie didn't wake up.

It was the Colombian. "All right. I can live with your request. But I'll pick the place and situation. You make sure Vincente and his friends suffer and die today. And Christie stays in the game."

"Call us by one p.m."

The call ended.

"Damn you!" he muttered. He couldn't wait to put a bullet in the Colombian's head.

It soured him further that he had committed to killing seven more men to save Harry. No. To save all of them. To save his life with Christie.

No one was following them so he assumed the Colombian was driving ahead of them. He might have changed vehicles, and he had the two men who helped kidnap them to help with surveillance. Maybe they were using two vehicles, or even three.

He thought about the Colombian and his associates. The guy that had held a shotgun on Christie at the first rest stop acted like ex-military. He could have been hired to help. But the woman and man holding Harry were sloppy, indicating they weren't hired but had a personal motive. The young man wearing the C-4 vest also wasn't a professional so for him it was personal. It seemed likely that at least Harry's two captors and the young man were related to the Colombian.

If so, it pointed to a whole family in on revenge. Risky. He remembered the photo of Marita. If that had been Christie, her brothers wouldn't hesitate to go after the killers either.

They had no choice but to keep going for now. Hopefully Christie's brothers or Colonel Jeffries would find Harry so they could end all of this. Then he could send Christie home and hunt down the Colombian.

He wasn't looking forward to California.

# CHAPTER 18

ANGEL DROVE THE REST of the night and through the morning. Used to days with little sleep, it didn't bother him. He arrived in Vail at noon.

It was overcast, but the sun managed to send rays through a few breaks in the clouds. He thought it was beautiful the way the light created changes in color in the green forest and in the clouds. It reminded him of Renata. She always found happiness in nature's beauty, a trait he admired in her and one he had taken on himself.

He found the address without difficulty and drove up the driveway without hesitation. Extremely observant, he prided himself on picking up details that most missed.

Almost immediately he spotted the guard lying fifty feet from the driveway in the woods, nearly hidden by the trees. He stopped, put on gloves, and walked carefully through the forest, searching for footprints or anything that might give a clue as to what had happened.

It was easy. Based on the shoe prints, he guessed a woman had killed the man. He squatted by the body, seeing the bruising around the eyes, nose, and especially the neck. The guard had possibly surprised the woman, maybe even captured her, but he had not taken her seriously enough. She had bludgeoned him to death.

The guard deserved to die for that sloppiness. Angel didn't feel he was being sexist with that thought. In fact he had trained some very capable women.

He walked back to the car, drove up to the house, and saw another man lying half off the porch. Striding up to the body, he inspected it. Two bullets in the back.

He traced the trajectory, and again found the same woman's prints east of the house. She impressed him even more. And the fact that she had killed two men took her out of his refuse-to-kill category of *innocent women and children.*

He walked west from the porch, the way the dead guard had been facing, and found a man's shoe prints. It didn't take long to trace them to the backyard, the third dead guard, and then to where the man and woman met, and split up.

They had approached the rear corners of the house. The balcony. Smart.

He also discovered boot prints. A half-dozen, leading east, along with the same woman's and man's shoes, along with a new set of woman's shoes. The wolf in him wanted to investigate the boot prints immediately, but he couldn't afford to leave his car in the driveway that long. Instead he carefully noted the direction, the sun's position in the sky, and let it go.

Inside was a mess. Too many bullets. Very sloppy. Garcia and Hernando had tried to defend themselves and died for their failure.

He felt no remorse over their stupidity. Garcia had never been known for his intelligence. The man was also a coward. Diego had been planning to get rid of him on this trip anyway.

Garcia's wife and children were missing. Not killed. Striding out the front door, he got into his car and left.

He headed east, using the sun to get his bearings. In a mile he came to a house that appeared vacant. Vail had a lot of house rentals. Parking in the street a block to the west, he took out a Glock and entered the woods.

He headed north, searching for the tracks coming from the west. He didn't find them. They must have driven to the house. Taking a risk, he crouched and walked up to the side wall and peered through several windows. Empty. It was a curious puzzle. He loved it.

Once he was back on the road he called Diego and filled him in.

At the end of it, Diego asked, "What do you think?"

Angel appreciated the question. Diego treated him with respect, an equal, and knew his expertise deserved it. "Do we know who was with Steel in Colorado?"

"His girlfriend and her brother Harry."

Angel considered that. "It's unlikely that it's just a coincidence that Steel and Christie are here, and a man and woman killed Garcia. But why?"

"I have no idea," said Diego.

Angel had no solution to that question either. "A group intervened, I'm guessing after the fact. I doubt we'll find Garcia's wife and children."

"How can Steel know that we are here? It makes no sense. And who intervened?"

Angel knew Diego was worried. "I think a third party is involved. Someone betrayed us. Perhaps the group was watching Garcia, and Steel interrupted their plans."

"Talk soon, amigo." Diego hung up.

Angel settled back in his seat. They were on a timetable, but he had to be patient. Needing more information, he decided to start at the beginning. Steel had been at the Macky Auditorium at Colorado University in Boulder, protecting a woman speaker. He drove the highway east through the mountains.

Details again caught his attention.

A black SUV on a scenic overlook had a smashed-in rear passenger window. A police car was parked on the passenger side. The officer stood beside the vehicle's front passenger door, his head stuck halfway in through the open window.

Angel slowed to note the SUV license plate, and then drove on. He called Diego and asked him to contact their connection in the police department to see what he could obtain. In Mexico or Colombia he would have stopped and questioned the police officer. Here it would invite more risk and attention that he didn't need.

Diego called back in ten minutes with the police report. "The SUV was rented by Steel. He and Christie left the auditorium parking lot, leaving three men dead. The men were attacking Afia Ameen. Christie's brother, Harry Thorton, was also at the scene. Someone spotted a small white pickup with a cargo bed cover leaving the area."

Diego paused. "What do you make of it?"

Angel considered the information. "It's a mystery, but if Steel and Christie killed Garcia we all have to be careful."

"I will warn Vincente to be on guard until we know who the opposition is. My brother is clever, not stupid like Garcia. If Steel is coming to us, all the better. Good hunting, Angel."

Angel kept driving, enjoying the mystery. However something about this job made him uneasy. In his decades of working with Diego he had never hesitated. Never questioned. But he couldn't deny a small feeling of uncertainty about this case. When he asked himself why, he had no answers.

In an hour he reached Boulder and found the University without incident. The parking lot on the side of the Macky Auditorium was taped off. It had to be where Steel had been attacked.

Not seeing anything useful, he drove away and pulled out his phone. He hit a number on speed dial.

A woman answered, her voice soft and loving. "Angel."

"Renata."

"I'm worried about you," she said.

"I'm fine." She was always worried. He thought it was due in part to being confined to a wheelchair and spending too much time in her head. But he loved her more than his own life and never held it against her.

They were twins and had always been close. No matter what happened in their lives, they would always have each other. She was the reason for his sanity and success.

He said, "We think Jack Steel and Christie Thorton killed Garcia and might go after Vincente. An unknown group intervened. And a white pickup truck was seen outside of Macky Auditorium in Boulder Colorado. Harry Thorton was also working with Steel and Christie."

He stopped just before the highway junction and pulled off onto the shoulder. "North or south?" His sister always did best when presented with choices.

"North feels better," she said. "But the white pickup doesn't seem right."

"Maybe they switched vehicles."

"I sense a very dangerous situation here, Angel."

He excelled in dangerous situations and wasn't worried. "Thank you, dear sister. I promise to be careful."

"You're welcome, dear brother." She paused. "Do you think we could take a trip?"

He smiled. "Of course! Anywhere."

"I'm excited!"

"Me too. I will call soon." He hung up, wondering where she wanted to go. It would come to her, like everything else did.

She had received strong premonitions for as long he could remember. At first she had been terrified of them, but eventually she learned to harness them.

When they were children, their parents had been killed by the Colombian cartel for refusing to sell their farmland. Taking Renata's advice, he had pushed his sister in her wheelchair down ten miles of muddy roads to the nearest town. Eventually they ended up living on the streets in Bogotá.

With her guiding sight, and his smile and toughness, they had survived. Even thrived. He eventually commanded a small gang of thieves, never telling them his brilliance was in part driven by his sister's gift.

Years later he was introduced to Diego. They were a successful team. And he told no one about Renata or her premonitions. If he had, she would have been murdered by his enemies long ago. He had hidden her from everyone in the cartel, as she had requested, only seeing her in secret.

She could guide him, and he could watch over her and provide for her. Oddly, her gift of premonitions didn't work for herself.

As soon as he had been able to afford doctors, he had her examined thoroughly to find out why her body continued to weaken. The doctors found a benign tumor, inoperable due to its location near the spine and base of the brain. It was the reason she was confined to a wheelchair.

They had tried many therapies, including scores of alternative healing strategies, but nothing helped. He often wondered if the tumor somehow gave his sister the ability to have premonitions.

The tumor had continued to grow, creating more pressure in her brain. Then last month doctors told her that she had anywhere from a few months to a year left to live. That often gave him sleepless nights.

He drove back onto the road, turned north on the highway, and punched it. Clearing his thoughts, he focused. His work for Diego was usually almost too easy so the complexity of this case made things more interesting. Someone had taken a dangerous risk to kill a senior cartel member. After discovering who it was he would begin the vendetta against Steel's people. The wolf in him would do what it did best. Hunt and kill the prey.

He drove over the speed limit for a half hour before he noticed something unusual. Two black SUVs with tinted windows appeared ahead of him. They looked identical. Finding it curious, he followed them out of instinct as they continued on the highway northwest. When they reached Estes Park, they pulled into a gas station.

He pulled over to the side of the road, watching. The men that got out to pump gas were dressed in all black. Short haircuts. And purposeful in how they moved, reminding him of military personnel.

After they finished, one of the SUVs continued northwest on highway thirty-four and one headed northeast on it. He could only follow one of them, so he called Renata, watching the two vehicles quickly pull away from him.

After explaining the situation, he said, "Northeast feels better to me."

"I agree with your choice, Angel."

"Thank you, dear sister. Talk soon." He hung up, feeling safe and ready as he always did in these situations. Sometimes he felt all the years around Renata had strengthened his own abilities to *see* things.

He sped onto the highway. Canyons appeared, with more peaks, and there were a few straight sections. Traffic was light. In a minute he spotted the SUV far ahead on a curve.

He slowed down, keeping as far back as possible without risking losing them.

The overcast sky seemed to reach down and touch the tops of the mountains. He enjoyed the scenery, not green like the jungle-covered landscape in Colombia, but beautiful nonetheless. With many hiding places for bodies.

After thirty minutes the SUV pulled onto the shoulder a half mile ahead of him. He pulled over too, watching them.

The front passenger got out with a pair of binoculars, watching something farther up the road. Angel leaned over, pulled his binoculars out of the glove compartment, and scanned the road ahead.

Several miles away on a curve he glimpsed a pickup, but it quickly disappeared. It was dark colored—not white. Perhaps the kidnappers had switched vehicles.

The SUV remained parked. It looked like the men were waiting for the pickup to reappear. Another of the men got out, a cup in hand, and leaned against the SUV.

It might be a while. No matter. He was patient.

Forty-five minutes later they were still there. It didn't appear that they were sure the pickup belonged to the kidnappers, because they hadn't called in the other SUV. Whatever their assumptions, he had a good feeling about the pickup.

From the glove compartment he took out his box of badges and selected a U.S. Marshal's badge. He attached it to his belt. It was a stretch, but most people wouldn't question his presence, nor even know what a U.S. Marshal's job entailed. Too many TV shows and movies took liberties that the general public absorbed as fact. And he had perfected his American accent long ago.

Leaning back, he did a quick body scan, relaxing all his muscles. Calm helped him operate efficiently. He was ready. And if anything occurred that surprised him, he would call Renata.

# CHAPTER 19

STEEL DROVE MOST OF the night.

Christie took over in the morning, allowing him to sleep until noon. It was midafternoon when they arrived in Three Rivers, California. The overcast sky threatened heavy rain, but so far only a light drizzle hit their windshield.

Christie pulled into a gas station to get gas and supplies. Steel checked in with Clay, who sounded tired. No news. Next he called Colonel Jeffries to see if there was anything new regarding Harry. The colonel had nothing to report but wanted to know where they were and what vehicle they were driving.

"We're about to go after the second target," said Steel. "We'll need witness protection for a woman. If we get the ISIS information, you better deliver on Harry."

"Who's the target and where are you, Steel?"

He heard the colonel's frustration. "We'll keep you posted."

"That's not good enough." Jeffries sounded angry.

"Find Harry and I'll answer all of your questions." He hung up.

Christie returned with a map, fruit, nuts, juice, and water. They pulled the car into the back of the lot. Steel retrieved a pair of binoculars from the duffel bag in the trunk. While they ate he filled her in on the calls with Jeffries and Clay, and the earlier call with the Colombian.

"He wants us to cut up Vincente and his men just like they cut up Marita's face." He chewed slowly. "While they're alive."

"He's sick." She shook her head. "How can he verify that anyway?"

"I think he's ahead of us and scouts out the scene after we leave."

"He's crazy." She took the juice bottle he offered and slugged a drink. "What else?"

"He said if we don't do it, they'll cut up Harry."

She stopped eating and stared at him.

He shook his head. "The man and woman with Harry are amateurs so I don't think it would be easy for them. You have to have a certain mentality for senseless torture. Either training, no values, or a disturbed mind. I couldn't do it just for revenge."

"Good. I can't either." She glanced at him. "And I don't think I'd be in love with someone who could."

Another thing was bothering him. "Let's assume Garcia, Vincente, and Diego came here to meet with the ISIS terrorists. If so, they might have sent someone to check on Garcia if he didn't answer calls, which means they might have already discovered that he's dead."

"They won't know it's us."

"I don't see how they could." He chewed some nuts. "We continue for now. Before we kill Vincente and his men, I told the Colombian that we want Harry set up for the drop to Dale and Clay. They might be able to get to Harry before we have to do anything. It's our best shot. The Colombian will call us by one."

They hung out there for another quarter hour. Steel worried that the Colombian had lied to him.

But the phone rang on schedule.

The Colombian sounded gruff. "It's going to be in the mountains. Give me the phone number for Christie's brothers. I'll call them and tell them where to be. You can check with them in fifteen minutes. There is no way they are going to rescue Harry before you take out Vincente. You are running out of time."

Christie gave the Colombian Clay's phone number and he hung up.

Steel grimaced. "He's boxing us in. I don't trust him, but we have no choice. Wait a few minutes and call Clay."

Clay answered on the first ring, sounding relieved. "The Colombian told me to park on highway thirty-four before it enters the mountains and wait for further directions. I'm close to it and will call you when I get there." He hung up.

Clay called Christie back in ten minutes. "It's freshly paved so it fits what Harry gave us. I'm thinking I'll go in a few miles and see if I can spot anything. Dale is in another rental car so he can wait here in case I'm wrong."

Steel's hopes rose. But he didn't like the idea of Christie's family at risk in three different locations. "Be careful, Clay. This guy is very smart and dangerous."

"Roger that. Talk soon."

Steel looked at Christie.

She stopped chewing. "You're worried."

"Seven men." He didn't state his deeper concern of her getting another injury or dying.

She patted his hand. "You're smarter and we're a better team. And we're desperate." She slugged down some water. "What's the plan?"

"We watch their hotel and wait for them to leave. The Colombian said they're going to visit a winery and Sequoia National Forest. The forest would be better for us, but I doubt they'll go there in the rain. The winery would be harder and too public. We might have to wait until they leave and ambush them on the road."

He dreaded an Op like that. Too many risks and unknowns. It wouldn't be a controlled situation.

"Let's put on the ponchos." Christie opened the trunk and got them out. They were dark green.

It took them fifteen minutes to reach the hotel address in Lemon Cove. The hotel had private grounds, and the entrance was a U-shaped drive up to the front door. Christie drove past it on the highway, and then pulled onto a frontage road adjacent to the property. The street was lined with trees. Perfect to park and wait.

Steel called the hotel to verify that Victor Sanchez was still checked in. He was, and they settled in. The terrain was flat so Steel could watch the hotel entrance with the binoculars. The rain increased slightly.

Two black sedans with dark tinted windows pulled into the hotel entrance. Through his binoculars Steel saw seven men and a woman in a yellow raincoat exit the cars. One of the men matched the photo of Vincente that the Colombian had sent them.

They waited an hour. Finally there was movement. The black sedans left the hotel entrance.

He put down the binoculars. "They're on the move. Hang back."

The rain was steady now, the temperature in the upper forties. Steel thought about calling Jeffries but decided to wait. The sedans followed the winding highway northeast in the direction of Sequoia National Park. It surprised him.

"Late afternoon on a weekday with steady rain; there won't be many visitors to hike the trails." Christie followed the sedans at a distance.

In a half hour the sedans reached the park entrance, stopping to get a permit. Christie waited until the cars drove in. Then she pulled up to the kiosk too. The park was open twenty-four-seven and the attendant gave them a trail map.

"Why would they go here in the rain?" asked Steel. It felt too easy to him.

"The woman. She's never seen it. And she has a new raincoat so she's making him go." Christie smiled at him. "Women have power over their men, Steel."

"Don't I know it."

Despite his concerns, he couldn't help but marvel at the size of the trees and their majesty. He wished they were here under different circumstances. He hated what was coming. Worse, he didn't want Christie here.

"Stunning. I've always wanted to see these trees." Her eyes showed no joy.

For a few moments fury erupted inside him at the Colombian, but he let it go. Otherwise he would get sloppy and put them both at risk.

The park road wound like a snake, the forest turning darker as they went deeper. The sedans repeatedly disappeared and reappeared ahead of them like phantoms among the massive pillars of red bark.

They followed the winding road for another hour. Only a few cars passed them. They stopped before reaching the parking area for the General Sherman tree. The sedans continued on to a lot marked for the handicapped that was adjacent to the tree. Christie parked on the road a good distance away from the lot.

Vincente and his girlfriend got out of the lead car with umbrellas. The girlfriend wore her bright yellow raincoat, Vincente a long black one. They posed together in front of the General Sherman tree as the driver from their SUV took photos. No one exited the second car.

"Call Clay," said Steel.

Christie did, but Clay had no news.

Steel didn't like it. The Colombian wasn't delivering. But they had little choice about it, other than refusal. And right now that didn't feel wise. He could never face Christie if it resulted in Harry's death. One more Op. Then either Jeffries, Clay, or Vincente would provide a way for them to get out from under the Colombian's control.

Christie leaned forward to gaze through the windshield at the height of the General Sherman tree. "That tree is thousands of years old, and yet humans think we're so important."

"Sequoias are disease resistant and have the thickest bark of any tree." He stared at the tree, feeling sick inside that they were in a place of serene beauty with violence waiting for them.

Christie extended her hand and he held it.

"I wish we were here with Rachel and my brothers," she said. "I know you do too. We'll have to come back."

"Yes." He sat back. "Let's kill Vincente only if we have to. If we can get the ISIS information, and Jeffries or your brothers can find Harry, we can end things here." He vowed to make that happen.

"The Colombian said this was the last hit." Her tone didn't sound hopeful.

"I don't trust him either."

"We'll have to find him, Jack, or he might release our photos to the cartel."

"I was thinking the same thing." He turned to her. "If Jeffries can find a relative for Marita that fits the Colombian, we'll be able to end this."

The rain came down harder.

Vincente and his entourage hurriedly got back into their car. Christie quickly drove north on the park road, stopping in a small turnaround. It didn't matter, because the sedans drove south, back toward the entrance.

Steel hoped they weren't going to a winery now. "We might have to take them here on the road."

Christie quickly turned around and followed. But the sedans entered the parking lot for the Giant Forest Museum. The rain was heavy now, the parking lot dark and empty except for the two SUVs.

This time Vincente and his girlfriend exited their sedan with their driver and another man. All four wore raincoats and carried umbrellas. The four men in the rear car also exited, also dressed in raincoats and holding umbrellas as they walked behind Vincente.

The whole group followed a dirt trail into the Giant Forest. They quickly disappeared in the rain.

Steel sat patiently, formulating a plan.

Christie prodded his arm. "What are we waiting for?"

"Let them get farther along on the trail. It will make things easier on us."

After ten minutes they pulled up the hoods on their ponchos, got out, and opened the trunk. Steel took the backpack Jeffries had given them and stuffed the G28 sniper rifle and its silencer inside it. Christie slid a knife into her back waistband. They both grabbed zip ties, spare mags, and silenced Glocks.

Steel held his gun down by his leg, while Christie shoved hers into her waistband. She grabbed a SIG and carried it alongside her thigh.

They walked down the trail. Steel stopped to glance at the trailhead map. Running through options, he suddenly knew what he wanted to do. He led Christie twenty yards in on the trail to the south side of a large tree.

The rain beat against their ponchos with a steady patter. His voice was calm as he spoke.

"Okay. The trail goes north, then east and loops clockwise back to here. Go off the trail immediately, heading northeast. Eventually you should be able to see the girl's yellow raincoat. Find a good place to target the trail and stay put.

"I'm going off-trail due east to get ahead of them on the trail. I'll move fast, and with the sniper rifle I hope to even the odds. There's a good chance they'll run back to the exit once I begin shooting, and you can target them from off the trail." He paused. "Promise me you won't engage them until I do. We have a big advantage with surprise and we want to maximize it."

She rested a hand on his chest. "I promise, Steel."

"If anything looks wrong or suspicious, hide and wait for me to come to you."

"I will." Her eyes didn't waver off his.

"No mercy. Don't worry about saving Vincente if it puts you in danger. Stay low, be careful." He looked at her eyes—steady. "Ready?"

"One hundred percent."

He hugged her, and then left, moving fast, using the large trees for cover. Unable to take his mind off her for the first minute, the terrain quickly forced him to focus. The ground was slippery and he couldn't see clearly for more than fifty feet.

Running around the giant sequoias made him realize how an ant must feel crawling past the foot of a human. The forest felt like something out of Alice in Wonderland. Surreal. Even more so because he was hunting people amid this beauty.

Ferns, grass, and undergrowth covered the ground and the forest birds were silent in the rain. Pine trees filled inbetween the scattered sequoias, but little of their scent reached him through the rain.

The rain pelted his face, shoes, and lower legs. Yet he remained mostly dry.

In a quarter mile he came upon a big tree with a knot at its base about five feet high. Tucking the Glock into his belt, he climbed up to stand atop the knot. There he took out the G28 and attached the silencer.

Slowly he scanned the woods ahead and to the north with the rifle. Nothing. The rain made it difficult to see much. However the yellow raincoat of Vincente's girlfriend would stand out even at a distance.

He climbed down and walked around the tree to take another view with the rifle to the north. Still nothing. Deciding to continue, he ran parallel to the trail.

His plan was to hit Vincente and his men hard. Kill all of them if he could. Without Christie's help.

It was a risk, and she would be angry with him later, but he couldn't stomach seeing her wounded again or worse. He would use the rifle to box Vincente and his men in. If one or two managed to escape via the trail, he felt confident Christie could handle them.

He had adjusted to the fact that she was a pro. However she was injured, which always compromised skill sets. Thus he planned to make sure Vincente and his men all died before they reached her. Ironically, even without the Colombian blackmailing them, he wanted to kill these men for what they had done to Marita. Their depravity had set all of this insanity into motion.

In another five minutes he stopped again to view the trail west and north, expecting to see the girlfriend's yellow jacket. He didn't see anyone. Triggers went off in his head. The odds of not seeing anyone were low.

Abruptly the visit to Sequoia National Park in heavy rain felt like a set-up. Vincente had known they were coming. How? Panic hit him as he ran due north. He had sent Christie into a trap.

# CHAPTER 20

CHRISTIE HAD AS DIFFICULT a time separating from Steel as he did from her. But it would be foolish to stay together. Knowing he was out there, moving ahead of her, gave her confidence that they could do this. And if Dale and Clay could rescue Harry, then there was only the Colombian left to deal with.

She watched Steel disappear before she ran off the trail into the rain. Her shoes had good soles but she was still careful. She didn't want to lose her balance on the wet ground.

Every time she saw a massive sequoia she felt awe, but those sentiments were rapidly shed as she hunted the killers. Darting from tree to tree, she constantly scanned northwest and north for moving figures, searching for the girlfriend's yellow raincoat or anything else that might yield the whereabouts of Vincente's thugs.

After a half mile she slowed. To the north the path remained hidden by rain and low ground cover. She saw a hint of yellow. Impulsively she gripped the SIG and stopped on the east side of a sequoia, trying to think about the situation like Steel would.

The yellow coat wasn't moving. Maybe Vincente and his men were standing beneath a tree, waiting to see if the rain would ease up.

Another idea sent shivers down her back. Maybe the girlfriend had taken the coat off and they were using it as bait to draw them closer. That would mean Vincente had found out about them.

If so, Vincente's men might be hidden somewhere in a circle radius of the yellow coat. Most likely to the west or south—closer to her. That made her press herself into the trunk and carefully study the landscape between herself and the raincoat. Slowly she scanned the forest ahead and to the west several times. Nothing out of the ordinary.

She wiped rain from her eyes. The next large tree ahead of her would give her a good vantage point of the trail.

The steady rain filled the air with gray, and Vincente's men were all wearing black raincoats. Hard to spot. But their pants would be soaked if they stopped using their umbrellas. Her own shoes and pants were soggy, her legs wet and cold.

She hesitated, remembering Steel's advice on waiting for him if anything looked suspicious. But if it was a trap, and he followed the trail back to her, he might be in as much danger as herself. She needed to get closer for a better assessment.

Crouching, she jogged toward the next tree, watching the ground to avoid stepping on sticks. Puddles were forming on the soil. The rain wasn't letting up.

By the time she reached the next massive sequoia, tension crawled down her limbs. She couldn't see the trail and needed to move around the tree. Keeping her back to the trunk, she drew the Glock and pointed it behind her—so she would be able to shoot anyone trying to sneak up on her.

She slowly kept moving. Her SIG followed the round trunk. The tree had deep furrows, and sometimes the trunk jutted out at ground level. Then she had to step over or go around the bulge. She couldn't hide then, making herself an easy target.

A quarter of the way around the tree she glimpsed the yellow coat again. Fifty yards away. The rain made it difficult to see it clearly. It looked like it was hanging from the low branch of a tree.

The woman wasn't wearing it. Maybe she and Vincente hadn't gone any farther. Where were they?

A cluster of seven giant sequoias surrounded her, each big enough to hide all of Vincente's men. They could be all around her. Waiting. Watching. A number of the trees had dark cavities at ground level, big enough for someone to squat in and not be seen unless you were close.

Unsure what to do and where to go, she stood still for a moment. She heard muffled shots to the east. Steel. Focusing, she slowly continued around the trunk. She felt vulnerable, knowing every tree was a possible hiding place. Ahead of her a bulbous area at the base of the trunk—two feet high and three feet wide—forced her to stop. She would have to step around it.

Glancing throughout the grove, she slowly edged forward.

When she reached the foot of the trunk, she stopped with a jolt. A man holding a silenced pistol stood on the other side of the bulge, staring at her.

# CHAPTER 21

STEEL STOPPED RUNNING AND paused behind a tree. Using the rifle, he scoured the landscape east, north, and west. No sign of the yellow raincoat. The trail wasn't that far away—even if the rain hid it from his eyes.

Vincente must have stopped a short distance in to ambush them, perhaps never intending to lure them in very far. Christie could be facing seven men. That spurred him to change course a second time. Northwest.

As he ran, he took the silencer off the rifle and put both into the pack, threw it on his back, and drew the Glock. The rain shortened the distance that the rifle was useful and he would be in close quarters soon.

He tried to discard worries for Christie. She could handle herself.

Yet images of her lying on the ground or tortured by Vincente made his legs fly. He was taking a risk. He had no idea where Vincente's men were hiding, and he wouldn't be of any help to Christie if he was shot.

Three minutes later he slowed down, stopping close to a sequoia to wipe moisture off his face. Squatting, he gazed ahead. No movement. No figures. No sign of the yellow raincoat.

Remaining low, he moved farther around the tree to increase his viewing angle west. As he rounded the trunk, a figure appeared kneeling beside another sequoia to his right, aiming a pistol at him. He launched himself backward onto his back, firing as he fell.

The man ducked out of sight.

Rolling over, Steel scrambled to his feet and ran around the tree trunk in the opposite direction.

Another man rounded a massive tree to his left. Fast runner. Coordinated. Steel took a shot on the run—missed the swerving man—and kept going. Halfway around the tree he found a small crevasse in the trunk and ducked inside.

Pressing his back against the inner bark, he squatted, gun pointed out. He considered running to the nearest tree across from him. His back would be exposed to at least one of the gunmen so he stayed put.

His hope was that the men would chase him. If not, he might be here a while, leaving Christie on her own. That reality sent his thoughts spinning.

Faint shots sounded to the west.

He might have to take another risk.

# CHAPTER 22

C HRISTIE RECOVERED FROM A millisecond of shock and leaned back, firing her gun at the same time the man shot at her.

The man mirrored her reaction. Neither of them scored a hit. She stumbled back, keeping her gun aimed forward, but the man never came. Whirling, she ran around the tree to come up behind the enemy.

Her left arm and gun were pointed ninety degrees out from her at the forest, the Glock following the curve of the tree. She estimated three to five seconds.

She slipped once and hit the trunk with her shoulder. Grunting, she pushed off and kept going. Glancing out at the other trees, she almost missed the man running straight at her around the tree.

He was slightly farther out from the trunk, due to one of the trunk's bulbous feet. He saw her at the same time. Stopping, she slapped her back into the tree and fired three times with her leading gun. Aware of his gun going off, she expected to be hit.

He went down in a heap. Neck, chest, and head wounds.

Surprised she hadn't been shot, she looked down. Two bullet holes had scored her poncho beneath her armpit.

Another sequoia in the grove was directly across from her to the west. She ran for it. There was movement in her right peripheral vision. Diving to the ground onto her side, she aimed both guns right.

Thirty feet away a man was running at her—firing.

She shot out his legs and kept shooting as he went down until he didn't move. She had to assume Vincente and his men would have heard her shots.

Rattled, she scrambled to her feet and looked around. Then she sprinted for the tree ahead of her. She made it, and carefully slid around the trunk, ignoring the pain from the cut in her lower back. Vincente's men might be working in pairs. If so, one pair had to be attacking Steel. That left two more men, plus Vincente and his girlfriend.

Slowly edging around the tree, she stared at the trail sixty feet away.

Vincente's girlfriend was on her back, her hands raised protectively over her face. Sobbing. She wore a dark sweater and slacks.

Vincente stood above her, his feet straddling her as he bent over to slap her and backhand her.

Christie assessed him. One-eighty, mid-forties, five-foot-ten. Cretin. She wanted to put a bullet in him just for beating his girlfriend. Vincente's driver stood on the trail fifty feet south of his boss, staring off into the woods. Unsure where the rest of Vincente's men were, Christie didn't shoot. They had to have heard the shots so this had to be a trap.

Keeping a pine tree between her and the two men, she ran to it. She held both guns close to her chest, wary of an ambush. The beating rain disguised her footsteps, but it also meant it would be harder to hear Vincente's men.

Ahead of her a giant sequoia stood close to the trail. She darted to it. Taking a deep breath, she slowly crept around the tree counterclockwise. She wanted to end up behind Vincente and his girlfriend.

The trail quickly came into view. The girl was crawling through puddles, still crying. Vincente wasn't in sight.

The trap.

Christie edged out a few inches farther. Fifty yards south, Vincente strode along the trail with his driver, headed toward the parking lot. Leaving his girlfriend? Harry's image came to her. Vincente had to be stopped. Helping the woman would have to wait.

She hesitated. Vincente's other men might be hiding in the surrounding trees. Where was Steel?

The girlfriend became aware of her and turned, her mascara running in the rain, her eyes wide. Korean. Five-foot, one hundred ten pounds, late twenties, black hair. Stupid. And soaked. Her wet clothing clung to her athletic frame.

The woman lifted one hand to Christie. "Help me," she whispered.

Christie ignored her and strode forward, sighting her guns on Vincente's back.

Something slammed into her side and her shoulder banged into the tree. She lost her balance and her ribs screamed. Vincente's girlfriend knocked her arms aside and punched her in the ribs again.

Christie tried to raise her guns, but the woman tackled her to the ground away from the path and behind the tree. Pushing Christie's arms aside and kneeling on them, the woman punched her in the face.

Grunting, Christie's survival instincts and training kicked in. Her hands were useless if she hung onto the guns. She dropped the weapons and writhed violently.

One of her arms slipped free, then the other. Feinting a right punch, she used her left to hit a lower rib. The woman gasped.

Simultaneously twisting, Christie used her left knee to thrust the woman off her. Both actions made her cry out in pain. She rolled away from the Korean and pushed to her feet.

Vincente's girlfriend was already standing and smiling. She threw a sidekick. Twisting again, Christie blocked the blow with her arm, while driving an elbow down at the woman's knee. She missed as the Korean jerked her leg back. The woman snapped her foot into the side of Christie's head and she stumbled back into the tree.

The woman came at her again fast, fists held up like a Thai kickboxer.

Christie remembered what Steel had taught her, and what she had practiced a hundred times in the VR sims. Pulling the knife, she stepped to the side, slashing the blade in an upward arc. She scored the woman's forearm while twisting away from a knee kick. Dropping to one knee, she stabbed the woman in the thigh.

The woman screamed and kneed Christie in the chest.

Groaning, Christie fell to her side and kicked the woman's injured leg. The woman cried out and fell to all fours.

Footsteps on the path.

Christie scrambled over the wet soil and picked up both guns. Beyond the tree trunk, she glimpsed Vincente and two of his men running toward her, all holding machine guns. Seeing her, they stopped and fired.

Still on her knees, she ducked behind the tree as their bullets bit the trunk and the soil near her feet.

The Asian woman was lunging at her, swinging the knife.

Christie fired twice at point blank range. The woman slumped heavily into her, her head falling on Christie's chest as if she was taking a nap. It sickened her, but she had no time for remorse. She pushed the woman off her and hastily rose.

Running clockwise around the tree, her fingers tightened on the triggers. She fired as soon as she saw the mens' clothing. She hit the man to the right of Vincente first—in the back of the shoulder—he dropped to his knees.

Vincente and the other man stopped and turned toward her, firing, bullets tearing up the tree. Running out at an angle from the trunk, still firing, Christie hit Vincente in the arm and leg, the other man in his chest and stomach.

Both men collapsed. She put two more bullets into the man on his knees who was trying to rise. He fell dead.

Her chest heaving, she walked up to Vincente and kicked his gun away. She put another bullet into the second man to make sure he was dead. Keeping her SIG aimed at Vincente, she ejected the Glock mag, stuck the gun between her upper arm and torso, pulled out a spare magazine and reloaded.

Her thoughts were with Steel now. Two men were missing. She looked around quickly to make sure they weren't charging her. Safe.

Kneeling on Vincente's chest, she placed one gun muzzle into his open palm, the other against his forehead. "I want to know how you're contacting ISIS. When and where. If you don't talk, I'll start putting bullets in you."

"Go to hell."

She fired into his palm. He shouted and recoiled.

Switching gun positions, she ground the other muzzle into his good palm, the second into his forehead. "When, where, how."

He gasped in pain. "My brother is always careful. He told us nothing."

"Where's your brother?"

"Las Vegas. That's all I know. What do you want? Money?"

"Marita. Remember her? The DEA informant?"

"That's all this is about? That stupid whore? Your military left her behind. They didn't care about her so why do you?" He gasped in pain. "I have money in the house. Lots of it."

She stood up, remembering the photo of Marita's face on Steel's phone. The man sickened her. "I don't care about your money. And I don't want to end up like Marita. Neither does anyone else."

Holding his bloody hand in front of his face, Vincente cringed. "Wait! Wait! Diego will never let you live if you do this. He will find you no matter where you go if you kill me."

"We're counting on it." She shot him twice.

Without pause she ran to pick up her knife and headed east. She wondered what she had become. That thought slipped away as panic sent adrenaline racing through her. Faint shots again to the east. All she could envision was Steel in trouble, and being too late to help him.

# CHAPTER 23

AFTER HEARING MORE SHOTS to the west Steel decided to act. The two men would be coming from different sides. They would be cautious, but they would come.

He could see only a few feet in either direction. If one of them saw the crevice in the tree, they might circle wide and fire at him from the protection of another tree. He listened for anything that didn't fit the pattern of the rain.

Taking a calculated risk, he edged himself to the right side of the fissure so he could see farther in the direction he had arrived from. That man had been closer to his position and should show up first.

Ten feet away, the man's gun hand came into view. Aiming for the man's hand, Steel fired twice. The man shouted, his hand disappearing.

Shifting to the other side of the crevice, Steel didn't see the other man. He leaned out. Neither killer was in sight. Leaving the backpack, he stepped out. Still no killers in sight. He ran back the way he had come.

He spotted the wounded man running toward another tree. Three shots in the back brought him down. Continuing counterclockwise around the tree, gun arm extended, he kept his finger ready on the trigger.

In three seconds he spied the other gunman pressed close to the tree, edging around it. The man whirled, but Steel fired repeatedly until he went down.

Grabbing the backpack from the crevasse, he reloaded the Glock on the run and headed for the entrance to the park. Christie had to be a prisoner or dead. His limbs stiffened.

A figure ran at him in the rain. At first he didn't lower his gun. Then he recognized her. Eyes wide, heart pounding, he ran to her and held her, careful of her injury. His world was safe again.

In a minute he asked, "Are you all right?"

"Good enough," she whispered.

"How many?"

"Six."

He kept the surprise off his face. How had she succeeded against six killers? And how close had she come to dying again? "Vincente's girlfriend?"

"She was in on it and almost killed me. Thai kickboxer. I had to kill her."

He heard something beneath her words that bothered him. "Let's get out of here."

They ran, but he quickly slowed to a jog. It was obvious she was in pain from the way she favored her side. When they reached the parking lot, they found it empty except for their vehicle and the two SUVs.

He drove.

Shivering, Christie wrapped her arms around her torso. He cranked the heater and turned all the vents toward her.

"Wipe the guns down completely, whatever you used to shoot anyone. Same with the knife." He drove farther into the park. At a higher elevation he parked and got out with her. They wiped the grips, barrels, and stocks a second time, and tossed the weapons over the guard rail. They still had three Rattlers, a SIG, and the G28.

Back in the car, driving toward the exit, he scrutinized her. "Where are you hurt?"

She barely looked at him. "Some bruises. You?"

He didn't believe her. "I'm fine. Now tell me where you're hurt or I'll stop until you do."

Her voice had an edge. "All over. Ribs, the cut on my back, my face, and chest."

He felt sick inside. "All the Thai boxer?"

"Yes."

"I'm sorry."

"Your training saved me." She took a deep breath. "It's all right."

"No, it isn't." He softened his voice. "It's not you I'm upset at."

"I know."

He let it go. "Did you learn anything?"

"Diego is in Las Vegas. Vincente had no information on the meeting with ISIS." She stared at her hands in her lap, her voice quieter. "Vincente thought raping, torturing, and killing Marita was nothing. Offered me money. I didn't see how we could drag him out injured so I killed him."

"You had no choice. He might have given us a bargaining point to get to ISIS, but that's Jeffries' problem now." He was aware of her taut face, the lost look in her eyes, and her trembling hands.

"How are you, honey?" he asked gently.

"I feel like a hired killer."

Stopping the car, he reached over, grasping both of her hands tightly, knowing what she was feeling and not wanting this to stain the rest of her life. "You're saving Harry and our families and I'm proud of you. These men can't be allowed to live, and they don't deserve to have more chances to hurt us or anyone else. It's why I had to kill Gustavo Alvarez."

"Thanks for the reminder."

Her subdued emotions worried him. "You're not a killer. This is self-defense. It bothers you because you have a good heart and you're a good person. I'd be more worried if it didn't affect you."

Tears rolled down her cheeks. He leaned over and held her. He remained like that for some time, holding her in silence and stroking her head and back.

"Thank you," she whispered at length.

He pulled back and continued driving. The Colombian was as good as dead.

# CHAPTER 24

HARRY HAD SPENT AN enormous amount of energy trying to break free of the zip ties.

After managing to get his arms around his butt and feet, it still took numerous efforts to break the ties. Mainly because he couldn't drive his elbows hard enough past his torso while lying on his side. But he eventually broke them.

The ankles ties had taken another serious effort. He had to bend over from the waist in the bed, pulling on them until they finally gave way. His elbows were bruised from his efforts and his fingers ached. He shoved the remnants of the ties toward the front of the bed near his feet so they wouldn't be visible.

His ankles and wrists were sore and he was tired. Impatient. Food and more water would help that.

He hadn't eaten since breakfast the previous day. Refusing the poor-quality plane food when they flew into Denver, he had decided to wait for dinner. The restaurant they were originally going to eat at had healthy food, unlike many. Conscious of his weight, he liked to stay lean.

Sleep in the truck bed had also been hard to come by. In between dozing off now and then, he wasn't always sure if they were moving or parked somewhere—with his captors waiting for the order to kill him. He doubted the woman had it in her. Her brother did though. He heard it in the man's voice.

He tried to prepare for his escape by using one of Steel's methods, where he visualized repeatedly what he was going to do.

He envisioned the tailgate opening. He would be curled up, his hands partly hidden and his legs pulled up close so he was hunched over in a ball.

Steel had made him practice this escape variation in a pickup repetitively. Harry remembered thinking at the time it was overkill. Now he was glad for Steel's obsessiveness regarding readiness for all situations.

He also counted on the brother and sister being tired and sick of everything. Sick of him. If his plan worked, this was the last time he would be held caged up in the truck bed.

Sometime later, he wasn't sure how long but it felt like hours, the truck seemed to creep along on a road that wasn't smooth. Maybe dirt or gravel. He listened for any sounds, but nothing distinct reached his ears.

The truck stopped.

Quiet.

He prepared himself.

Another long interval went by. Several hours if he had to guess. Finally he heard the key in the tailgate lock.

He kept his eyes closed and his mouth slightly open, his left hand against his back while his right was beneath his waist. Trying to hide the absence of the wrist zip tie, he concluded his captors wouldn't be able to see the missing ankle zip tie. People often operated on expectation, and one thing Steel had always insisted on in training was paying attention to minute details.

The tailgate creaked open.

The brother and sister talked softly in Spanish as the shotgun was shoved into his neck again. He ignored it and didn't flinch, keeping his eyes shut and his body relaxed.

His captors continued talking in Spanish.

Two fragments he understood: "...ataque al corazón..." and "...necesita agua..." *Heart attack* and *he needs water*—they were worried about him. He prepared himself.

The shotgun was removed from his neck, replaced by two fingers taking his pulse. The brother. A few drops of water were dribbled past his lips at the same time. The sister.

He exploded.

Grabbing the brother's wrist with his left hand, he gripped the edge of the tailgate with his right and pivoted his entire body on its side, swinging his bent legs out into the woman, knocking her down, while hanging onto the brother's arm, twisting it and pushing him away.

He half fell out of the cab. The brother tried to bring up the sawed-off. Harry struck out with his left fist as hard as he could, hitting the man's stomach. The guy dropped the shotgun and collapsed to his knees at Harry's feet.

Harry kneed him in the jaw and the man fell limp to the ground.

Sensing an attack from the woman, he whirled. Searing pain hit his left upper arm. The woman gaped at him, her wide eyes showing she was as frightened by what she had done as by what he might do. With his right hand he pushed her down hard.

That left her knife sticking in his arm. He looked at it. Small. One edge switchblade. He pulled it out by putting pressure against the dull side and dropped it to the dirt. His arm hurt like hell and he groaned. She had hit the triceps. Blood soaked his shirt.

Bending over, he picked up the shotgun and sat on the lip of the open gate, pressing his left arm against his torso. The wound still sent blood down his side.

The sky was clouded, but it was light out. Early evening. They were parked on a circular dirt plateau, maybe fifty yards across and hidden from the road. Hues of gray and green covered the surrounding mountain slopes, some of which had white-capped peaks. Beautiful.

Harry took a deep breath, glad to be on his feet. A tiny section of the east side of Boulder was visible. A small cluster of antlike buildings far to the southeast. He had been right about his kidnappers driving north.

A large outcropping of rock hid them from the road, but a dirt road circled out past the outcropping. He could walk or drive out. The mountain road wasn't visible even miles away. The kidnappers had picked a great hiding spot.

He was still on his own, but he was free. *Not bad, Harry.* Game over for the crazy family. He would use their phone to call his brothers. A smile crept over his face as he imagined Christie and Jack hearing he had escaped. It made the pain in his arm bearable.

He would wait before involving the police. Jack and Christie might have been forced into something ugly and might need time to sort it out.

The woman crawled to her brother, cradling his head in her hands. She glanced up at him, fear in her eyes.

"Take off your masks," he said.

She pulled hers off, and then her brother's.

She was attractive, as was her brother. The resemblance between the two was obvious. Chiseled features, straight jet-black hair, high foreheads, and narrow chins. And he had been right about her age. Maybe late twenties.

For some reason Harry felt sorry for the woman. Stockholm syndrome, he mused. Things weren't turning out as she expected. The brother blinked, gazing up at him with obvious hatred.

Hearing an engine, Harry whirled around, gripping the shotgun.

A black SUV slowly pulled around the outcropping, and then forward, stopping twenty feet from him. The SUV passengers couldn't have seen the pickup from the road, which meant they were actively searching for him.

He wasn't sure if that was good or bad.

Four men wearing black hoods, fatigues, and boots jumped out of the SUV, remaining behind the vehicle doors. The HK416s in their hands worried him. They reminded him of Steel's Blackhood Ops.

Harry stiffened, ducking down with the shotgun.

The woman blanched and gaped along with her brother at the men, but neither of them moved.

One of the men called out, "Harry Thorton!"

"Who wants to know?" He held the shotgun ready, thinking he would shoot their legs from ground level. There was no way he could compete with HK416s standing up.

"U.S. Army. We're here to take you to safety, sir. It's over."

"Prove it." That sounded hopeful but felt too easy.

"Christie Thorton said you would trust us if we gave you one secret only she knows."

"I'm listening."

"You wet the bed until you were twelve."

"Amen to that." Harry rose and set the shotgun on the truck bed, and then lifted his right hand to show it was empty. "It's great to see you guys."

The soldiers strode forward in front of the SUV, appearing relaxed, their guns aimed at the dirt. They glanced at the man and woman on the ground. "We're happy to finally find you, sir."

He heard another engine and turned with the soldiers. A black car with tinted windows slowly pulled around the outcropping, stopping twenty feet short of the SUV, but broadside to it.

A man got out. Wearing a black suit and sunglasses, he remained behind his car. He had a slightly brown complexion and appeared fit.

Harry's immediate reaction was that the man was an ally of his two kidnappers. He would have shouted to the soldiers, but they had already pivoted, their guns aimed at the man.

All four soldiers formed a line facing the car.

"Identify yourself!" snapped the lead soldier.

The man held up a badge in his left hand. His voice had no accent. "U.S. Federal Marshal Covington. Are you all right, Harry Thorton?"

"Show your right hand!" said the soldier.

The marshal held up his empty right hand.

The lead soldier relaxed, his gun still up. "U.S. Army has jurisdiction here."

"You need to provide me with ID so I know who you are and that you're legit." The marshal craned his neck. "Harry Thorton, are you alright?"

Feeling better about the man, Harry heaved a breath. He held up his right hand. "Fine. Yeah, they're good. I'm going with them."

The marshal clipped his badge back onto his belt, his hands resting on his hips. "All right. Then, soldier, I need your superior to call my superior and straighten this out."

The lead soldier nodded. "I can arrange that."

The soldiers lowered their guns halfway.

The lead soldier began walking forward. The marshal walked along the side of his car, but rounded the front of it with a surprising burst of speed. In a flash the marshal's hands dipped beneath his suit coat, appearing again with silenced Glocks. He fired at the soldiers. They all went down before they could get their guns back up.

Harry had never seen that kind of accurate and fast shooting with both hands simultaneously. It stunned him. Even Clay wasn't that good. Four shots. Four dead.

He grabbed the shotgun and dropped flat to the ground to fire at the man's legs from beneath the truck. No sign of the killer, but he heard a thump. The killer had jumped onto the pickup.

Harry twisted to his back, kicked the tailgate closed with his foot, and aimed the shotgun straight up along the back of the pickup. Glancing at the woman and her brother, he saw they were staring up at the rear of the truck.

"Drop the gun, Harry, or I'll kill the man and woman."

"Be my guest." Harry wiggled sideways to get most of his body beneath the back of the truck in case the man stuck his gun over the edge of the topper. Harry also noted that the killer was now speaking with a Hispanic accent.

"You two, lie on your bellies and close your eyes or I'm going to shoot both of you right now."

Harry watched the man and woman follow the killer's directions. The man was eliminating any help from them.

"You know, Harry, I think I'll just wait up here. That shotgun is going to become heavy after a while. And while I wait, I'm going to call in reinforcements."

Harry heard the soft sound of a phone making a call.

"Yes, my friends. We're on thirty-four, at the end of a short dirt road on the south side, halfway to Estes. See you soon." Another number was dialed. It must have been on speaker this time, because Harry could hear it clearly.

He considered trying to stand up but didn't see how he could survive that. His only other option would be to crawl to the side of the pickup and try to surprise the man. He heard some motion on the topper. Then a nearby thump. He craned his neck to look behind him.

The killer was lying on his belly on the ground, beside the rear tire near Harry's head, his Glocks aimed at him.

"Harry, I'll shoot your shoulders, your arms, and then your head if I have to." The man smiled. "Wouldn't you rather live to fight another day?" The killer lifted his chin. "Toss the shotgun to your left or I begin shooting."

Harry did as he was told.

"Tuck your hands into your belt, and don't move."

Harry obeyed.

The man stood up smoothly and walked around the end of the pickup, one Glock aimed at Harry, the other at the brother and sister. His voice sounded calm and his friendly smile reflected that too.

The word that came to Harry was *psychotic*.

The man walked around Harry, past his feet, and stared down at him. "Ah, you're already hurt, Harry. So sorry to see that. We don't have time for a long conversation since we have to leave."

The killer spoke to the man and woman in Spanish. Harry couldn't follow it, but the man and woman rolled over onto their backs.

The killer eyed them. "Hermano y hermana?"

The woman nodded, wide-eyed. Her brother stared up at the killer with fear evident in his eyes too.

The killer said, "Nombres. Rapido."

The brother said, "Juan y Isabella."

"Apellido!"

Juan was silent. The killer aimed his gun at Isabella.

"No!" Juan held up a hand. "Aguilar."

The killer glanced at Harry. "How rude of us to speak Spanish. We want Harry to understand everything. Isabella, take your phone out of your pocket, sit up, and toss it over the edge behind you. Juan, do the same."

The two did as ordered, and the killer said, "Now lie down again." When they did, he said, "Isabella, are you the one who hurt Harry?"

"Yes."

"Tough woman." He winked at Harry. "Why did you kidnap Harry?"

Tears flowed down Isabella's face, but she said nothing.

"Perhaps to get Jack Steel and Christie Thorton to kill Garcia? A vendetta?"

Isabella continued her silence.

Harry realized the killer knew more than he did about what was going on. He had questions but kept silent too.

"Ah, it must have been painful to see a loved one die." The killer turned to Juan. "Anything you wish to say about vengeance, Juan?"

Juan shook his head.

The killer sighed. "Children, Juan?"

Juan didn't answer, and the killer pointed his gun at Isabella's leg. "Should I shoot her?"

Juan said quickly, "Three."

"Wonderful. All boys?"

"Two girls and a boy. Please, señor—"

The killer cut him off. "I bet they're a handful. If you wish to see them again, you will do exactly as I say. Turn over onto your stomach, Juan, arms at your sides."

Juan complied.

Isabella didn't move, but she placed her hand on her brother's back. "Por favor!"

The killer seemed to hesitate as he aimed his gun at Juan.

Harry didn't get it. Maybe the guy was deliberating on what to do. "You don't have to kill us," he said.

The man's brow furrowed, but he shot Juan in the back of the head. Juan collapsed.

Isabella gasped, her hand flying to her mouth, her face twisted. She rolled to her side, her hand on her brother's shoulder. "No no no."

Harry assumed they were all going to die here so he rolled over and reached for the shotgun. Something slammed into the back of his right shoulder and he collapsed where he lay.

"Help him up, Isabella or I'll have to shoot you both here. Hurry. I won't repeat myself."

In seconds her hands slid beneath Harry's cut arm. He groaned but tried to help her. His arm ached, his shoulder burned, and he was groggy and weak. His knees wobbled as he rose to a kneeling position, and then stood, leaning against Isabella for support.

"Walk over to the car. Keep up. Follow me." The man walked backward in front of them, still smiling as if he was out for a stroll, aiming the two Glocks at them.

Harry relied on Isabella to stay upright. Shuffling along, he wanted to attack the killer. His legs had no strength to charge.

The killer stopped near the trunk of his car and opened it. "Harry in first, on your side. I apologize for the cramped conditions. I'll try to get you out soon for a nice chat."

"Go to hell." Harry glared at the man.

The man lifted the Glocks slightly, shaking his head as he smiled.

Harry sat on the lip of the empty trunk and slid in on his left side. That position made the knife wound ache, but it protected his more severely injured right shoulder. The assassin was arrogant and Harry wanted to kill him. It gave him a reason to cooperate. As he lay on his side, facing the killer, Isabella climbed in too, also facing out.

"Perfect," said the killer. "Nice and cozy. Get acquainted. Talk soon." He shut the trunk.

# CHAPTER 25

HARRY PASSED OUT. WHEN he came to, the woman was quiet. He wondered how long he had been out. It felt like a few minutes, but it could have been much longer.

He tried to adjust his body to get more comfortable—and groaned. Too painful. His right shoulder was stiff and his chest was wet. Hoping the bullet might have gone through, he gingerly felt around for an exit wound with his left hand and found it. Lucky.

The killer was psycho, dangerous, and very skilled. His first reaction was that they were going to die. The car wasn't moving. Maybe the killer was waiting for the people he had called.

He heard a faint crash. When he realized what that meant, it sickened him. In another minute he heard another faint crash.

"Do you know who the killer is?" He waited a minute, impatient over Isabella's silence. "Well?"

"He has to be from the cartel." Her voice was gruff.

"You sent Jack and Christie to kill the cartel people that killed Marita." She didn't answer, and he said, "Look, I need your help. I'm losing blood and getting weak. We have to stop that right away."

"Why should I help you? You made it possible for that man to kill my brother!"

"Your family made it possible." His jaw clenched. "You put my whole family at risk, and because of you I've been shot and you stabbed me!"

She didn't reply.

He cut off another angry outburst and said calmly, "If we don't work together, we won't have any chance of surviving this."

More silence. Then a sullen, "What do you want me to do?"

"Bandages."

He was aware of her slowly turning to face him. In moments he could feel her breath on his face.

The car began moving.

Her voice was matter-of-fact. "Just so we're clear, I was trying to stab your heart. I missed."

"Lucky me."

"I'm not sorry for hurting you," she said.

At least she was honest. "Truce?"

"For now."

"Before you bandage me, can you look for an emergency trunk release? It's usually a small handle where the hood joins the frame. It might be attached to the underside of the trunk with a clip or Velcro."

"I know what they are." She sounded annoyed.

"Feel behind me too. See if you can push out the back seats. Don't pull the release or do anything with the seats now that he's driving."

"I'm not stupid."

He almost gave a sarcastic reply, but instead said, "Sure."

She had to squeeze over him. As she searched for the release and checked out the back seats, he groaned over the pressure against his shoulder. He noted that she offered no apologies for causing him more pain.

In moments she moved off of him and resumed her position on her side. "No release, and there's a solid metal plate between the trunk and the back seats. There's no way to get out."

He sighed. The killer had modified his trunk to hold prisoners. "See if you can rip my shirt into strips."

"I will cut my blouse into strips," she said.

"Did you say cut?"

"I picked up the switchblade and shoved it into my bra when I helped you up. You were lying on it."

"Great!"

"I don't need your praise."

"Of course." He was already tired of her.

He heard her cutting her blouse. He started using another technique Steel had taught him. Imagine every possible scenario you can think of, and then pick the one that feels like a winnable strategy and rehearse it endlessly. They had practiced a hundred times how to escape from this situation in the VR sims too.

He couldn't wait to wipe that stupid smile off the killer's face.

# CHAPTER 26

C LAY COULD FEEL WORRY burrowing into his gut. It was hard to shake it off. It was early evening—still light out. Closing in on twenty-four hours since Harry had gone missing. And they had nothing to show for their efforts.

As the eldest brother he felt responsible for his siblings. Dale and Harry would find that laughable, as capable as they were of taking care of themselves. But the feeling was still there nonetheless. Christie would understand it more. Women seemed to be more nurturing.

Christie and Jack were in a nightmarish situation, and the stress in his sister's voice told him Harry was in trouble. The idea of losing a brother and sister over the next few days choked him up.

Being tired didn't help. Dale had rented a second car so they could cover more ground. They had driven north all night and all morning, eventually heading back south and driving east and west on side roads. For most of it he had felt aimless.

They should have brought the police in right away. Steel was operating as if this was one of his covert Ops. The police might have found Harry already. Several times he thought about calling them himself, but the kidnapper's threat that they were ready to die for their plan made him hesitate.

If the kidnappers were stopped by the police and Harry died, he would never forgive himself. The threat of releasing their photos to the cartel concerned him too. Their lives would never be the same.

Continuing west on highway thirty-four, he waited for a call from the kidnapper to get directions to find Harry. He didn't believe it was going to happen.

His phone beeped and he answered.

"They call yet?" asked Dale.

"Not yet, Dale. I'll let you know as soon as they do."

He hung up, feeling as impatient as Dale sounded. His brother had been calling every five minutes. Dale loved Harry as much as he did. They were close as a family. That the three of them had somehow survived their tours in Afghanistan without serious injury had been lucky. They considered themselves a miracle family.

Christie's brush with death last year had put tears in his eyes. He had never thought things could get that dangerous stateside. Now he knew.

He had looked forward to hiking in Estes with his siblings, but now he just wished he was back in Montana with his wife and children. Home was his refuge and the center of everything he ever wanted in life.

As much as he liked Christie's partner, Steel, the man had brought danger to their family. Steel was what Clay had always admired, the soldier's soldier. Special Ops. A true hero dedicated to protecting the innocent and their country. And last year Steel had taken down a presidency, remaining nameless in the process for security reasons.

But now Clay found Steel's career less than appealing. He didn't want his siblings to worry for the rest of their lives about some unknown threat from Steel's past. Worse, the current situation could even place his own wife and children, or even his parents, in danger.

His folks lived on an idyllic ranch in Montana, their values and lifestyles simple. Solid. Their whole family lived that way. Christie seemed to have strayed the most. But they had all served in the military in some capacity, emulating their father's abiding loyalty to it as a veteran.

The one thing Clay did know about Steel was that the man would do anything to protect Christie and their families. And from what Christie had told him, enemies always underestimated him.

He rolled down his window, letting in the cool mountain air. It was quiet. The new blacktop kept his tires quiet too. The peaks to the west, south, and north were all beautiful, rising up in gray, brown, and green collages that normally would have inspired him.

One thing he dreaded was having to tell his parents that one or more of their children had died. He aimed to make sure that didn't happen.

His phone beeped. Meera. "Hey, love," he said.

"Hi, darling. News?"

"None." He was glad to hear her voice.

"Don't give up. You can find him, Clay. I know you can. I believe in you. Always."

"Thanks." Her ability to be direct was one of the many reasons he had married her.

Named after a great female Hindu mystical poet—whose work was popular in India—Meera was also a poet. She actually made a living from her writing. Her unflinching support never failed to amaze him and always made him feel better during rough moments.

"Tell the boys I love them and that I'm having fun," he said.

"They would be proud of their father, as I am."

"Thank you, Meera." His boys were twelve-year-old identical twins that he adored.

"I'll let you go so you're not distracted, Clay."

"I miss you. Tell the boys that too."

"Always, love."

He hung up, feeling inspired. She did that for him.

Somewhere ahead he heard a sound that seemed out of place. Almost like a faint crash. Maybe a car accident or road construction.

He was heading toward Estes Park, east of Rocky Mountain National Park. The crisp air was in the sixties and a mass of gray clouds was just beginning to cover the peaks.

He called his brother. "Hey, Dale, I just heard something. I'm going to check it out."

"What was it?"

Dale sounded eager for anything other than the same old lack of news.

"I don't know. Stay close by until I can investigate it." He stomped on the gas, his imagination running wild with speculation. And hope. Saving Harry also meant saving Christie and Jack and ending this mess.

A half mile later he heard several distinct crunches, similar to what he had heard before, but louder. He was getting closer. Slowing to a crawl, he listened carefully. Nothing.

He stopped on a short straight stretch of road and rolled down all the windows.

A car appeared far ahead of him on a distant curve on the road, also heading west. Expensive. Black. Tinted windows. It disappeared around a bend.

He didn't recognize the make or model from where he was parked. Dale would have been able to. He hadn't seen the car before and wondered where it had come from. Maybe a scenic overlook. It wasn't a pickup so he doubted it was the kidnappers.

He kept driving, accelerating and listening.

In a half mile a dirt road appeared to the left. It was narrow and hard to see at first, but on instinct he braked hard and backed up. The road felt about right for where the sounds might have come from. A fifty-foot-high rock wall to the right and a steep drop-off to the left bracketed the road. It couldn't go very far in because there were cliffs and peaks all around it. In fifty yards the road turned right, past an outcropping that hid the rest of it.

Maybe it led to a private residence. But there was no sign posted. The road had no guardrails. The idea of having to back out on it unnerved him. He hated heights. Like driving on a road such as this, or standing next to a drop-off. But Harry's life was on the line.

He gripped the steering wheel and turned onto the road. The vertical rock wall to his right was about two feet from his car, and he had no more than two feet from the steep slope on his left side. He kept his eyes glued to the center of the road.

When the road veered right, he followed it at a crawl, sweat running down his back. The road narrowed so that he had only one foot of clearance on both sides of the car. He kept the passenger sideview mirror almost scraping the pale rock on the right side.

After fifty feet he had to stop. His bunched shoulders and clenched fingers needed a rest. Cautiously he cracked his door. A drop of five hundred feet greeted his eyes. He hastily shut the door, dizzy and nauseous.

"Geez!" He wished he had walked in instead. Now he was committed. He might be walking out, because there was no way he was backing out.

White knuckling it, he drove, holding his breath as the road narrowed a little more. Sweat beaded his forehead and soaked his shirt.

"You stupid idiot," he said to himself.

He envisioned the left wheels of the car slipping off a crumbling edge and his car tumbling down the mountainside. He was sure he was going to die.

"Idiot!" he repeated over and over.

For a moment he thought of his life. Math teacher, husband, father. All he wanted in life was to be a good family man, and a stupid decision was jeopardizing that. "Idiot!" he said again.

But in another fifty feet, just beyond a big overhang of tall rock, the road veered right a second time, ending in a decent-sized circular dirt space. Big enough to turn around in.

Stopping the car a short distance in, he exhaled and sat back. "Clay, you have survived another day."

Exiting the car, he took some deep breaths, his aching hands still trembling. He grabbed his hat and the binoculars he had brought for the hiking trip and walked forward. An excellent tracker, a skill learned from his father on many hunting trips when he was a boy, he scoured the ground.

Multiple tire tracks.

Avoiding walking on any of them, he followed the tracks and saw where the vehicles had parked. Near two sets of tire tracks he spotted bits of red. That alarmed him. He didn't have to touch them to know what they were.

Dismayed, he stopped to call Dale. "Get up here fast, little brother. I found something serious. Take highway thirty-four west, and about halfway to Estes there's a narrow entrance to a dirt road on the left. South side. Go slow. It's dangerous."

"I'm coming, Clay!"

He hung up, knowing Dale would drive like a maniac to get here.

Examining the ground, he saw boot prints and shoe prints. And marks that could have been bodies dragged across the ground. One set of shoe prints had to be a woman's. They were too small to be a man's.

Remembering the crashing sounds he had heard—and feeling sick to his stomach at what it might mean—he forced himself to carefully walk back to his car. Then he strode to the south edge of the tiny plateau.

Even though he could guess where things had probably ended up, he didn't want to trample the evidence in the dirt. And he wanted to search the whole perimeter anyway.

He needed to see straight down, but he couldn't make himself lean over the edge to do it. Going down on his knees, he put his palms close to the edge and peered over the precipice.

A drop of two thousand feet greeted him. Nothing but stone. Gasping, he rocked back on his heels and closed his eyes for a few seconds.

Figuring he had a quarter hour before Dale found him, he speedily crawled along the edge. He didn't want his little brother to see him crawling around on the ground. He would never hear the end of it.

Stopping every five yards to take a look over the edge, he arrived at the northwestern lip in ten minutes. Straight across from where he had parked his car. Nothing to note thus far.

Careful to not crawl over any prints or marks in the dirt, he remained just to the side of the first tire tracks he came to that led up to the edge. He leaned forward and stared.

A smashed up blue pickup truck and a black SUV rested on their sides down the distant slope. From what he could make out there were bodies down there too. No one would have survived that fall. He concluded the victims had been dead before they were thrown over the edge.

He took off his hat and sunglasses. Laying down, he propped his elbows on the edge and scoured the area with the binoculars. "Not you, Harry. Not you. Please, God. Not my brother."

He counted four black-hooded men and a Latino. It was likely that the Hispanic was one of Harry's kidnappers. The hooded men were a mystery. They reminded him of Steel's Ops. Steel had said Colonel Jeffries had sent men to search for Harry so maybe they were U.S. military. Dumped like trash.

Feeling sick to his stomach, he crawled back a few feet , grabbed his sunglasses and hat, and stood up. Anger replaced concern. Harry could be down there, beneath one of the vehicles. But his gut said *no*. The female partner of the dead kidnapper was missing too.

He remembered the car he had seen ahead of him on highway thirty-four. If it was the cartel, and they had the woman and Harry, they would torture the woman to get the name of the man running Steel's blackmail. And they would torture Harry to punish Jack and Christie. But how could the cartel figure all this out so fast?

He carefully studied the area by the cliff edge, finding the drag marks where someone had pulled bodies along the ground. Whoever had done this was ruthless.

Backing away from the tracks, he retreated the way he had come, walking a few yards in from the perimeter so he felt safe without walking over the evidence.

By the time he reached his car, Dale was pulling the red Malibu in fast. As if he was coming off a racetrack. Dale had always been fearless. Clay had thought it would get him killed someday. But to his credit, Dale also had a strong survival instinct.

Dale's car skidded to a stop when Clay held up a hand.

Clay strode to Dale's open window and leaned on it. "Let me get my gun, you turn around. I'll explain on the way. Keep out of the center of this plateau or you'll destroy evidence the police are going to need."

He hustled back to his car, while Dale carefully turned the car around. Clay retrieved the SIG Sauer, and Dale pulled up. Clay tossed his hat in the back seat and got in, realizing he was going to be staring down the edge of the drop-off all the way out.

"What about your car?" asked Dale.

"No way am I driving it out of here, and we don't have time for you to do it." He looked at the drop-off, and then at Dale. "I think I'm going to be sick."

Dale grinned. "Get out and walk behind the car."

"We don't have time."

Dale's smile vanished. "What's wrong? What did you see?"

"Death, and lots of it." He hunched over toward Dale. "Get us on thirty-four heading west. I think I saw the car that has Harry. If I'm right, the driver of that car just killed four of Colonel Jeffries' soldiers and one of Harry's kidnappers and dumped them and their cars down the mountainside."

"Hell." Dale gunned the engine.

"Don't kill us." Clay gripped the dash with his right hand and twisted away from the drop-off. Closing his eyes, he tried to think of something nice. Meera.

"Do you want to hold my hand, big brother?"

Clay knew Dale was probably grinning. "Keep both hands on the wheel, you idiot! And look at the road!"

# CHAPTER 27

ANGEL SHOULD HAVE FELT elated, since he had Christie's brother and one of the kidnappers in the trunk. Tossing the truck, SUV, and bodies down the mountainside would keep all of it hidden, or at least slow down any investigation.

Things were going smoothly, even by his standards—which were high. Except he had reservations about killing the Colombian man and the four soldiers.

He was glad he had placed a little seed of hope in the Colombian man's heart before shooting him. Renata had told him that was very important for their souls to have a better death, and he always listened to her in everything.

Still the killings bothered him and he wanted to talk to her about it. In all his years of killing for Diego, he had never doubted himself before. Why now?

The answer came to him quickly. These latest victims were not his usual targets. Diego's ruthless competitors were murderers, but the young Latino was an ordinary guy who loved his sister, as he loved Renata. And the soldiers looking for Harry were not bribed or caught up with the cartel. Honorable versus despicable. It also explained the uneasiness and uncertainty he had experienced before this job.

He called Renata.

"How are you doing, dear brother?"

"Excellent, for the most part." He explained what had happened, and finished with, "Do you see any danger coming my way from this?"

She was silent for a few moments. "I see a flash of red. Maybe a car."

Angel considered that. Someone might have seen him exiting the dirt road. He could run and hide or face them and end it. "I favor facing them."

Renata was quiet again and Angel waited patiently. It was never wise to rush her if she needed time to explore options.

Her voice was cautious. "If it doesn't turn out as expected, leave. I sense you will be in more danger by staying."

As always her advice resonated to some degree with what he was feeling. "I agree."

"You said *Excellent, for the most part.* Something is bothering you."

"I hesitated in killing the Colombian. I doubted myself. And even killing the soldiers bothered me, Renata."

"We have been on a dark path together for a long time, Angel. I began feeling remorse months ago about our work for the cartel, and you are beginning to feel it too. We need a change."

Her words struck a chord in him that was unsettling. "What are you thinking?"

She paused. "I've never been to the Bahamas. Would you be happy there with me for a few weeks?"

"I would love the Bahamas!" he exclaimed. She loved snorkeling in the ocean because of the beautiful fish, and her body could be free of her chair.

He added, "When I return I think we need to find a new home close to the ocean, where there is warm water and good snorkeling."

"You would do that for me?"

"Of course!" Renata was often alone, with little to do, and he realized abruptly it was time for him to give back to her. Especially since she might only have a short while left to live.

He felt guilty that it had taken him so long to see this obvious truth. "Get one-way tickets. Don't use our real names. Pick one of our aliases."

"You will leave your job?"

He considered her question carefully, realizing that his recent reservations over killing were related to deeper desires. "I need to get out. I won't tell Diego or anyone. We'll just leave. He'll never find us."

"He will feel betrayed, Angel. He will never stop hunting you. You will have to kill him, dear brother. The other cartels will turn against him for killing Antonio anyway, so they will be happy if he is gone."

"Antonio's son might put a contract out on my head for his father's death."

"I don't know how, but I see that resolving itself."

"That would make us safer. Talk soon, dear sister."

"I look forward to it."

He hung up, considering his betrayal of Diego. He didn't want to kill him. The man had treated him like a brother. But Renata was his sister. There was no comparison. And Diego's wish to enslave him for as long as possible was based on the man's greed and thirst for power, not for any concern about him.

His rearview mirror showed a mile straight stretch of road with no cars following him. He maintained speed until a small side road allowed him to turn off. He parked far enough from the highway to be able to see it, without easily being spotted.

While sitting there, he regarded the majestic slopes of the mountains, their blend of bluish hues, and their size. Priceless. Feeling privileged, he enjoyed the view. The scenery calmed his emotions.

In fifteen minutes a red car flew by.

He gave them a short head start, and then drove back onto the highway and followed them, slowly putting together a plan. Wondering who it was, he realized he might not want to kill them. But if he died or was caught, Renata would be alone with no family.

He refused to imagine her in a nursing home. He had always taken care of their finances and other matters, thus she would not have access to their money, nor be able to find it. It was another mistake to have not given her that information.

He had no choice now. To protect his sister, he would have to kill anyone who threatened his life or his freedom.

# CHAPTER 28

CLAY FELT FEAR CREEP into his bones. Outside of heights there wasn't much that could produce that sensation in him. But the killer following them had achieved it. He wished he had called Meera again.

"You're sure it's him?" Dale sounded incredulous.

"Not one hundred percent, but close enough. Don't change your speed. We don't want him to know we've spotted him. At least not yet." He had noticed the car far off the road, sitting and waiting. Dale had used the rearview mirror to watch it follow them onto the highway.

"Should we call the police?"

Clay had considered that. "They won't be here before he makes his move."

Dale scoffed. "He's damn arrogant to think he can do us the way he did—"

"Four Special Ops soldiers who knew how to handle themselves?" Clay shook his head. "What kept you alive in Afghanistan? I always thought your arrogance would send you back in a body bag."

Dale's voice calmed. "We had a team leader that told me I was going to die on my first mission unless I stopped talking and started listening. This guy had a lot of mission successes so I shut up and listened."

"So I'm going to tell you now, little brother, I'm more scared of this man than anyone I ever faced in combat. If I'm right, he just killed five guys, he somehow knows we're following him, and he has no issues with trying to kill us. He has high confidence, high skill level, and has done this before."

Dale licked his lips. "What are we going to do?"

"He has to hit us before we reach Estes. He might try a drive by and shoot us while passing, but that can get sloppy."

Clay took the SIG Sauer out of his belt and grabbed an extra mag from the glove compartment. "I think he'll do something more creative. Whatever he does, please listen to me, agreed?"

"Yeah, okay, Clay, I'll listen. Just promise me we're going to nail this guy and free Harry."

"That's the plan, little brother. Get your gun ready."

Dale pulled the Glock from his belt and set it on his lap. "He's hanging a quarter mile back. What's he waiting for?"

"No traffic and a straight stretch."

They rounded a corner into just that.

Dale glanced at the rearview mirror. "He's coming up fast now, Clay."

"Get ready to brake hard if he tries to pass us and duck your head down. I'll be the shooter." He released his seat belt and twisted sideways in his seat, the SIG pointed at Dale's door. He braced his right foot against the floor board.

Dale took off his seat belt too. "He's making his move, Clay!"

Through the rear passenger window, Clay watched the car accelerate, trying to time his next words: "Brake hard, Dale!"

Dale slammed on the brakes just as the killer's car pulled even with them. The killer's passenger window was open, and in the fraction of a second that they were eye-to-eye, Clay glimpsed a machine gun aimed at him.

They stopped, tires screeching.

Fifty feet past them the black car also braked hard, burning rubber too. The black sedan slowly pulled over into their lane, and then off onto the shoulder and parked.

Clay wasn't sure what was happening. "Back up onto the shoulder and keep it running. He's got a machine gun. Maybe an FN P90. Be ready to do a U-turn and run."

"Hell." Dale backed up onto the shoulder, but kept the car running and in drive.

"What kind of car is that?" Clay ran through scenarios in his mind. He tried to ignore the steep drop of the terrain past the shoulder.

"Looks like a Chevy SS, but the logo is missing and the trunk seems customized. I'm not sure."

It was the first time Clay had ever heard Dale say he didn't recognize the make and model of a car.

The man got out of the car, smiling and holding the P90 in one hand, pointed up at the sky.

Clay guessed he was Hispanic, but light colored. "Dale."

Dale backed up another fifty feet.

The killer tossed the machine gun through his open driver's door window, and then held up both empty hands. Next he took off his suit jacket, laid that on the open window, and slowly turned around, still smiling.

His black dress shirt was fitted, betraying no lumps. No guns were tucked into his belt.

"Do you think he wants to bargain with us for Harry?" asked Dale.

"He didn't kill five men to bargain with us." Clay knew he was viewing a rattlesnake pretending to be a corn snake. The man had jet black hair and looked strong, but not bulky. He moved fluidly, effortlessly, with a smile that would be taken as friendly in any other situation.

The killer walked casually to the trunk of his car and stood directly in front of it, facing them.

"Let's take him," said Dale.

"That's what he wants. It's a trap." Clay swept his gaze up and down the man's body.

"He's unarmed." Dale sounded eager.

"He just killed four Special Ops soldiers." Clay sensed there was something they weren't seeing, but he couldn't figure out how the man could come at them. Even if the killer had an ankle holster, they would have two guns on him. The idea of Harry lying in the man's trunk, maybe the woman too, made him angry. The car's tinted windows hid anything else inside.

"Maybe there's another shooter in the car." Clay decided that had to be it.

Dale turned to him. "We're so close to Harry, big brother. We gotta try, don't we?"

Clay agreed. They had to try. "Okay, Dale. Drive up slowly and be ready. If he goes for his machine gun or a car door opens, we back up. There's no way we can compete with a P90."

"You got it." Dale slowly eased the car forward, his right hand on the wheel, his left on the SIG Sauer resting on his thigh. "I say when we get close enough, we shoot without waiting for him to move."

"Agreed. But let's play his game first. When I tell you to stop, be ready. Wait for my signal."

"He's going down." Dale gripped his gun.

"Don't hit the trunk, in case Harry's in there."

Dale frowned. "Crap. That's why he's standing there, isn't it?"

"I think so."

"You're the best shot, Clay. I'll go high, you go low."

"That's a deal."

Dale slowly pulled up until they were seventy feet from the man. The killer was still smiling and standing casually, as if he was waiting for friends.

Clay felt a needle of fear in his chest over the man's carefree attitude. He said softly, "Stop."

Dale stopped the Malibu.

Clay opened his door, holding his right hand high to show it was empty. He was left-handed like Dale. Though he could shoot just as well with both hands. He kept the SIG hidden, down at his side.

The killer smiled and called out to them. "So good to meet you, Clay and Dale. You want your brother Harry back alive, correct?"

"How the hell does he know our names?" asked Dale.

Clay was caught off guard by that too. He worried that the killer also had the names of his wife and two boys. He wanted the man dead.

The killer kept talking. "I would like to give your brother back unharmed. All I want is to talk."

"What do you think, Clay?" whispered Dale.

"He's lying. Forget it." Swinging one leg out, his gaze on the killer, he stood up. The killer's hands slid slightly behind his back. It sparked a sense of urgency in Clay and he whispered, "Now, Dale."

He swung his gun up, and Dale stuck his gun out the window, leaning his head out, but their movements seemed eerily slow in comparison to what Clay saw before him.

The killer brought his hands out faster than them and strode forward, gripping two silenced Glocks and firing before they squeezed off a single shot.

Clay couldn't figure where the guns had come from, but instinctively knew he wasn't going to be fast enough. He launched himself backward to get the door between him and the man's guns, firing his gun on the way down, aiming at the killer's head—the only thing still in his line of fire.

Dale shouted. Clay thought he heard his brother get off one shot, but he saw Dale either lean sideways or fall over, he couldn't be sure which.

He hit the ground hard on his back and grunted. His sense of where he was escaped him for a few moments. He couldn't register sound. The top of Dale's head was visible on the passenger seat.

Too dizzy to get up, he stared beneath the car frame. He saw the killer's dress shoes twenty feet away, approaching the front of the Malibu on Dale's side. Knowing Dale had only seconds, Clay rested his hand on the pavement and fired the SIG under the car at the man's ankles. His vision was clouded and his hand trembling, but he emptied the gun, moving his hand in a line left to right.

His hearing partially returned. He heard retreating footsteps. A car door opened and slammed shut. An engine roared. He got out the extra magazine, ejected the empty, and loaded it. His hand still trembled as he sat up.

He couldn't figure out what was wrong until something trickled down the side of his face. Gingerly he put his fingers up to his head, feeling a furrow of skin dug up along the side of his skull. The bullet had just grazed him.

"Clay, you have survived another day," he murmured. The killer was not only fast, but accurate with both hands. He remembered glimpsing something else on the way down to hitting the ground, but he was too consumed with Dale to remember it.

He called out, "Dale? Dale!"

Silence.

Panicked, Clay rose to his knees, his shoulder against the car for support. He saw the other car speeding away, already far down the road. There were three bullet holes in the windshield of the Malibu, all about where Dale's head had been.

Dale lay half in the passenger seat, his left hand bloody, along with his left shoulder. But his head seemed free of wounds.

Using the car door to pull himself up to his feet, Clay leaned in to examine his brother more carefully. And froze. There was a gouge on the left side of his brother's neck. Blood seeped down his back, staining his brother's jean jacket a dark color.

"Dale!" Clay knew he had seconds.

He took off his jacket, then his t-shirt, which he ripped in half. Pushing the thick end of the torn shirt against his brother's wound, he wrapped the rest around Dale's neck as hard as he dared to stop the blood flow without choking him.

He called 911 and gave his position. Estes Park had a medical center. He had looked it up in case they had any hiking accidents.

Once off the phone, he used his other hand to check Dale's pulse on one of his wrists. Nothing. "Dale!"

He turned his brother onto his back and began chest compressions with one hand, while keeping pressure on the wound with the other. Five minutes later he was still working on his brother when the ambulance and police arrived.

They asked him to move out of the way so they could take over. Dizzy again, he wobbled on his feet as he stumbled around the back end of the car. His skin was suddenly cold and clammy.

One of the medics steadied him by holding his arm and guiding him to the back bumper of the ambulance. He sat there while they checked his vitals and head wound.

Dale's gun was lying on the street by the front door of the Malibu. Guilt flooded him. He was responsible. It was his plan that had failed.

Abruptly he remembered what he had seen. When the killer had stepped forward, it seemed like part of his trunk lid was open. But the main trunk had remained closed. The man had a small compartment built into the outside of the trunk that blended perfectly with the trunk's design. That's where the guns had come from. That's why they never had a chance.

The killer was in Steel's class, someplace he and Dale didn't belong.

Dazed, he watched while they worked on his brother. *Please let my brother live.*

Sometime later they placed his brother on a stretcher, his body covered with a sheet. He stared, feeling numb.

Dale had survived Afghanistan, but not Colorado. And now he would have to tell Christie and his parents that he had gotten his little brother killed, when he was the one who was supposed to protect him.

Tears ran down his face.

# CHAPTER 29

HARRY WOKE UP TO Isabella whispering his name. Disoriented in the dark, he was quickly brought back to reality by his throbbing shoulder and arm.

"What happened?" He was surprised he had passed out again.

"I think someone tried to rescue us."

He was instantly annoyed. "You should have woken me up."

"I tried. Anyway, what could you do?"

Frustrated, he asked, "How do you know someone tried to rescue us?"

"We stopped and there were muffled words, and then muffled shots. Then our car left."

His heart raced with thoughts of being rescued. "It had to be my brothers or the Army."

"They're dead now."

That sent a sliver of panic into his chest. "What are you talking about? How can you be sure?"

"Okay, I'm not certain. But the killer got away."

"Maybe they're just wounded." He hoped his brothers weren't lying facedown on the road. If they died trying to save him it would haunt him for the rest of his life.

Isabella continued to cut up their shirts, working on his shoulder bandage first. Tying several pieces of cloth together to make a binding, she folded two small pads of cloth that she put over the entry and exit wounds. She tied them in place by looping the binding around his neck and armpit. To find the wounds she accepted him guiding her hands with his.

Harry appreciated that she was gentle with him.

She made a similar bandage for the knife wound. He had to shift his weight for her to get the patch binding under his arm. In another life it might have been a fun game at a singles party.

When she finished, he said, "Thank you."

She remained silent.

"Let's talk about our plan." He needed to get himself focused.

"He's going to shoot us. What can we do?"

He heard the hopelessness in her voice. He had to stave off his own sense of doom. "It's likely he intends to torture us to learn whatever he can, and maybe to punish Jack, Christie, and your family. When we've suffered enough, he'll kill us. That's his plan. We're going to have our own plan."

She spoke grudgingly. "What kind of plan do you have?"

"How good are you with your knife?"

"My father showed me how to use it. I'm pretty good."

"Did your father organize the kidnapping?" She didn't answer, and he asked, "Is Marita your sister?"

She remained silent for a few moments. "You said you have a plan."

He let it go, but her silence indicated he might be right or at least close to the truth. "When he stops to let us out, he'll think we have no weapons. He'll be less worried about me because I've been shot. All that adds up to less caution on his part. I'm hoping he lets us out at the same time. If so, I stumble, pretend I'm very weak, and then charge him. You come in fast and stab him."

"I will try," Isabella said softly.

"Don't try. Do it."

"Do you want the knife?" She sounded irritated.

"You have a better chance of surprising him. Stab his eyes, face, whatever is close, and don't stop until he's down for good."

That sounded crude and brutal even to him. She didn't respond so he worried she wouldn't even be able to try. "Do you think you can do that?"

"If I stab him a million times it will not be enough for what he did to my brother."

He cleared his throat. *Not Snow White.* "Have you always been this tough?"

Her voice had an edge. "Typical man. You think women are weak."

"I'm glad you're tough. Women have to be. My sister is."

She was quiet again for a minute. "I had some bad experiences with men. In our country many men are still sexist pigs. My father said I would have made a good soldier." She paused. "Do you have a family?"

"My wife died of cancer. No kids."

"I'm sorry."

"Thanks. She was an amazing woman." It took him a moment to recover as images of his wife swept through him. He hadn't talked about her for a long while. "Let's say instead of taking us both out, he takes me out of the trunk first or takes you out first. Either way, you're on your own. This guy is fast and very good with his hands, so you're going to have to surprise him any way you can."

"I'm not sure I can do that." Her voice revealed no confidence.

"If you visualize how you might do it, the movements, where you'll stab him, something real that you can do, it will make it easier to carry out."

She sighed. "I will practice it over and over in my mind."

"Perfect." Thinking of all the possible scenarios, he didn't think they had much chance of escaping. His wounds and physical condition played a part in that. But he said, "We'll make him wish he had never seen us."

"I hope you're right."

"So do I. So do I." They were both quiet for a minute. He thought he heard her crying. "I'm sorry," he said softly.

She sniffled. "I was thinking of Juan. His children and wife will suffer now. It makes me sick to my stomach. We caused all of this."

"His death was horrible to watch." He painfully reached out his left hand to touch her arm. "His children have a great aunt to help them with their loss."

"You don't know anything about me!" she said angrily, pushing away his hand. In a minute she added softly, "Gracias."

"It's okay. You're right, I don't know anything about you. But I trust my instincts and I know you care about your family, Isabella."

"You seem like a good man too, Harry."

They were both quiet this time. He yawned. "I'm going to try to get some sleep. If you're awake, and he stops, next time wake me up."

"I will, believe me. I don't want to face that animal alone."

Thinking out loud, he said, "If anyone lived through that last stop, they'll call the police. Canine units will smell us in the trunk. He might try to kill us and dump us somewhere before he gets to a roadblock."

She spoke softly. "That's pretty bleak."

"Sorry. I'm not trying to scare you, but we have to be prepared. He won't shoot us in the trunk. There's too much risk of a blood scent, which dogs would definitely pick up. Just be ready to act any time you can. We'll only get one chance at him."

"I will do my best."

"That's all you can do." As he closed his eyes, he wanted to buoy her up, and whispered, "You have a nice name, Isabella." Instantly he thought it was a stupid thing to say to someone that had kidnapped, drugged, and stabbed him.

"I like Harry too. It's a strong name."

As he drifted off, he started to think that maybe they were both feeling the Stockholm Syndrome.

# CHAPTER 30

ANGEL DROVE AWAY FROM the gunfight knowing he had been lucky. Renata had saved him again. He had recognized Christie's brothers immediately from the photos Diego had given him the day before.

Ego might have kept him in a gun battle with the two brothers. However his sister's warning and hundreds of past instances that supported the accuracy of her sight had made him flee as soon as Clay had fired at him from beneath the car.

As it was, he had a small nick in his left ear that he put a bandage on. He carried a first aid kit in the glove compartment.

Clay was an excellent shot and had almost killed him while falling backward. The man had reacted instantly to his guns and was a worthy opponent. Dale was less skilled and more brash. Angel had shot him several times. He had hit Clay with one bullet but didn't know if it would be fatal.

He was lucky there were no bullet holes in his car. That would have forced him to dump it, and probably kill the two in the trunk. He was just as lucky that Clay had not shot his foot or ankle.

Considering what had happened, he felt twinges of remorse again over killing. Two brothers trying to save a third. Decent people, not cartel scum. He didn't feel good about it. It was going to be difficult carrying out Diego's vendetta.

Emergency sirens.

He quickly found a side road to pull onto. In less than a minute an ambulance and police car drove by. Pulling back onto the highway, he accelerated.

He called Renata and filled her in.

She was quiet until he finished. "I'm glad you listened to me! I was worried you wouldn't, you're so headstrong at times."

"I know better than to outguess my sister. Should I hide or try to leave Colorado?"

"Get out of that state."

"I have two hostages in the trunk. Dogs will find them."

Renata didn't hesitate. "I sense if you go fast you will be fine with your usual precautions."

"All right. Thank you, dear sister."

"I'm checking flights for the Bahamas! I'm so excited, Angel!"

"That's wonderful! Talk soon." He hung up, happy for her. She hadn't sounded this excited in years.

And it was good timing because he was becoming more interested in a new life too. Killing had been his path for decades, but he had always known that at some point age would increase his odds of failure and he would have to walk away. He had never expected his conscience to push for it too.

He had plenty of money stashed away for the two of them. Maybe he could even meet someone he could trust and love as much as his sister. Those thoughts surprised him. He must have carried a deep unconscious desire to get out of the cartel for some time now.

He called Diego, but the call was not pleasant. He filled him in on what had happened since this morning.

Diego sounded stressed. "Vincente is not answering his phone. I sent men to find him, but I fear the worst for my brother. I am still meeting with our friends tomorrow."

"Do you want me to help you?" Angel knew he had no choice anyway.

"Yes. I have my men, but so did Vincente and I think it is likely he's dead. I would also like to meet the two you have captured, Harry and Isabella." Diego paused. "I think I will do some digging. The Aguilar family seeking vengeance, tied to Steel and our cartel. It shouldn't be hard. Leave your captives alone until you arrive here. We will have fun with them and send Steel a message."

"I'll be there. Don't worry, Diego."

"Gracias, Angel."

He hung up and tromped on the gas to get to Estes Park, zeroed in on his escape now. On the outskirts of the small town he kept an eye out for a cabin with a driveway bordered by trees, which would offer privacy from the road and neighbors.

He spotted one and turned into it, driving right up to the cabin. No cars were there. He assumed on a nice day any occupants would be out hiking as long as there was ample light. It should give him a good hour or more.

To be safe, with a Glock tucked in his belt at his back, he went up to the front door and knocked. No answer. He walked around back to check the porch and hot tub. All vacant.

Hustling back to the car, he began peeling the plastic dip off it. He had it painted with plastic dip by a professional to ensure it would peel faster. With so much practice doing this, he was an expert and worked fast.

Beginning at the edge of a door panel, he carefully peeled enough of the black dip off so he could take off the panel's covering in a whole sheet without tearing it. Beneath the black was the original paint. White.

He had the whole car finished in a half hour. Then he buffed out edges and any telltale bits of leftover black with a microfiber towel. In ten minutes he was finished. It looked fantastic.

From the glove compartment he pulled out two Chevy logos and one SS logo, snapping one onto the front, and two onto the trunk.

When he had purchased the Chevy SS, he had the logos taken off and the trunk modified for his needs. He preferred the SS because it handled like a sports car and had a massive trunk.

After tossing all the black plastic dip peelings into a plastic bag, he stuffed it under the back porch of the cabin. Back at the car he stripped off his shirt and pants, grabbed the suitcoat, and stuffed them along with his dress shoes beneath the porch too.

Grass grew in front of the porch. When he stepped back he was pleased that none of the clothing was visible.

Returning to the car, he opened the back door. On the back seat were a pair of hiking shorts, hiking boots, and a yellow cotton t-shirt. A western hat rested on top of the pile. He put it all on, except for the hat.

Moving fast, he replaced the Glocks in the secret trunk compartment, and then walked to the front passenger door, opening it. He lifted up a corner of the carpet on the floor, revealing a thin square of sheet metal, which he also lifted up. A shallow depression appeared in the floorboard metal. He slid the FN P90 into it, covering it with the sheet metal and carpet.

Lastly he reversed the magnetized plates on the front and back of the car so he had a different license plate showing. It was registered to an elderly man. He drove out of the driveway, not seeing anyone, and smiled to himself.

Closer to town he pulled into the back of a hotel lot. His tinted windows blocked viewing and there were few pedestrians near the rear parking spaces.

He opened the glove compartment and took out a small bag. In it was an expensive wig of curly gray hair, gray eyelashes, a gray moustache, and a small bottle of Ben Nye Spirit Gum Adhesive for prosthetics. He applied the adhesive to all four hair pieces. As soon as the adhesive was tacky, he used his mirror to apply them to his head and face. Having done this many times before, it went smoothly.

He put on his sunglasses and hat, and then checked himself in the rearview mirror. Perfect. An old white man with a tan driving a white car, instead of a forty-something dark-haired Latino killer in a black car. He had a matching California driver's license.

One last touch. In the glove compartment was a cheap bottle of strong liquid perfume. He took it out, unscrewed the top, and got out. Canine units might smell his two hostages in the trunk, but the police would focus on a black car driven by a Latino with black hair. Still he dumped the whole bottle of perfume along the crack of the trunk so it would settle into the edges. Dogs hated perfume.

As he drove out of Estes, heading west, the sun was poking through the afternoon clouds. Beautiful.

He thought about Steel. If the man had killed Vincente and his men, he was very good. Special. And since Steel had killed his share of men, Angel had fewer qualms about killing him.

One of Diego's comments came back to haunt him. The one about having fun with Harry and Isabella. Diego meant torturing and raping Isabella as his men had tortured and used Marita. He wouldn't participate, but it soured his mood about delivering her to Diego.

She didn't strike him as a killer, like Vincente's girlfriend. He would have to find a way to kill her cleanly to spare her Diego's injustice. Both of his captives.

# PART 4

## OP: DIEGO & ANGEL

# CHAPTER 31

GUILT SWEPT STEEL AS he listened to Clay talk. It was his fault the brothers had been involved, his mess they were trying to sort out. And now Christie had lost a brother. She could easily lose another. As an only child he couldn't imagine the pain she was feeling. He could only relate to it by assuming it was as painful for her as when his parents had died.

Staring at the phone, she placed it on her leg, her face pale. She winced as Clay described how Dale had died. Clay sounded distressed.

It tormented Steel that he had brought such misery into the lives of the woman he loved and her family. Anger at the Colombian made him clench his fist.

Tears rolled down Christie's face.

They had driven out of Sequoia National Park and into a nearby small town. He pulled into the lot of a restaurant and parked at the back.

Clay finished with, "I gave the police the killer's license plate and the location of where he killed the soldiers. They're going to put up roadblocks so no one can get out of the area. I kept you two out of it, said I didn't know where you were, and that we bought the guns off the grid for self-defense while we were looking for Harry. They took the guns. I don't think I'll be charged with anything since the guy attacked us. Being ex-military helped."

Steel leaned over. "I'm sorry for your loss, Clay. It's my mess to clean up. Take care of yourself."

Clay asked hoarsely, "Do you know who the killer is?"

"It can't be the Colombian so the only other option is that the cartel somehow learned that we killed Garcia and that Harry was kidnapped. I don't know how they did, but it's the only explanation that fits."

"Steel, I'm holding you responsible for killing the SOB that killed Dale. The killer knew our names. He could be coming for our families."

Steel heard Clay's anger. "He's as good as dead. You have my word."

"You take care of my sister, Steel. You hear me? I can't lose anyone else over this."

He swallowed. "I will, Clay. One quick question. Any sign of the woman that Harry said was one of the kidnappers?"

"None."

Christie picked up the phone. "Don't chase this guy, Clay. He's a professional killer." She heaved a breath. "I'm sorry, Clay, for all of this." She rubbed her forehead, her voice trembling. "Have you called our folks?"

"That's next. You should go home, Christie. Mom will need you." He hung up.

Christie had tears in her eyes. "I can't believe Dale is gone. My little brother."

"I feel sick about it too." He held her, her face on his shoulder.

She sniffled. "It's my fault. I got them involved."

"No. It's my fault. My mess they got involved in."

She pulled back, wiping her eyes. "How did the cartel find Harry so fast?"

That troubled him. "They shouldn't have known that I was in Colorado protecting Afia, much less about the Colombian's blackmail. Yet Vincente knew we were coming."

Her chest heaved. "What if the police don't catch the man who has Harry?"

That worried him too. "Then our best bet is to go after Diego, the other name Garcia gave us, and find out if he sent the killer. If so, we can take Diego and trade him for Harry. The Colombian might still be planning to release our photos to the cartel, but if I'm right that his family is helping him, and his daughter is in the trunk with Harry, he has a strong reason to bargain with us."

"We were supposed to be hiking today with my brothers. Now one's dead and Clay is a mess. I could hear it in his voice."

He said gently, "Clay is a marine. He's tough. He's just concerned about his family. In time he'll be okay. I don't think either of your brothers would have accepted being kept out of the search for Harry." He paused. "I have to call Jeffries, then the Colombian."

The colonel listened in silence while Steel filled him in.

"I need to talk to Clay," Jeffries said curtly. "Give me his number."

Christie did, and asked, "Will the military be active in this now? Can you help us?"

"And answer questions about why Special Ops were operating in Colorado?" Jeffries sounded bitter. "I would love to help, but we're completely out now. We can't lose any more people or clean up another mess like this."

Steel said, "I'm calling the kidnapper next. Any news on family connections to Marita?"

"DEA found an uncle who she had some contact with in the past. The guy has three sons and a daughter. His name is Carlos Aguilar. Colombian Special Forces. And he subsequently trained people at their famous School of Lanceros. He's currently living in Mexico and has an export business. He hasn't applied for a visa or entry permit so if he's here it's under an alias too. I'll text photos and names of his family now."

The photos and names came through, and Steel showed them to Christie.

Jeffries continued. "You owe me, Steel. I want intel on the ISIS operatives, and I want to know if Diego's assassin killed my soldiers. If so, I want him and Diego dead."

Steel's neck grew hot. He didn't owe Jeffries anything, but he kept that to himself. "If we get info on ISIS and the assassin, I'll pass it along. In return I need supplies."

"Let me know when and where. Now I have to organize a coverup." Jeffries hung up.

Steel turned to Christie. "Carlos Aguilar fits. I'm guessing we saw two of his sons when they first abducted us, and the other son and daughter have Harry. It's too much of a coincidence. If Carlos was a trainer at the School of Lanceros, he's one of the best." It felt good to put a name to the Colombian. Now more than ever he wanted the man dead.

"He's the reason Dale is dead and Harry is stuck with a killer." Christie said it with venom.

"I want to kill him too. But we have to talk to him."

She punched the number.

The Colombian answered. "You didn't do what I requested for Vincente and his men. I checked. You never cut them up. They didn't suffer, so Harry will."

"Screw you, Carlos Aguilar." Christie's face was livid. "We know who you are, your connection to Marita, and about your family." There was silence, and she continued. "One of my brothers died while trying to rescue Harry and I'm holding you personally responsible."

There was a slight pause, and then, "Who shot your brother?"

Steel put a hand gently on Christie's forearm, his voice matter-of-fact. "Carlos, I have some more bad news for you. A cartel killer found your children with Harry and killed your son. Christie's brothers saw no sign of your daughter where your son was killed so it's likely the killer has Isabella along with Harry."

"You're lying."

"Christie's brothers found your dead son and his blue pickup dumped over a cliff on the mountain. They tried to rescue Harry, but the cartel killer shot them up. One brother died, the other is injured. For the moment I'm guessing your daughter may be alive."

There was a long silence. "Forgive me if I don't believe you." Carlos hung up.

Christie pursed her lips, her eyebrows hunched.

Steel sat back. "He'll verify whatever he can. It's what I would do. He'll try to call his children. When they don't answer he'll start to worry that we're telling the truth."

"How would he verify our story?"

Steel thought about it. "I'm guessing he might have left another of his sons behind in Colorado to either kill Harry before the hand-off or make sure the hand-off occurred without a problem if he went through with it. It could take a while."

"Can you hold me?" Christie stared at the dash.

Steel reached over and put his arms around her.

"I just need some quiet," she whispered.

He sat with her, not saying anything, but fearing that their relationship had taken a blow it couldn't recover from.

# CHAPTER 32

C ARLOS CALLED BACK IN an hour. "I'm aware of the road-blocks around Estes, and people have died. That is all."

Steel had to calm himself before he spoke again. "You're a pro. Your daughter isn't answering her phone. Neither is your son. That's no coincidence. If you don't work with us, your daughter is as good as dead."

There was a long pause, then, "What do you want?"

"I have a plan. Do you want to hear it?"

"I'm listening."

"Garcia gave us one more name. Diego. I'm guessing you already know him. We capture him together and exchange him for Harry and your daughter. Then we kill all of them so our families are not running and hiding from the cartel for the rest of their lives. This means you end your vendetta against us or I will hunt you down and kill you, and the DEA will release photos of your children to the cartel." Steel didn't mean the last part, but he had to say it.

Christie glanced at him but didn't speak.

Carlos was quiet again for a few moments. "You think my daughter is still alive?"

"Yes. And I think it's highly likely the killer will escape the police in Colorado and bring Harry and your daughter to Diego. You can't take Diego by yourself, and your remaining two sons aren't qualified—especially the younger one. You need us.

We need each other. Unfortunately my trust in you is zero at this point. You lied about releasing Harry. But I believe if you want to save your daughter and your family, you'll be willing to compromise."

"If we work together, then no more secrets. Nada. Comprende?"

"Agreed." Steel didn't care what lies he told the Colombian.

"I want to know why your military got involved."

Steel had expected that question. "They were tracking the Alvarez cartel. They learned that whoever took over after Gustavo Alvarez was still meeting with splinter ISIS terrorists to hit the U.S."

"Why can't your military help?"

"Our military was trying to find Harry. The cartel hit man killed four of their Special Ops soldiers. Our government doesn't know about the military effort to find Harry, and they won't find out about it. They definitely won't let the military intervene further. If we get any special branches involved, like the FBI or CIA, I think Harry and your daughter will end up dead." He saw Christie's lips purse.

"The son I lost is Juan. How did the cartel find my children so fast?"

"I asked the same question. It makes no sense." Steel allowed anger into his voice. "You knew about Diego, didn't you?"

Carlos didn't hesitate. "Yes. He is the most senior member of the Alvarez cartel. Gustavo Alvarez was his nephew."

Steel remembered Gustavo's words, that his family would seek retribution for his death. It drove another needle of guilt into him for Dale's death. "How come you weren't going to send us after him?"

"I wanted to kill him myself." Carlos paused. "Diego's assassin is Angel and he is legendary. They call him El Lobo—the wolf—because once he's sent to track someone to kill, he never fails. He and Diego were both part of Marita's torture and death."

Steel heard anger and fear in Carlos' voice. Christie's face tightened.

Carlos continued. "Diego is very controlling and will demand that Angel bring Isabella and Harry to him untouched."

"That works in our favor," said Steel. "It gives us time."

"All right," said Carlos. "We move forward. I will let the vendetta against you die with Vincente. Diego has a meeting tomorrow at nine a.m. I never knew what it was for or who with, but it must be with ISIS."

"Where?" Christie asked curtly.

"Diego is staying at the Wynn Las Vegas under the name of Roberto López."

Steel spoke up, already knowing the answer to his question. "Do you think Diego will risk meeting Angel in Vegas with two captives?"

"No, Diego is too cautious for that. Most likely he will meet Angel somewhere out in the desert. I still want to take care of Diego myself, but I won't involve myself or my family with your ISIS problem. We should rendezvous in Vegas tomorrow morning. I'll contact you." Carlos hung up.

Steel looked at Christie. "I don't like any of it. And I still don't trust Carlos. I think he learned these guys were helping ISIS and felt good about it. Now he's trying to separate himself from that."

Christie bit her lip. "I still want to kill him. But I agree with you, for now we need his help. What about Clay? He'll never forgive me if I don't tell him and something happens to Harry."

"Yeah. Call him. Fill him in on everything. If he wants to get involved, have him meet us in Vegas in the morning. He can fly in from Denver."

Christie called Clay. Steel closed his eyes, listening to her voice. Anger and sadness. It tortured him. When she finished, she handed the phone to him wordlessly and stared out the window.

Steel sent a text to Jeffries for a time and place to meet in Vegas. Finished, he glanced at Christie. "How are your ribs?"

"Pretty sore."

"You could have a cracked rib." He wished he could take her pain away.

"I could use some TLC," she said quietly.

"You're going to get it. Let's get some dry clothes, first aid, and then drive to Vegas."

He massaged her hand with his. "I think the cartel was coming for me out of revenge for Gustavo Alvarez. That's why they found Harry so fast. They were already planning to kill us before Carlos started all this. This is all my fault."

"It's the killer's fault, not yours."

He didn't respond.

"I'm scared, Jack."

"I know."

"Not for myself." Her voice softened. "I'm scared I'm going to lose another brother and that our lives won't be the same." A tear rolled down her face.

"I'll do whatever it takes to protect your family. I promise." Even as he said those words he wasn't sure he could deliver. He had to find a way. Whatever it took.

If Christie lost Harry, their relationship might not survive it. He wasn't sure they would survive the loss of Dale. His whole life and world was crumbling around him and the best he could do was to ensure that Christie and her brothers survived his mess. He vowed to make that happen.

Her voice trembled, her face lined with fatigue and sadness. "I'm terrified that I'm angry enough to change into someone I don't respect anymore."

"I will always admire and love you, no matter what."

She looked at him. "We had to talk Clay into this hiking trip. He's a homebody and doesn't like being away from Meera and his boys. He insisted on doing all the trip planning and that we only do safe hikes. He didn't want anyone to get injured. Instead of family fun, he had to watch his brother die."

"I'm so sorry, honey." Wondering if Clay or her family would ever be able to forgive him, he felt another piece of their relationship falling apart.

She pulled on his shirt until he leaned over and held her again. Her voice was a whisper, her head on his shoulder. "I never got a chance to say goodbye to Dale, to hug him one more time. I'll never see his smile again."

Anger and sadness welled up inside him. Anger at himself for bringing this to her life, and sadness for her. He wanted to take it all away from her, but all he had were words. "Dale was a hero."

She cried quietly.

# CHAPTER 33

CARLOS HAD TO REMAIN calm. Otherwise anger and sadness would overwhelm him and he would put more of his family in danger.

He felt numb. His son Mario had verified what he could in Colorado, enough to support what Steel had said. There was no logical reason that both Juan and Isabella would not answer phone calls from him and Mario. He had to accept it. Juan was dead because of his vendetta. In addition, Juan's children were now fatherless and his son's wife without a husband. If he also lost Isabella, it would crush his heart.

Inside the cartels there was always someone who was greedy or desperate for money. Thus, long ago—after spending a hundred thousand for information from a few people inside the Alvarez cartel—he had learned that Diego was one of Marita's killers. With another similar investment he had also learned about Diego's meeting with ISIS.

Originally he had planned to kill Diego after the cartel boss met with ISIS. He wanted ISIS to strike back at the U.S. But now he couldn't risk playing that game. Isabella's life was on the line.

Ironically he had not known about Diego's plan to avenge his nephew Gustavo Alvarez. If he had, he would have waited before doing anything on his own. Instead for nearly a year he had made plans, while waiting for Diego and his men to travel north so he could set his own vendetta into motion.

The best he could hope for now was to kill Diego, save his daughter, and walk away with his two sons. Steel might live, but he couldn't risk any more of his family.

And if Diego survived their attempt to kill him, they were all as good as dead anyway. He wanted desperately to kill Diego and Angel, but a seed of fear filled his belly. He had heard of Angel's reputation.

Worst of all, how could he face his children now?

He had driven out of Sequoia National Park hours ago, after finding Vincente and his men dead. Mario was in Colorado, waiting instructions, while Pedro was tracking Diego in Las Vegas. Mario would grieve for Juan but accept it. However Pedro had been close to Juan and would want revenge even more than himself. It made him question how much of the need for revenge his son had learned from him.

A single tear escaped his eye. Juan. He would never see his son's smile again, never hold him, never talk to him. His thirst for revenge had harmed the very people he was committed to protect.

Another tear rolled down his cheek for Isabella. She had seen her brother executed. She was the light of their family. Even with her temper, she had always been the healer and peacemaker in their family.

Deep down he had known she never wanted to help with his revenge, but he had been so blinded by hate that he had ignored her pleas to put aside vengeance. And when she could not convince him to let it go, he had just as easily accepted her demands to join him. She couldn't bear to see all of them risking their lives and not be part of it. Yet without her, the tender heart of his family would be gone.

Suddenly he was glad to have Steel's help. The man was one of the best, as was Christie. The way they had taken out Vincente and his men was impressive and spontaneous. They knew how to improvise.

His window was down and he heard several crows cawing in the distance. Perhaps mocking him for his reckless stupidity.

*What have you done to your family, you fool?*

# CHAPTER 34

STEEL DROVE ALL THE way to Las Vegas, where they purchased some fresh clothing. Designer jeans, a blue blouse for Christie, and a black short-sleeved shirt for him. Along with first aid supplies, pain relievers, socks, tennis shoes, and food.

They found a cheap hotel and showered, and he rebandaged Christie's back wound. Afterward they collapsed on the bed and slept for a few hours, rising early to eat a breakfast of fruit, nuts, and jerky inside the room.

Steel gazed at her, seeing the bruise on her ribs before she pulled on her blouse. There was also a bruise on her left cheekbone. He let it go. If she had a broken rib she would have trouble moving and breathing so it was probably just bruised.

Still it upset him to see her hurt. "You look good. How do you feel?"

"I'm tired, but otherwise I'm all right." She gave him a small smile. "It was nice to wake up in your arms."

"I look forward to more of that when we're done with all this." He returned her smile but didn't feel it inside.

She pushed some nuts around on her plate with her fingers. "I keep seeing Dale. In my dreams, in my thoughts. I remember one time when Clay and I got into a fight, and Dale jumped between us, laughing. He kept laughing until we started laughing. He was the light side of our family."

A single tear escaped her eye and she wiped it away. "I wonder when we'll have the funeral."

Her pain wrenched his gut. He gently put a hand on her shoulder. "He was a wonderful brother and I'm so sorry he's gone, Christie."

Her chest heaved. "I want them to pay, Jack. All of them."

"We end it today." The horrible possibility of someone else in her family dying in the coming hours flashed through him. He wanted to keep her and Clay out of the approaching fight, but they would never agree to it.

After Christie finished eating, she spoke in a hard voice. "Today we rescue Harry."

He felt pressure over the low odds of saving Harry but kept it to himself. "Tell me what happened with Vincente's men."

Her eyes flicked up at him, and then she described it. Her ability to escape a very dangerous situation a second time surprised him. "You didn't follow directions."

"I did the best I could."

"You did as well as I could have." He meant it. "Let's go meet Colonel Jeffries' man."

As they gathered their things, he went into the bathroom to get their ponchos, which they had hung the night before to dry. He saw the bullet holes in Christie's poncho and just stared.

They left the hotel and drove southwest out of the city, past the suburbs until they were on a deserted dirt road where they parked on the shoulder. They waited by the trunk of their car.

The sun was already up, the air dry and hot, and the sky blue. Arid land. Scattered bushes. Occasional hedgehog and foxtail cacti. A black-tailed jackrabbit chewed on vegetation fifty feet away. A few ravens circled in the sky.

In a different situation Steel wouldn't mind taking a hike to see what other wildlife he could find. He had a Glock in his belt beneath his shirt, while Christie carried a SIG Sauer beneath her blouse against her back.

In twenty minutes a black SUV approached them from the east. It pulled past them, made a U-turn in the road, and went by them again. Making one more U-turn, the SUV parked on the shoulder behind them.

Two young men got out. Dressed in shorts and tees and wearing sunglasses.

One of the men said, "Colonel Jeffries sends his regards."

Steel and Christie followed them to the rear of the SUV. One of the men opened up the door, revealing a large duffel bag which he unzipped.

Steel liked what he saw. An M3 MAAWS with three anti-tank rounds, ear muffs for sound protection, another set of silenced Glocks, five Rattlers, a pair of SIG Sauers, two phones with Bluetooth earbuds, four car trackers, and two knives. There was also another silenced G28 sniper rifle.

"Are we good?" asked the soldier.

"We're good." Steel zipped it up. When no traffic approached in either direction, he carried it to the trunk of their sedan.

One of the soldiers held up a small tracker. "Colonel Jeffries says it's nonnegotiable."

Steel gave a small wave. "Agreed."

The soldier squatted and attached it to the underside of the front of their car frame. When he stood, he said, "Good luck."

Steel nodded. "Thanks."

The SUV took off, and they leaned against the trunk, waiting.

Christie edged up to him. "Kiss?"

He obliged her for a few seconds and pulled back. "You okay?"

"Harry's life is on the line. Our lives are on the line."

"We've come this far. We can jump a few more hurdles." He had to believe they could.

"I still want to take a road trip with you." She tousled his hair.

"You get whatever you want when this is over."

She smiled, pain showing in her eyes. "Hmm. I'll remember that."

He couldn't smile back, amazed that she still wanted to be around him.

She gazed at him. "You need to let it go. You're not responsible for Dale's death."

"I brought your family into this mess. It's on me."

"Oh, Jack." She wrapped her arms around him, her head on his shoulder.

A silver pickup truck approached from the east and they pulled apart. The vehicle soon pulled off the road in back of them. Three men exited the truck.

"Be ready." Steel recognized their size and shape from the first night. Their faces also matched the photos Jeffries had sent. He wanted to put bullets into all of them.

Carlos was in his fifties, stocky and strong, with a moustache and a cowboy hat. He looked self-assured. This man could be dangerous. Like his two sons, he wore sunglasses.

Mario was in his thirties, strong, with easy strides. He and Carlos wore boots, western shirts, and jeans. Mario wore a small western hat and had a toothpick in his mouth. Pedro, in his twenties and lean, had on a hoodie, shorts, studs in his ears, and sandals. Unlike Mario and Carlos, Pedro had longer hair tied back in a ponytail and was shorter.

No weapons were visible so Steel relaxed. He stared at Carlos, despising the man that had put him and Christie into so much danger. However he kept his mouth shut, waiting to see what would happen.

Approaching them with a son on either side, Carlos grimaced as he stopped a few yards away. "I told my sons they get to say whatever is on their minds to you, just once, and that's the end of our vendetta."

Mario took off his sunglasses, his voice and eyes steady. "I will never forgive you for what happened to Marita, but I can let that go if you help us save Isabella."

Steel heard the man's conviction and levelheadedness. A professional. He believed him. He turned to Pedro. Smaller and shorter. He remembered the intuition he had days ago when Pedro held the dynamite. The young man was willing to do anything, which made him reckless.

Pedro took off his sunglasses and his eyes narrowed. "I honor and obey my father so I too will let it go. I loved my brother Juan so I hate Angel even more than I despise you. But if Isabella dies, all bets are off."

Steel wasn't surprised. Carlos wouldn't be able to control his son if things went bad. "The cartel has her, not us."

Pedro's eyes narrowed. "Because you let Marita die, the cartel came after you and now they have Isabella instead."

Steel remained quiet. Young and hot-headed, Pedro wasn't skilled enough to be a threat to him.

Carlos took off his sunglasses, glancing at Pedro. "I will honor my word, and so will my sons. The vendetta is over. Now we try to save my daughter and Christie's brother."

"First I get to say something." Christie stepped forward. "Jack tried to save Marita, but she was scared of him because he was half-delirious when he killed Gustavo Alvarez. He protects women. It's his business. And if you come after him again, we'll kill all of you."

She flicked her hair back, eyeing Pedro. "Your father already knows what we're capable of."

The three men looked at her, and Carlos said, "You remind me of Isabella, how protective she is of us. She never wanted this vendetta."

Christie's voice softened. "I want the cartel men dead as much as you do. I'm sorry about Juan."

Carlos' voice was gentle. "Gracias. And I'm sorry about your brother."

Christie grimaced. "His name was Dale."

He tipped his hat to her. "I'm sorry for your loss of Dale."

Mario lifted a hand. "I didn't know Dale, but if he was anything like my brother Juan, I understand your loss."

Christie stuffed her hands in her pockets. "Thank you."

"We're going to make them pay," spat Pedro.

Christie nodded to him. "Yes, we are."

Steel stared at Carlos, still not trusting him and wanting to kill him. For now he stuffed his feelings. "First things first." He opened the trunk and the duffel bag. "We have a sniper rifle for you, Carlos, if you want it."

Carlos eyed the weapons. "Excellent."

"Our biggest advantage is that they won't be able to identify you three so the element of surprise is on our side." Steel studied Mario. "I'd like you to find Diego's hotel room and get a photo of the ISIS connection."

"I told you we're not involving ourselves with your ISIS problem." Carlos' tone was emphatic.

Steel kept his voice calm. "These men want to kill innocent people. You were a trainer at the School of Lanceros to stop things like this. I also think you're going to have a problem leaving the country after this is over. You kidnapped someone and were involved with murder, among other things. All that goes away if you help us. We'll make sure all of you get out safely and any possible charges disappear."

"Lies," said Pedro.

"Papá, I don't mind doing it." Mario waved a hand. "ISIS is something we shouldn't support for any reason. And I want to come back here."

"How can we trust you will keep your word or that your government will support us?" Carlos shook his head. "Marita took the same risks and it cost her everything."

Steel pulled out his phone and dialed Colonel Jeffries, putting him on speaker. "Sir, Carlos and his sons will help us track the ISIS connection, if you can guarantee they'll face no charges and can leave the U.S. safely, and return for visits and travel if they like."

"You help us take down ISIS and you have my word. No charges, no problems leaving and returning. No retribution."

"Your name is?" asked Carlos.

"Classified," said Jeffries. "Steel can vouch for me."

"Thank you, sir." Steel hung up.

"So an unnamed officer gives us his word, which can just as easily be denied," Pedro said with disgust.

Mario remained quiet.

"I understand it's the best we will get." Carlos put his sunglasses back on. "All right."

Steel eyed him. "You know where Diego is planning to take Isabella and Harry, don't you?"

"Yes. Diego has a place in the desert. I'll show you on a map." Carlos stepped closer to him. "I've hated you for so long that it feels odd to finally meet you in person. But if you help us save Isabella, I will find it easier to believe your story about Marita."

Steel didn't give a damn what Carlos believed about him anymore. "I'll do whatever it takes. My daughter could be next. It ends here. Today. And if you help save Harry, I won't put a bullet in your head."

Carlos extended his hand and Steel took it. It meant nothing to him.

Carlos lifted his chin. "If you really tried to save Marita, then I owe you an apology. But the dead don't talk and no one else knows what happened in the jungle."

Steel kept his expression neutral. "I might have the same reaction if I was in your shoes."

Carlos nodded. "Then we understand each other."

They discussed Diego's hideout and their strategy. Afterward, Carlos and Mario grabbed weapons and left with Pedro, driving back to the city.

Steel leaned against the trunk. Christie pressed against him, holding his waist.

He gazed into her eyes. "You were pretty tough with your comments."

She trailed a hand gently down his face. "I'm getting used to it. Maybe it's the new me. Does it bother you?"

"Not at all." He wrapped his arms around her, amazed at her strength.

She held him while she dialed her brother. "We're ready, Clay." Pocketing the phone, she said, "I need some time alone with him, honey."

# CHAPTER 35

STEEL WAITED IN THE car, having mixed feelings about Clay joining them. Christie's brother had flown in overnight and was nearby. It wasn't long before a black sedan drove up from the east and parked close behind their car.

Steel adjusted the rearview mirror and sat close to the open passenger window.

Clay got out, a large bandage wrapped around his head. No hat. Christie strode forward to hug him. She pulled back from him, wiping her eyes, and they exchanged quiet words for a few minutes, talking in low tones.

Steel watched them in the mirror, assuming they were talking about Dale. His stomach knotted again, knowing he was the reason for their brother's death.

Clay straightened, his voice louder. "You're beat up."

"You don't look much better," said Christie.

"If you're injured you should sit this one out, Christie."

"Then so should you, Clay."

Their voices were amped up. Steel guessed Clay wanted him to hear them. He was glad Clay voiced concerns for his sister. He wanted Christie out too.

Clay's hand flew up as he continued. "We lost our brother and I don't want to lose my sister too."

Christie shoved her hands in her pockets. "Jack is my family, Clay. Like it or not, I'm staying."

"I don't like it."

Steel had heard enough. He got out and walked up beside Christie. "Words can never tell you how sorry I am about Dale."

Clay stood with his fists bunched at his sides. "Your mess got my brother killed, and now you're going to get my sister killed."

"It wasn't his fault!" snapped Christie.

Steel shook his head at her. "No, he's right. I accept responsibility for Dale." He turned to Clay. "Christie performed as well as I could have in both Ops thus far." Ironically his efforts to protect her in the Garcia and Vincente Ops had put her in more danger, and she had handled it. "Anyway, I'll be the one inside on this Op."

Clay stuck his hands in his pockets, his voice gruff. "Okay. What's the play?"

Christie explained what they needed from him.

Clay gave a dismissive wave. "Do we have to work with the scum that kidnapped Harry and got Dale killed?"

"I don't like it either, but we need them to take Diego," said Steel.

Clay shook his head. "When this is over you're going to kill Carlos, aren't you?"

Steel was aware of Christie watching him. "Yes."

"Secondly, Christie," said Clay, "Angel is dangerous and I'm a marine with combat experience. I should be facing him, not you. Are you trying to protect *me* now?"

"No." She stared her brother down. "I want to be with Jack. That's final and not up for debate, Clay."

"You always were stubborn." He stared at her for a few moments, and then motioned to Steel. "Angel is at your level. He's one of the best I've ever come across. Watch out for the trunk compartment. Watch out for surprises. Don't expect anything to be what it seems."

Steel didn't like hearing any of it.

Clay eyed Christie. "If this goes well, are you going home?"

She took Steel's hand. "Of course. Mom and Dad need our support."

Steel opened the trunk. "Take your pick, Clay."

Clay examined the arsenal. "You look ready for war."

"We're going to bring it to them." Steel knew they would use all of it.

Christie picked up a Rattler. "We're getting Harry back today, and we're going to bury all of these animals."

# CHAPTER 36

HARRY WOKE UP NESTLED against Isabella. She had one arm draped over him. It was almost amusing, except that they could both be dead soon.

His wounded shoulder and arm ached and his legs were cramped. He tried to stretch his right leg by lifting it above Isabella and extending it into the corner of the trunk. It helped. He was thirsty and hungry but didn't expect food or water from the killer.

Isabella stirred and quickly pulled back her arm and moved away from him a few inches.

"Good morning, Isabella."

"How are you feeling today, Harry?"

Surprised she cared, he said, "Sore and stiff. But I'll be okay." He doubted he could even throw a punch. Maybe with his left hand.

The car stopped.

He stiffened. "Get ready."

A door opened, then shut. Preparing himself, he tensed. Then the car began moving again. He didn't know what it meant, except that their opportunity for escape or death had been postponed once more.

Isabella released a breath. "I just want it to be over, one way or the other."

He agreed, but said, "We're making more turns so I think we're in a city."

"I'm scared, Harry."

"I am too, but I'm more angry than scared. Where do you have the knife?"

"At my back tucked into my jeans. My blouse will hide it."

"Perfect."

Her voice quieted. "Do you think we have any chance to get away?"

He couldn't be honest with her. "My brothers and sister will be looking for me. They won't quit until they find us." Truthfully, he wondered if any of his siblings were still alive.

"Others will be searching for me too."

He doubted it mattered. "Steel will eventually find us so the more time we have, the better our chances."

"How can you work for that man and be friends with him?" Isabella sounded disgusted.

"He tried to save Marita. I know the story and I'll tell you if you want to hear it."

Her tone became harsh. "I don't want to hear your lies."

"Why do you think his protection agency was protecting Afia Ameen? A woman who has a fatwa on her head? He would never have abandoned Marita to the cartel. He was betrayed by our own military down there..." His voice trailed off. He didn't have the energy to argue with her.

The car stopped again. Quiet.

Footsteps. The trunk opened and a Latino man stared down at them. Not the killer.

Harry glimpsed a dimly lit garage of some kind behind the man, who was average in size and build. He felt a spark of hope. Anyone would be easier to face than the killer.

He couldn't effectively punch the man with his stiff shoulder. And he would never get out fast enough over Isabella before the man drew his gun. No doubt that the man would be armed. They needed an advantage.

"We have to use the bathroom," he said.

The man smiled. "Tough, amigo. You're not getting out."

Harry hoped Isabella could stab the man with her knife. He lifted his chin slightly to her. Giving a tiny nod, she slowly allowed her left hand to slide to her back.

"Chiquita." The man ran his left hand along the side of her thigh, toward her hip. "Maybe we have a little fun while we're waiting, huh?"

Isabella said something harsh in Spanish.

Harry recognized one of the words—*puerco*—pig. She tried to push the man's hand away, but he blocked her arm with his right hand, his left sliding up her blouse.

Impulsively Harry kicked out his leg, hitting the man's upper left arm, the toe of his boot sliding into the man's cheek.

The man stumbled back, swearing in Spanish, and pulled a gun from behind his back. He stepped forward, aiming the pistol at Harry. "You're going to pay for that, gringo."

"How do you think your boss will react when you spoil his party?" Harry said quickly.

Hesitating, the man swore again. "Later, gringo. I will remember this when we all have fun with both of you." He slammed the trunk shut.

Quiet.

"I'm sorry you had to go through that, Isabella." Harry cleared his throat. "I was worried he would find your knife before you had a chance to use it."

To be honest, he had acted out of anger. Stupid. It might have been their one chance to get free. Steel had often told him sometimes you had only one opportunity. He had to believe they would have another.

"Gracias," she said softly. "I shouldn't have reacted to him as I did. It was my fault too." After a little while, sounding resigned, she said, "Okay, tell me Steel's story. I'll listen, but I can't say I will believe it."

"Sure." He started talking, telling the story as Christie had told it to him.

When he finished, she was quiet for a minute, and then talked softly. "When I first saw what they had done to Marita, I threw up. I wanted to forget about it. It was so terrible. But then my father wanted revenge, and so did my brothers. They wouldn't let it go. I couldn't let them do this alone so I pretended I wanted revenge too. All this hate and violence. It makes me sick."

He decided to press her. "What did your father want from Jack and Christie?"

"He told them to kill the Alvarez cartel people or he would kill you."

He thought about it. "Maybe it was a blessing in disguise."

"How could it be? My father forced Jack and Christie to murder people."

"If your father hadn't sent Steel after the cartel, the cartel might have blindsided him and Christie. They might be dead now. Instead they surprised the cartel."

It was a few moments before she responded. "Are you saying that just to make me feel better?"

"No, I mean it."

She sounded resigned. "The cartel must know what is going on."

"Yeah, the killer is probably bringing us to his boss."

"They will do to me what they did to Marita."

He heard the fear in her voice. "Not if I can help it."

"Thank you, Harry." She put her hand on his arm. "You are one of the good ones."

"If I forget about the kidnapping, drugging, and stabbing, then I think you have a good heart too, Isabella."

They were quiet for a few minutes.

"Do you have any dreams, Harry?"

"I'd like to build a house on some land and do beekeeping and grow herbs. You?"

"I'd like to write a book about authentic Mexican cuisine. I'm a chef." She paused. "I hope we both live to see our dreams come true, Harry."

"Me too." He doubted either of them would live through another day.

# CHAPTER 37

ANGEL HAD TAKEN OFF his wig and the rest of his disguise before he reached Las Vegas.

He had arranged for one of Diego's men to meet him a mile from the Wynn and drive his car around while he met with Diego. It wasn't prudent to leave the car unattended in case Harry and Isabella made too much noise and were discovered. He also wanted to see the hotel entrance from a distance to judge the best way for Diego to exit it.

The walk gave him a chance to stretch his legs and wake up after driving all night nonstop to get here.

While strolling toward the hotel he was observant of everyone around him. Tourists, a few police officers, and employees. All mixed together on the sidewalks, overflowing out from the casinos, hotels, and other venues.

He detested the glitz and phoniness of Las Vegas, but Renata had told him to suggest it to Diego as being the safest. She was always right.

He stopped across the street from the Wynn, got out his phone, and called her. It gave him a chance to scan everyone within a block of the Wynn in all directions without being obvious. Superb at noticing people that were out of place, he was especially looking for Steel, Christie, and her brother Clay. Though he doubted they would be out in the open here.

As the phone rang he paced and moved his lips as if he was talking, while taking quick peeks up and down the sidewalks.

Nobody seemed suspicious. But he did enjoy watching a young man with long hair and wearing a hoodie skating down the sidewalk across the street, weaving in and out of pedestrians. That took skill.

Renata answered and she sounded excited. "I found us a nice beach house in the Bahamas, Angel! It's so beautiful. And private like you wanted. It's on one of the smaller islands."

"Wonderful, dear sister." He chuckled. "Now can we make sure I am available for the trip?"

"Of course! I was just so excited I had to tell you."

"Gracias. I'm in Las Vegas. One of Diego's men is driving my car around with Harry and Isabella. I'm across from the Wynn, about to enter to meet Diego and go to the meeting with his friends."

"Don't attend the meeting, dear brother. It's best if these people don't know you. That's not my sight, just logic."

He thought about that. "I'll tell Diego that I'll follow him into the desert and see if anyone tails him. He will appreciate that cleverness."

She was quiet a few moments. "I sense they will be waiting for you in the desert."

He smiled. "It's going to be an adventure."

"You're crazy! Even though I've heard you say it a thousand times, it still makes me nervous."

He became serious. "Do you sense anything else I should be worried about?"

"I don't trust Diego. I think he would not hesitate to hurt you if you refuse to carry out his vengeance."

He knew she was right. "I look forward to the Bahamas, dear sister, and a new life." That idea made him feel warm inside.

"It's so exciting! Call me if anything doesn't feel right."

"I promise." Putting his phone away, he crossed the street whistling. Carefree in his stride, smiling at everyone who passed him, he still ran his gaze carefully up and down the block. Nothing caused alarm.

He strolled into the hotel's main driveway entrance, noting the limos, the parking lots, and the trees lining the drive. Many places to hide. But Steel would never choose to have a shootout in a busy public place.

After entering the main lobby, he bypassed the registration desk and strode down the corridor to the villa Diego had rented. Along the way he noted everyone, but all he saw were tourists.

To him the hotel was decadent. People were starving in the world while these fools pretended that all this *show* meant something.

The three billion spent on the building was obvious in the colorfully designed floors, shining wood, wall art, and beautiful architecture. But he scorned the empty lies it told. That it was all here to welcome guests as friends, to make their lives easier. Or that guests were important and powerful if they were surrounded by such opulence, when in fact the hotel owners cared nothing for anyone. All they wanted was your money.

At least the cartel was blunt about their business and not pretending they were trying to help anyone. However Diego liked to live high and paying three-thousand a night was nothing for him. The drug lord also liked to gamble.

Diego was born into the Alvarez cartel, whereas Angel had fought his way in. If the rich tourists in the hotel spent a week on the streets in Mexico or Bogotá, their pathetic weakness would be revealed.

His musings brought back memories of Bogotá; his family's farm and his parents. He rarely thought of them anymore and was surprised those memories had surfaced. Another sign that he was ready for a new life.

He walked to the villa door and knocked. One of Diego's men answered, hastily stepping aside for him to enter. Diego was standing on the outdoor pool patio. They embraced each other.

Remembering Renata's warning about Diego, Angel kept his face calm.

Diego's eyes glistened. "It was as I feared. They killed Vincente, his girlfriend, and the six men with him, even though my brother was prepared and had set a trap." He hung his head. "My beloved brother, gone."

Angel was impressed. He had guessed as much, but to hear it from Diego's mouth made it real. Vincente was smart. Which meant Steel and Christie were formidable.

"I am sorry, Diego. There are no words that can bring Vincente back, but I hope in time your fond memories of him will help your heart heal." He meant what he said. If he ever lost Renata, it would crush him.

Diego lifted his head. "You always know what to say to make me feel better, Angel." His eyes hardened. "Will we be prepared to take Steel?"

"We have always been better than..." He avoided saying *Vincente* and instead said, "...our enemies. We will kill all of them, have fun with the leftovers, and then bury them. Afterward I will continue hunting the rest of their families."

"Good. The ISIS contact will be here in a half hour." Diego's eyes glinted. "Soon we will have our revenge on the government and people of this country."

"I've had a little taste and I'm ready for more." But ever since he had decided to leave the cartel he didn't care about retribution anymore. He was looking forward to his new life.

Now he just wanted to kill Steel so the man didn't hunt him when he left the cartel. One more fight. He had been a good friend of Gustavo Alvarez so that obligation spoke to him too. But Diego and his continuing vengeance meant nothing to him now.

"What is your plan?" Diego spoke softly, as if the villa was bugged.

It reminded Angel of Diego's paranoia. The cartel leader trusted no one and that practice had kept him alive. He would have to be careful. "I will skip the meeting, make a quick trip to our storage locker, and return to see who follows you. I'll arrive last, with our cargo. We know they are coming. They won't try anything here or in the city. If I can surprise them from behind, that will give us another advantage in addition to what we have planned."

Diego frowned. "What about my exit from the hotel?"

"Make it easy for them. Have the valet bring your car to the main entrance of the hotel. We don't want them to miss the party."

Diego smiled. "Always a step ahead of our prey, El Lobo."

Angel returned the smile, curious if Diego had any clue that the wolf was leaving him. Over the years, several times he had almost told Diego about Renata, but she had always cautioned him against it. He was thankful he had kept her a secret.

Diego clapped his arm. "I will see you soon, amigo. And after this is over we can have fun with your two captives."

Angel forced a smile and left. He found Diego's enthusiasm about raping and torturing Isabella repulsive.

On his way out he spotted someone in the lobby who didn't quite fit. Latino. Male. Thirties. The man stood too stiffly. Ex-military. Perhaps related to Isabella. It didn't matter.

Leaving via a different exit, he walked aimlessly through a few shops to make sure no one followed him. Once he was back outside, he walked another mile down the boulevard before calling Diego's man to bring his car.

Steel's group would know his description, but they would not recognize his white car. Its tinted windows ensured they couldn't see him in it either.

He considered the coming battle. The last big one of his career with the cartel. And the most important. There was a good chance Steel's people would kill most if not all of Diego's men. He would kill Steel, and sometime during the fight he would have to kill Isabella and Harry to spare them Diego's twisted plans of torture.

He considered his future with Renata. She was right. He had to kill Diego too.

# CHAPTER 38

CLAY FELT HE HAD given in too easily to Christie. Just the thought of her facing Angel, even with Steel and the others, worried him sick. The man was evil and would be prepared.

Christie had told him many times that Steel was the best of the best, but he had never seen the man in action. It did console him that they had taken care of two cartel leaders and their hired guns without serious injuries.

Dale still weighed heavily on his mind. And the call to his parents had been one of the hardest things he had ever done. They took it quietly, but they would grieve deeply.

He called Meera and she answered immediately.

"How are you, my love?" she asked.

"Better. Sad. Afraid. I want to kill them all today."

"I know, Clay. This has all been very hard on you and your family. All of you are heroes."

"Heroes don't get their little brother killed."

"You did your best, Clay. You always do. Everyone knows you would have died to save Dale. No one blames you."

He choked up. "Thank you."

"Me and the boys are going to spend some time with your parents. It will help them."

"Thank you, honey."

"Please be careful, Clay. Your two boys need their father."

"I'm coming home. I promise you that. I can't wait to leave this hell behind."

"I love you."

"You too. See you soon." He hung up, feeling impatient.

In three minutes his phone rang and he answered it. Mario. Carlos' son had found the room Diego had registered in as Roberto López and watched who came and went.

"You are up, Clay." Mario sent a photo to Clay's phone.

Clay looked at the photo. "Are you sure this guy is the ISIS contact?"

"He fits the profile, Clay. It's a best guess. I could be wrong, but I don't think so. How many Middle Eastern guests is someone like Diego going to have?"

Clay started his rental car. He was parked fifty feet from the main check-in entrance to the Wynn.

The man Mario had photographed exited the hotel entrance. All Clay had to do was get the license plate of the man's car and follow him. He would pass the intel to Steel, who would contact Jeffries, who then would inform Las Vegas FBI and give them the vehicle description and plate, along with Clay's location.

When the FBI took over following the terrorist, Clay would rejoin the others in time for the assault on Diego. Steel didn't want to contact the FBI directly since they would want to question him and interfere with the Diego fight.

Mario came out and tipped his cowboy hat toward the departing ISIS terrorist. Then he headed toward the parking lot and his vehicle to join his father for the assault.

Clay felt a flash of anger as he watched one of the men that had kidnapped Harry walk away. "Working with a criminal," he muttered.

He studied the ISIS operative walking down the sidewalk. Average in every way. Height, weight, and a non-descriptive face. Wearing a brown collared shirt and white pants. Late twenties.

Middle Eastern in heritage, but from what country he couldn't be sure. But secretly a terrorist.

He wondered if the man was on the FBI's watchlist. It would be easier and save everyone time and trouble to just run him over.

Wheeling the car out slowly, he stopped at the front hotel entrance, waiting for the terrorist to walk farther ahead. The man reached Las Vegas Boulevard and took a left down the sidewalk.

Clay quickly pulled up to the street and watched as a white van stopped in the road a half-block down. The terrorist got into the front passenger seat. At this distance he couldn't make out the van's license plate.

He pulled out to follow the van, thinking Christie should have been following these guys. Much easier, with much less risk.

His teeth jarred and the side of his body slammed into his door as a grinding crash of breaking glass and twisting metal filled his ears. His rental car was jolted sideways up over the curb. Shaken, he looked out the passenger window.

A silver SUV with a push bar and tinted windows was already backing away from his car. He ducked down reflexively in case they were going to shoot him, but he heard the vehicle speed off.

Opening the door, he got out, kneeling, while reaching for the SIG beneath his shirt at his back. He didn't pull his gun. The white van and SUV were racing down the boulevard. The SUV turned off the boulevard, quickly lost to sight, while the white van remained on the road, disappearing around a bend.

Standing, his legs shaky, he walked in front of his car to assess the damage. The front passenger tire was leaning at an angle. Undriveable.

"You idiot!" He had just let everyone down while they were risking their necks, and he had no easy way to rejoin them. Taxi, Uber, or rental car.

A blue pickup pulled over and stopped ahead of his car. He tensed, his hand going back to the SIG again.

Mario leaned out the driver window. "Get in, Clay."

Surprised, he hustled to the passenger side of the truck and got in, not looking at Mario. "White van. I couldn't get the plate number."

Mario stomped on the gas in silence. At the next intersection they saw the white van two blocks down at a stoplight. Veering around a slow-moving car, Mario hit the gas hard to catch up. When he was a half-dozen cars behind the van, he slowed down and settled back into his seat.

"Binoculars, paper, and pen in the glove compartment, Clay. Get the license plate."

Clay had the binoculars up to his eyes in seconds. "Got it." He wrote down the number on the paper and put the binoculars away. Grudgingly he said, "Thanks. I'll call Steel." He got out his phone.

"You were made following Diego's ISIS contact, either by the terrorist's associates or Diego's. Either way, the terrorists will know someone is on to them." Mario's voice was steady. "What if they call their associates and warn them?"

Clay hesitated, annoyed. "We work the plan. I call Steel, give him the plate number, and he calls the military, who call the Las Vegas FBI. Supposedly they're ready to move and we'll hand off, and they can take over."

Mario waved his toothpick. "I don't like the plan."

Clay felt impatient. "Why? It's solid. We're not letting them walk."

"Even if your FBI captures these men alive, how will they get information about the other attacks from them?" Mario shook his head. "If the other terrorists are not caught and they kill hundreds or thousands, that will be our legacy."

Anger filled Clay's throat. "What the hell else can we do?"

"I say we grab the one who met with Diego and then go help our families. We can find out later from the terrorist where the other ISIS operatives are going. Their targets and timetables. And then inform your military."

Clay didn't like it. "What makes you think a terrorist will be any more willing to talk to us?"

"We'll make him."

"You mean torture." Clay frowned.

"My father is an expert. We play rough in Colombia too, Clay."

"Any delay puts my brother and sister at more risk. You've already done your share of hurting my family." He couldn't keep the bitterness out of his voice.

Without taking his eyes off the road, Mario said, "This takes me away from my brother and father and puts them in more danger too."

Clay didn't know what to say. He felt boxed in. A foreigner was more concerned than he was with stopping terrorists in his country. What if Harry or Christie died because he wasn't there? Damn it all to hell!

"I'll let you decide, Clay."

He took a deep breath and thought about being a Marine. What it meant. No choice. "Let's take them down." He put his phone away. Sweat poured down his chest and it wasn't because of the heat. A Rattler lay near his feet. He was glad they had that kind of firepower.

Mario glanced at him. "I respect that you and your brother tried to rescue my sister, and I'm sorry your brother Dale was killed."

Clay couldn't answer as anger and grief hit him again.

"My father told us what Jack and Christie did against Vincente and Garcia. They are quite skilled."

"Yeah." Clay hoped that held true.

"Angel is that good too. Maybe even better." Mario's voice became somber. "My father said goodbye to us today."

Clay suppressed a sarcastic reply. "What do you mean?"

"In case one or all of us don't survive the day."

Clay's stomach sank. He might never see Christie or Harry alive again. "As soon as these guys get out of the city, let's run them off the road and take them."

"I am planning on it."

# CHAPTER 39

S TEEL SAW TOO MANY variables and unknowns, which put them all at risk. Angel worried him the most. Just from the little he knew about him, the man was always prepared, smart, and inventive. And after Garcia and Vincente's deaths, the assassin would assume they were coming for Diego.

The sun was bright, the sky clear.

He licked his dry lips, wishing he was with Christie. Worry for her slid into his thoughts, but he had to let it go. So far she had handled herself as well as he could have. For this Op he had sidelined her as much as possible. Hopefully they wouldn't even need her. One last hurdle.

Pedro had been successful in planting the tracker on Diego's car while pretending to skateboard. But according to Carlos it had been too easy to follow Diego. Steel guessed Diego's driver had been told to not lose any tails.

He was parked on the southwest edge of the Las Vegas suburbs, waiting for Carlos' call. They needed to be sure Diego was heading to the desert hideaway Carlos had shown them.

While he waited, Colonel Jeffries called. He had informed Jeffries earlier that Diego's assassin, Angel, had killed his men. Jeffries wanted to help.

"I called in the favor," said Jeffries. "The drone just looked at the canyon hideaway." He described the intel from the drone.

"Perfect." Steel wasn't surprised.

"I want all of them dead for killing my men, Steel."

"That's the plan, colonel. I have one more request."

"Name it."

"We don't need any Las Vegas police coming out to investigate a gun battle."

"I'll run interference, tell them it's an Army exercise. Good luck." Jeffries hung up.

In twenty minutes his phone rang. Carlos.

"They're headed in your direction, Steel. Still driving slow."

"I'm leaving now." He pulled out onto the highway, driving fast. Checking his watch, he figured he had a half hour before Diego arrived.

The dry red and brown landscape led into the hills and mountains to the west. Near the foothills he exited onto a dirt road, still heading west. Soon he was a mile north of the dead-end road leading to Diego's canyon hideaway.

He stopped to look south at the canyon entrance with the binoculars. The drone had picked up snipers. He quickly picked out a path that would maximize his chances of avoiding being spotted.

Driving across the intersection, he headed straight into the desert. Sagebrush and cactus dotted the low hills that led to higher elevations. He drove as fast as he could without risking hitting the bigger rocks and cacti, and to minimize the chance of getting stuck in the sand.

Cactus wrens flew from his path, and once he spotted a greater roadrunner fleeing far ahead of the car. He didn't like driving over the desert, knowing it was a more fragile ecosystem than it appeared.

Halfway to the foothills he turned southwest.

It took ten minutes of careful maneuvering to reach a medium-sized hill he had picked out. He drove around to the west side of it, and up the back of it, parking the car at an incline.

Getting out, he looked east. He couldn't see the road so the car would remain hidden from Diego and his men.

Slinging the silenced G28 over his shoulder, he stuffed the Glock into his belt. The binoculars, M3, and the three rounds went into the bag Jeffries had given them. He ran. Up and down the sides of small hills, steadily gaining in elevation while hoping no one spotted him. Sweat covered his torso and limbs and his shirt was soaked with it.

Two-thirds of the way up he slowed to a fast walk. The climb had worn him down.

Larger rocks provided more cover for him as he made his way south toward the canyon. A quarter-mile later he stopped by a boulder, got out the binoculars, and scanned the slopes above him that overlooked Diego's house. He searched for the snipers the drone had spotted.

On the canyon ridge a man sat with a rifle behind a rock, facing south. The sniper never looked in his direction. He knew why.

Swinging the binoculars farther west and slightly higher in elevation, he searched for the second sniper. He glimpsed the rifle barrel of the second spotter aimed in his general direction. The man's shoulder was visible. The backup for the lower sniper. There was no time to circle above the second sniper.

Unslinging the rifle, he knelt and took aim at the higher spotter through the telescopic sight. Then he swung the gun to target the lower sniper. He repeated this maneuver three times, noting the distance he had to move the rifle barrel, the change in elevation, and how long it took him to do it. A half second if he did it right.

Aiming at the shoulder of the higher spotter, he fired. Immediately he swung the rifle and targeted the chest of the turning lower sniper. He squeezed the trigger again. The second target slumped to the ground. Swinging the G28 back to the higher sniper, he saw the man crawling on the ground. He shot him twice and the man lay still.

The air was dry and his muffled shots were noticeable. It was likely that the third sniper the drone had found had heard them. It didn't matter. He was committed now.

Moving fast, he picked up the bag and crossed the last quarter-mile of terrain until he reached the top of the sloping hill. He was just north of the house, a quarter mile above it. Stopping near the dead man, he remained in the shelter of the rock. It was safe to assume the other sniper across the canyon knew he was here.

Taking the binoculars, he poked his head out to scan the rim on the far side of the gorge. A glint of metal made him pull back just as a bullet bit the rock near his cheek. Blood ran down his face from a cut caused by a flying rock chip.

He crawled to the other side of the rock and used the rifle scope. A glint of metal stuck out from the back of a boulder across the canyon. The shooter was hidden. At least he was safe in this position.

He scanned up and down the far side of the canyon to ensure no other snipers were posted. The drone should have seen any others, but he wanted to make sure.

Angel had to be in charge of Diego's security and planning. The assassin would have wanted two snipers on the north side, knowing the sun wouldn't be in a shooter's eyes on this side of the canyon. It was what Steel would have done too.

There were no cars or people below yet. Just Diego's house. The one-story building was rectangular and ran east-west. It would be hidden from the driveway until an intruder was past the canyon choke point.

There was another narrower, lower entrance to the canyon south of the road entrance. It would also divert any potential flooding away from the house in the rainy season.

Swinging his binoculars east, he spotted three SUVs driving down the dirt road he had taken. They turned into the dead-end road and approached the canyon. It had to be Diego and his men.

Farther north he saw Christie's red rental Camry. There were other cars behind her. He wasn't sure if it was traffic, Pedro, Carlos, or Angel. Mario was supposed to take up the rear, but his blue truck was absent.

Using the Bluetooth, he called Christie. She picked up, and he said, "I'm set up. Tell Carlos they had two shooters on the north side, and there's one left on the south side that I can't get to. I'll watch the cars behind you. Go a quarter mile past the driveway and pull over onto the shoulder. Tell Carlos there's another entrance into the canyon south of the entrance road that he might want to take. Call me back ASAP."

"Got it." She hung up, but quickly called back. "Carlos said Mario had to help Clay. Clay's vehicle was taken out by someone helping the terrorists. They're going to try to come, but they'll be late."

That bothered him. Mario and Clay had military experience they needed. "All right. Hang on."

He watched the cars following her as she stopped on the shoulder. Two vehicles went by her. One stopped. Carlos. He and Christie remained in their cars.

A beat up old brown sedan made the turn into the driveway. Pedro.

An expensive-looking white sedan drove past the driveway, past Christie and Carlos, and kept going.

Steel said to Christie, "Angel might be in the white sedan that just went by you. If it turns around be careful."

"Got it. Do we assume Angel still has Harry and Isabella?"

"Absolutely. Keep the line open." He looked north. No other traffic.

He scanned farther south. The white sedan had pulled onto the shoulder a mile away and was making a U-turn in the road, heading north again. "Heads up, Christie. Has to be Angel in the white sedan coming north. Remember, Clay thought Angel had an FN P90 when they were attacked."

She responded immediately. "I'll tell Carlos."

He held his breath, hoping Angel wasn't going to try a drive-by shooting. But the white sedan passed Christie and Carlos without incident, and then pulled into the driveway, heading toward the canyon.

Carlos waited a minute before driving his truck into the desert south of the driveway. Christie turned her car around and stopped on the opposite shoulder, ready to drive in.

Satisfied, Steel opened the duffel bag and pulled out the M3. He wanted the scene under control before Christie entered the canyon. Lying down beside the rock, he set up the G28, observing the SUVs arriving below.

An idea came to him. Grabbing the sniper rifle, he moved back from the edge fifty feet, and ran east in a crouch parallel to the cliff edge. In twenty yards he stopped by another rock.

Using the rifle scope, he gazed across the canyon. The sniper on the opposite side was still hidden, but one of his hands was visible on his rifle, which was pointed east. Probably at Carlos. He aimed at the man's hand—and squeezed the trigger. The sniper's hand and gun disappeared behind the rock.

Uncertain of his success, he scrambled back to his bag and the M3.

Below him the three SUVs had parked single file in a line parallel to the house. The men emptied out of the SUVs on the driver's side, opposite him. He counted twelve, including Diego. They stood around as if waiting for something. Maybe for Angel.

That didn't fit. The shooter across the canyon must have informed Diego that a sniper had killed two of their men and had just shot at him. Why weren't they acting more concerned?

Some of the men were occupied with something inside the vehicles. Even if they had high caliber weapons, Steel could easily control the situation from up here.

He was tempted to begin firing on them but wanted to wait until Carlos was in position. Without Mario and Clay bringing up the rear, it would be too easy for the men below to escape. And he wanted all of them dead.

Pedro's car barreled through the choke point, flying past the SUVs and house. In fifty feet it made a skidding turn. Diego's men drew machine guns from the SUVs. Pedro did a circle three times in the dirt, creating a cloud of dust before he came to a stop broadside to the parked SUVs. Then he revved his engine.

Diego's men unloaded on him with a barrage of bullets.

Steel watched the young man crawl out the front passenger door and kick it shut so he had two layers of metal between himself and the bullets. Temporary safety, but high risk. Pedro's tactic seemed like a suicide move. Still it was buying Carlos time to get to the canyon. Steel continued to hold off firing, wanting Carlos in position first.

Angel's car appeared. The assassin drove in, stopped, and backed his vehicle so that the trunk ended up close to the canyon wall, across from the SUVs.

Steel understood why. The man was cautious, ready for escape, and not tying his fate to the SUVs or Diego's men.

Everything below appeared too easy and convenient. "Christie, don't come into the canyon. Something's wrong. Tell Carlos to watch for booby traps."

"Roger that."

He couldn't see her car. The bluff hid it. He had convinced her to bring up the rear, hoping most of the fighting would be finished by the time she arrived. Making a snap decision, he put down the rifle and loaded a round into the M3.

The shooting below stopped abruptly. Maybe Pedro was dead.

"Jack Steel!"

The sniper across the canyon must have called Angel or the assassin just *knew*. Keeping the M3 on the ground, Steel peered over the edge. Angel stared directly at him while standing behind his car on the passenger side, his arms up in the air as if imploring him to listen.

Steel pulled his sniper rifle up as Angel kept talking.

"It is an honor to meet such a worthy opponent. I saw your skill with Garcia and heard about it with Vincente. It will be a great privilege to kill you and your family, and then bury you. Thank you for coming. I will bring Isabella and Harry out, Jack.

Do you wish to see them? They are in my back seat. If you shoot at us, I will put bullets into their heads." Angel ducked behind his car.

Steel kept his emotions in check. A sense of urgency had him hoist the M3 to his side, keeping it out of sight, but ready to go. Placing the ear muffs over his ears, he readied himself for firing.

He grimaced. If he aimed the M3 at Angel or his car, he could kill Harry too. A diversion would help. He spoke softly: "Christie, tell Carlos and Pedro it's a go."

He peered over the edge. Angel had the rear passenger door open and was leaning into the car. What was going on? None of it made sense to him. Maybe Angel planned to use Harry and Isabella as shields.

Diego stared up at him from the far side of the lead SUV, smiling, something in his hands.

He finally understood. Grabbing the M3 and rifle, he slid his legs over the edge of the canyon and jumped. He hit the steep slope ten feet down and slid farther on his back. An explosion rocked the cliff just above him. The blast pushed him down faster.

Two more explosions went off along the top of the cliff.

His side slammed into a small boulder but he managed to hang onto his weapons. It took a few deep breaths to gather himself. Christie yelled his name on his Bluetooth. He couldn't respond. His ears rang and his body trembled. He looked at the vehicles below.

Angel had an RPG-7 on his shoulder, aimed at him.

Steel rose to his feet in a crouch and jumped, still holding both weapons.

Angel fired the RPG.

The boulder behind Steel exploded as he landed on his back on dirt and gravel, sliding down the hill. He was numb as bits of soil and rock rained down on him. Fifty feet down, a clump of rocks provided a brake for his slide. His feet hit them hard, his legs taking the impact.

Machine gun fire erupted and bullets traced lines in the slope on either side of him. He bent his knees to move closer to the rocks his shoes rested against. The barrage prevented any lateral movement.

His chest heaved as he studied the landscape left and right. The rocks gave him little protection. If he sat up they could easily shoot him. Expecting Angel to fire another RPG, he braced his legs to jump again.

Movement brought his attention to the right. Pedro was crouched behind his car and flinging something at the lead SUV. A grenade.

The young man scrambled away from his vehicle, farther into the canyon, as his car exploded. Angel must have fired an RPG at it.

Pedro's grenade exploded under the lead SUV, sending it into the air.

Rifle fire erupted from the other side of the canyon. Carlos. That seemed to lessen the barrage being aimed at Steel. He partially sat up and fired the M3 at the middle SUV. The blast from the M3 reverberated off the ground and his whole body felt like it had taken a punch.

The round exploded, destroying the SUV, taking a number of Diego's men with it. Dust filled the air, clouding his view. Men were running for the last SUV and the house.

Above the dust Steel saw Carlos scrambling up the smaller gully to the south on the far side of the canyon. He grabbed the sniper rifle and went to his belly, edging out until he could fire at Diego's men below. The explosions would bring Christie into the canyon, but he was still pinned down by Diego's men. He picked off one and looked for a second.

Then he glimpsed Angel aiming the RPG at him again.

# CHAPTER 40

C LAY'S SKIN CRAWLED WITH worry. They had driven highway fifteen south out of Las Vegas, but to reach the others they needed to be going west. He looked at Mario. "You should know that our military gave Steel kill-on-sight permission with these guys."

"I'm ready." Mario reached down to the floor by his feet and picked up a silenced Glock.

"There are cars coming from both directions." But Clay pulled out his SIG, resting it on his thigh. It reminded him of his encounter with Angel, which didn't help his nerves. Traffic was light on the highway, but it only took one car to see them and call the police.

"Stay away from your door and watch traffic in back. I'll watch the approaching traffic."

Clay grabbed the inner side of his seat and leaned toward Mario, looking out the rear window.

Mario sped up closer to the white van but didn't crowd it.

A car was approaching from behind, and Clay said, "You have to wait."

They waited for the car to pass them, giving it time to drive a quarter mile ahead of the white van. Clay looked out the rear window. The closest car behind them was barely visible. "Do it!"

"Can't. Cars approaching."

Clay glanced out the front window. Three cars in a row. In a minute the approaching cars passed them, and he glanced back. The car behind hadn't gained on them. "Clear in back," he said.

Immediately Mario pulled out, accelerating hard. He veered into the side of the van, hitting it hard just behind the driver's door.

The van teetered.

Mario immediately hit it again, sending it toppling onto its side. The van slid across the shoulder into a six-foot-deep gully where it was mostly out of view. Mario angled to the shoulder and braked hard, speedily backing up so his pickup was half off the shoulder and leaning down into the gully. The truck blocked any view of the rear half of the van from approaching highway traffic.

Clay jumped out, the SIG up. Mario circled around front. The van's driver door opened.

Clay saw a gun barrel pointing out, followed by the driver. He fired with Mario. A half-dozen shots sent the man collapsing inside. The passenger was trapped.

Hustling to the rear door of the van, Clay waited. Mario carefully approached the driver's door. They both eyed traffic.

The car that had been behind them was closer. Clay smiled and gave it a thumbs-up, keeping the SIG behind his thigh. The car kept going.

The back door of the van clicked softly. The man he had followed earlier crawled out, a pistol in his hand.

Clay hit him in the back of the head with the butt of his gun and the man went down. "Back here!"

Mario appeared with duct tape. They bound the man's ankles, hands behind his back, and taped his mouth. The terrorist was light enough to pick up by his ankles and shoulders. They dumped him into the truck behind the front seats.

"Check the van for anything." Mario headed to the front of the vehicle.

Clay searched the back. It was clean. Hustling to the pickup, he got in, eyeing traffic and their prisoner.

Mario soon returned to the driver's seat. "Clean. Nothing."

"Same."

Waiting a moment for three oncoming cars to pass them, Mario wheeled the truck in a U-turn and headed north, gunning the engine. The whole episode had taken minutes.

Clay was relieved no cars had stopped at the van or were following them. He finally relaxed his shoulders. *Clay, you have survived another day.* Dale's image was in his mind and he swallowed. "Knocking over that van took skill. What did you do for the military in your country?"

"Counter-terrorism. You?"

Clay glanced at him. "Marines. Army sharpshooter before that."

"My father is an excellent shot too."

Holding back a harsh comment, Clay asked, "What do you do when you're not kidnapping people?"

"I'm an engineer. My dream is to design and build a big bridge."

"Huh. How did you get off work?"

Mario hesitated. "Vacation time."

Clay thought of Dale and had to hold back another angry comment.

"What do you do, Clay?"

"I teach high school math and run a small beef ranch. Wife and two kids."

Mario nodded. "I hope to have such a family someday."

Clay thought of his siblings and worry replaced his anger. "On to the real show."

Mario's voice was a whisper. "Isabella and Harry."

# CHAPTER 41

A QUARTER MILE FROM THE canyon entrance, Christie heard the first explosion. It had come from up above, not below. Worried that Steel had been ambushed, she gunned the car.

"Jack!" she yelled into her mike.

Panicked when he didn't answer, her nerves were rattled further when two more explosions occurred. As she entered the canyon she saw Pedro's car on its side in the hazy distance.

Men were running for the house and the last SUV. Smoke and fire came from the other two SUV wrecks and dust hung in the air.

Christie focused on Angel, visible to her left. Six feet, one-eighty, mid-forties. A charming smile. Psycho.

Angel stood in front of his white sedan, aiming an RPG at the north canyon slope. Jack. Furious, not knowing if Steel was alive or dead, she spun the wheel, aiming for the assassin.

Angel saw her and swung the RPG toward her windshield. She ducked and floored the accelerator.

Dropping the weapon, Angel flung himself off the ground and onto the front hood of his car. Christie just missed him but clipped his front bumper. Braking hard, she watched him roll across his car as she skidded past.

She had purposefully avoided hitting his car head on. Harry and Isabella were probably still in the trunk. Her car stopped just past Angel's.

Ducking as she opened her passenger door, she scrambled out and hustled to the front end of the car, using it for cover. Glancing toward the SUVs, she saw one man in the smoke carrying a machine gun. She fired a burst from the Rattler. His body crumpled to the ground. She peered over the hood of her car.

Angel crouched near the trunk of his car, firing south with two Glocks in his hands. Fifty yards away Carlos was crouching amid large boulders.

Christie stood and fired the Rattler across the top of the Chevy. Angel had already ducked, holding one gun just high enough to fire at her. It was either crouch or take a bullet. She went low.

The man was so smooth and practiced in his movements that he reminded her of Steel. A needle of anxiety distracted her. Steel hadn't answered her call. Then she was firing at Angel again.

***

Harry heard the explosions outside and prepared himself. Either Jack and Christie or Isabella's family were making a rescue attempt. Maybe all of them. From inside the trunk it sounded like a war. Perhaps the military had found the cartel killers.

He touched Isabella's arm. "Ready, Isabella?"

"Sí, Harry." She sounded sad.

"What?"

Her voice was barely a whisper. "I don't want to die."

"We're not going to die." A sense of protectiveness for her rose in his chest. He wanted to pound the killer into the ground. Unlikely he would get the chance.

She spoke softly. "I wish we had met under different circumstances."

"Maybe it's for the best we met this way."

Her hand found his. "You like getting stabbed, drugged, and shot?"

He dredged up optimism. "We might never have met other-wise, Isabella. I think it was meant to be. Which means we're going to survive this."

"Thank you for being so positive."

He squeezed her hand. "De nada."

The trunk banged open. The gunshots outside were much louder. Harry squinted at the bright sunlight outlining the cartel killer. The man held two Glocks, was still smiling, and crouched while firing in two different directions.

The word *maniac* occurred to Harry.

The man didn't look at them as he spoke. "Get out now or I will shoot you both where you lay. Fast!"

Isabella rolled over inside the trunk and climbed out. With his left arm, the man grabbed her around her waist, pinning her arms to her side while still firing his left Glock. He spoke calmly. "Now, Harry, or I'm going to kill you."

Groaning, Harry slid forward in the trunk. His shoulder and side ached fiercely from being in one position for so long. He clumsily climbed out, hunching over due to the pain and stiffness of his wounds and cramped limbs.

The killer pushed him in the back toward burning vehicles and a house beyond them. Stumbling forward, Harry waited for the killer to push him again. In two steps he did. Whirling, Harry lunged at the man.

Harry felt slow and clumsy with his injuries, and the man seemed incredibly fast. An elbow to his neck stunned him. Falling heavily to his knees, Harry waited for a bullet.

Instead he saw Isabella swinging her knife at the man. The killer seemed to move effortlessly out of the way of her blade, backhanding her across the face. She cried out and fell to the dirt.

Enraged over seeing her hurt, Harry lunged at the man's legs—and received a knee in the jaw for his efforts. He slumped to the ground. Isabella's head rested on the soil not far from him, her eyes locked on his. Strangely, as he stared into her eyes, he thought it was a good way to die. *The Stockholm Syndrome has claimed you for good.*

***

Christie remained behind the car, her Rattler fixed on Angel. He was using Isabella and Harry as shields so there was little she could do except duck down when he fired at her. Popping up again, she saw Harry charge Angel, then Isabella stab at him. Both were beaten down by their kidnapper without any effort.

The Rattler barked in her hands as she fired high. She was unwilling to risk a low shot that might hit Harry or Isabella. Angel ducked out of sight again. Panic. Maybe he was killing Harry and Isabella.

"Harry!" She heard rifle shots to the southeast. Carlos was coming up fast.

Machine gun fire from the SUVs made her duck down again. She waited a moment, then peered over the hood again.

Angel ran away from the Chevy—crouching low to be out of Carlos' sight. While running toward the last intact SUV, he fired both guns, forcing her to duck down. His agility, speed, and accuracy again surprised her. She had to get to Harry. What if he was bleeding out?

***

When Christie's car had entered the canyon, Steel risked sliding down the hill on his butt. He dug his heels in when he reached rocks big enough for cover. From there he took shots at Diego's men. They were on the run. He continued working his way down. It was slow going because dust and flames made it difficult to scan the battlefield.

The incline became more gradual so he knelt and used the scope.

Diego had disappeared. He spotted Angel firing at Christie while running for the rear SUV. He took a quick shot. Missed. The killer was fluid, very fast, and seemed aware of everyone's position. Steel lost sight of him in the smoke and dust.

Running hard for the burning lead SUV, he used it for cover as he fired at several of Diego's men crouched in front of the house. He knocked one down, but needed to duck shots coming from a side window of the house.

Swinging south, he glimpsed two motionless bodies on the ground near Angel's car. He swallowed hard.

*** 

Christie stood and fired through smoke and fire in the direction of the third SUV. One of her rear tires was flat so she wouldn't be able to chase the vehicle.

The SUV backed out in a roar, turning fast and skidding. The driver, hidden by the tinted glass, gunned the engine and the vehicle threw dirt as it headed for the canyon exit. Diego and Angel were making a run for it. Panic and disappointment filled her in equal measure.

Guns stuck out of the SUV passenger windows, sending bullets into the rear window of her car. Diving to the ground, she glimpsed Carlos kneeling near the trunk of Angel's car. He was firing at the escaping SUV and put bullet holes in the rear window. The SUV kept going.

Thoughts of Harry dying before she could reach him forced her to stand. She fired the Rattler in arcs at anyone beyond the burning SUVs in front of the house.

Running to Harry then, she reached him at the same time Carlos did. They both dropped to their knees, continuing to fire toward the house through the smoke and fire.

Christie panicked. Isabella was lying on her side, cradling Harry's head in her arms, whispering his name. Harry's eyes were closed and blood covered his tattered shirt. His shoulder was wrapped up, the bandage matching the color of Isabella's shredded blouse.

"Mija." Tears on his face, Carlos rested a hand on Isabella's shoulder.

"Papá." Isabella was sobbing. "Juan…"

"I know," he said softly. He stood, calling out loudly, "Pedro!"

A faint "*Sí*" came from the direction of Pedro's burning car.

Christie put fingers to Harry's neck and found a pulse. Something snapped inside her. Teary-eyed, she put another magazine in the Rattler, rose, and strode for the house, firing nonstop. What gave her courage was that Carlos was beside her, stride for stride, firing a Glock.

# CHAPTER 42

STEEL SIGHTED ON THE side window of the house. As soon as the shooter appeared again he fired. The shooter disappeared inside. Slowly he approached the house. The front door was open, the bodies of half of Diego's men scattered in front of it. By the time he reached the porch, Carlos stood on the far side of the door.

Christie knelt below the front steps, aiming into the house through the open front door. Steel's gut wrenched when he saw tears in her eyes. Harry and Isabella had to be dead. Fury burned inside him, but he maintained calm. They might have blown it and allowed Diego and Angel to escape.

Yet he was sure Angel had planned another trick. If he had the M3 he would fire a round into the house and burn it down, but the extra rounds were on top of the ridge. He didn't have time to get them.

"Be careful of booby traps," he whispered. He went in first to the right, Carlos going left. Christie entered last, moving left and center.

It was obvious no one spent time in the house. The main room was empty of furniture and the walls bare. The unfinished wood floor had stains on it. A place for Diego to torture and kill his enemies. A few wood chairs were placed by the walls. A dead man lay on his back near the side window.

Two hallways led away from the main room, one far left, the other far right. Carlos went left, Steel right—Christie followed him.

Hurriedly they searched the rest of the house. Nothing. And no basement.

Steel pounded floors, listening for a hollow sound to indicate a hidden tunnel. Carlos searched the other side.

They returned to the living room.

Steel didn't want to ask, but he had to know. He faced Christie. "Harry and Isabella?"

"Alive," she said, her face a little brighter. "Sorry, I should have said something."

"That's good to hear." He heaved a deep breath, but it made no sense to him either.

"Diego and Angel escaped." Carlos sounded disgusted. "We failed."

Steel thought about it. "Did either of you see Angel or Diego get into the rear SUV or enter the house?"

Christie and Carlos exchanged glances.

"Come on." He hustled out the front door, pointing Carlos to the west corner.

Steel strode to the east corner of the house, which had been closest to the rear SUV. Glancing around it, he saw two of Diego's men lying on the ground, bullets in their backs. Christie followed him past the bodies, her Rattler aimed at the rear corner of the house.

When they reached it, Carlos was already in back of the house, digging with his boot at something on the ground. An iron ring appeared, but Carlos didn't pull on it. Instead he took off his belt, and then gestured to Steel to do the same.

Taking both their belts, Carlos fastened them together, and then looped one end around the iron ring. Sitting on the ground, his boots facing the ring, he motioned them to get back.

Steel retreated to the corner of the house with Christie. Carlos leaned back on the taut belts, his weight pulling up a manhole cover until it was vertical.

No explosion.

Steel strode forward and aimed his Glock down the shaft. Rungs led down a vertical cement shaft and at the bottom a steel door faced south. Bitter disappointment filled him that Diego and Angel had escaped. The Alvarez vendetta wasn't over.

Christie's and Carlos' drawn faces mirrored his sense of failure.

A phone rang. Steel looked more carefully. It was attached beneath the bottom rung of the ladder.

"A trap," said Carlos.

# CHAPTER 43

AS SOON AS THEY entered the dead-end dirt road, Clay saw the SUV shooting out of the canyon, speeding toward them.

Mario stopped the pickup. "Now what?"

Clay didn't like it, but they had no choice. "I'm guessing their windows will be bulletproof. The Rattler can probably punch through, but we still might not stop them. Pull up a hundred yards, stop broadside, and we'll get out and shoot out their tires."

Mario gunned the engine and sped toward the hurtling SUV. A quarter mile away he wheeled the truck broadside, stopping in a swirl of dust.

Clay grabbed the Rattler at his feet and handed it to Mario, who raised his eyebrows. "I'm good with the SIG."

Clay jumped out of the cab and ran behind the tailgate.

Mario exited and crouched behind the front fender.

Clay wondered if Christie and Steel were hurt, if Harry was alive, and if Diego and Angel were in the SUV. He had tried to call Steel and Christie to no success. All of it tightened his hand on the Glock and made him determined to stop the SUV. It brought back memories of Dale's death. He settled his palm on the tailgate and aimed at the front driver's side tire.

Fifty yards from them the SUV veered off the road on Clay's side. Mario let loose a spray of bullets at the front passenger tire.

Clay did the same. The tire went flat, but the SUV kept going, quickly broadside to them.

The passenger windows came down and machine guns fired at them, their staccato loud.

Diving to the ground, Clay fired into the front passenger window. Mario fired into the rear window. Clay emptied his gun and loaded another clip. The SUV was pulling away.

Rising to his knees, Clay fired at the rear passenger tire, hitting it.

Slumping down onto one side, the SUV hit a bump, tilted and rocked to a stop. The engine whined as the driver gunned it, but the two flat tires spun on the dirt and couldn't get traction.

Both passenger doors opened on the near side.

Mario ran out into the desert, loaded another clip into the Rattler, and fired.

Clay saw it was too late to run for cover. Falling to his belly, he fired at the two men coming out of the SUV. Mario did the same. Bullets hit the truck near Clay as he kept shooting.

The two men went down.

Clay lay there, shaken. Slowly he pushed to his feet. Mario still had his cheek glued to the stock of the Rattler. Keeping his arm outstretched, Clay aimed his gun at the SUV as he slowly approached it.

When he could see inside, he stopped. Four bodies. Two on the ground and two in the vehicle. It was over.

He let the gun fall to his side and took another look in the cab.

Mario was soon by his side. "Good shooting."

"You too. But bad luck."

Mario raised an eyebrow. "Why?"

"I don't see Diego or Angel." Clay swung to face the canyon. "We better get in there in case they need us."

They ran for the truck. Clay noted that the distant gunfire from the canyon had ended. Worry for Harry and Christie made him run faster.

# CHAPTER 44

S TEEL RETRIEVED HIS BELT from Carlos and put it on. He then climbed down the shaft, stopping above the bottom rung. The phone could be wired to explosives.

While hanging on to a lower rung, he reached out and gently felt around it. Nothing. It was attached to the ladder rung with a simple wire twisty. He undid it and hastily climbed back up. The shaft reminded him of his own tunnels on his property in Virginia.

Once out, he backed up with the others to the side of the house. Then he answered the phone, putting it on speaker.

No explosion.

"Jack Steel, that fight was magnificent. You were excellent, as was your team. I assume you are out of the tunnel entrance?"

Steel's hand tightened on the phone over hearing Angel's voice. "We are."

"Excellent. Cover your ears. I am going to remotely detonate a small explosive to cave it in."

They covered their ears as an explosion occurred. When they looked, dust and smoke rose out of the shaft. Angel's concern for them made no sense to Steel. The man must need something.

"I have a deal to discuss with you, Jack Steel."

He kept his emotion out of his response. "What do you want?"

"I have decided to end my career with the cartel. They don't know this, of course, but I am through. Just as you are committed to care for your daughter, I have someone that needs my care and attention. The vendetta of Diego includes all of your family, and also all of the family of the Aguilars. It will not be difficult to track down Isabella's family members."

Carlos winced.

"You said you had an offer," snapped Steel.

"I will kill Diego for you and reveal another attack he has already set into motion against your families, if you agree to allow me to disappear."

"You're killing Diego for your own protection." Steel had no intention of letting the assassin walk after killing Dale.

"Yes, but Diego's death benefits both of us, because the Alvarez vendetta dies with him. And learning about the other attack benefits only you."

"Why should we trust anything you say?" Christie said vehemently. "You killed my brother, Dale."

"So Clay lived? I am glad to hear that. I also made sure Diego couldn't harm Isabella or Harry. With my help we can end the vendetta. I saw things were not going our way so I deliberately avoided shooting anyone. I could have easily killed Harry and Isabella.

"Diego also wanted the explosive attached to the shaft's outer lid, but I told him it would be easier to track you to your family if we didn't do that. I don't kill people with bombs. I also left the phone. Think about it. I can kill your family members with a sniper rifle at my leisure if I want to. Why would I bother with all this drama? My past promise to Diego to kill all of you dies with him."

Steel still didn't trust him, but some of his statements rang true. "Your word is meaningless."

"And if I kill Diego, end the vendetta, and tell you now about a future attack on your family, what is my word worth then?"

"You're lying. You might have killed Diego in the tunnel." Christie sounded bitter.

"He left before me. You had me pinned down."

"How can we trust someone who raped and tortured Marita?" snarled Carlos.

"I have never raped a woman, nor tortured one," said Angel. "Diego and his men did that, not me. I could not deliver Isabella to him for that very reason and decided to kill her here instead of turning her over to him. I'm even happier that she is still alive."

Carlos gazed at the dirt, his face livid.

"Hang on." Steel muted the phone. "He's a killer, but I think he wouldn't be talking to us unless he meant this." He shrugged. "We can go after him, but like he said, he's good enough to pick off our family members any time he wishes."

"He killed Juan." Carlos said it softly, his head still lowered.

Christie touched his arm. "He's a murderer, but he could have easily put bullets into Harry and Isabella. I was surprised he didn't. We don't have to trust him, but maybe he can help us. We can kill him later."

Steel agreed with Christie's assessment, but kept silent.

Carlos lifted his head. "If there is any chance he can help end this, then I say we take his offer." He looked at Christie. "As you say, we can always kill him later."

Christie wiped sweat from her face and looked at Steel.

Steel put the phone back on speaker. "All right, we're listening."

"You agree to the terms?"

"Yes." He had no problem lying to a killer.

"Diego has a group hunting for your wife and child. They are very, very good, and are used when Diego wants his victims to suffer before they die. They are called *La Manada*—the pack. I used to lead the pack, and I trained them. They are waiting on Diego's orders to attack, and he's waiting on me to give the signal."

Steel felt immediately on edge. Perhaps the pack was already close to Rachel and Carol. Carol had said she wasn't followed, but she wasn't a professional. "How many are they and how much time do we have?"

"Seven men. I can give you a twenty-four-hour warning."

Steel considered that. "If you kill Diego, will the pack leave my wife and child alone?"

"Even if they hear Diego is dead, their reputation demands they finish the job. But I can delay killing Diego to give you more time."

Steel thought about it. "All right. Wait for our decision. Call us in twenty-four hours."

"One more thing. I want you to call your military. A trade. I will give them the ISIS targets in exchange for your military forgetting about me."

"I can't promise anything, but I'll see what I can do." He hung up. Something else occurred to him. "Carlos, I injured a sniper on the south canyon wall. Did you see him?"

"I put a bullet into him. I'm going to check on my son." He hurried away.

A vehicle entered the canyon and Steel ran with Christie to the front of the house. He was relieved to see Clay and Mario.

Clay jumped out of the truck cab. "We stopped the SUV headed out, but no Angel or Diego." He hugged Christie, and the two of them hustled to see Harry.

Mario started to follow them, but Steel stopped him with a hand on his shoulder. "Isabella is fine. Let's drive out of here, fast, and see if we can spot any vehicles to the south or north. Angel and Diego escaped through a tunnel."

Mario frowned, but then returned to the truck, waiting for Steel to get in before wheeling it around.

Steel glanced behind the seat, and then at Mario.

"The terrorist," said Mario.

They shot out of the canyon. When they were clear of the cliffs, Steel scouted south and Mario north, but neither of them saw anything.

"They're gone." Steel let it go. Angel and Diego could have had motorcycles waiting and perhaps ridden them west out of their tunnel.

Mario drove back to the canyon in silence and left him to see Isabella.

Steel walked toward Pedro's destroyed sedan, wondering if the young man was dead. He didn't see how Pedro could have survived the blast. Pausing, he called Jeffries and filled him in. He also asked for a medevac helicopter and cleanup crew. He finished with, "I want protection for my ex-wife and daughter."

"We can do witness protection, but no bodyguard service."

He wanted to punch Jeffries. Unwilling to put his daughter and Carol into hiding for the rest of their lives, he let it go. "All right, I'll let you know. Angel wants to do a trade. The ISIS targets for the military leaving him alone after this is over."

"I'll call some people." Jeffries hung up.

Striding past the burnt car, Steel found Carlos kneeling beside his son. Pedro was lying facedown with his eyes closed. A piece of metal stuck out from his right thigh and blood marked the dirt around the leg. Carlos had tied a tourniquet around his son's thigh. Steel noted the Kevlar vest Pedro had on. Smart.

Carlos looked up. "He's still alive, but he needs medical attention right away."

"A medevac helicopter is on the way to take him to Nellis Air Force Base." Steel saw the strain on Carlos' face. *What did the man expect to happen when he involved his children in this mess?* "I hope he's all right."

Not wanting to talk to him further, he left to join the others. Mario was striding toward him, and stopped, still chewing a toothpick.

"Thank you for your help, Jack. After today, and after talking to Isabella, I'm less inclined to think you let Marita die." Mario stuck out his hand and Steel grudgingly took it.

"Her face still haunts my dreams at night, Mario."

Mario grimaced. "Mine too. I often ask myself if I could have helped her in some way."

He left Mario and called Carol to check in with her. She sounded all right, so he called Wyatt.

Wyatt had met Carol and Rachel in Billings and had spotted someone following her. Wyatt allowed the tail to follow him to his place, intending to take Rachel and Carol out after dark through tunnels on his land to a friend's house. The tail had gone by his driveway and disappeared. Steel told Wyatt about the pack. His friend thought luring them to his place gave them control over how they met. Steel agreed and thanked him.

Feeling better about Carol and Rachel's safety, he hung up.

He found Christie on her knees at Harry's side. Her hair was a mess, her clothing dirty—but she was still beautiful to him. That saddened him for some reason.

Harry had his eyes open, his head resting on Isabella's lap, his shirt in tatters. Clay knelt nearby.

"Helluva ride, boss." Harry had tears in his eyes as he looked up. "Dale died for me."

"It's not your fault, Harry." Clay's voice choked with emotion.

Steel rested a hand on Harry's shoulder. "I'm sorry, Harry. I know he'll be dearly missed by you and your family." He took a deep breath. "I can't tell you how good it feels to see you alive."

Isabella stared up at him. "I'm sorry we did all this to you, Jack." She wiped her eyes. "I believe what Harry told me about Marita."

Her genuine concern made it easier to stuff the angry words he wanted to hurl at her. "I'm glad you're okay."

"Harry is a very good man." Isabella stroked his hair.

"Stockholm syndrome." Harry smiled, but then sobered. "Before he left us that maniac killer said, 'Stay down if you wish to live. Good job, you two! You were fantastic prisoners!'"

Isabella waved a hand. "Sí. Está loco. He could have easily killed us."

Steel exchanged glances with Christie.

Clay stood up. "We have to talk, Steel."

Steel understood and walked with him to the pickup truck.

Clay led him to the passenger door and opened it. Pushing the passenger seat forward, Clay revealed the ISIS operative lying in back, staring at them.

Clay explained what had happened. They dragged the man out and carried him to the house.

Steel kicked the front door shut once they were inside. "Let's take him to the back."

Clay walked backward. Steel followed until they were in one of the rear bedrooms. It was bare like the rest of the house, save for one chair. They sat the man on it. Steel waited while Clay left and returned with duct tape, shutting the door behind him. Clay taped the man's legs and chest to the chair.

Steel tore the tape off the terrorist's mouth. Pulling the OTF knife from his belt-sheath, he held it by his thigh. "You either tell us what we want to know or we hurt you for as long as it takes until you do. Your choice."

The man remained silent, hate evident in his eyes.

The door opened and Carlos entered. Striding up to the side of the prisoner, he faced Steel.

"I owe you, Steel. My daughter is alive because of you and Christie." He eyed the prisoner. "I have experience with torture in my country. Give me the knife and I will get the information you seek."

Steel wanted to, but he didn't trust Carlos. "I'll do it."

"I know you can do it. Por favor?" Carlos held out his hand.

Steel hesitated, and then set the knife in his palm. Following Clay out, he shut the door. They returned out front, where Christie strode toward the house.

She walked into Steel's arms and held him tightly.

"Everything all right?" he whispered.

"Perfect now that I can hold you." She rested her head on his shoulder. "I need a bath and massage and a few other things."

"Ditto." He heard a helicopter in the distance.

She touched his face, where the rock chip had cut him. "We'll have to clean that." She turned to Clay. "I'm going to say goodbye to Harry."

Steel watched her walk away. "She's tough, Clay."

"Always has been. Three brothers, so you can blame us if you want."

"I'm sorry, Clay. For everything."

"You went through hell to rescue Harry, Jack, so I'm grateful."

Steel noted the reservation in Clay's eyes and voice.

They joined Christie and Mario and watched as Harry and Pedro were carried on stretchers by Jeffries' men out to the helicopter, which had landed outside the canyon. Isabella elected to go with them in the chopper.

In twenty minutes Carlos came out of the house, striding past the burnt SUVs. He stopped in front of them. "It's finished. It's not good." He held out Steel's knife.

Steel took it, noting it was clean. "Let's hear it."

Carlos eyed all of them. "They want to remind America that you are not safe anywhere. They want to sow fear for five days in a row. The one in the house was supposed to take a rifle to a national park and kill as many people as he could with his partner. The park had not been specified, but he had chosen Yosemite."

"People will say anything under torture," said Clay.

Carlos waved a hand. "I agree. But I gave him a little hope. I told him that if he told us where the other targets were, and it turned out to be true, he would live. Diego was supplying them with logistical help and weapons, so this man had to know where his associates would attack and what they would need."

Steel was impressed. "Do you trust him?"

"Of course you can never be certain, but based on twenty years of interrogation my heart says it's true. I used the knife at the end to verify what I could." Carlos looked at each of them. "There are two operatives for each site. Mario and Clay already killed one of the Yosemite operatives, the other is in the house. The Yosemite attack was for four-thirty p.m. today. Four more attacks will occur at the same time of day, one attack each day, to keep the country on edge."

Steel frowned. "Something like this took major planning."

"Makes no sense." Clay studied the ground. "The ISIS guys we stopped were driving south, but they would have needed to take a private plane to reach Yosemite on time for their attack today."

Carlos stuck a thumb in his belt. "He got nervous when he saw you follow him. He decided to change the day and location."

Steel agreed with Carlos; it wasn't good. "The other terrorists may move their schedule up as much as a day when they don't see any news about their associates in Yosemite, especially if they were supposed to maintain contact with each other. Any idea of the weapons supplied for the other two attacks?"

Carlos pushed back his hat. "Machine guns and bombs."

"Any descriptions?" asked Christie.

Carlos shook his head. "Our prisoner only had phone contact with the others. Once the attacks began, they were to have no contact."

"Where are the other sites?" asked Steel.

"Mall of America in Minnesota, St. Croix River Crossing Bridge in Wisconsin, New York subway, and Walt Disney World in Florida. He didn't know the order."

"What do we do about the prisoner?" asked Clay.

Carlos glanced at him. "It's taken care of."

Clay nodded. "Good."

Carlos turned to Steel. "I am going to visit Pedro at Nellis Air Force Base to make sure he will be all right. We can give you three a ride to the airport in Las Vegas. It's on the way."

Mario and Carlos walked away to get the truck.

Steel took Christie's hand and walked toward the cars, noting the bullet holes in her Camry. The weariness in her features matched her beat-up car.

He called Jeffries and filled him in on the ISIS targets, finishing with, "They've put a lot of planning into this. Expect the worst."

"Good job. Your country owes you."

He didn't mention Angel's request to Jeffries. They didn't need the assassin for the ISIS target locations now. Besides he didn't trust Angel, and six murders demanded justice.

Her smile weary, Christie squeezed his hand. "I'd like some ice cream to celebrate freeing Harry."

"I think we can manage that." He didn't think he could celebrate anything until Diego and his men were dead.

# CHAPTER 45

ANGEL LOVED THE WIND in his hair. After exiting the half-mile long tunnel, he drove the Zero FX electric motorcycle hard over the hilly terrain. The bike made no noise and was a joy to ride.

When he had arrived in the west-leading tunnel, only one of the two bikes had been present. Diego must have fled before him and, as always, had kept his destination secret.

The Zeros had a hundred-mile range so they were perfect, but it also meant it was futile to try and find Diego now. The cartel leader was going to a storage facility in a small town, where a car waited for him. Angel was doing the same.

As he rode he contemplated his last fight and his call to Steel. Not long ago it would have bothered him that he had failed to kill Steel. He would have pursued Steel, Christie, and their families obsessively. But he wasn't climbing up the cartel ladder anymore so his reputation didn't matter to him.

All that mattered now was creating a new life. In fact it had been fortuitous that he had not put a bullet into Christie or Harry. Steel would have come after him if he had, and he didn't want someone that skilled to chase him for the rest of his life.

In truth he was glad he hadn't killed anyone on Steel's team in the last fight. However on the way to the tunnel at the back of the house he had shot two of Diego's men in the back. That hadn't bothered him. He had hoped to find Diego just ahead of him, but the coward had probably ducked out early in the fight.

It was amazing that in a matter of days he had gone from accepting killing as part of his life to wanting to walk away from it completely. And he was relieved that he had found a way to spare Isabella rape and torture at the hands of Diego and his men.

He had to plan things carefully now. Before he killed Diego, he would move Renata to someplace new, to ensure her safety. Even though she was hidden, he still wanted to be cautious.

To avoid an open contract on his head, he would have to kill all of Diego's men to make sure none of them could tell the other cartels about his disloyalty. The cartels would just as soon kill each other, but they hated traitors no matter what family they belonged to.

As he rode he recalled the fight, his choices, and Steel's nimble responses. The man was excellent in sensing when to act and how to maintain safety. Christie had also impressed him. Even Harry and Isabella had done their share.

He felt magnanimous about ending his part in the vendetta. After all, the bad guys needed someone with Steel's skills to keep them in line. He smiled over that.

He heard a helicopter in the distance. Steel must have called in help for their wounded.

In fifty miles he reached his destination, a small town to the west. Driving up to a storage shed, he opened it and traded the Zero for the parked car. Another Chevy SS. Blue instead of white, with the same modifications as the other SS. He drove west.

Diego would head back to his California ranch, where he had privacy and security, and direct the pack from there. Diego expected him to chase Steel, but instead he would go to California and then call Steel.

He was about to call Renata when his phone rang. It was her.

Smiling, he answered. "Yes, dear sister."

"Angel, we have Renata and we're bringing her to the ranch. Diego will call you shortly, but if you don't fulfill your part in the vendetta, we'll slice up your precious sister's face."

Stunned, he couldn't speak at first. He recognized the voice of Diego's man. Diego must have been planning this for a long time, having him followed and discovering that he had a sister. The man's treachery preceded his own.

He kept his voice calm. "I want to speak with her."

"You get thirty seconds."

Renata sobbed on the phone. "Angel, I'm sorry, dear brother. They threatened to cut my face so I told them you wanted a new life and planned to leave."

He sensed the phone was on speaker so he said, "Dear sister, you would have told them everything anyway. You made a good choice."

"You will make a good choice too, dear brother."

"I will, Renata. I—"

Diego's man interrupted him. "Wait for Diego's call, Angel."

The call ended.

Panicked thoughts ran through his head.

In minutes his phone rang. Diego.

"I'm sorry, Angel, but when we met at the Wynn today I sensed something was wrong. I had your sister picked up. When you began disappearing over the years, I had you followed. That's how I learned about Renata." Diego paused. "My men saw you leave your hostages alive in the canyon. I felt betrayed. Renata confirmed my fears when she told my men your plans."

Angel searched for a way to make it less personal for Diego. "I didn't leave the hostages alive to betray you, but to stop Steel from chasing me."

"Still a betrayal, my friend." Diego paused. "You know I cannot allow you to leave the cartel. You know too much and I need you."

He thought on that. It sounded as if Renata hadn't told Diego that he planned to kill him. That might help him later. "I have served you like a brother for many years, Diego."

"Yes, and I have paid you well. Bring Steel to me alive and kill the rest of his family. Kill Christie's family too, and the Aguilars who engineered Garcia's and Vincente's murders. Otherwise we will do to your poor sister what we did to Marita. You remember that day, don't you?"

He clenched his jaw. When he first joined Diego's cartel, he insisted he would never kill innocent women and children. Probably the love of his sister had taught him that perspective. Diego had never complained. He wanted Angel's skills for his more dangerous opponents.

Angel kept his voice calm. "I'm disappointed in you, Diego."

"As I am in you, Angel. You are going to join the pack, and if Lucas doesn't call me hourly, we begin hurting your sister. Lucas will contact you to coordinate your first assignment with them. You have three days to kill all of our enemies and bring Steel to me alive. I want them all to suffer like Marita before they die. Send me photos."

The line went dead.

Angel's usual calm evaporated and he pulled the car over to the shoulder and got out, yelling incoherently at the sky and desert as he stalked back and forth.

After calming himself, he whispered, "How did you miss this, Renata?"

But he already knew the answer. Regarding herself, she was as blind as anyone else. It was up to him to keep her safe. And he had failed. He guessed this must be what his victims felt, a sense of helplessness and loss.

He considered returning to the canyon and killing everyone there. It was doubtful he would succeed. And he had given his word to Steel, an honorable man. Whereas Diego was scum.

Sitting down against the front tire of his car, he stared out over the desert. Renata could not help him now. If she revealed her skills to Diego, he would keep her prisoner forever, and use her ability to keep himself in power. But she might do it anyway if her brother died and she had no one to protect her.

Renata's face was beautiful. To think of it cut up by Diego and his men sickened and angered him. It was probably why she had given in so quickly. It was the one part of her body that made her feel normal.

Her words filtered back to him. *You will make a good choice too, dear brother.* She was telling him to trust himself and everything would be okay.

His phone rang. Lucas. He had trained Lucas. The man was ruthless and very skilled. That fact used to give him pride. Now it just bunched his shoulders.

Lucas was curt, giving him an address to meet.

Getting into the car, he turned around and headed east. He had a long drive ahead of him. Flying was too risky after the Colorado shooting. Clay would have given his description to the police. Besides he wanted his car with him.

Of one thing he was certain. Diego would never let him live after this vendetta was over. Perhaps the pack had orders to kill him. He could trust no one.

And Renata's life was on the line.

He loved her more than his own life and would do whatever it took to get her back.

# PART 5

## OP: ISIS

# CHAPTER 46

THE CAR RIDE WAS painfully quiet, with everyone staring out windows.

Mario drove, his father in the front passenger seat. Steel sat behind Carlos, with Christie beside him, her head on his shoulder, her eyes closed. Clay sat on the other side of Christie, behind Mario.

Steel thought it couldn't get any more strained or odd than to have former kidnappers-and-victims-turned-allies in the same vehicle.

With his eyes he traced the curls of Christie's brown-and-blond streaked hair, the soft lines of her face, her lean body. Again he questioned what kind of life he was giving her. It couldn't be worth all the misery and pain he had brought to her and her family.

After ten minutes, Carlos said, "I will help with Diego's pack. Diego and his men threaten my family as much as yours."

"I appreciate that." Steel wanted to clear the air. "You knew about the cartel hiring ISIS long ago, and you wanted ISIS to hit the U.S. out of revenge."

Carlos remained quiet.

"Papá?" Mario stared open-mouthed at his father. "How could you support terrorists killing the innocent?"

Carlos rested a hand on his son's shoulder. "Because I was blinded by hate."

"You're getting off easy." Christie sat up, glaring at him from the back seat. "Harry was shot and stabbed because of you, Dale died, and you almost got me and Jack killed."

Clay's hand tightened to a fist on his thigh, but he remained silent.

Carlos turned in his seat. "And your government, the one you love so much, did they tell Steel to get our beloved Marita out of Colombia?" He gestured. "Did they even tell you her name, Steel?"

The memories were still painful and Steel swallowed, remembering that night. "That was part of the problem. I didn't know if she was the informant or not."

Carlos nodded. "Christie, your government was fine with allowing my dear niece, who never wanted to hurt anyone in her life, to be used like a piece of meat by Gustavo Alvarez in his bed, while risking her life. And they were fine with her remaining behind so long as Steel got out, which cost her rape, torture, and her life. Your government is responsible, and so yes, I wanted your people to suffer. I wanted to strike back in any way I could. Misguided, yes, but for a reason."

Christie's shoulders slumped, her voice less harsh. "I just want to end all of this."

Carlos seemed to sag too. "As do I. That's why I offered to get information from the ISIS prisoner. To end this and to make amends."

Mario glanced in the rearview mirror at Steel. "I will help with the pack too."

"Thanks." He wouldn't turn down any guns at this point.

They drove another ten minutes in silence, until Clay stared at Carlos, his voice calm. "Harry said something to me. If you hadn't forced Steel to strike at the cartel first, they might have blindsided our families and most likely killed more of us."

Surprised, Steel stared at Clay. He found himself fighting Clay's words, not wanting to give Carlos any absolution for what he had done. Carlos hadn't chosen to abandon his vengeance—it had been forced upon him.

Carlos said softly, "I appreciate your words, my friend."

"Harry also said he never would have met Isabella if she hadn't kidnapped him." Christie squeezed Steel's hand and rested her head on his shoulder again.

Clay frowned. "He also said she stabbed him."

"Harry's an idiot, Clay." Christie closed her eyes. "You know he's always been a pushover."

"Harry always finds the positive." Steel looked out the window, still wanting Carlos dead. He wondered how Christie and Clay really felt.

Carlos' eyebrows rose. "Harry must have a heart as big as Isabella's."

"I'm not surprised Harry likes Isabella after being stuck in a car trunk with her," said Mario. "My sister has a strong personality."

Clay cleared his throat. "I'd appreciate a ride to Nellis Air Force Base to see my brother."

Mario waved a hand. "No problem."

"I want to come too." Christie nestled into Steel. "I want to see my brother, Jack."

"That's a great idea, honey. I have to get to Wyatt's to prepare. We'll meet up there."

"Can we stop for ice cream?" she asked.

"Sí. Why not?" Carlos pushed back his hat. "I would like some food too."

*** 

Mario dropped Steel off at McCarran International Airport. They stopped at a gas station first, where Steel washed the blood off his face in the restroom and bandaged his cut. He gave Christie a quick hug and kiss, and she left with the others.

That she could still love him after what she had been through, and what was still to come, amazed him. Yet as they said goodbye, his sadness returned. Something else to push aside.

He felt impatient to get to Billings. Wyatt would move Carol and Rachel off his property tonight, but he didn't like the thought of the pack showing up on Wyatt's doorstep when his friend was alone.

His phone rang. He tensed when he heard Angel's voice.

"Did you call your military?" Angel's voice was calm.

Steel kept his voice neutral. "We extracted intel from the ISIS operative that met with Diego so we didn't need you."

Angel was silent a moment. "How many targets did he give you?"

"You tell me."

"Five. Now tell me the targets he gave you."

Steel ran through the list.

"He gave you a false one. I can give you the real target in exchange for your military forgetting about me after I leave the cartel."

"I'll call them. Call me back in five." Steel hung up and called Jeffries, explaining the situation.

"Do you trust him?" asked Jeffries.

"No, but this could be real. He wants out of the cartel and wants you and me to leave him alone. He's caring for someone, maybe a family member, and doesn't want to worry about being hunted."

"I talked to my superiors. No way are they letting him walk after killing four of our own. Play him. Tell him sure, give us the target and we'll forget about you. Call me." Jeffries hung up.

Angel called back. Steel didn't mind lying—he agreed with Jeffries. "Okay, give us the target and they'll leave you alone."

"The Mall of America is not a target. Tomorrow they hit the Skywalk on the Grand Canyon."

Steel frowned. "Do you know how?"

"Diego hid weapons near the site that the ISIS operatives can retrieve."

Steel believed him. "What about Diego and the pack?"

"I'll get back to you." Angel hung up.

Steel filled in Jeffries, and the colonel said, "The guy's desperate. He knows we're going to hunt him down. Worse, what if he's playing us? Maybe he's not leaving the cartel and he's trying to get us to pull people from the Mall of America while ISIS hits it."

Steel doubted Jeffries' concerns, but agreed with taking precautions. "I can't argue with any of that. Keep the MOA on alert. To be safe, Skywalk should still be alerted."

"We could shut it down for a few days. Say it's maintenance issues."

Steel didn't like it. "Don't. If Angel was truthful, and you shut down Skywalk, you could tip off the terrorists. They might hit another place or even hit Skywalk another day. If it stays open you have a chance of ending it today."

Jeffries said, "I'll call and tell them to beef up their security without warning anyone off. Bomb detection will arrive there ASAP."

"The terrorists could move up their timetable to today at any of their sites."

"Acknowledged. Thanks, Steel." Jeffries paused. "How far are you from Skywalk?"

"A few hours." He knew what was coming.

"You have experience spotting operatives, Steel. You're one of the best. Why not drive up today and make sure it's safe? At least for today. Scout the area for a weapons cache too."

Steel hesitated. "There's something I need from you then."

"Name it."

"Send a helicopter to an address near Billings and take my daughter and ex-wife to a secure location until this mess is over."

It was Jeffries turn to pause. "All right. Consider it done. But I expect to be filled in on everything, and I want Angel and Diego dead at the end of this."

"Then we have the same goals."

# CHAPTER 47

S TEEL RENTED A JETTA and drove fast. Jeffries had lifted some of the stress from his shoulders by agreeing to take Carol and Rachel out of the equation. But he still had a knot in his stomach.

Diego and the pack threatened to ruin their lives. That wouldn't end until the cartel vendetta was finished. He vowed silently to bury all of them.

And he still held anger at Carlos—Christie had been cut, beaten, and almost killed twice because of the Colombian. More than that, he still worried that Carlos would release their photos to the cartel.

He called Wyatt and filled him in on the helicopter coming for Carol and Rachel. Then he settled back to focus on driving.

If Angel was telling the truth, he didn't think the terrorists would wait until tomorrow when they learned their counterparts for the planned Yosemite massacre were missing.

Highway ninety-three took him over the Colorado River. The bridge safety walls hid views of Hoover Dam. He entered Arizona. White clouds formed shadows on the low mountains, while the landscape created a contrast of burnt orange, reds, and browns dotted with cacti and shrubs.

Soon he was passing through acres of Joshua tree forest. The branches of the yucca trees ended with bushy clumps of evergreen needles reaching up to the sky as if in prayer.

A golden eagle floated high in the sky and a northern flicker flew across the road ahead of him. He made a mental note that this was a place Rachel would like to see. That put a lump in his throat.

Pushing the speed limit, two hours later he arrived at the parking lot for the Grand Canyon Skywalk. Two-thirty p.m. He pulled his OTF knife from its sheath and slid it beneath the driver's seat. The Glock too. It was a relief that he didn't have to worry about Christie.

As he walked to the visitor center the heat reflected off the pavement bathed his skin. Turkey vultures circled overhead in the blue sky.

Guards with leashed dogs were visible, as well as Hualapai tribal police in the parking lots and building. The guards were smiling and seemed to blend in enough to not warn off any potential terrorists.

He purchased one pass and rode the half-full bus to the Skywalk center, not seeing anyone of interest on the bus. When it stopped, instead of entering the building he walked past all the tables in the outdoor eating areas. If the attack did come at four, he still had time to look outside first.

Police presence was also visible in the eating areas and along the canyon edge ahead.

Search dogs and their handlers stood at the building entrance. The dogs could sniff out ammunition and guns so he thought an outside attack was more likely. ISIS operatives were often on suicide missions. Maybe one of them planned to create confusion outside, and then the other would try to get inside the building to create havoc there.

Not seeing anyone suspicious among the tables, he strolled down closer to the canyon. The plateau descended slightly to the edge. Large rocks embedded in the ground formed natural steps and convenient places to sit and rest. Some people walked up to within a few feet of the lip overlooking the four-thousand-foot drop to the river below.

He carefully strolled closer to the edge, making sure no one was tailing him. The drop to the first slope of the wall was about eight hundred feet. The canyon was majestic, breathtaking, but he couldn't enjoy it.

To his left the horseshoe-shaped cantilevered Skywalk appeared full. A dozen people stood along the canyon edge between him and the wood security fence, which prevented people from getting closer to Skywalk.

None of the tourists looked questionable.

If Skywalk was a target, he expected automatic weapons, not bombs. If the terrorists wanted to create more fear, they would escalate the gravity of the attacks over the five days. The brochure said Skywalk could hold over eight hundred people. He hoped it could handle a bomb if he was wrong.

He ambled farther south, watching everyone. Tourists were scattered over a quarter mile south of Skywalk, their numbers thinning the farther he walked.

His watch read three-fifteen p.m. He was running out of time. He wanted to be on Skywalk at four.

A quarter mile farther south, beyond where most of the tourists were congregated, a tall man sat close to the edge, staring at the canyon. Steel was curious. Perhaps he was a single tourist that didn't like crowds. Deciding to investigate further, he walked at an angle away from the canyon, pretending to be heading for higher ground.

He kept the man in his peripheral vision. Turning, he put his hands on his hips and looked at the canyon. The man was a hundred yards away, sitting on a large rock, his back to Steel. He seemed to be working at something, his arms moving slightly.

"Hell," he muttered. He had no time to waste on being discreet.

He made a beeline for a spot thirty yards north of the man. From the man's side-profile Steel put him at thirty, six feet, two hundred pounds, with dark curly hair and dark skin. European. Wearing long pants, tennis shoes, and a baggy green polo shirt.

Steel slowed as he got closer, trying to see what the man was doing. He glimpsed a nylon rope in the man's hand for a brief moment. The man bent over, a large day pack resting by his feet.

Steel checked his watch. Three-thirty.

The man turned and stared at him but didn't move.

Keeping his gaze averted, Steel pretended to be taking in the canyon. Walking away, he headed toward the Skywalk building. He couldn't cover the distance between himself and the man faster than the man could shoot him—if he had a gun. He needed help.

Several times he checked over his shoulder. The man was still sitting, but not watching him. Maybe waiting until a few minutes to four.

Striding farther away from the canyon, he made his way up to the road that the tour bus used. From there he jogged toward the Skywalk building.

Before he reached it, he stopped and punched in the Skywalk number on his phone to report a man with a gun down by the canyon edge. After giving a description and location, he hung up and hurried to the Skywalk building.

He was satisfied to see police officers scurrying in the direction he had seen the man. If the man was one of the terrorists—which he thought likely—the police should be able to deal with him.

Once inside, he headed for the Skywalk entry line. He didn't think the gift shop and restaurant merited attention. The dogs would have found a bomb. That left the possibility of an attack of some kind on the Skywalk itself. It would get better publicity, but he didn't see how they could get a weapon onto it, unless Diego had managed to have one hidden there too.

He had to give up his phone at the metal detector station and put disposable booties over his shoes to protect the glass bottom of the outdoor walkway. Then he stood in line with several dozen people, waiting for vacancies to open up on the Skywalk.

Peering over the shoulders of the people ahead of him, he scanned the tourists already on Skywalk. Beginning with the end of the walkway and working back, he searched for single males that stood out in any way.

The ten-foot-wide, horseshoe-shaped bridge extended seventy feet out over the rim of the canyon. It was crowded. The brochure said they limited the number of people to one hundred twenty and it appeared to be at maximum capacity.

As he surveyed the walkway, his gaze rested on one individual.

Halfway down the first section of the walkway, a young man with shades leaned against the inner Skywalk rail. Alone. The man checked his watch several times in the course of a few minutes. Six foot, dark tanned, wearing shorts and a loose shirt.

The man checked his watch again. Steel wanted to bolt at the man. Maybe the watch was meaningless, but he couldn't help his reaction.

He quickly scanned the rest of the walkway to the entrance but didn't see anyone who fit the profile. There was a small knot of tall tourists on the left side that blocked his view of a few people beyond them.

He smiled at the security guard standing at the entrance ahead of him. "What time is it, miss?"

The guard glanced at her phone. "Three-fifty-five."

"Thank you." Due to the number of people in front of him it didn't seem likely that he would make it onto the Skywalk in time.

He glanced at everyone in line once more. His gut said he had to be on the walkway, one way or the other, by four. Pulling out his billfold, he said to a family of four ahead of him, "I have to leave in fifteen minutes. I'll give you twenty each—eighty bucks—if you let me cut in front of you."

They eagerly took the money from him. Two people in their sixties did the same. A man and his girlfriend in their twenties shrugged and just let him go ahead without taking any money. By then he was at the head of the line.

The man he was watching slowly meandered to the far side of a young woman looking over the inner rail. The woman partly obscured Steel's view of the man so he couldn't see if he was talking to her or not. Maybe the man was with her. Maybe not.

The security woman waved him through. "You can go, sir."

He hurried past her, weaving through the people in front of him, keeping his gaze on the solitary man. The man reached under the back of his shirt and Steel rushed forward. Grabbing the man's wrist, he strong-armed him against the rail.

"What are you doing?" blurted the man.

"Leave him alone!" said the woman.

"What's your relationship with him?" asked Steel.

"My husband." She came closer. "Get off of him!"

Steel lifted the man's shirt. No hidden weapons.

A shout made him whirl around. Farther ahead, a man near the outer railing was stabbing one of the tall tourists in the back with a black knife.

Steel released his suspect and bolted for the terrorist. Late twenties, average in height and weight, wearing jeans, a loose, short-sleeved blue shirt, trim beard, and sunglasses. Maybe Middle Eastern descent. Fluid movements.

People were scrambling away from the man, who stopped in mid-attack when he saw Steel charging.

Machine gun fire erupted from the canyon edge below to the south. People screamed.

The terrorist pushed his shocked victim against the rail, grabbed one of his legs, and slid him over.

The tourist shouted.

Steel leapt forward and grabbed one of the falling man's ankles, his stomach against the rail as he held the man's weight with both hands.

The terrorist came at Steel from the side, his black knife raised.

Steel kicked into the man's abdomen, sending the terrorist flying back.

Two other tourists rushed forward and grabbed the dangling man's ankles.

Steel released the victim and chased the attacker, who had fled, leaving a trail of cut arms and necks in his wake. Victims were either bent over in pain or lying on the glass floor. Steel guessed the terrorist's knife was ceramic, which would get it past the metal detector.

More shots from down below. People shouting. The side glass on the opposite side of Skywalk was punched by bullets. Tourists toppled.

More shots.

Quiet.

Steel needed to jump over one woman who had collapsed. He landed just beyond her head.

The terrorist was within his reach, but the man grabbed a boy and jerked him into Steel's path. Steel jumped again. While airborne he whirled around the boy—a move he had practiced in the VR sims. When he landed, the man was slicing at him with his knife in a backhanded arc.

Steel raised an arm for protection, blocking the man's arm with his forearm. Hitting the terrorist in the ribs, he aimed a low kick at the man's knee.

The man lifted his leg to avoid the kick and swung a reverse roundhouse with his heel aimed at Steel's head. Ducking and charging, Steel jammed his shoulder beneath the man's raised leg and pushed the terrorist up against the outer rail.

Gasping, the man drove his knife at Steel's back.

Stiff-arming the man's wrist, Steel gripped it. Squatting, he lifted the man's standing leg and tossed him over the side.

Not bothering to watch the terrorist fall, he strode toward the other side of the walkway, mostly vacated by people fleeing for the exit. Three tourists lay on the glass floor, wounded by bullets. Police were coming onto the walkway.

Steel looked over the side. Several hundred yards to the south, along the canyon edge, police officers and EMTs were swarming to help a half-dozen people lying on the ground. The sight dismayed him. He assumed the terrorist was dead.

Hurrying off the Skywalk with other patrons, he blended in and soon exited the building. A shuttle bus was parked in the nearby lot with its door open. Climbing aboard, he took a seat, watching police vehicles arriving.

In twenty minutes he sat in his own car and drove out.

As soon as he was out of the park, he called Colonel Jeffries and filled him in, ending with, "You better assume timetables will be moved up at the other sites. I'd expect bombs after this."

"Angel was telling the truth," said Jeffries.

"I'd still keep the Mall of America on alert."

Jeffries agreed and hung up to make calls.

Settling into his seat, he decided to wait to tell Christie. She had enough to worry about with Harry in the hospital.

It bothered him that the terrorists had hurt people, and it gave him another reason to kill Diego. Even though Angel had helped save lives here, it wasn't enough to change his mind about killing him.

# PART 6

## OP:
## THE WOLF & THE PACK

# CHAPTER 48

ANGEL SAT IN THE driver's seat of his Chevy SS, waiting for Lucas to speak.

Lucas sat in the front passenger seat, with two of his men in the rear seat. Angel's past student wore a short-waisted leather coat, jeans, and a simple white shirt. He also had a moustache, jet black hair, a strong chin, and dark eyes. Handsome.

However Angel found him repulsive at the moment.

Angel had driven thirty-five hours to reach a suburb in Richmond, Virginia and was exhausted. But that didn't bother him. All his worry centered on Renata.

Earlier he had met Lucas a few miles from the target's address. They had driven together to the target's neighborhood. Angel again wondered if Diego had told Lucas to kill him.

A second car with four more of Lucas' men was parked behind them.

Lucas spoke softly. "Diego wants you to take care of the American general who sent Steel to kill Gustavo last year. Send him photos." He handed a photo of the general to Angel, who quickly handed it back.

"It will be a pleasure to kill the man who ordered my friend, Gustavo, killed." Angel smiled. "It's good we can work together again, Lucas."

"It is."

Angel stared ahead. "Diego wants General Morris to suffer. How much time can I take?"

Lucas smiled at him. "Thirty minutes."

"Perfect." Angel left the keys in the ignition and got out. It was good to stretch his legs and the night air was crisp. Stars dotted the sky.

He was not as relaxed as he usually was before a job. Renata was not guiding him and he wasn't as confident of what to expect or what might go wrong. Certain this was a test by Diego, he felt he was safe from Lucas for now. When they went after Steel, Lucas would make his move against him. He had some time to think things through.

He walked down the quiet street, noting the big houses, the nice lawns, and the decor of the neighborhood. Orderly. Peaceful. He wanted his life like this, quiet and peaceful. Thoughts of Renata flashed through him and he had to put them aside.

The house appeared to his right, and he walked up the long sidewalk to the front door. It was ten o'clock and dark outside. Lights were on inside. Dressed in a suit, he looked professional. He counted on his smile to be disarming, as usual.

Still he would be surprised if anyone answered the door this late. Through the window to the side of the door he glimpsed an elderly woman dressed in a nightgown staring at him.

Before he could ring the doorbell she opened the door, smiling.

"Good evening, ma'am." He returned her smile. "I appear to be lost."

"Well come in then and I'll get you a cup of coffee." She stepped back, allowing him to walk in. "It's so good to see you again. We'll have a nice visit."

He shut and locked the door after he entered, realizing she had Alzheimer's or some other kind of dementia. Convenient and sad. She had to be General Morris' mother. Morris was in his sixties and the woman appeared to be in her late eighties.

"Come along." She slowly led him down a hallway into a living room.

The general was sitting on a couch, wearing a bathrobe and watching TV, a plate of pizza slices on his lap. Morris was tall and slender, with ebony skin, graying hair, and glasses.

Angel noted that the light from the large TV was perfect for what he had in mind. No other lights were on.

"He said he's lost, Tommy."

"Who are you talking about, Mother?" General Morris turned and instantly paled. He put the slice of pizza in his hand down on the plate. "Mother, why don't you go up to bed now? I'll be up later to check on you."

"All right, dear." She touched Angel's arm. "It was so nice to see you again."

"And you, ma'am." He watched her climb the stairway at the other end of the room. Then he drew one of his Glocks and sat on the far end of the couch, his gun casually pointed at the table.

"What do you want?" Morris put the plate of food on the coffee table and reached for the remote control.

"Leave the TV on." Angel waited for Morris to sit back again. "I want nothing, but my employer wants you dead for engineering the Op that killed Gustavo Alvarez."

"You're from the cartel?"

"Sí."

"You'll never get away with it."

Angel smiled. "I don't want to. Let me explain some things to you."

Morris's eyebrows hunched. "I'm listening."

"I don't want your military chasing me. I made a deal with them earlier today in exchange for information on ISIS activity in the U.S. However the cartel has my sister and they're blackmailing me to kill you, among others."

Morris sat back. "And?"

"I have a plan, but we have to hurry."

"Why?" Morris straightened.

"There are other men here."

"How many?" Morris frowned.

"Seven. If I don't kill you, they will. And if I kill them, they won't do their hourly check-in calls, which will result in my sister's death."

Morris talked calmly. "I could get help here fast."

Angel gave a slight shake of his head. "Then my sister dies so I cannot allow that."

"I could run out the back door."

Angel shrugged. "Same result."

Morris sighed. "Alright. How do we get out of this?"

Angel talked, Morris listened.

Afterward the general said, "What happens if it doesn't work?"

"We both die."

"I see." Morris lifted a hand. "Okay. Let's do it."

The general slid off the couch to the floor, lying on his back. He stared up at Angel. "Are you an honorable man?"

Angel smiled. "I am tonight. Now close your eyes, open your mouth, and slow your breathing."

From his pockets he pulled out several small bags of materials. He had used them once before when Diego had insisted he kill a woman who had stolen money from one of his drug couriers. Angel hadn't wanted to kill the woman. Her story of needing money to help her invalid brother had moved him. Taking a risk, he had faked her death, sent a photo to Diego, and driven the woman to a boat and helped her disappear.

On the drive out to Lucas he had picked up some of the necessary products.

Quickly he applied Ben Nye Spirit Gum Adhesive to three areas of Morris' face and one on his neck. Using scar wax, he formed a rough small circle for a bullet wound and three narrow oblong pieces for knife wounds.

He applied the wax pieces to the general's forehead and cheeks, quickly smoothed the edges, and then used a brush to rapidly apply colors from a small pallet. Blue, brown, and black—to simulate wounds. A small bottle of theatrical blood filled in around the edges. Straightening, he was satisfied with the effect.

He drew a switchblade, opened it, and bent over again. Pulling up the general's pant leg, he made a small cut on his calf. The man was tough, handling the pain without showing any reaction.

Using another brush, he smeared some of the fresh blood around the wounds and the general's face. Finished, he took all of the materials and dumped them in the general's kitchen trash. He walked back into the living room to see how the general appeared to him. The TV cast a dim light onto Morris' face, enough to see him, but not enough to see too clearly.

"Perfect." Angel used his phone to snap a photo of Morris and sent it to Lucas and Diego. "Remember, do as I told you or they will come again, guaranteed. Don't move and keep your eyes closed and mouth open for at least twenty minutes."

He walked to the front door and opened it. On the front step stood Lucas, two of his men on the sidewalk below. None of them held guns. Angel showed no surprise. It was something he would have done if he had been in Lucas' position.

"Diego wants me to verify," said Lucas.

"Be my guest." Angel listened from the front door as Lucas disappeared into the other room.

There were two soft thumps. Silenced gunshots. And a last sound that might have been a groan or a body falling.

Angel didn't react, smiling at the two men on the sidewalk. He kept his right hand near one of his holstered Glocks, ready for anything.

Instead of concern for himself, he found himself worried over who would take care of General Morris' mother if the general was dead. *You would be proud of me, Renata.*

It seemed late in life to finally find his heart again, which he had lost when his parents had been murdered so long ago. Renata had kept it alive all these years. She had saved him with her love. He vowed to save her.

Lucas returned, his gun put away, and clapped him on the shoulder. "Good work, Angel. A true master. I had to kill the old woman. She came down to say goodnight to her son."

Angel wasn't sure if Lucas was lying. Did he put two bullets into General Morris or did he truly kill Morris' mother? Or perhaps he put one bullet into each of them. The idea that Lucas had killed the old woman or the woman's son bothered him deeply. It reminded him of his relationship with Renata, and how she depended on him.

Whatever Lucas had done, he wanted to kill him for it. But not yet, not with Renata at risk. Instead he strolled with him back to the car, the two men tailing them.

As they neared his car, he saw Lucas' other four men standing beside it. He prepared himself, but he didn't think Lucas was ready to kill him. At least not here.

"I need to sleep," said Angel.

Lucas' eyes glinted. "I have always wanted to drive one of your cars."

"You have the address to Steel's family?" asked Angel.

"We have a long drive." Lucas smiled. "Montana."

"Wonderful." Angel returned the smile.

Lucas pulled out his FN Five-Seven pistol and held it near his thigh.

Angel knew his former student appreciated the lighter weight and light recoil of the FN, but Lucas' real motive was to show off—FNs were expensive.

Lucas' six men suddenly had guns in their hands too.

Angel didn't move, his two Glocks still in his side holsters beneath his jacket. He could have drawn his weapons faster than any of them, and he was still tempted to fight all of them here. But the check-in calls to Diego worried him. Unsure how to make that work all the way to California, so Diego didn't become suspicious and hurt Renata, he decided to wait.

He stood quietly, watching carefully for any signs.

Lucas turned to him. "Angel, I'm sorry, but I'm going to have to ask you to get into the trunk of your car. This way I don't have to hurt you."

The other men all held their weapons half-raised in case he reacted. He still thought he had a chance to kill all of them, but the image of Renata wouldn't let him risk it. It didn't seem likely, but Lucas could just shoot him in the trunk of his car. He felt Lucas needed him for something. Before he cooperated he had to find out what that was.

He relaxed his body. "You know Diego will eventually betray you too, Lucas."

Lucas didn't seem surprised. "Of course."

Angel shrugged. "He's mad. Wanting to kill a U.S. Army general and killing Antonio. The other cartels will go after him."

Lucas' eyes glinted. "I agree, Angel. I've already had talks with Antonio's son about joining his cartel."

"Then why kill me?" Angel prepared himself, aware of the men around him, their stances, the exact angles of their guns, and their distance from him.

Lucas lost his smile. "Diego ordered that, but I'm not going to kill you. He wanted Steel brought back, but I'm going to finish Steel in Montana."

"Diego will not accept disobedience."

Lucas responded calmly. "Of course not. That's why I'm going to take you back to California instead. I will let you rescue your sister, which you will only achieve by killing Diego and his men. And if you succeed..." He shrugged. "We both win."

Angel considered Lucas' tone of voice, facial details, and posture. He concluded that the man would keep him alive for now.

"We owe everything to you." Lucas put his hand on Angel's shoulder. "Antonio's son wants Diego to die slowly, as I am sure you do. But I have to ensure you don't interfere here, my friend. You could try to take all of us now, but there would be no check-in calls to Diego and your sister would be hurt. You must really love her to have hid her for so long."

Angel walked up to the trunk. He understood. He would be blamed for killing Diego and his men. Lucas would then kill him and take over the cartel, and also manipulate Antonio's son and eventually have both cartels. Smart. And dangerous.

"Your guns, Angel, and your phone."

Slowly taking them out, he handed them to one of Lucas' men. "You really think the seven of you can take Steel and his friends?" He looked at Lucas and his men. "I've seen this man at work and he's as good as I am."

Lucas smiled. "Diego sent up more men. Steel will not have a chance. Now get into the trunk. I have to call Diego or he will hurt your sister."

# CHAPTER 49

S TEEL DIDN'T LIKE IT that they hadn't heard from Angel. It had been over twenty-four hours and dusk was only a few hours away. He had called Angel but hadn't left a message. Maybe Diego had killed Angel or something else had gone wrong.

It was too risky to depend on the killer for anything at this point. For all he knew Angel had joined the pack and was on his way here to kill all of them. They had to be prepared.

One piece of good news had come from Colonel Jeffries. Earlier in the day, undercover FBI agents had foiled a bomb attempt on the St Croix River Crossing bridge, killing two terrorists in the process. There had been no attack at the Mall of America. It verified Angel's information as accurate.

The attacks were moving west to east and escalating as Steel had predicted. Minimizing the terrorists' success, and Diego's revenge, gave him satisfaction. Everyone at the table with him felt the same way.

Even though he had flown in Saturday night, everyone else had just arrived early afternoon today because Pedro and Harry had complications at the hospital. Steel had told Christie to stay with her brother overnight; he would never forgive himself if Harry died while Christie came to see him. Also he doubted the terrorists could mount an attack as soon as Saturday night. By Sunday morning both Pedro and Harry were stable, and thus everyone had joined him.

Carol and Rachel had already been picked up by Jeffries' helicopter and taken to Malmstrom Air Force Base in Montana. Steel had missed any chance to talk to them.

He looked at Wyatt, who sat at one end.

The six-foot-two burly man had a bushy beard, graying sideburns, and hair that reached the base of his neck. His rugged appearance fit his dark flannel shirt and jeans. In his sixties, his eyes were bright and clear. A fixed blade knife was strapped to his belt, along with a holstered Glock.

"What's the plan, Jack?" Christie sat next to him, her hand resting on his on the table.

He regarded everyone, thinking on it. Carlos, Mario, and Clay sat across from him and Christie. Five of them. That gave him confidence. Also his early arrival had allowed him to explore Wyatt's land and plan their strategy.

He took a deep breath. "Carlos, Mario, and I will hide in the forest. Christie and Clay will stay inside Wyatt's barn, monitoring the security system and keeping us updated. If these men are as good as Angel, they won't use the driveway and they won't be conventional. If you're not sure who you're aiming at, ask for the signal—one hand up, five fingers spread."

He modeled it with his hand, and then turned to Wyatt. "Anything I'm missing?"

Wyatt gave a broad smile, his voice grainy. "Just me."

Steel shook his head. "This isn't your fight."

"But it's one worth fighting, Jack. Besides I finally get to test out my security system." Wyatt clasped his hands on the table and looked at Christie. "If they try to come up the driveway, I have buried spike strips that are automated. Jack and I also buried explosives in the road in the meadow area in case any vehicles get past the spikes. I'll show you the switches by the computer station."

Christie let go of Steel's hand. "We don't need two people inside."

Steel kept his voice neutral. "You're injured enough to seriously hamper your abilities in the forest and in one-on-one encounters. If you're on the computer, then Clay can worry about anyone trying to get into the barn."

Christie looked annoyed but remained silent.

"I think it's a good plan." Clay glanced from Christie to Steel. "Any idea of when they're coming?"

"I doubt they want a daytime fight. I'm guessing the attack will be tonight. If not, we'll stay alert for at least another day." Steel emphasized his next words. "If Angel shows up, assume he's the enemy."

Wyatt opened a worn topographical map which was rolled up on the table. "As you've seen, my place is situated in the corner of two sloped forested hills on the north and east sides, with forest also out front. The back of the house is built into the east bluff face, the long side of the barn is built into the north bluff face. There are tunnels leading from the barn north, south, and east. There's also a tunnel connecting the house and barn."

He traced them on the map. "The illusion for people who don't know my tunnel network is that we can only escape out the front of the house or the main barn entrance."

He looked up. "I'll wait south of the spike strips and take out as many of them as I can from any stopped vehicles. Then I'll hunt them from behind with the sniper rifle. We'll let whoever's left converge to the meadow and get them in a crossfire there. The element of surprise is heavily in our favor."

"We know the pack is seven men." Steel looked around at all of them. "If Angel is with them, and we have to assume he is, he could come in anywhere. He's a wild card and we have to be ready for the unexpected."

"What if they bring in grenades or explosives?" asked Clay.

"They want us to suffer." Steel shrugged. "No easy deaths. Smoke bombs or tear gas could be a possibility, but nobody will be in the house and the barn is a fortress. I'll cover the north forest."

He expected the main assault to come from that direction. "I'll let them go by me and attack them from behind, driving them down to the house."

"I'll leave the front house door open," said Wyatt. "If they go in to escape us, we can use the tunnel from the barn to get into the lower level of the house."

Carlos looked thoughtful. "I'll sit on the east side of the driveway south of the meadow so I can see the area in front of the house and the barn."

Mario pulled a toothpick from his mouth. "I will take the east hill. From there I can help Jack or my father."

Steel nudged Christie. "Your analytical skills are key to letting us know where to go and what we're facing."

She continued to frown. "I'm not an invalid."

"You're injured." Clay lifted a hand. "It's okay to sit out the heavy lifting on this one. You've done enough. I had a hard enough time convincing Harry that he wasn't invited." He nodded to her. "I'll provide the muscle on the switches."

"Wonderful." She scowled.

"Trip-wires or pit traps could be set off by wildlife so we elected not to use them." Wyatt stood. "Let's take a quick trip to the barn so you can get outfitted and see the tunnel network."

He led them out the two-story house, and across twenty yards of short grass to the barn. The solitary barn door was the size of a house door and located on the end of the building closest to the house.

Steel appreciated that the land had been cleared a hundred feet south of the house and barn, leaving three-foot-high meadow grass. That gave good visibility to the south.

He also noted the keypad and deadbolt entry on the barn door, like his own in Virginia. The interior was different though. The three sides of the barn that were exposed had a thick steel inner wall, like the outside, with cement in between. The computer array on the first level included four wall-mounted viewing screens that showed different camera angles of the driveway and property.

"I have a more redundant security system than you have, Jack." Wyatt smiled. "If someone disables a perimeter camera or laser sensor, then another line of sensors is triggered farther in."

Wyatt led them to the middle of the barn, which had exercise equipment, a virtual reality station similar to Steel's, and a series of built-in cabinets.

Stopping in front of a wildlife painting on the north wall, Wyatt tilted it enough to reveal a hidden, embedded keypad at eye level. He punched a code into it, and a section of the wall slid up, revealing a large rectangular safe at waist level. It had a fingerprint keypad, and Wyatt pressed his thumb on it and the front slid up.

Steel stared like everyone else at the large arsenal of guns, rifles, machine guns, scopes, night vision gear, ammo, and other ordnance.

"Take whatever you like." Wyatt grabbed one of the sawed offs—a Mossberg Shockwave—a G28, and night vision goggles, setting it all to the side. He nodded. "I like to be prepared for anything. I've got Kevlar vests for everyone in another locker. Be sure you take enough ammo. I also have wireless radios with throat mikes so we can all communicate in whispers if necessary."

"Now we're talking." Clay rubbed his hands together.

Carlos picked up an M40, an older bolt-action sniper rifle based on the Remington 700. M40s had eventually been replaced by the Mk 13 for the Marines and Special Operations snipers for longer range targets in countries like Afghanistan.

Carlos shook his head. "Amigo, you're ready for an army."

Wyatt clapped him on the back. "Always. Let's go over the tunnel system in case you need to use it." He patted Christie's shoulder. "Then I'll show you the security system."

Walking a little farther, Wyatt stopped by the shooting range but turned his back to it. In the north wall there were built-in shelves, and on the inside bottom corners of each shelf were wood supporting brackets. Below the third shelf from the top he pulled the bracket out, revealing a black button which he depressed. He then snapped the bracket back in place.

A four-by-six-foot section of flooring along the wall slid back, revealing stairs going down.

"I'll keep this open while we're in the tunnels so we can move fast. To close it you just hit the button a second time." Wyatt led them down to the lower level.

Large and finished, it had a steel wall with a steel door blocking off half of it. Wyatt punched a code on the keypad by the door, used his fingerprint, and opened the four-inch-thick door.

A panic room. Complete with food-lined shelves, a corner latrine, dry goods, and other necessities.

Steel was impressed. "You've thought of everything, Wyatt."

Wyatt smiled. "If we need to, we can hole up here for weeks. I can contact the outside, and I've got a hidden tunnel in here. But I don't think we're going to need it."

He closed the door and led them to a bookshelf in the northwest corner.

"Here's how it works." He pulled the bookshelf out from the wall. It swung easily on hinges, revealing another steel door with no handles and a keypad. "Here's the code." He punched the number slowly for all of them to see and continued talking.

"Then I use my fingerprint on the pad. I turned off that feature so any of you can use the tunnel system. There's also a locked door at the bottom of every exit shaft. Use the same code to open them. Just remember, if you leave any doors open, anyone can enter from the outside. The rule is that tunnel doors are always kept closed."

Pushing the door open, he revealed a dark, bricked tunnel. "This leads west thirty feet to a crossroads leading south and north a hundred yards. You end up south of the field a good distance or up the north hill. If you go south, you'll first come to another junction leading left below the meadow to the base of the east hill."

He looked at all of them. "Happy hunting."

***

Steel worked the ropes in the barn and then moved to the virtual reality station. The preceding days of too little sleep had left a residual effect on his ability to respond. He wanted his body sharp when the pack arrived.

Wyatt's state-of-the-art virtual reality station was much like his. Sensors high on the wall at the four corners of a very large floor pad allowed room-scale tracking. A wireless motion-tracking controller completed the setup.

Wyatt had confided in him before the others had arrived that he had supplied the VR program and tech to the Army's Blackhood Ops, retiring after that project was completed. Upon hearing that, Steel was even more impressed with Wyatt's skills.

He put on the full-body haptic suit, boots, gloves, a headpiece, and goggles, and ran several VR sims in a dark forest with multiple attackers. The suit delivered pain on a scale he could select, and also simulated flat or uneven surfaces, hills, and temperatures.

He ran scenarios with guns and hand-to-hand combat with two to eight attackers for several hours, as he had for over three years. The workouts over the last few days had sharpened his reflexes enough that he felt ready. When he finished, he stretched his legs and back.

Christie and Clay spent the time with Wyatt at the computer station, going over the laser and camera feeds, how to switch computer screens to different cameras, and how to activate the automated spike strips and explosives buried in the driveway.

A little after ten p.m. Jeffries called Steel with news of an attack on General Morris that had just occured. Morris had managed to call an ambulance, even though he had taken a bullet. The general was in the hospital, unconscious and in critical condition. Steel told everyone to go to bed. Given that Morris was two thousand miles away, there would be no attack tonight.

***

The next day everyone traded off on keeping watch, exercising, and waiting. By late afternoon Colonel Jeffries called. There had been an attack on the New York subway, but the terrorists had blown themselves up in a mostly empty car when confronted by SWAT. Only two passengers had died. More people had been injured at Skywalk, but Steel was glad to hear only one had died. Disney World was the last target. They were going to keep the amusement park open.

Later Steel walked with Christie on Wyatt's land adjacent to the house. The air was cool and they both wore light coats. The scent of the pine trees was strong.

Somewhere above them a Steller's jay gave its harsh, scolding call. In the distance a buck deer stared at them.

Christie held his hand.

"You don't think we can do this." She stopped, staring at him.

He leaned against a tree, pulling her in close. "We still have to find Diego and take out him and all of his men before they return to Colombia or Mexico. If they get out of the country, this will never be over. Then we'll have to go into witness protection."

She pressed into him. "You know what I think?"

"What?" He stared into her eyes.

"We'll be okay. There's enough of us here. Even if Angel is with them, they have no clue what this place is like. If we keep one of them alive, we can find out where Diego is and go there tomorrow."

"I was thinking the same thing." He swallowed.

"What else? I can see it in your eyes, Jack."

"Your brother thinks I'm too much of a risk for you." He agreed with that sentiment. The more he had thought about it the more he had been driven to the same inescapable conclusion.

Christie scoffed. "Clay has always felt protective of everyone in our family. I'm going to talk to my brothers. They'll be okay.

They can't say much when Harry might be falling in love with someone who almost killed him."

"I agree with Clay. All of this mess is because of my past life in Blackhood Ops. Dale's death, your injuries, the threat to your whole family is—"

She cut him off. "You were protecting our country. You risked your life. Your job is to stop terrorists. I can accept the risk that brings."

"I can't." He looked away. "I think of Rachel and Carol, what I've put them through."

"Steel." Her tone was strong. "You are who you are, and that's why I love you. You've done nothing wrong. This is probably the only loose end from all your Ops that could come back to haunt you, so let's end it."

He hugged her tightly, and then pulled back. "When I go after Diego, you're not coming." The sadness filled his chest again.

Her lips twisted as she stared at him. "What else?"

"After tonight we need to go our own ways."

She stared at him, open-mouthed. "You're saying we're through?"

"Yeah."

The setting sun sent red hues through the clouds.

# CHAPTER 50

ANGEL SLEPT FOR THE first twelve hours of the drive. It was uncomfortable, but when he woke up he felt rested. His watch said ten a.m. He stretched, moved his body as much as possible, and thought about how to save Renata and kill Diego. In late evening he settled down again for another short sleep. When he woke the second time it was three a.m.

He estimated they would be near Butte, Montana. In another hour it sounded as if they had turned onto a gravel road. Not much longer after that the car stopped.

Listening carefully, he heard car doors open and shut. No one talked. They had to be arming themselves. Since he had trained all of them, he guessed they would have night vision goggles, Kevlar vests, AK-47 rifles with thirty-round mags, knives, radio gear, and pistols. Probably tear gas and smoke canisters on chest straps as well.

A final light *bang*—a trunk shutting—and then quiet. Waiting another minute, he began working.

When he had the trunk modified, he also made sure he had a way out in case this scenario occurred. On the passenger side, in the front part of the wheel well, there was a piece of smooth metal. He pressed it as hard as he could. It was kept in place by a strong spring and bent in just enough to reveal a small compartment. He couldn't see it, but reached in with his other hand, grabbed the trunk emergency handle that was there, and pulled. There was a small click.

He turned onto his side to face the back of the car. With his right foot he raised the trunk. No guard.

He climbed out quietly, relieved to be out of the confinement of the trunk. There were two other cars parked on the side of the dirt road, one in front of his and one behind.

Closing the lid, he twisted the small decal on the trunk that hid the number pad for the secret compartment. Punching in the code, he had it open and his silenced Glocks in hand in seconds. There were two extra magazines, which he pocketed.

Running up the adjacent hill, he was glad for the pine tree cover. He liked the quiet, the distant dark shadows of mountains against the lighter sky, and the stars in the sky. There was some moonlight, but scattered clouds blocked much of it.

The air was cool, the ground soft and quiet too. Perfect.

In the distance an owl gave a loud *oowhoo!* several times. Renata would love it.

It reminded him of his father's farm. He and Renata often had sat on the porch at night—listening to the jungle and talking —before their parents were killed. A flash of rage at the cartel erupted inside him, surprising him. Perhaps he was finally ready to pay them back.

Taking a deep breath, he sorted out his priorities.

He needed Lucas alive for the check-in calls when they drove to Diego. Steel had to die so the man wouldn't hunt him forever. His agreement with Steel had to be broken. Weighed against Renata's life, it was a small price to pay. He couldn't see any way out of it. Everyone else was expendable.

Lucas and Steel were both very skilled. And for once he did not have Renata's guidance in a dangerous situation. For the first time in decades he didn't relish the challenge that lay ahead of him.

# CHAPTER 51

CHRISTIE WATCHED THE MONITORS with Clay, who seemed content to sit in a chair with his hands locked behind his head, his eyes closed. It was four a.m. She was tired of watching camera feeds too, but it still annoyed her.

What really bothered her was sitting inside while Steel was risking his life. His decision to end their relationship didn't feel real, but he meant it. She also believed he loved her deeply and felt he had to protect her. In that respect he was just like Clay. Stupid.

She turned to her brother, her voice strained. "Jack said we're through."

Sitting up, he opened his eyes. "I'm sorry, Christie. I really am. But maybe it's—"

"For the best?" She bit off the words. "Damn your arrogance, Clay! How would Meera feel if you dumped her while you were in Afghanistan? How do you think I feel? Have you ever asked yourself that?"

"It was his choice, Christie."

"You didn't help, Clay, always rubbing it in his face that it was his fault I was hurt, his fault Dale died, his fault for everything. Judge, jury, executioner. You're perfect, Clay."

He cleared his throat, got to his feet, and walked up to her. "Okay, Steel's a lot like me. Protective to a fault. But if I was in his shoes, maybe I'd do the same thing if it was Meera instead of you."

"Don't you think Meera and I worry just as much about our men? Jack could have died at Skywalk and I didn't even know he was there." Her eyes misted. "I love him, Clay. He's every bit as important to me as Meera is to you."

He gently held her shoulders. "Then fight for him, sis."

"I plan to." She wiped her eyes. "I'm not letting him off this easy. And by the way, do men always have such rotten timing on these things?"

"I think so."

A sensor beeped and she brought up the camera feed for the north perimeter.

Clay looked at the wall monitors, put on his radio, and talked into his throat mike. "Heads up, Steel and Mario, you have a group coming in from the north."

Christie donned her radio too. "I count a dozen men." She frowned over the numbers. "Moving fast with night vision gear."

Another sensor beeped. The driveway.

She pulled up the camera positioned a hundred feet in on the driveway. The road was straight, three-quarters of a mile long, and ran through pine forest. "Intruders coming up the driveway."

She grimaced. Angel had not only lied to Steel, he had also brought a small army with him. They couldn't let anyone drive up to the house or Steel and Mario wouldn't have a chance.

The vehicles appeared moments later. The two lead SUVs were larger than the third.

"Three SUVs driving fast." She turned to Clay. "Time it!"

He waited two seconds and then hit the switch for the spike strips. Her face taut, Christie watched the monitor.

The lead SUV hit the second strip and veered off the road, its tires shredded. It managed to stop upright in the grass. The second SUV hit the first strip, tilted, and fell onto its side, sliding along the dirt.

Swerving off the road, the last SUV plowed through brush until it was past the spike strips. Then it veered back onto the road.

Christie's limbs stiffened. A dozen men exited the two stopped vehicles, all holding machine guns and wearing night vision gear. Three men fell to the ground before they got off the road. Wyatt.

The rest of the men speedily disappeared into the forest.

"Nine men coming in on the west side of the driveway with night vision gear and machine guns," she said.

Steel and Mario hadn't responded so she assumed they were already moving to engage the first group. On the camera feeds she watched the remaining SUV accelerate down the driveway.

"Keep going," she murmured. "Get ready, Clay."

"On it." He kept his finger on the switch, waiting for the sensor to alert him to throw it.

The SUV reached the meadow and veered off the road into the grass bordering the driveway. It was going to pass right by the buried explosives.

"How did they guess that?" asked Christie.

"Smart." Clay watched the monitor.

"Carlos!" Christie watched as the SUV veered erratically back onto the road, and then in seconds swerved toward the grass again.

"The driver and front passenger are down," said Carlos.

"Good shooting, Carlos," whispered Christie.

The sensor for the explosives lit up on the computer console. Clay flipped the switch.

The blast barely hit the front left fender of the SUV, throwing dirt and smoke into the air. Veering sideways off the road, the vehicle managed to stay upright with its front tire blown. It came to a sudden stop and men piled out.

Christie counted four exiting the SUV; one toppled immediately into the grass. Carlos again.

The other three killers crouched and ran through the meadow. They had deciphered Carlos' position from the shots and kept the SUV between them and his location. In seconds they would reach the cars parked in front of the house. Then they would either try to breach the house or barn.

Christie worried they would go up the hill after Steel.

"I'm coming up behind the group from the SUVs, Carlos," said Wyatt. "South of the tunnel exit."

"I'll stay here and we can pick them off when they're out in the open." Carlos sounded assured.

"I'll be ready," said Wyatt.

Christie ran from the computer station toward the open armory safe.

Clay shut off his radio. "Where are you going, Christie?"

Not wanting to distract Steel and the others with their chatter, she shut off her radio too. "That's way more than they can handle, Clay."

He hastily followed her. "Steel said we need to stay inside."

"I'm not going to do them any good in here. You've got two boys at home, Clay. You stay here and coordinate everyone."

"Yeah, right. I'm not going to sit around and watch monitors while you risk your life."

She took off her windbreaker, put on body armor, and covered it with the jacket. Grabbing a silenced SIG Sauer P320 compact and Rattler, she stuffed extra mags for both into her pockets. Lastly she put on night vision gear.

Clay stood by her, already pulling his jacket over a Kevlar vest. He picked out an HK416 assault rifle with an optical scope, a SIG, and extra mags.

She faced him. "Do you want north or south?"

"Since you're injured, the hill will be easier for me so I'll take north. You go to the southern tunnel exit, hook up with Wyatt, and hit the men in the meadow."

She rested a hand on his shoulder. "Thanks, Clay."

He grabbed her and hugged her. "Hell, you're my sister. What else am I going to do?"

She pulled back. "Be careful. I'm going to watch the cameras a bit longer."

"Good." He hustled down the stairway leading to the lower level, speaking into his throat mike. "I'll be coming out the north tunnel, Steel."

Christie hadn't wanted to tell Clay what she was going to do. Returning to the cameras, she saw two of the killers from the meadow already beside the front house door, which had been left unlocked. They were quickly inside. Their partner had to be ahead of them.

She had a minute.

Grabbing a pump shotgun, she checked and saw it was loaded with buckshot. Slinging the Rattler over her shoulder, she hurried to the barn door. Sliding back the deadbolt, she quietly slipped outside, shutting the door behind her.

Running to the closest parked car in the turnaround, she knelt behind its front driver's side tire. Even that little bit of exertion caused her bruised ribs to ache.

The men came out of the house in seconds. Remaining low, they approached the closed barn door. One of the killers tried to open it. When it didn't budge he took something from his belt to place on it.

Rising just above the car fender, Christie fired the shotgun twice at the killer closest to the door. Legs and head. He collapsed to the ground.

One of the killers rose and aimed his machine gun at her, but he took a bullet in his neck and dropped to the ground. Carlos.

The third man knelt and fired at her. Bullets hit the front of the car.

Falling to her belly, Christie shot below the frame at the third man's legs. Yelling, he fell to his belly. The man still managed to fire his machine gun at her, hitting the dirt beneath the car. Christie scrambled toward the rear tire, crouching low.

She unslung the Rattler. When just past the rear bumper, she knelt and fired a burst at the man. He collapsed into the grass. The man with the neck wound was lying on the ground, groaning.

Standing up, she ran forward. To ensure she didn't have to watch her back she put bullets into all three killers.

Quickly she punched in the barn access code, opened the door, deadbolted it, and ran across the barn. Dumping off the shotgun, she practically ran down the steps to the lower level, and then to the tunnel access.

Pulling back the bookcase made her groan. She punched in the code and pushed the door open.

The tunnel had no lighting so she used her hands to feel her way along the wall as she ran to the first junction. It helped that she had experienced moving fast in similarly dark tunnels on Steel's land.

At the first junction she went left.

Ignoring the pain in her ribs, she kept running. Passing the junction leading east, she continued south. In another hundred yards she reached the exit door. She punched in the code and opened it. Steel rungs led up to the tunnel entrance.

"Exiting the south tunnel, Wyatt."

No reply.

Closing the door, she climbed to the top, her ribs aching again.

Carefully she pushed the manhole cover up an inch, but she didn't see anyone. Pushing it farther, she climbed out, quietly closing it. Taking two steps to a tree, she pressed herself against it and drew the Glock, keeping the Rattler slung over her shoulder.

Scanning through the night vision gear south, east, and west, she didn't see anyone.

The intruders had to be farther north already. She assumed Wyatt was following them.

Slowly she rounded the tree trunk and looked north. Far ahead of her, men were moving at a quick pace. Crouching, she dashed across the soft ground from tree to tree, pausing each time to estimate the distance to the men ahead of her.

At the third tree she stopped. A slight rustle behind her sent panic into her limbs. She dove to the ground, her Glock aimed back, as silenced bullets hit the tree trunk.

# CHAPTER 52

STEEL STOOD ON A tree branch ten feet off the ground, his back pressed against the south side of the trunk. Holding a silenced Glock, he kept it vertical in front of his chest. He hunched his shoulders to stay hidden from anyone coming from the north.

He had climbed up as soon as Christie had alerted him of the north perimeter assault.

Somehow ending things with her had given him a sense of calm. Even if a deep sadness lay buried, he was focused. Still the numbers of men Diego had sent against them felt overwhelming. He had planned for eight, not thirty.

On its far side the north hill ran down to a dirt road. That would be the point of entry. It would take Lucas's pack only five minutes before they reached his location.

Shots were fired down by the barn. Christie or Clay. He didn't dare even whisper in case the pack was closer than he thought.

When he heard Christie telling Wyatt she was coming out, his calm seeped away. At least she was with Wyatt—the man knew what he was doing.

Mario would be coming toward him from the east, Clay from the west. He had to hold the center. That left Christie, Wyatt, and Carlos to take care of nine men, with surprise still heavily in their favor. The sooner he could help them the better.

What nagged at him was that he didn't know if Angel would be with the pack or with the SUV assault. The man was unpredictable and liked to work by himself. Thus it made more sense that he would come in alone. But where?

Not far away he heard the loud calls of a Great Gray Owl, the largest owl in North America. He listened to its loud *oowhoo!* calls. It brought up a surge of anger again that he had to be here with guns ready to kill people. He wanted to end this insanity, and the men who had brought it to him.

A small rustle made him look left.

A crouched figure holding a machine gun appeared twenty feet east of him, moving down the hill toward the house.

Slowly lowering the Glock, Steel aimed for the man's hips in case he was wearing Kevlar. Wounded was as good as dead if the wound was serious. Trying for a head shot through the trees was too risky. A tree trunk hid the man for a moment.

When he came into view Steel fired two quick shots. The man collapsed, his head hidden by a tree trunk. Steel pulled his gun back to his chest, deciding to remain where he was. It would be hard for anyone to locate his position in the tree, even if the intruders had a short spread between them and heard the shots.

He spotted another figure thirty feet away to the west. Almost even with him. He began a countdown of five.

At *three* a shout from the man he had shot interrupted him: "Está en el árbol!"

He jumped to the ground, landing on a spot to the east that he had previously picked out. Bullets thudded into the tree behind him.

Running in a crouch to the next tree, he threw himself on the ground to give himself a better angle on the man he had shot. The killer was sitting up, downhill from him, swinging his machine gun toward him. Steel fired three times. The man slumped into the dirt.

Bullets thumped the ground near him. Without waiting, he scrambled farther east to a log, hurdled it, and sat on the far side, his back to it.

To his east a man was running toward him but fell abruptly as if he'd been punched in the back. Mario. Though Steel couldn't spot his location.

Muffled machine gun fire came from Mario's direction. Another man was darting from tree to tree, heading in Steel's direction. Steel peered over the log to the west. The other killer was running toward him just as fast.

Rolling to his knees, he spotted a large boulder north of his position. It would give him a good vantage point for both men. A risky run though.

Glancing east and west, he tried to time his dash for when the two men were hidden by foliage. He fired one shot at both men, to make them duck for cover, and then bolted.

No shots rang out. He would make it.

He reached the boulder in a dead run, rounded it on the west side, and found himself face-to-face with Angel.

# CHAPTER 53

C LAY CLIMBED THE METAL rungs in the tunnel exit, hoping he was behind the intruders.

He pushed the manhole cover up a few inches and peered out. West, east, and north were clear. Pushing it up all the way vertical, he climbed out. He quickly checked south down the hill. Safe.

Closing the cover, which was camouflaged with grass, he hustled to a big tree for cover. Muffled gunshots sounded to the east. Steel and Mario were already engaging the enemy. Christie was right, their friends needed help. But he didn't enjoy imagining her facing nine guys with just Wyatt and Carlos.

The odds here were worse than in the canyon when they had tried to take Diego. If Christie had chosen to go home, he would have too. But he couldn't bear the thought of her dying here. Nor could he face his family if he abandoned her.

He had wanted to call Meera, to hear her voice one more time, because he felt there was a chance he could die. That idea had lodged into his brain as soon as Christie said she was going out. There were too many men, even with the tunnels.

Numbers often won battles, and they were heavily outnumbered. Yet he wouldn't give in to fear. And if he was going to die, he wanted to kill Angel for killing Dale. He wanted that man dead more than anyone he had ever wanted to kill in his life. But he still feared him.

Kneeling down, he unslung the HK416 and did a quick check east along the slope. He stiffened when he picked up a figure about a hundred yards away heading south. Sighting with the scope, he aimed for the man's head and fired. The man took a nosedive into the ground and didn't move. That gave him hope.

A bullet bit the trunk near his face.

He jerked back. Another man was moving toward him from the east. Fifty yards away.

He didn't have a clear shot, so he swung the carbine vertical and switched sides to make sure no one was coming at him from the west. Clear. Leaning farther out on the west side of the tree, he looked north. Another figure appeared, heading toward him.

That unsettled him. He was in front of the line of killers. He debated going back down the tunnel, but there was a high probability they would see him. If he locked the door, he would be limited to the barn, which wouldn't help anyone.

Sighting on the man to the north, he took a quick shot. The man was protected by trees, but he wanted to slow his advance. He swung east again. The other killer appeared thirty yards away, mostly hidden by trees. His location put him in a dangerous position for a crossfire from the two men. He had to move.

Twenty feet away from him, downslope and east of his position, a massive pine had collapsed. Its shallow roots had pulled a big chunk of ground out with it in an eight-foot-diameter rootball. It would give him better protection than what he had now. And a better angle on the intruder coming from the east.

Making sure nobody was sighting on him, he sprinted, keeping low. Bullets whined around him. He kept going. Something nicked his upper left arm. He almost cried out.

Reaching the rootball, he slid around it to the south side and stepped into the shallow depression left by the pulled roots. Immediately off balance on the uneven ground, he teetered backward. Grabbing one of the broken roots, he clung to it. Regaining his balance, he glanced over his shoulder. And froze.

He was standing on a one-foot-wide ledge that dropped into darkness. Dizziness gripped him. The terrifying prospect of falling paralyzed him for a few seconds. *Damn acrophobia!* Hanging tightly onto the root, he cautiously leaned backward to see what was below him. A thirty-foot drop to a hill with an eighty-degree slope.

Sweating profusely, he pulled himself back into the rootball, cursing that he hadn't scouted the hill more thoroughly the day before. He had assumed the whole face of it was a gradual slope, as it appeared from Wyatt's house below.

He slung the HK416 over his shoulder and drew the silenced SIG. His actions were slowed by his fear of falling backward. Edging out on the east side, he aimed the SIG northeast.

A bullet whined near his face.

He fired blindly twice, just to make the shooter cautious, and pulled back.

Slowly edging out on the other side, he felt nauseous thinking of the drop-off. He spotted the enemy there heading farther west. They had to be talking to each other, intending to get him in a crossfire.

He shoved the SIG into his belt, took the rifle off his shoulder, and sighted on the man. His left arm ached. He wasn't sure how bad the wound was and he didn't want to look.

Timing the intruder's spurts between trees, he kept his finger on the trigger. When the man appeared, he fired three quick shots, one into his legs. The man fell down but crawled along the ground. Clay shot the man in the head, and immediately glimpsed another man coming from the northwest.

He turned around, his back to the rootball, to see if he could move faster by pivoting his feet. His gaze slid down past his toes and dizziness assaulted his senses again. *Bad idea.*

Closing his eyes, he took a deep breath and slowly turned until he was facing the roots again. He spotted the shooter to the east darting to a tree closer to the edge of the precipice. He fired two quick shots. The killers would soon be able to shoot him at will from behind trees and he wouldn't have a chance.

He had to get out.

Panicked, he tossed the rifle over the drop-off and drew the SIG. Twisting so his back was to the rootball, he slid down to his butt. His feet and lower legs hung over the edge. He hesitated.

Images of his boys and Meera forced him to move. Slowly twisting, he gripped one of the exposed roots to slow the downward movement of his legs, but they rapidly slid over the edge anyway.

Panicked, he dropped the SIG and grabbed at roots—and felt a sharp pain in his left arm. His chest slid over the drop–off. He desperately grabbed for anything he could find. His legs dangled over emptiness. *I'm going to die.*

To his right he saw movement. He let go of the roots with his right hand, grabbed the SIG, and fired three times. His left arm burned and he couldn't hang on. Releasing the root, he clawed at the edge but found only crumbling soil in his fingers.

He was airborne then, with only emptiness beneath him.

# CHAPTER 54

CHRISTIE SAW A BLUR twenty feet behind her. She fired, but the man had already pulled back out of sight. Keeping perfectly still on the ground, she aimed her SIG at the tree.

The killer fell into view, landing heavily on the ground and not moving. His eyes were open in death. She gaped at the corpse.

"Christie, Wyatt coming out. Don't shoot."

"Roger that."

She scrambled to her feet as Wyatt strode out from the tree. He held a knife in one hand, the Mossberg Shockwave in the other, the rifle slung over a shoulder, and his Glock holstered. Nodding to her, he veered off to her left, running west.

Taking a deep breath, she was thankful Wyatt had been watching her back. She peered north. Eight killers left. Three appeared fifty yards ahead of her, moving fast. To join a crossfire with Carlos and Wyatt she had to get closer.

She stuck the SIG into her jeans and brought the Rattler off her shoulder.

Picking out a large pine, she ran hard, continuing to move from tree to tree. While she ran she caught fading glimpses of Wyatt still moving west. Trees soon obscured her view of him.

In five minutes she stopped behind a tree. Still ahead of her fifty yards, two attackers were kneeling at the edge of the clearing. She put her back to the tree and whispered, "Carlos, Wyatt, I have two ahead of me at the edge of the clearing. Status?"

Wyatt came back first. "I'm farther west. Take them."

Carlos followed with, "I'm east of the driveway and have two others in sight. Let's both fire in three."

Looking again, she now saw only one man at the edge of the clearing. Edging around the tree, she glimpsed the missing man to the east, running between trees, trying to work his way behind her. She didn't have a good shot at him and headed north.

Muffled shots northeast of her. Carlos.

Running, crouching low, she tripped. That confused her because the ground seemed level. Flying face forward, she landed on her stomach, still gripping the Rattler. Her calf burned. She realized that she had been shot. Why had they aimed so low?

She painfully crawled forward to a tree and drew herself to a sitting position, her back to the trunk. With her other hand she drew the SIG.

Machine gun fire sounded to the northwest, followed by Wyatt's Mossberg booming three times.

She put a tiny bit of pressure on her right foot. Sharp pain shot up her leg and she gasped. She hated alarming Steel but panic overwhelmed her.

"I'm shot, calf wound, two men trying to circle me," she whispered. "Just south of the clearing."

No one came back to her, making her wonder if anyone else was still alive.

# CHAPTER 55

STEEL ALMOST COLLIDED WITH Angel. The cartel assassin was running toward him, both of his Glocks held vertically in front of his shoulders. Steel immediately fired point blank.

Angel was already twisting sideways, swinging his left hand at Steel's face. Steel blocked it with his free hand while trying to head-butt him.

Angel moved his head sideways and brought both guns down. Steel dropped his Glock and used his hands to push Angel's Glocks wide. Charging forward, he took Angel down hard to his back.

Angel dropped his guns, his hands moving in rapid-fire strikes at Steel's neck and ribs. Steel grunted, rolled off him, and kicked sideways, hitting Angel's stomach.

They both scrambled to their feet, eyeing their guns.

Aware that he had little time before the other two men were upon him, Steel charged. He grappled with Angel, trying to get leverage. Both of them tried to trip the other, or stomp on feet or knees, trading and blocking strikes.

Angel caught the side of Steel's neck with a knife hand. Steel staggered sideways but managed to raise a leg and kick Angel's ribs. They squared off a few feet apart, hands up, both in martial arts open stances, exposing only side profiles.

Footsteps to the east.

Steel rushed Angel with a flurry of hand strikes aimed at his face and neck—and then dove sideways to the ground. He grabbed his Glock, rolled, and shot the man charging from the east, first in his legs, then his chest.

When he twisted to his back so that he could fire on Angel, he heard Christie's call for help.

Angel had already disappeared behind the far side of the boulder. The man from the west appeared, but before Steel could shoot him, the man toppled. Angel.

Surprised, Steel didn't move, keeping his gun pointed at the boulder. He didn't trust the cartel assassin.

"Truce?" Angel's voice was a whisper.

Steel hastily rose. He considered bolting sideways to fire on him. "You lied." He put another mag into his gun.

"Diego has my sister. The men here have orders to kill me. Lucas, their leader, needs to remain alive for hourly check-ins to California or Diego will do to my sister what he did to Marita."

"Who shot Morris?" Steel stepped quietly to the opposite side of the rock, his Glock level.

"Lucas. I tried to save him."

Steel didn't detect a lie but Angel was a pro. "Proposal?"

"We finish them here, capture Lucas, and take care of Diego."

"Why should I trust you?" Steel didn't.

"I just shot one of Lucas' men, and I'm coming out, guns lowered." Angel stepped out from the boulder, his barrels pointed at the ground. "Either shoot me or we help each other finish this. You will need me to find Diego. He has his ranch under a company name."

Gripping his Glock, Steel took off his night vision goggles, for once seeing the assassin without his smile. He stepped closer. "My people don't get hurt."

"I know who they are. I'll finish on the ridge here, you go below. Find Lucas. Leather coat, moustache. Keep him alive. Alert your people."

Steel's gut said, *Do it*. "Go."

Angel whirled and ran west, soon lost in the trees.

Steel ran hard, Christie's last words still in his ears. "I'm coming, Christie," he whispered into his mike. She didn't respond.

Panic. No one would be there for her and he was too far away. His training overtook his emotions and he wove in and out of the trees in a wild dash down the hill. Another figure appeared ahead of him in the trees. One of Diego's men.

Still, to be sure he whispered, "Signal."

The man didn't respond, instead whirling when he finally heard Steel's footfalls. It wasn't Lucas. Steel shot him twice on the run. At the barn he noted the three bodies near the door.

It was too risky to cross the clearing so he ran west along the hill, remaining inside the tree line.

Softly he called out, "Christie, Carlos, Wyatt. I'm coming in along the west side of the clearing. Mario, join Carlos. Angel is a friendly, I repeat, Angel is a friendly."

No one responded.

# CHAPTER 56

C LAY WANTED TO YELL. Instead he kept his mouth shut as he dropped through the air, landing hard on his feet. They slid out from under him, sending him into a tumbling roll for twenty feet into a pile of large rocks. His lower body hit them hard with a definitive *crack!*

He lay in a confused tangle of limbs and gulped for air. Moving his arms slowly, he could tell his left leg was at an odd angle. Surprised he had survived the fall, he didn't try to move his torso or legs.

He had lost the SIG and his night vision goggles.

He surveyed the slope above, unsure anyone could see him down here. Either way, they would come down along the side of the small cliff and find him soon enough. He wasn't going anywhere.

His rifle lay a dozen feet away. The SIG was a little closer. He tried to crawl toward it—and gasped. Sharp pain stabbed his leg. *Either suffer the pain or die.*

Rolling to his right side, he clawed at the dirt with his right hand and pushed with the heel of his right leg, inching himself toward the gun. Knifelike pain assaulted his leg. He gritted his teeth. Maybe he had a compound fracture. He definitely didn't want to see that.

Small rocks tumbled down the hill north of him. Someone was coming.

"I've got a broken leg and need help," he whispered.

No replies.

It took him a few seconds to realize he had lost his earpiece and throat mike too. The sound of falling rocks seemed closer. His outstretched hand was still three feet from the SIG. He pushed harder and reached for it, but a boot kicked the gun away.

He stared up. A stranger stood above him wearing night vision goggles and aiming a gun at his head.

A thump sounded. The man let out a weak gasp as he slowly slumped to his knees, and then fell forward over Clay's chest and head.

Clay gasped as the dead weight jerked his broken leg. Had to be Steel or Mario who had shot the man. That eased his nerves.

Another body slammed into the dirt just above him and rolled down into his injured leg. He groaned.

Working as quietly as possible, it was all he could do to move the body atop his face down to his chest so he could breathe a little easier. It didn't help that his left arm ached and was weak.

No one called to him. That worried him. He might have to get out of here on his own. But who had helped him? Maybe they didn't know he was down here. It seemed too risky to call out.

Rocks skittered not far away. He hoped it was someone friendly. He closed his eyes to feign death. In seconds the body lying over his leg was lifted off. Clay opened his eyes. A shadowy figure pulled the body off his chest too.

A familiar face loomed one foot above his.

A cold fear settled into Clay's stomach. *I'm finished. I'm sorry, Meera.* Fury replaced his fear. "Damn you."

"I probably am damned for how many I have killed." Angel stared down at him. "Steel and I have a truce. I'll let them know you are here, Clay."

Clay just gaped at him.

"I am sorry I killed your brother Dale."

Clay wanted to scream at the man. "I still want to kill you."

Angel nodded. "Sí. I understand. I would too if someone had killed my brother."

"Go to hell." He paused, swallowing hard. "If my sister dies here, I'll hunt you down."

"I will do my best to protect her, Clay." Angel disappeared into the darkness but tossed something against Clay's leg before he left.

Clay reached down and felt the SIG. He gripped it and held it against his chest. Settling back, he felt as if he had just climbed out of a snake pit without a scratch. It wasn't over. Steel and the others still had to win tonight. Then he could return to Meera and the boys. He would cheer over that later.

"You have more lives than a cat, Clay Thorton," he whispered.

The stars above him made him relax and allowed his thoughts to wander. He hadn't been able to protect Dale or Christie during Harry's kidnapping. Seeing Steel's overprotectiveness with Christie had helped him see it in himself a little differently too. It wasn't always good or noble. Like Christie had said, sometimes it was just arrogant.

He heaved a deep breath. Even if Christie lived, he wasn't sure what he would do the next time he saw Angel. The man had saved his life. Meera would tell him revenge wasn't healthy. And, crazy as it was, he couldn't deny feeling hopeful now that Angel was on their side.

A tear filled his eye. He still couldn't believe Dale was gone.

He hoped Christie was as lucky as he was. He couldn't take another loss.

# CHAPTER 57

CHRISTIE SAT AGAINST THE tree, waiting for the killers to reach her. She held the SIG in her left hand, the Rattler in her right. Keeping her attention fixed north, she would have to trust her ears for the guy coming from the east.

Hearing Steel's voice earlier had given her satisfaction and relief. However he was too far away to help her. That left Carlos to the east. She concluded Wyatt wasn't coming back. And Mario was too far away, like Clay. It bothered her that her brother hadn't responded either.

The killer to the north appeared near the edge of a tree trunk. The night vision goggles gave her just a glimpse. He had to be able to see that she was sitting. Trading the Rattler for the SIG in her left hand, she aimed at his shoulder and fired.

The man disappeared from sight.

*Soft footfalls?*

Before she could turn, a gun muzzle pressed into the left side of her head.

"Drop the guns."

Swallowing, she allowed both guns to slide from her hands.

"Put your arms up."

She obeyed. Her wrists were gripped hard by two men and she was dragged onto her back and through the woods. Her extended arms pulled on her bruised ribs and she gasped.

"We have her," said one of the men.

"Why are you dragging me south?" she asked. Steel would hear her and come, but she doubted he would be in time.

One of the men hit her with his gun butt and she lost consciousness.

# CHAPTER 58

JACK HEARD CHRISTIE'S MESSAGE. It tightened his jaw. He had no idea how many of the killers were left, or where they were, which made any tactical assessment practically useless. All he cared about was finding Christie.

The only reason he could come up with for Diego's men dragging her south was to cut her up like Marita before they killed her. A message to him, to make him suffer. He would never recover from it.

Skirting the west edge of the clearing, he ran hard. His Glock followed his pumping arms as he found the quickest path through the trees, simultaneously scanning for anyone ahead of him.

He almost ran past Wyatt.

His friend sat behind a large log, the Mossberg on his lap, his head hanging down. Stopping, Steel saw three bodies in the grass on the other side of the log. Wyatt had blood near his neck. An upper back wound.

Steel gently shook him, but Wyatt just mumbled, "Get her."

Sliding over the log, he ran faster, aiming southeast. He wondered about Carlos and Mario, who had both been radio silent for a while now. It didn't matter. As he ran it seemed as if the emotional weight of the last few days turned his legs to lead.

Dread and fear filled his mouth. He wanted to call out to her, to let her know he was coming. Tears would have filled his eyes if he stopped running.

By the time he saw the four figures they were mostly hidden by a clump of trees. He caught only snatches of them as he ran flat out, charging full speed.

A smoke canister erupted outside the cluster of trees, quickly hiding the figures.

"Stop now, Steel, or we put a bullet in her head." The voice came through his earpiece.

He stopped abruptly, his chest heaving. They had to be using Christie's radio gear. "What do you want?"

"Drive a vehicle down the driveway. Only you in it. Do as we say and we don't cut up her face. Take more than five minutes and we kill her in the worst way."

"Okay, I'll do it." The clearing was his only choice for their timetable so he aimed for it.

Running hard, he played out rescue scenarios in his head, unsure how to make one work. He didn't need to tell anyone what was happening. They would have heard Lucas as easily as he had.

A figure stepped out from a tree to his far right—and went down just as fast under rifle fire. Carlos.

Steel entered the dark meadow at a dead run. Lucas must have told his men to kill him if they could, or he was playing a game with him.

Halfway through the field another man stood up with a gun, and again went down just as fast.

He made it to the vehicles in the driveway, pulled out the keys for his, and got in. The rear-end fishtailed as he drove out of the large circular turnaround and south down the driveway. "I'm coming with the car, Lucas."

"We'll tell you when to stop. Be ready."

He looked at his Glock on the passenger seat. Nothing inventive came to him.

A half mile down the driveway came the order; "Stop!"

He braked hard, skidding to a halt on the east edge of the road.

"Open all the doors, driver's side last, toss your gun into the woods, and get into the trunk."

He reached over the front seat and pushed open the rear passenger door. Shoved open the front passenger door. Pulled the trunk release. Getting out on the driver's side, he held the Glock down by his leg. He kept the front door open and opened the rear driver's side passenger door.

Eyeing the woods across the road, he sidled to the back and opened the trunk wide. Stepping back, he kept the car between him and the trees. "I need to see her, and that you've let her go before I get into the trunk."

"No deal."

He took a chance. "Then shoot her and I'll be coming for you with my team. Yours is finished."

Four men appeared just inside the edge of the woods. Christie was propped up by two of them, her head hanging down and one leg dragging. Fear gripped him.

"All right, we compromise, Steel." They set her down with her back against a tree, her head hanging down. One of the men leaned over her. "Speak, so he knows you're alive."

"Don't do it, Jack." Christie's voice was strained.

The man straightened. Steel noted his leather coat and moustache. Lucas.

"Get into the trunk, Steel. We'll come out, you toss the gun away. Last chance."

There was no doubt in his mind that they planned to kill Christie no matter what he did. He glimpsed a flash of movement in the trees behind the killers. Climbing into the trunk, he knelt down, still able to see Christie. "Move out of the forest to the car," he said.

"Toss your gun first, Steel."

He dropped his gun to the ground near the trunk.

The men moved out of the trees, two of them stepping toward the front of the car. They would quickly be out of his field of vision. One of those men went down first, leaning forward and toppling as if shot in the back of the head. The other man flew forward, as if punched in the back.

Steel rolled out of the trunk, landing in a crouch. Picking up his gun, he fired at the man beside Lucas, sending him to the dirt. He straightened as Lucas turned to shoot Christie.

Angel slammed into Lucas from behind, knocking him to the ground on his stomach. The assassin stepped on Lucas' gun arm, forcing him to release his weapon, while keeping a foot on his back, his gun pointed at his head.

"Sloppy work, Lucas," said Angel. "I am disappointed."

Steel ran to Christie and knelt beside her, searching her face and eyes as she lifted her head.

Leaning forward, she weakly held him.

"You're siding with Steel?" spat Lucas. "The cartels will kill you for this."

Angel turned to Steel. "She is all right?"

"I am now," she whispered.

Steel picked her up in his arms and she rested her head on his shoulder. He looked at Angel. "How did you know?"

"I trained them. If it is too difficult to reach your target, then you take the target's prize." Angel grimaced. "Diego has mine."

"Clay?" Christie gazed at Angel, her voice weak.

Angel nodded to her. "A broken leg. I saved his life."

As strange as that seemed, Steel didn't care. He was relieved Christie and Clay were alive. One more job and the nightmare was over.

# PART 7

## OP:
## THE ALVAREZ CARTEL

# CHAPTER 59

CARLOS FOUND HIS SON. Mario had been shot early on, but the Kevlar had saved him, leaving him with a wound in his upper back. When he was shot he had fallen and hit his head, remaining unconscious for a few minutes and disoriented when he had come to.

Everyone helped carry the wounded to the clearing on makeshift stretchers, giving what first aid they could. Wyatt was barely conscious, but he managed to wink once at Steel. Steel could never repay what the man had done for him.

Clay was in pain, but glad to see them, and glad to learn Christie was alive. He held her hand while she sat next to him.

Clay also confirmed, grudgingly, that Angel had saved his life. It made Steel respect Angel's word more, but he wouldn't leave him alive after they killed Diego.

Mario, Wyatt, Christie, and Clay would wait in the field for the medevac helicopter Colonel Jeffries was sending. The colonel was also sending a cleanup crew for the bodies.

When Carlos first saw Angel, he glared at him, raising his rifle. Angel raised his Glocks.

Steel stepped between them, facing Carlos. "We need Angel, like it or not."

His face taut, Carlos hesitated but then walked away.

They took what weapons and ammo they needed out of the armory safe, including a Kevlar vest for Angel, and closed the tunnels, safe, and barn. They left the bodies of Diego's men where they had fallen. They were all accounted for.

Angel sat in the car with Lucas, while Steel walked away from the others and called Jeffries again to fill him in.

"Angel wants a clean slate for his help killing Diego. He also wants to know if you're going to honor the agreement for the ISIS attack." Steel waited, already knowing the answer.

"He killed four of my men," snapped Jeffries. "I'm glad he helped us out, but my men are going to pick him up when they get your wounded."

"We can't do this without him. Unless you want Diego funding more ISIS actions, we need Angel." He paused. "Did General Morris make it?"

"General Morris woke up. He said Angel tried to save him, but that doesn't change things." Jeffries was silent a few moments. "Angel gets a chance to redeem himself by helping you kill Diego. But then he's ours. Where are you going?"

"California. He wouldn't say where."

Jeffries' tone was terse. "I expect a call as soon as you know."

Steel hung up, deciding not to say anything to Angel. He left the burner phone with Christie and took another from Wyatt's armory. He didn't want Jeffries tracking him.

Lucas made a check-in call to Diego on speaker before they left, telling him that Angel was dead and that he was bringing Steel to him in Angel's car.

Angel held a knife to Lucas' throat while he talked. Lucas was told beforehand that if things went well, they would let him live. Steel didn't think anyone, including Lucas, believed that. But when facing death it was natural that you grasped at any opportunity to stay alive.

Diego told Lucas that he didn't have to call again until he was an hour away.

Angel drove his Chevy SS, with Carlos in the front passenger seat. Steel sat in back with Lucas, who had his hands zip-tied behind his back, zip ties on his ankles, and his seat belt on. Duct tape covered his mouth.

Steel remained silent, thinking of Christie. Tears had rolled down her cheeks because she worried he wouldn't survive the last assault. Her injury left no room for debate about her coming. He wouldn't have allowed it anyway.

He had said goodbye, leaving no doubt that they were through. His ex-wife, Carol, had paid a price while he was in Blackhood Ops, but Christie's price had been even higher.

Still a pain had settled into his chest. He had to ignore it if he wanted to function at the level needed for what was coming.

They had a sixteen–hour ride ahead of them to Diego's ranch in northern California and would arrive sometime after ten p.m.

Carlos broke the silence an hour into the trip. He turned to Angel. "You're driving fast. You want to get there early."

Angel nodded. "Yes. An hour early so we have an edge. Diego is paranoid and will be ready far ahead of time. Every advantage will help."

Carlos pulled out his Glock and rested it on his lap, aiming it at Angel. "You're a killer and deserve to die."

Angel remained quiet as he drove, watching the road.

Steel stiffened. "We need him, Carlos. We'll never find Diego in time on our own. Our families will be at risk."

"I have a hard time looking at you, Angel." Carlos said it matter-of-factly. "You killed my son, Juan, as if he was nothing."

"There was no honor in what I did." Angel sat back. "My parents were killed by the cartel for not selling their farm to them when I was ten years old. And I ended up joining the cartel as a young man. I think my anger made me feel violence was justified."

Angel sighed. "I didn't participate in Marita's death, and I am glad I didn't hurt Isabella. I began to feel during this vendetta that I couldn't do this work anymore, but unfortunately my realization was not in time for Juan."

For another minute Carlos kept the gun aimed at him, and then put it away. He was silent and didn't speak for a long time.

They took turns driving and sleeping.

Twelve hours later Angel was again behind the wheel, driving, and Carlos asked, "Who are you trying to save?"

"My sister, Renata. She's confined to a wheelchair and depends on me. She has no one else. I took a risk having Lucas tell Diego I was dead, because he might kill her."

Carlos looked out his window. "My son, Pedro, is going to live, so I am going to put this vendetta business away. But if I ever see you again, I cannot promise that I will not kill you. I bear some of the responsibility for bringing my children into this, and now I just want it over. If Diego and his men and their vendetta die today, then I will have to live with Juan's death. Killing you will never bring my dear son back to me."

Angel grimaced. "I will have to live with knowing I have deprived you of someone you loved as much as I love Renata."

Steel said grudgingly, "You tried to save General Morris."

Angel spoke softly. "Sí. But I failed there too."

Steel leaned back. "Our military informed me that General Morris lived. His mother was killed."

Angel lifted his chin. "Then that gives me some satisfaction."

Steel didn't want to say his next words, but felt Carlos needed to hear them. He didn't want him to put a bullet into Angel before they took Diego. "You saved Clay and Christie today."

"A debt to pay for killing their brother." Angel glanced at Steel in the rearview mirror. "Your military will hunt me, correct?"

"They'll wait until after we hit Diego."

"I expected as much." Angel tapped the steering wheel. "I offer you this, Carlos. If Renata dies today, you can kill me. I will have no heart to go on."

Carlos stared at him, and then turned away. "Then I would be just like you. I think it's better if your ghosts haunt you." He paused. "Let's be honest. None of us trust each other."

No one contradicted him.

Angel was silent for a half hour, and then he glanced over his shoulder at Steel. "I am jealous of you, Steel. You have a courageous woman that loves you, and you live a life of honor. That is something to treasure."

Unable to answer, Steel remained silent. Angel's words caused more pain than he expected.

"I had a wife that loved me," said Carlos. "She was always under threat from the cartels when I worked in Colombia, but she accepted the risk. Ironically she died from cancer and not a bullet."

Steel leaned forward. "How did you handle that, putting her in constant danger?"

"It was her choice to love me and stay with me, and I couldn't dishonor her wishes."

*** 

Diego's ranch was north of Hopland, a small town in northern California. Angel explained it was a vineyard and horse ranch of two-hundred-fifty acres, including a ten-thousand-square-foot villa, a guest house, pool house, and worker buildings.

Angel continued. "He also owns the surrounding land so he has complete privacy. The driveway into the villa is on the north end, but a dirt road exits the property on the south end too. There is an outdoor horse arena there. That's where Diego takes his enemies for sport."

Steel didn't like it. The situation wasn't contained and provided too many opportunities for someone to escape.

When they left San Francisco, heading north, Angel said, "We're an hour early so we don't need Lucas to check in with Diego." He paused. "I have a plan."

"You know Diego's setup," said Steel. "What do you recommend?"

"The Russian River flows along the back of his property, with trees on either side of it. Right across from the villa at this time of year it is low, easy to cross. There's a farm service road on the other side of the river that parallels it. We drop you off there, Steel, then Carlos on the south side of the vineyard. I will leave the car on the dirt road leading into the north driveway and go in on foot from there.

"I know the routine of the guards and can make sure none escape out front. Diego will have at least twenty men. If even one of these men get out, you and your families and me and Renata will be hunted forever. Kill anyone on the grounds. No one here is innocent."

Carlos scoffed at him. "Does that include migrant workers, maids...whoever we find?"

Angel didn't hesitate. "Workers will not be on the grounds now. Diego will have sent everyone home that is not part of his organization. So yes, anyone there should be killed."

Carlos faced forward. "I do not kill the innocent."

Steel was glad to hear Carlos voice his own values but kept that to himself. He would reach the villa first, which put more pressure on him to save Angel's sister. He wasn't sure he wanted that responsibility.

Angel lifted his chin to him. "I trust you, Steel. Whatever happens, no one is to blame. I let Diego capture Renata."

Carlos grunted. "Let's do it."

Angel stopped on a dirt road. "We're here."

The river was visible to the west. There was a full moon with some clouds still blocking most of the light. Steel got out, needing to stretch and yawn to wake up. Carlos and Angel did the same.

Angel opened up the trunk and dragged Lucas out of the car. They took the weapons bag out, shoved Lucas into the trunk, and shut it.

Steel grabbed a SIG, a Glock, and a Rattler, all silenced, with extra mags that he stuffed into his coat pockets, along with a night vision monocular. He gestured to the car trunk. "Lucas?"

Angel shook his head. "We'll kill him on the property, not here." He turned to Carlos. "You should know that Lucas and his men participated in defiling and killing your niece. His death is in your hands."

Carlos' eyes narrowed. "You waited to tell me to make sure I wouldn't kill him earlier."

"Sí." He turned to Steel. "Wait until you hear us draw their fire."

"Will do." Steel gripped the Glock and Rattler and hurried off the road.

Angel drove away with Carlos.

Crouching, Steel ran across a short field, heading toward the thick tree line along the river. Once there, he moved from tree to tree, using the monocular to see if Diego had guards this far east of the villa. None were visible. He spotted a gravel sandbar, where the river narrowed and appeared passable.

Taking off his shoes and socks, he rolled up his pants. A Western screech-owl gave its accelerating *bouncing-ball* call in a series of short hoots. He couldn't spot it in the trees around him.

A normal life.

One more job.

He hurried down the short bank and into the river. Only a foot deep and moving slow, it was still cool. After walking through twenty feet of water he reached the sandbar. Hurrying up the opposing river bank and into the tree line, he sat there to put on his socks and shoes.

Twenty feet away, on the shore of the river a raccoon was washing something in the water.

Rising in a crouch, Steel peered west. The villa was a white silhouette four hundred yards away. Remaining low, he ran through rows of grapevines to a small grove of trees. On the other side of the trees a strip of grass lawn ran up to the rear patio of the Mediterranean-styled villa.

He spotted two guards, two hundred feet apart, on the north and south corners of the villa. They would be able to see each other, and alert everyone if one went down. It bothered him that only two guards were stationed out back. If Diego was truly paranoid, two guards didn't fit the scenario of a villa on high alert. The south guard was closest and carried an AK-47.

Dropping to one knee, he scanned the surrounding area for any hidden guards. He spotted one above the north guard, standing in the shadows of a second-story balcony alcove. Moving from tree to tree, he stopped twenty feet from the north corner guard. From his vantage point he could see the balcony guard too.

However there was no clear shot through the trees to the south corner guard. He would have to take the balcony guard first. North guard second, south last.

Keeping his back to a tree, he listened for a sign that Angel or Carlos had begun their assault.

# CHAPTER 60

CARLOS CROUCHED, THE M40 held in both hands. The field had a slight downward slope so he had a good view of the villa a quarter mile away. It also meant he would be visible should someone look in his direction.

He ran between grapevine rows until he was a quarter mile farther in. Then he knelt, keeping his head just below the vines. The scent of rich dirt filled his nostrils. Angel had asked him to wait ten minutes before he attacked.

All around him clumps of deep purple grapes hung thick on the vines in large clusters. He picked one grape and tasted it, the juice tart in his mouth.

Considering how much his children's lives would be affected if he failed, he was determined to kill Diego. Diego and Lucas were also the last of the men who had tortured and killed Marita.

To think that he was working with the assassin who had killed Juan seemed sick to him, but without Angel, he and Steel would not succeed. They needed the killer's skills and knowledge of Diego. He would put a bullet in Angel later tonight.

He checked his watch. It was time.

Using the rifle's night vision scope, he surveyed the north driveway leading up to the estate and the area around the front of the villa. Six men. He swung the scope away from the house, south along the river frontage road to the horse stables and arena. No one.

He heard noise from the north driveway and angled his rifle back along the way he had swung it. Halfway across the field, he stopped abruptly.

A man was kneeling in the vineyard, a hundred yards from him, aiming a rifle in the direction of the driveway. Carlos shot him once in the back, and the man went down.

Swinging the rifle toward the house, he was alarmed. The men he had seen earlier had disappeared. They would have heard the shot, but it seemed unlikely that they all had reacted that fast. He needed to get closer.

Rising slightly, but remaining in a crouch, he zigzagged toward the villa. Stopping approximately where he had shot the man, he knelt, checking up and down the rows of vines. The man had disappeared. A sinking feeling in his gut matched his tense limbs.

Five men stood up in the field around him, aiming guns at him.

"Drop the gun."

Knowing they were going to kill him, he ignored the command. Deciding who to kill first, he planned to fall on his back and start shooting.

A sharp electrical sensation hit his legs and the rifle slid from his hands. He dropped to the ground, realizing he had been Tasered. They were on him in seconds, hitting and kicking him until he lost consciousness.

***

A quarter mile from the north driveway, Angel parked the Chevy SS on the side of the road. Grapevines grew south of the road, a line of large oak trees on the north side.

Opening his door, he got out, immediately spying the toe of a boot sticking out from behind a tree. It was quickly pulled out of sight. He understood what was coming, but there was nothing he could do.

A dozen men slipped out of the shadows of the trees, and out of the vineyard, all aiming guns at him.

Raising his hands, he smiled and said, "Tell Diego I have a gift for him in the trunk."

They approached him quickly, taking the keys out of his hands. Leaving the trunk of his car closed, they herded him into the back bed of a pickup truck and made him lie facedown. He was aware of someone driving the Chevy SS behind them.

Lucas must have tipped off Diego in the check-in call. However the fact that they had left Lucas in the trunk suggested Diego had other information too. From Renata? He had no idea what she had said to Diego, but he doubted he or his sister would live to see the morning.

What saddened him most was that he had failed Renata. She would never have a chance at a new life, free of violence and sick men. Ironically, until recently he had been one of those sick men.

# CHAPTER 61

S TEEL WATCHED AS THE pickup truck, loaded with men, swept around the curve in the road a hundred feet south of the house. It headed away from him, south along the river. Some men in the truck were firing guns into the air.

Angel's Chevy SS and two SUVs followed. It suggested they had captured Angel, and perhaps Carlos too. He had to move fast to take advantage of the gunfire.

Keeping the Glock in his right hand, the Rattler in his left, he waited for the guard to stroll past him to the north so his back would be to him. Striding out of the trees, he aimed at the balcony guard and shot him the same moment the guard spotted him. Pivoting, he put a bullet into the turning north corner guard. Dropping the Glock, he went to one knee, brought up the Rattler, and fired a quick burst at the south guard who was turning toward him.

The guard fell dead.

Picking up the Glock, he ran around the north side of the villa, gun extended. There was only one guard, running toward him, his rifle facing sideways. Steel shot him twice, and then stopped in front of the villa and knelt. Using the monocular scope, he scrutinized the nearby beach house, the driveway all the way west—what little he could see through the bordering trees—and the northern vineyards.

He swung the monocular along the same path in reverse and saw movement far out in the southern vineyard. A group of men were dragging someone toward the stopped pickup truck. Had to be Carlos. Diego's men were still shooting off guns. But even if they hadn't heard his shots, they would check in with the villa guards soon.

He hurried to the front door. Unlocked.

Striding inside, he already guessed what he would find. He needed to be sure. A high ceiling, tiled floor, chandelier, large paintings, and decorative furniture gave the entryway an image of refinement. The complete opposite image of the crude and brutal Diego.

On the far end of the room was the back door. To the right a large open stairway led up to a short, second-floor balcony that connected hallways on either side. Moving across the large entryway, he stopped even with the central corridor and checked left and right.

Right led to the kitchen. A soft ceiling light lit up a massive butcher block. At the end of the left hallway he saw another larger room, which was also half-lit.

Going left, he kept close to one side of the hallway, pointing the Glock ahead of him. Closed doors appeared on both sides in the corridor. He moved past them, speedily reaching the end, where he peered around the corner. Another large room, empty except for expensive sofas and high-backed chairs.

The corridor continued on the other side of it to another darkened part of the villa. He went faster then, through all the rooms on the first floor, ignoring the kitchen, then up the stairs and through the second floor.

All empty.

He ran down the stairs, stopping abruptly at the bottom, detecting movement at the end of the corridor leading to the kitchen. A man and woman in their thirties stood side by side, facing him. Striding toward them, gun raised, he saw they were unarmed. "Who are you?"

"Cook and maid," said the man.

He had to kill them. Leaving even one person alive meant the cartel might come after their families. Had they heard anything about Angel? Had they listened to Diego talking about him? His finger tightened on the trigger.

The cook wrapped his arms around the maid and they both closed their eyes. "Please, señor."

Remembering Angel's words, he felt conflicted over the possibility of shooting someone who was innocent. In the end he couldn't live with it and backed away from them into the entryway room.

Glancing at the front door and opposite corridor, he hurried to the back door. In the glass door he saw reflections. He hurled himself to the right, twisting and falling to his back as he raised his Glock and fired. Glass shattered above his head.

It was the cook and maid, both holding guns. He shot them multiple times.

After staring at their crumpled bodies, he rose and hurried out the back door and ran for the trees bordering the river. Once among them he ran as hard as he could, paralleling the frontage dirt road.

A quarter mile down he reached the next set of buildings, which appeared to serve as storage for equipment. Gunshots to the south made him run harder.

He wasn't going to be able to do anything unless he was willing to die. He owed his life to his daughter Rachel more than to Angel or Carlos. Still, if Diego lived the cartel leader would hunt his family, Christie's, and hire terrorists.

Letting it go, he settled into a smooth rhythm of flying legs and arms.

Another shot.

He passed a gun range that was empty. But it would explain away any shots that even distant neighbors happened to hear.

In another hundred yards, stables and a corral appeared. The arena was thirty yards farther south. It was easily big enough for rodeo and riding competitions. A distant line of trees to the south and west further isolated it from prying eyes.

A few small trees grew a short distance from the corners of the arena providing shade, along with two roofed wooden stands on the west corners. One of the stands looked big enough for a small band. The other had a grilling station.

On the east side, closer to him, was a large viewing stage for an audience. It had three open sides, a roof, and was three feet above the ground.

High outdoor lamps lit the arena.

He hid behind a tree, counting ten of Diego's men standing around the arena's three-board, five-foot-high fence. All armed with pistols, shotguns, or AK-47s. The audience on the stage was hidden to him. But if Diego was as paranoid as Angel said, he would have the rest of his men surrounding him there.

Without hesitating he ran across the bare ground to the closest clump of trees adjacent to the arena's northeast corner. Risky, but he needed to see more if he was going to do anything. Shadows and the night gave him cover.

He reached the trees and no shouts arose, so he examined the stage. Diego stood in the middle of it, smiling, a microphone in his hand. Ten men—five on either side of him—all held machine guns.

Scanning the fence, Steel now counted a dozen men. Two had been standing in the shadows of the corners.

A black tarp covered something in the arena's southeast corner.

Carlos lay in the center of the arena on his back. Angel stood close to him, facing the stage. Lucas knelt in front of them, also facing the stage, his wrists and ankles still bound with zip ties, his mouth taped.

What bothered Steel most was Angel's sister.

Renata sat in a wheelchair, twenty feet to the left of Angel. The lighting showed off her long dark hair and her beautiful face with delicately chiseled features. Her body seemed thin and frail in the chair. A simple but elegant dress covered her from her neck to her ankles. She was staring at Angel, her face taut.

Another shot rang out as one of the men along the fence targeted the dirt near Angel's feet. Angel didn't flinch and ignored the shooter, while staring at the stage.

As Steel watched, Angel flicked his left pinkie up and down three times, as if he was signaling him. That Angel had spotted him was impressive, but Steel had no idea what the man thought he could do.

Kobayashi Maru. *Stay calm, assess options, look for a solution.*

Diego held up a hand, his amplified voice cutting through the silence. "My arena tonight is filled with champions and traitors, but only one of you will survive."

He gestured to Angel. "You made Lucas tell me he was returning with Steel. Why? To put me off guard? And then you bring in an old man with poor skills to help you."

Diego shook his head. "And Lucas, when you told me Angel was dead, I had no use for his sister anymore. I was going to carve her up and have some fun, but then she told me her secret, and why Angel always had so much success."

"I knew my brother was alive." Renata glanced at Diego. "Just as I understood that Lucas had betrayed you."

Diego smiled at Angel. "I was right, you did have an angel watching out for you all these years. I asked Renata to prove herself, and she told me about the betrayal Lucas was planning. After a few hours of talking with Antonio's son, her words proved true. I would have forgiven you if you had simply returned with Lucas, but you betrayed me too."

Angel waved derisively at Carlos. "I never brought this man. When Lucas called you, he thought his men had killed me, but I killed Steel and captured the traitor to bring to you. Why would I risk my sister's life? And do you really think I would bring an old fool to help me fight you?"

"That did puzzle me." Diego lifted his chin to Carlos. "Who are you, old man?"

"None of your business." Carlos said it softly, but with defiance.

Diego's eyes narrowed and he smiled. "Carlos Aguilar. The man who sent Steel to kill Garcia and my brother, Vincente. I did some checking. Steel, our cartel, Colombians. It was an easy puzzle. Trying to avenge Gustavo's whore, Marita. We will take our time with you and you will die slowly over many days. With Lucas."

The drug lord pointed a finger at Angel. "Perhaps I was too hasty in judging you, Angel. But we will have to talk about how the Americans were able to stop all the terrorist attacks too."

Lucas wagged his head as if he wanted to talk.

Steel got ready, not thinking, just reacting.

Diego gave an order in Spanish. One of his men slipped through the fence and walked into the arena without a gun. He pulled the tape off Lucas' mouth, stepped back, and waited.

"That is why I gave you the warning in the check-in call." Lucas spoke forcefully. "Angel is the one who wants to kill you, Diego."

"I know Angel is very skilled, but are you saying he was going to kill all of us by himself?" Diego chuckled and looked at his men on the stage. A few of his men smiled with him.

Diego gave another order, and in the southeast corner a man pulled the black tarp off what it was hiding. A bloodied corpse tied to the fence. "Antonio's son supported Renata's claims, Lucas, and your betrayal."

"Steel is here!" Lucas jerked his head north. "Have you talked to your house guards recently?"

Diego frowned and gave an order to one of his men, who brought out a phone and made a call.

Steel lifted the Rattler, aiming it for the center of the stage. Remembering Angel's signal, he reconsidered and took out the SIG and Glock. Risky. And something he had never practiced before. But he wanted all of these men dead and he needed help.

Diego's man on the stage lowered the phone and shook his head.

All eyes were on Diego, who glared at Angel. Diego turned back to the guard. "Try again."

The man put the phone on speaker, the ringing audible.

Gripping the gun barrel of the Glock, Steel tossed it as high as he could between the trunks of two trees, out over the arena, toward Angel and Carlos. He immediately tossed the SIG too. Angel and Carlos would have roughly three dozen bullets between them. It would have to do.

Steel strode toward the stage, the Rattler leveled. The fence gave him some cover and walking instead of running gave him a few more seconds before someone noticed him. He glimpsed Angel striding casually for the guns, catching them in midair and tossing one to Carlos.

Steel shot the closest two men on the fence in the back and then ran in a crouch. He fired at Diego, but the drug lord had already ducked behind his men. Three of the guards closest to Diego went down.

Steel tried to follow Diego with his gunfire, but the cartel leader had ducked behind a podium.

The guards on the stage scattered, raising guns to fire back, forcing him to forget about Diego and spray across the stage as he ran for cover.

Something punched him in the back. He stumbled to the side of the stage, wondering if the bullet had pierced his Kevlar.

Hoping to minimize the number of guards that could shoot at him, he knelt there. Guards on the far end of the stage had their own men in their line of fire. Steel loaded another magazine. Lifting the gun just above the stage floor, he fired without looking, hoping to hit the legs of the remaining men.

Guards shouted and fell with *thumps*! Steel pressed the trigger until the Rattler was empty.

He risked a quick glance above the stage floor. Diego had disappeared. The door in the back of the stage was cracked open. Four of Diego's men were upright, cautiously advancing toward him. Two in front of the stage, two hugging the back wall. They all fired at him.

Bullets chewed the edge of the stage.

Dropping the gun and ducking, Steel glanced at the arena. Shots were coming from all sides.

Carlos was kneeling and firing at guards. He took a hit, wobbling. Angel ducked, twisted, and crouched, moving from his feet to his knees as he shot Diego's men. Jumping protectively in front of Renata's chair, he jerked back as if he'd taken a bullet in the chest, but he managed to stay upright.

Lucas was trying to hop across the arena on his bound feet. Carlos whirled and shot him in the legs, sending him to the ground.

The three of them weren't going to be enough, but Steel wanted Diego. He heard boots on the stage. Frantically he crawled to the side wall as fast as he could. To the east he spotted someone running into the trees.

There was a crash of splintering wood as if someone had broken through the arena fence. Simultaneously Rattler staccato erupted. *Jeffries?*

Steel rose, flattening himself against the building wall. One of Diego's guards jumped off the stage, swinging his gun toward him. Before Steel could move, the man collapsed in a heap at his feet. He picked up the man's AK-47, and looked at the arena.

Carlos lifted his chin to him. "Get Diego!"

Steel ran, his legs flying, chasing the shadow he had spotted entering the trees by the river. Unsure what direction Diego would flee in, he aimed himself in one possible intercept course. He remained in the shadows, preferring the dark.

Pumping his legs hard, he watched the trees and brush, while listening for any telltale sounds.

A slight sound to the right.

Steel ducked behind a tree, rounding it fast.

Diego stood on the other side, gun in hand. To avoid taking a bullet, Steel veered into the drug lord, knocking him into the tree trunk. He blocked Diego's gun hand with his rifle, but Diego had a knife in his other hand and swiped it at his right arm, cutting it.

Dropping the AK-47, Steel tried to stiff-arm Diego's neck. Diego dropped his gun to block his strike and kicked at his knees.

Stepping out, Steel drew his OTF knife and swiped at Diego's neck. Diego bent back and drew a second knife. The cartel leader smiled at him, and then attacked with a series of stabs and slashes. Steel hastily retreated. Diego was very fast with his hands, but his footwork was slower and less practiced.

When Diego paused, Steel rushed him and slashed his left arm.

Diego dropped one knife but attacked again.

Retreating in a circle, Steel waited for the man to tire. When Diego's movements slowed, he rolled to the side, slashed the cartel lord's ankle and then rolled away.

Diego pursued him, limping.

Steel rose and stepped away from a wild swing by Diego. He managed to slash the man's wrist. Diego gasped and dropped the knife, stumbling back, bleeding and limping.

Steel bent over and picked up Diego's gun.

Diego held up a hand. "I can get you millions. Whatever you want."

Steel pulled the mask off his face. "All I want is peace. This is for Marita and Dale." He shot Diego in the heart and head, and the cartel leader collapsed.

Breathing hard, he stood over the man who had caused so much misery. He wanted to shout or curse, but he was too weary.

Silence. No more gunshots.

Dropping the pistol, he picked up the AK-47 and ran toward the arena, unsure what he would find. He stopped just before the stage.

In the center of the arena Angel carried Renata in his arms. The assassin strode toward the north fence, in the direction of his parked Chevy SS.

Near the fence Steel was surprised to see Mario. Carlos leaned against his son with one of his arms wrapped around his son's shoulders. Carlos stood over Lucas, who stared up at him.

"You deserve much more than this." Carlos shot him in the head. He then turned to Angel. "Stop!" He fired a bullet into the ground by Angel's feet.

Angel stopped and slowly turned to face Carlos, looking resigned. His left hand had blood on it, and the front of his shirt had a hole in it; the vest had saved his life.

Steel aimed his gun at Carlos. A flash of anger erupted in his throat and he wanted to shout at both of them. Carlos had nearly sent Christie to her death twice, and caused both of them hell, and he and Angel were responsible for Dale's death. He remembered his promise to Clay. He didn't trust either man.

Carlos didn't look at Steel, but he asked, "Diego?"

"Dead." Steel tightened his finger on the trigger.

Carlos glanced at him. "I saved your life in the meadow at Wyatt's, Steel. And here."

Steel swallowed as Mario stared at him, holding his gaze. A son who would lose his father. He had to let it go.

Footsteps sounded on the stage and he turned, gun ready.

Limping around the corner into view, Christie appeared, her eyes wide and face taut. Shocked, his thoughts racing, Steel swung his gun to Angel.

Christie followed his gaze and limped down the front steps, her machine gun pointed first at Carlos, and then Angel.

"You all want to kill me." Angel lifted his chin. "I saved Clay's life. I saved Christie's life. I spared Isabella and Harry." He looked at all of them. "If you kill me, then you have the burden of taking care of my sister, who has no one else."

"Put her down, you coward," spat Carlos.

"I am just as responsible for your son's death." Renata looked at Carlos, and then Christie. "And for your brother's death. Kill me first. Because if you kill my brother, I don't have a reason to live anymore." She stared at them defiantly. "We have killed, but we want out. Kill us both or let us go."

"Papá?" Mario said it softly.

Carlos' gun wavered as he stared at Angel and Renata. His hand slowly fell to his side. "Go," he whispered.

Steel looked at Renata, wondering if two killers could find redemption too. Who was he to decide? He lowered his gun.

"You both deserve to die." Christie fired a burst for three seconds.

Steel stared, but Angel and Renata remained standing. Christie had fired above their heads.

Lowering her gun, she waved them off. "I'm tired of killing."

Angel bowed to her, and then whirled and strode to his Chevy SS.

Steel thought allowing a cartel assassin to escape as crazy as everything else that had happened. But he could live with it.

Christie dropped her gun and limped into his arms, holding him tightly, her voice cracking. "If you say goodbye to me again, Jack, I won't return. It's my choice to stay with you. Not yours. You have to let me own it."

"I know," he said softly.

"Did you really think I was going to let you do this alone?" she whispered.

"How?"

"I asked Angel where the ranch was while you talked to Jeffries. Jeffries got us to San Francisco, where we rented a car. We entered the front driveway, saw the lights of the arena, and came back down to the south drive."

He kissed her cheek. "Your leg?"

"A medic on the airplane gave me pain killers and taped it."

"You might have ruined it."

"I'll live." She paused, still holding him tightly. "I get your life and accept it, whatever it brings. I'm not Carol, Jack."

"No, you're not. You're stronger than me, honey." The ache in his chest released and he heaved a deep breath. He understood fully now why Angel was jealous, and what Carlos once had with his wife.

The vendetta was over. Retribution could end. The killing could stop. All of it gave him such relief that he sagged in her arms.

They held each other like that for a while longer, and then Steel called Jeffries on speaker and filled him in.

"We owe you one, Steel." Jeffries' voice hardened. "I want you to hold Angel for us."

"We're beat up and he took off."

"I can make your life hell, Steel."

"I've had hell for nearly a week, colonel. I served up ISIS and Diego, and we all suffered losses. I don't work for you." He hung up.

Christie stood beside him, an arm around his waist. "You have a good heart and it's finally mine. Right?"

"One hundred percent." He smiled at her. For the first time in nearly a week it felt real again.

# CHAPTER 62

ANGEL ROSE OFF THE chair and threw his towel over his shoulders. After a late morning swim in the ocean he had dried off. And he had enough sun. The beauty surrounding him in sparkling water and waving palm trees did wonders for his spirit.

Walking across the white sand, he was soon inside the rental house. He poured himself a glass of lemon water from a pitcher in the refrigerator and sat down on a rattan chair, waiting for Renata's massage to end. Body work was a necessity for her due to her limited movement. He hoped the new therapist was good.

In minutes the bedroom door opened.

The Filipina therapist, Jasmine, pushed Renata out in her chair. Jasmine had long black hair and an athletic body covered with white shorts and a collared light blue blouse. Late thirties.

Renata wore a yellow silk robe that covered her body. She beamed at him. "She is fantastic, Angel!"

He smiled and stood, feeling a little self-conscious in his bathing suit, even though it went to his knees. Taking a hundred-dollar bill off the counter, he handed it to Jasmine. "Anyone who makes my sister happy makes me happy."

Jasmine smiled. "Renata is easy to please and I am happy to help her." She rested a hand on Renata's shoulder. "I'll come back in two days for your next appointment. And please consider what I said."

Renata lifted her hand slightly. "I don't need to think about it. I accept."

"Wonderful." Jasmine smiled at Angel and left.

Angel found himself watching her. She had a graceful stride, natural and not forced. He turned back to Renata. "What did you accept?"

"Her uncle is a well-known qigong healer in the Philippines and has seen tumors like mine respond to his treatments." She cocked her head. "We've tried a lot of things, Angel, but I have a good feeling about this. Maybe not that I will be able to walk, but perhaps my body can have more strength."

He shrugged, not wanting to get her hopes up. "Why not? When do we leave for the Philippines?"

Her eyes sparkled. "That's the beauty of it. Her uncle is coming here for three months."

"Perfect." He filled another glass of lemonade. "Thirsty?"

"Sí."

He brought her the glass, which she gripped in her right hand, still strong enough to hold it.

She winked at him.

"What?" He chuckled and sat down.

"Jasmine and you have many things in common, Angel."

He stared into his glass. "Renata, my history is not something I wish to talk about with anyone."

"Jasmine has a bad history too. She told me some of it. I think you both are ready to start over. There's no need for either of you to talk about the past."

Her love for him made him warm inside, and he wondered if it was truly possible to put his past behind him and have love in his life. "I have much to atone for, Renata."

"We both do, Angel. I helped you, remember?"

"How do we recover from it?"

She lifted her chin to him. "We help those in need."

He raised an eyebrow. "Doing what?"

She smiled. "Think on it. I'm sure you'll find a way for both of us."

He rose, fluidly crossing the stone floor to her and bending down to kiss her forehead. "You always make me feel anything is possible, dear sister. Thank you."

Renata laughed. "That's because it is, dear brother."

# CHAPTER 63

THE CHURCH WAS FILLED to capacity with seven hundred people.

Steel held Christie's hand, as she held Harry's. Christie's whole family formed an unbroken line across the pew. Each family member said a few words about Dale; his life, his spirit, and his easy laughter.

Through all of it Steel witnessed more fully what a close-knit family Christie had, and how much they loved each other. It still hurt to think that his life had disrupted that harmony and brought such pain and loss. He mourned for Dale too.

\*\*\*

Across the room, Carol was chatting with Mr. and Mrs. Thorton, who were both fit, slender, and in their seventies. The Thortons were allowing all of them to stay at their ranch house in Montana.

Steel had given them his condolences for Dale, and both of them had welcomed him with open arms. It had eased his guilt.

His gaze drifted to Isabella. She was talking to Clay, who sat in a lounge chair by the dining table with his broken leg propped up. Clay had a cast from his ankle to his thigh. His wife, Meera, sat beside him, her hand on his shoulder as the three of them chatted. Clay's boys were outside.

Steel wondered if Carlos had found some peace knowing his daughter was safe and happy, and that Mario and Pedro could live their lives in peace too.

Isabella had talked to him again about Marita and forgiven him. Her words had somehow allowed him to forgive himself. For the first time in a year he had several nights of sleep without her face haunting his dreams.

Colonel Jeffries had called him days ago, informing him that they had interrupted the bomb attack at Walt Disney World. An alert citizen had listened to the news release of expected terrorism and called about suspicious neighbors. Jeffries had actually thanked Steel.

The colonel had also relayed that General Morris had asked how he and Christie were doing. It all made him feel good.

"What do you think of Isabella, Jack?" Harry sat alongside him in an easy chair, his right arm in a sling. His shirt hid the stitches in his left arm.

Steel smiled. "She has a good heart, Harry. I'm happy for you." They were all healing, in more ways than one. He had stitches on his arm where Diego had cut him.

"I'm not saying we're going to get married, but it feels right." Harry cocked his head at him. "Strange how things work out, isn't it?"

"I think it's wonderful, Harry." Christie sat on the other side of Steel, also in an easy chair. Her lower leg was bandaged and crutches leaned against the wall. "I wanted to kill her at one point and now I might have a new sister-in-law."

She reached over, and Steel took her hand and smiled.

Harry turned serious. "I think of Dale all the time. See him smiling when I walk into rooms. But he isn't there."

"I see him all the time too, Harry," Christie said softly.

"I'm sorry." Steel had said those words a hundred times to Harry's parents and family.

Harry shook his head. "It wasn't your fault, Jack."

Harry's eyes and voice were sincere, and Steel believed him. Christie squeezed his hand.

"It wasn't yours either," he said to Harry.

Harry sighed, and then smiled broadly. "Christie had a smack-down talk with all of us about her professed love for you, Jack, and that we better leave it alone."

"Did she?" He eyed Christie, who blushed.

Harry continued talking. "I'm the last one who should point fingers, when I'm half-crazy about a woman who tried to kill me."

Steel raised his eyebrows. "So there are fringe benefits to working for me."

Harry nodded. "You got that right. I already told Isabella I'm still working for Greensave until we get enough money saved up to start the farm."

"That works for me, Harry." Steel realized Meera was standing in front of him.

Her brown skin shone, her eyes bright. Her long black hair fell onto a yellow blouse, a long white skirt beneath that. Slender. Calm. Elegant.

He liked her demeanor. He hadn't talked to her much and was glad she had approached him. He cleared his throat. "I'm sorry Clay got hurt, Meera."

She smiled. "Yes, but he will live. He is a protector, like you, so he worries about his family. I told him that if one man stands up and acts heroically, then we all need to support that man or soon there will be no one left to stand up."

Her voice softened. "He agreed, Jack, and will tell you that himself sometime before you leave. Thank you for standing up so many times for all of us."

He took a deep breath and smiled up at her. "No wonder Clay loves you so much."

She winked at him and walked away.

Christie squeezed his hand again. "Thank goodness I'm not the only one who thinks logically. Sometimes I think you men are too emotional."

He chuckled. "I think you're right."

Carol wandered over, sitting on the arm of his chair. Tall and slender, she wore slacks and a blouse, her hazel eyes studying him. "Jack, since everyone is saying it, I have to too."

He raised an eyebrow.

"I wouldn't want any other man to take care of our daughter. She's strong because of you, and she survived two years of kidnapping because of you. I survived last year because of you. We all accept the risk. And Rachel would never want any father other than the one she has."

"That means a lot to me, Carol."

"You mean a lot to both of us, Jack." She bent over and kissed his forehead, and then left to talk to Isabella.

He heaved a sigh, looking at Christie. "It's nice to be loved."

Christie winked at him. "Don't forget that."

Rachel hurried into the room from the outside door, stopping in front of him, her face lit up with excitement. Her red T-shirt was loose over her jean shorts, her skin glistening with sweat. "Dad, there's lots of birds here. Want to do a species-finding challenge?"

"Sure, why not?" He turned to Christie.

She waved him off cheerfully. "You better spend as much time as possible with her, because as soon as I'm healthy I'm going to demand our road trip."

Rachel looked at Christie. "Sometime we could do a species challenge too."

Christie beamed at her. "I'd be happy if you just taught me the names of all the birds you know, Rachel."

"Deal." She pulled on Steel's hand. "Let's go, Dad!"

He chuckled. Rising, he pecked Christie on the lips, and then walked out of the house with Rachel, her auburn hair shining in the sunlight. The sweet whistle of a western meadowlark greeted him. Grassy fields, forest, and nearby mountains made him smile.

"Rachel, I'm going to give you a one minute head start."

She smiled mischievously. "You're going to regret that, Dad."

He laughed. "I don't think so."

She walked away, looking for birds. As he watched her go he felt a swelling of warmth in his heart. They were all safe. No regrets. And he could relax.

He had put all Greensave assignments on hold for three months while everyone recuperated. Afia Ameen had contacted him through her protection agency, happy to hear he was safe. He had called Wyatt, relieved to hear the man was going to live and be healthy. Wyatt had said he was proud to help him—and that his door was always open.

He wasn't worried about anyone anymore. Just relaxed and at peace. He wasn't responsible for the choices others made, including Christie, but he could honor and cherish them.

"Come on, Dad!"

He walked into the grass, glad to have nothing to do but look for birds.

* * *

Want to see what happens next to Jack Steel?

When the head of Army Black Ops is murdered, Steel hunts the killers, and becomes the hunted.

SKIP THE FOLLOWING EXCERPT AND
BUY STEEL JUSTICE ON AMAZON.

* * *

## AUTHOR'S NOTE

*The Jack Steel series is in development*
*for a major motion picture!*
Hooray! I can't wait...

Thank you so much for reading my thriller! I wondered how it would feel to have someone you love with you on life-or-death Ops, and that idea began Steel Assassin. I hope you enjoyed reading the book as much as I enjoyed writing it.

Reviews help me keep writing, and encourage other readers to take a chance on a new author they haven't read before. So if you enjoyed the book, please leave a review. Every review, even a few words, helps!

Thank you!

~ Geoff

Turn the page to read an excerpt from Book 3
in the Jack Steel series

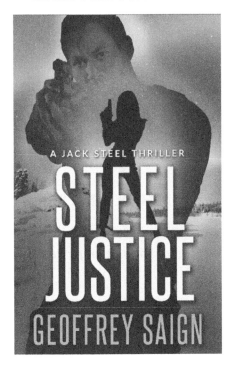

A JACK STEEL THRILLER

# STEEL JUSTICE

## GEOFFREY SAIGN

**Someone is murdering top military personnel and senators for a secret agenda. When Steel tries to help a friend, the killers put him in their sights. To stop a powerful mercenary organization from destroying his family and life, Steel is going to have to start a small war. He's also going to have to redraw the line of justice...**

## PART 1
## OP: GENERAL MORRIS

# CHAPTER 1

JACK STEEL SAT IN the lobby of the Richmond Marriott Hotel not looking at anyone in particular, but watching everyone. He was a half-hour early, but he wasn't busy today and felt he owed General Morris the benefit of the doubt. The lobby was cool, like its marble floor, so it made wearing his black shell jacket comfortable. Black jeans, a black T-shirt, and soft-soled hiking boots completed his outfit.

He picked up an outdoor magazine on a small nearby table and found an article on bison regenerating grasslands in western states. That interested him. He had a deep abiding love of nature and the current global warming and environmental degradation bothered him. He also wanted to appear occupied.

In a half-hour, precisely on time, General Morris strode into the lobby, ignoring Steel as he walked to the check-in counter. The tall, ebony general was dressed in a long black coat for the February weather and carried a single small suitcase. Graying hair and glasses gave him a distinguished appearance.

In minutes Morris left the front desk, and Harry Thorton arrived via the front hotel door. Six-three, broad-shouldered and lean, he was built like a linebacker. Wearing jeans, boots, a flannel shirt, and an insulated black shell jacket similar to Steel's, he strode to another lounge chair and sat down, not looking at Morris or Steel. His easy-going face appeared calm and relaxed.

As General Morris carried his overnight bag to the elevators, Steel got up and walked a half-dozen steps behind him. He ended up standing next to the general in front of the elevator doors, but didn't look at him.

An elevator opened, two guests exited, and Steel followed Morris in. When the doors shut, Morris looked at him, his hand extended with car keys.

Steel took the keys and nodded. "Just as a precaution, stay in your room tonight, sir."

Morris nodded. "Will do. I appreciate this, Steel."

"Glad to help out, sir. Anytime." Steel turned to him. "I appreciated the help from Colonel Jeffries last September. You authorized that and it made a difference."

The general said softly, "I was glad to help, Steel. We owe you for what you did."

The elevator stopped at the third floor. Before the general exited, Steel checked the hallway in both directions, and then led the general down to his room. Morris unlocked the door, and Steel pulled his unregistered Glock 19 and entered the room, quickly walking through the two-room suite, checking closets and the balcony outside. All empty, as expected.

Finished, he returned to the living room and looked at Morris. "No one knows you're here, so any visitors are suspect. Don't open the door for anyone, general."

Morris smiled. "I can do that."

Steel returned a brief smile. "I'll check in and keep you updated. Call if you need anything."

Morris set down his bag and looked at Steel. "Do you believe my theory is possible?"

Steel regarded the general. He liked and respected the man. "You oversee Army Intelligence for a reason, sir. Your concern is enough for me to take it seriously." He didn't add that he owed Morris help if he needed it, regardless of his feelings.

Morris stared at him. "How much do you believe in justice, Steel?"

Steel hesitated. "Sir?"

"How far should we go to ensure justice?" Morris' voice was calm.

Considering the question, Steel said, "You know what I've done in the past, sir. It depends on what's at stake."

"Some feel they are above the law. That justice doesn't apply to them." Morris stepped closer. "How can we win if that's true? If the law can't touch them?"

"We have to do what's right, sir. No matter what the cost."

Morris nodded. "That's why I picked you, Steel. We agree on that. No matter what the cost."

Steel asked a question that had been gnawing at him. "Why not bring in CID, CIA, or Army intelligence?"

Morris frowned. "I don't know who I can trust inside."

"Hell."

"You're lucky, Steel. You have a family. Take care of them. Keep them close." Morris shrugged. "I have a grandson I see too little of, along with his mother."

Waiting to see if the general had anything else to say, Steel said softly, "See you soon, sir."

"Goodnight, Steel."

Steel exited the room and walked down to the elevator. For ten minutes he casually stood there. The hallway remained empty except for a few couples in their fifties that exited rooms and disappeared down the hallway corners. A few took the elevator in front of him down.

General Morris' words about justice had set him on edge. He wasn't sure what the general was implying or what he wanted. Morris had a lot on his mind and perhaps had just wanted a sounding board. Maybe it was just a conversation.

Letting it go, Steel finally rode the elevator down to the lobby. Striding to the front door, he noted Harry rising to follow him out. Once outside, Harry split off from him and headed to Steel's nearby Jeep, where Christie was waiting. Steel didn't glance at

Christie—though he was tempted to. The sun was setting—it was five-thirty p.m.

Steel strode to General Morris' car in the lot, a black sedan with tinted windows, and got in. No one would be able to see who was driving, and the evening lack of light would make it even harder to ID who was behind the wheel in the general's car. Still, he pulled his Glock and set it on the passenger seat and pulled a Lycra hood over his head.

In thirty minutes he pulled into General Morris' attached house garage, one hand on the steering wheel, the other holding the Glock just below the dash. The garage was empty, but he checked to the sides and in the mirrors. When the garage door closed, he pulled on non-latex surgical gloves, pulled a rag from his pocket, and wiped down the steering wheel and car door.

He had visited Morris' large house earlier in the week. This time he entered it from the garage, his Glock leveled. Stepping into the hallway running from the front door to the back, he looked right. Harry and Christie were already entering through the back door, also wearing Lycra hoods.

Harry carried a Glock along his thigh, Christie a Sig Sauer P320. Both also wore surgical gloves. Christie wore jeans, a gray light jacket over a black blouse, and soft-soled shoes. Her brown-and-blond streaked hair was hidden by her Lycra hood. They nodded to him and he pointed up.

Christie led Harry through the living room entrance to the right and up the stairway along the wall, guns up, while Steel remained downstairs, carefully going through all the rooms and closets.

Finished checking the house, they all met in the living room. Steel shrugged. "Now we wait. Stay sharp. Stay on coms."

Christie winked at him, and Steel smiled.

"You got it, Steel." Harry nodded, his voice and expression also on the light side.

Steel watched Harry leave out the back door, while Christie climbed the stairs. All alone in the living room, he decided it was going to be a long night.

# CHAPTER 2

STEEL STOOD IN THE front corner of the darkened living room. He felt comfortable without having any lights on. Years of spelunking had given him almost a second sight in the dark. Another advantage over enemies.

It was nearly midnight and he was tired of sitting, so he was standing for a change, squeezed in between two bookcases. From his corner vantage point he could fire through the front entryway between the hallway and living room if anyone came through the front door. He also had a clear view of the far side of the room, where a second open entryway connected to the main hallway.

The stairway across the room led up four steps in the far corner opposite him to a small landing where the stairs turned and ran up along the side of the wall to the second-floor bedrooms. A wall at the top of the stairs blocked any view of the second floor.

The house was dark and Steel's clothing blended in. He had attached a silencer to the Glock, which was holstered. The surgical gloves on his hands ensured he didn't leave prints anywhere in the house. He also wore a throat mike and earpiece.

On-the-hour check-ins were all he permitted, so at midnight he murmured, "Harry?"

"Quiet," came the whisper back.

"Christie?" he murmured.

"Quiet." Her voice was calm.

Steel wondered about General Morris' theory again. Two weeks ago, on a Saturday, the acting Secretary of Defense, Marv Vonders, had died in his bathtub from a blow to his head as the result of a fall. Bathrooms were still the most dangerous place in a house, and the man had been sixty-eight, his death ruled accidental. A week ago, on a Sunday, Senator Seldman—a high-ranking senator on the Senate Intelligence Committee—had died from carbon monoxide poisoning. The seventy-year-old had accidentally left his car running in his garage, and his townhome bedroom was above it. He was found dead in his bed, his death also ruled accidental. Suicide had been ruled out based on the absence of a note, and the fact that Seldman had seemed engaged in his life.

Now a week later, on Friday, Steel was in General Morris' house to spend the weekend, to satisfy Morris' suspicions that the previous deaths were not accidental.

Besides heading up U.S. Army intelligence, in the past General Morris had also overseen the now sidelined Blackhood Ops. Morris had called Steel last week and asked that his protection agency, Greensave, guard him for one weekend. For some reason Morris didn't want to go through Army or any other security channels.

Morris had only said to Steel, *I trust you and you're anonymous in this.* The general hadn't offered Steel any intel that the previous deaths were anything but accidents—and Steel hadn't asked for it. Nor did Morris give any explanation about why he thought he might be linked to the other deaths and next in line for a murder. The elderly general was also paying cash so nothing could be traced.

As obsessive as Steel was with details and security, he still doubted the general had anything substantive to back up his concerns that two high-ranking government officials had been assassinated. However, Steel always operated on gut instinct so he couldn't discount the general's hunch.

Protecting Morris was the first protection gig for his company, Greensave, since the cartel business five months ago. They had all been a little banged up, especially Harry and Christie. But now his core team was healthy and eager to take on any assignment. Harry and Christie had spent the last months limited to exercising and practicing drills in the VR station to get themselves back into shape—something he had insisted on before taking on any new assignments.

His thoughts drifted to Christie, who troubled him more than General Morris' assassination theory at the moment. The question he had been pondering for months was whether or not to buy her an engagement ring. She hadn't asked for one, never even hinted at it. And he didn't need a ring to guarantee how he felt about her. But he still thought about it. They had been together for a year and a half and he couldn't see his life without her in it. He knew she felt the same way about him. They were both happy.

He considered his daughter, Rachel. She had just turned thirteen, and was doing well. However, a two-year kidnapping that she had survived always made him careful about any decisions involving her. Rachel liked Christie, so he didn't think his daughter would mind if they got married, but he didn't want to ask for her opinion—a teenager shouldn't have to make that kind of decision. It was up to him.

He could always ask Christie how she felt about a ring. But he didn't want to pressure her either. The choice of getting a ring seemed more difficult than planning General Morris' protection Op. He smiled over that. Not a bad problem to have.

"We've got company." Harry's voice was barely a murmur from the backyard. "Single male approaching the rear door. No weapon in hand."

"Copy that. Everyone hold positions. No coms unless necessary." Steel tensed and drew his gun, while edging to the front window to peer out past the drawn blinds. No one was visible in the street, front sidewalk, or at the front door. Yet a half-block down a car was parked on the side of the road, lights off. It hadn't been there earlier. That bothered him, since in this neighborhood everyone had their cars in garages and driveways. Especially at midnight. "Car in the street," he whispered.

He strode across the living room to the hallway, which ran from the front door to the solid wood back door. Bringing up the Glock, he aimed it at the back door. Deciding something, he quietly ran down the hallway and ducked into a den doorway near the back door, pressing his back against the inner wall, waiting.

A very faint scraping came from the door. Glass being cut. No alarms went off. Steel had asked Morris to turn off the house alarm system for the three-day weekend. He didn't want motion or sound detectors scaring someone away.

To make the deaths of Secretary of Defense Marv Vonders and Senator Seldman look like accidents, their security systems had to have been bypassed and then turned back on by potential murderers. The intruder here could be a burglar, but the chance of that on the weekend Morris was worried about being murdered was highly unlikely. Yet the fact that the man was cutting glass, which would leave evidence of a break-in, didn't fit the pattern of the other two deaths.

"The man just pulled a gun." Harry's voice was still a murmur.

"Hold positions." Steel abruptly decided General Morris had been right. Which meant someone had assassinated the Secretary of Defense and a senator on the Senate Intelligence Committee. Professionals. He felt a needle of worry for Morris, but he let that slip away to focus. "Everyone watch your six," he murmured.

The back door opened and someone stepped inside, quietly closing it. Steel tightened his trigger finger. There were some sounds of a door opening, followed by a soft metallic scraping. The closet door and the alarm system box. The intruder had to be disarming the security system. Morris had it installed decades ago and hadn't bothered putting it on the second floor, which would have made it harder to find and get to before the alarm went off. Still, someone had to have been in the house once already to know where it was. This had all been carefully planned.

Soft footsteps quickly passed his doorway, and Steel slid out halfway, knowing Harry would warn him if a second man was coming in the rear door. Speaking softly, he said, "Don't move or I'll put a bullet in you. No talking. Raise your hands."

The man stopped near the living room entryway and raised his hands, his right holding a pistol. He appeared six feet, average build, wearing a black leather jacket. At a lean six-two, one-hundred-ninety pounds, Steel wasn't intimidated by most men.

But he knew in fights size often didn't matter and he preferred caution. Remaining six feet back from the intruder, he said, "Slowly throw the gun into the next room."

The man complied.

Steel added, "Hands on top of your head, slowly, then drop to your knees, then to your stomach."

The man placed his hands atop his head, and then bent his knees.

The front door opened quietly and another man entered. Steel saw the glint of a gun in his hand.

In a flash the man in front of him rolled sideways through the entryway.

Steel fired once, sure he hit the man's left shoulder. Squatting and moving sideways to lean against the hallway wall, he fired twice at the man crouching at the front door and hit him in the chest and head. Ducking, he rolled through the den doorway, rose to a knee, and fired half a dozen times through the den doorway into the opposite hall wall, about waist-high. No sounds, no gasps, no falling body.

Bullets came through the living room wall, hitting the hallway wall. Steel rose and stepped to the side of the den doorway. When the shots ended, he glanced out and looked at the bullet holes in the two walls to estimate the position of the shooter. Stepping out, he fired another five shots into the wall while swiftly moving sideways toward the living room entryway.

Squatting low, gun extended, Steel peered past the doorway. The intruder wasn't on the floor. He edged farther out. No one on the upper stairway either. The man was likely on the first landing, four steps up, just around the corner before the staircase turned. He didn't hear any footsteps or creaking steps—and he had checked earlier—they creaked. But the gunshots might have disguised those sounds.

Gun up, he slid fast along the wall. The man still didn't come into view. Once past the doorway, he ran lightly to the front living room entryway. The man at the front door was dead. Crouching, then sliding to his belly, he silently crawled into the living room behind a sofa he had positioned there earlier. At the far end of it he slowly peered around it. He wanted to see if the intruder had a serious injury and if he could risk approaching him to question the man.

Three bullets bit the furniture and he ducked back. Crawling backward, he reached the hallway and stood up. Shifting his gun to his left hand, he stuck it around the corner and fired a half-dozen rounds into the far corner of the stairway landing.

Silence. He crouched, peeked around the corner, and saw a body slumped on the staircase. "Two intruders down. Hold positions. Check in."

After loading a fresh magazine into the Glock, he crossed the living room, his gun aimed at the man who was lying on his back. In seconds he bent over, pressed his gun into the man's neck, and took the gun from the man's limp hand. He ejected the magazine and round in the chamber and tossed them to different parts of the room. Then he quickly checked the man's pulse. Dead. Shoulder, neck, and chest wounds.

Something glinted from inside the man's partially open jacket. Pulling it open revealed a machete held against the inside lining of the jacket with elastic straps. That startled him. After ripping the man's button-down shirt apart, he quickly checked the man's neck, arms, back, and chest—no tattoos. Made no sense. The violent street gang, MS-13, hired out to kill, and they used machetes. But a Caucasian with no tattoos didn't fit the MS-13 profile of a Central American ethnicity with tattoos, which often included *Mara Salvatrucha* or *13* for MS-13.

It also worried him that no one had checked in.

Simultaneously shots came from upstairs and outside. Outside it was a muffled machine gun.

Steel swore under his breath and ran up the stairs. "Christie!" he murmured into his throat mike.

# CHAPTER 3

H ARRY CROUCHED IN A rear corner in the backyard, a fence at his back, an evergreen in front of him. Early February temps were above freezing, but chilly. Richmond, Virginia also had a rare foot of snow on the ground. Harry had dressed for it.

He wore hiking boots and wool socks for the cold and snow, and the flannel shirt and insulated shell jacket kept him warm. He held a silenced Glock 17. Steel had offered to buy him a Glock 19 as a wedding present, but he had refused. The slightly larger gun felt better in his hands. He also liked the two extra shells of the 17.

General Morris' backyard was a five-acre lot, with ten-foot-tall wooden privacy fences on the sides which began ten feet out from the rear corners of the house, running seventy feet back into the yard. Harry had decided to squat behind the row of Thuja Green Giant evergreens that paralleled the privacy fence. The hardy trees grew fast as narrow cones and provided good cover for him. The scent of pine filled the air. Across the yard was another row of the same trees.

He was thinking of Isabella. She had texted him before they had arrived at Morris' house, sending a photo of a simple wedding dress she had found on eBay. She also was going to try on her mother's wedding dress while she was in Mexico and text him a photo. Colombian, lean with black hair, chiseled features, a high forehead and narrow chin, Isabella was beautiful to him even in jeans and a tee. She was in Mexico for the next two weeks to visit her father and tell him of their plans to marry. She hadn't wanted to do it over the phone.

Harry understood that. Her father, Carlos, had almost gotten them all killed five months ago, and Isabella wanted to see what her father's reaction would be to her marrying one of the people he had targeted. She also wanted to spend time with her two brothers, Mario and Pedro.

Harry was supposed to marry Isabella in two months, if Isabella's father could attend—they had decided it was best to do it in Montana, where Harry's parents lived. The wedding was a somewhat hasty decision, but Harry knew it was right because all he felt inside was a glow. Isabella didn't want to wait either. They weren't eighteen-year-old kids; he was thirty, she was twenty-nine.

His inner glow was quickly replaced with cold caution when the man appeared. He spotted the intruder on one of his scans of the backyard with the night vision monocular glued to his eye. The MNVD gave him a fifty-one-degree field, which was enough. The intruder was sidling along the back of the house, coming from the south. It was dark, overcast with no moonlight, so he was glad he could give Steel a warning.

Steel's request to *watch your six* made Harry wary. Steel expected more operatives outside. The man was cautious to a fault, which was a good thing. Caution kept you alive. Harry had the skillset of an ex-marine, but Steel's abilities were at another level, which he hoped to match someday.

He peered between two of the evergreens. He had a good view along the north side of the house and across the backyard. Steel had felt the three of them were enough. But the sudden appearance of the intruder made Harry wary.

Once the man had entered the back door, Harry stood quietly and made his way closer to the house along the fence, remaining behind the row of evergreens. Steel had asked them to hold positions, but something about that didn't feel right; and Steel always advised following your instincts. Someone could be coming in the front door too. And if he had to charge the house to help Steel and Christie, he wanted to be ready.

He almost bolted to the back door when he heard the exchanges of shots, but he forced himself to hold back. He was glad he did when Steel asked them again to hold positions. That was hard to do when one of his best friends and his sister were in the house. Christie was as capable as himself, but he still felt protective toward her. Brotherly love.

Adding to his tension, five months ago in the cartel mess he and Christie had lost their brother, Dale. It had shaken both of them, and had made them even closer. They spent a lot of time together at Steel's house, training, sharing meals, joking. It made the loss of their brother much easier to handle than if either of them had been on their own.

Still, he found himself sweating over Christie's safety. He consoled himself with the fact that Steel was in the house. The man loved her as much as he did and would take a bullet before he let anything happen to her.

Steel's comment of *intruders* meant a second hostile had come through the front door. He decided not to check in. If someone was nearby, he didn't want to risk even a whisper.

Pausing, he glanced east and west along the fence. He didn't see any movement. Nothing across the yard. He considered things. There might have been more operatives in the parked car that Steel had mentioned, and thus a third hostile might be preparing to enter through the front door. He made his way quickly along the fence.

Reaching the end of the privacy fence and the last evergreen, he glanced around the fence to check the north side. Nothing. As expected.

Moving fast, he sidled along the north side of the house to the front corner. Peering around it, he didn't see anyone near the front door. He spotted the empty car a half block south of the house, parked on the opposite side of the street. The monocular didn't show anyone in the car. That made him nervous. The driver could be anywhere. It seemed possible that two men had come to kill General Morris. But he would expect at least a lookout in the car.

Pulling back from the corner, he crouched and listened. He had excellent hearing.

Silence.

He waited a few seconds more, and heard a barely detectable crunch of snow. What tensed his back is that it came from behind him. Not thinking, he leapt sideways, twisting so he would end up on his left side, facing the backyard. With his Glock in both hands, he began firing while he was falling, before he even had the man in sights. Another skill Steel had forced him to practice.

Silenced bullets chewed their way across the siding of the house where he had been squatting.

Harry caught a blur near the east corner of the house. The man pulled back out of sight, and Harry stopped firing after the third shot.

Rising quickly, he scrambled around the front corner of the house and crouched. Whoever was behind the house must have tracked his movements. The hostile might have come from the adjacent wooded lot behind General Morris' house. Harry took a deep breath. He had come close to being ambushed. Moving forward had probably saved his life.

He wasn't sure what the next best move was. Steel's code for problem-solving situations ran through his mind: *Stay calm, assess options, look for a solution.*

Taking a risk, he bolted across the front yard in a southwest diagonal, across the street, and toward the parked car. All the front yards on the block had a few large oak trees, and he ran from one to the next until he was closer to the car. He viewed its interior again with the monocular. Empty.

Settling on a position behind a tree, he waited. The killer was either going to run on foot out the backyard or return to the car. In a whisper he said, "Third intruder, machine gun, backyard. I'm across the street watching the parked car."

Gripping his pistol hard, it bothered him that no one came back on coms. What if more operatives had entered the house? He'd kill them all if they hurt Christie. His older brother Clay would help him hunt them down if need be.

He took a deep breath to calm his racing thoughts. His back was stiff, his hands clenched on his gun. Shaking his head, he sagged against the tree and waited.

# CHAPTER 4

C HRISTIE STOOD INSIDE THE bedroom walk-in closet, its sliding door open six inches. Keeping her body mostly concealed behind the inner wall, she could view the bedroom door and the north bedroom window. After two hours she was feeling warm. The nonsurgical gloves on her hands didn't help. Morris kept his house temperature at seventy-eight. Maybe because he was older.

Steel had put her in the bedroom, because out of the three positions for the Op it was likely the safest. That didn't annoy her. In fact she found it endearing that he cared about her. However it had made her smile earlier when she reminded him of who had saved who's butt in the cartel mess five months ago. He had smiled at her and winked. With his curly brown hair and light olive-colored skin, she thought he was handsome. His skin tone was from his Cajun creole heritage—Spanish, French, Native American, and Caribbean. An American mutt.

Lately he had been acting a bit weird around her. As if he was nervous. And his smile was off. He had something on his mind. Patient, she had decided not to press him. She knew he was head over heels about her, in a good, solid Jack Steel way. So whatever was bothering him wasn't something major, like an impending breakup. But she couldn't figure what else it might be. His daughter Rachel and his ex-wife Carol were doing well, and she and Steel were doing extremely well. She was getting along comfortably with Rachel, and the dogs were healthy. As much as she tried, she couldn't think of anything else that might be troubling him.

Sometimes Steel just made too big of a deal out of small things. His obsessive nature led to his excellence in black ops and protection work, but it also put more stress on him in simple relationship issues. She almost chuckled out loud over that. His issue. And he never made it hers, so she would just wait out the mystery.

The first shots from downstairs revved her pulse, but she held her position.

More shots downstairs.

She turned rigid, but forced herself to remain calm. It was hard at times not to be worried over Steel, but the last mess with the cartels had also taught her that worry wasn't a bad thing. Carelessness was. Still, in the back of her mind was the gnawing thought of her brother Dale dying only five months ago...

She slid the door open and stepped out of the closet, her SIG Sauer P320 compact aimed at the bedroom door. Quickly she crossed the room. On coms Steel requested they hold positions again so she paused just before the door. She debated if she should return to the closet. That didn't feel right.

Carefully she opened the bedroom door, peeked left and right, and stepped into the dark hallway. To her left the hallway led to more bedrooms. To her right the hallway ended in twenty feet, where it turned left to the top of the stairway, which was hidden by the wall. Stepping out, gun still up, she slowly walked right.

Faint whispers of sound made her glance over her shoulder. She barely glimpsed the dark figure rushing her, swinging something. The intruder must have come out of one of the bedrooms. With no time to turn, she collapsed and rolled forward on her side, aware of pain on her upper back. Something had cut through her Kevlar.

She had the gun up, but whatever glinted in the dark was swung back the other way at her. Jerking her hands back, the shiny object still hit her gun barrel, driving her arms to the side. Kicking out at her attacker's legs, she hit his knee, then scrambled back on her butt, swinging the gun up again. He kicked her hands, knocking the gun free, and she kicked her heel at the man's crotch. She missed, but not by much because the man groaned and retreated from her into the bedroom, partially bent over. The door was immediately closed.

Scrambling back, she swept her hand across the floor until she found the SIG. Her upper back was burning as she rose to her feet. Cautiously she approached the closed bedroom door.

Blows sounded from inside.

She quietly opened the door, knelt, and stuck her gun and one eye around the corner.

The killer was already whirling, releasing whatever was in his hand in a sideways motion. Jerking back, she heard the object thump into the door near her head—a machete.

She slid down to her shoulder onto the wood floor, arms and gun extended now, and fired at the kneeling man. They both exchanged shots. Bullets thumped into the door above her head, but the man collapsed and didn't move.

More shots outside. A machine gun. Brother Harry. Her heart raced. She wanted to run to him, but Steel would be ahead of her. And she wanted to make certain her target was down for good.

Rising, she stepped forward, gun still aimed, and sized the killer up—something she was good at. He matched her height at five-eight, thirty-five—four years older than her—and a fit one-seventy pounds. Thirty pounds over her. Caucasian. Dead.

# CHAPTER 5

STEEL TOOK THE STEPS up three at a time, gun ready, sweat on his brow over his worry and not the exertion. Slowing at the top to make sure he wouldn't be blindsided, he carefully peered around the corner. Empty hallway. Striding to the bedroom door, he glanced inside.

Christie was crouched over a body, her back to him, her Lycra hood rolled up to her forehead. His shoulders relaxed, but then tightened again when he hit the bedroom light and saw the machete and bullet holes in the door, and the slice across her back. He swallowed. She hadn't held her position. That unnerved him, but he shoved the emotion down. She knew what she was doing.

She rose quickly, facing him. "Harry?"

Harry's voice came over their coms from the street. "The intruder is making a run for the car."

Christie frowned, but Steel said, "I'll go. Check the upstairs and find out how this one came in. Make sure it's clear."

"All right." She winced slightly.

She had to be seriously hurt, but he couldn't wait any longer. Hustling back to the stairway, he took the steps down two at a time, at the bottom deciding on the front door. The inside solid oak door was still partly open. Stepping over the body, he glanced out. Lights were on in houses up and down the street. They had to get out before the police arrived.

A man ran from the southwest corner of the house toward the solitary car parked in the street. Steel felt an urge to let the killer escape and try to follow him, but their car was parked a block away and they wouldn't be able to get to it fast enough.

He aimed at the man's legs and fired twice. Falling in the street, the killer twisted and sent a spray of bullets at him. He ducked back into the house as the door took hits.

Two single shots were fired. Harry.

Silence.

Steel whispered, "Harry?"

"Hostile down," answered Harry.

Steel stepped out as Harry walked into the street, his gun targeting the killer. Steel remained on the front stoop to cover him.

Harry was soon beside the body and squatted. "He's finished, Jack."

Steel said quickly, "Grab his phone, a facial photo, and any ID. Check for tattoos. Hurry."

Steel checked the body near his feet. No phone, ID, or tattoos. But he found a machete. He snapped a quick photo of the man's face with his phone, and then hustled back through the house to check the body on the stairs. No phone or ID. After taking a photo, he hurried up the stairs three at a time, back in the bedroom in seconds.

Christie was sitting on the bed and didn't look up at him as she studied a phone in her hands. "The killer climbed up on the south side and cut through a bedroom window. Skilled."

Steel finally holstered his gun, got out his phone, and called General Morris—on speed dial. While he waited for an answer, he rolled up his hood and walked around the foot of the bed so he could see Christie's back. Her brown and blond streaked hair barely reached the slice across her upper back. The machete had cut through her Kevlar. He couldn't see how badly she was hurt, but the machete attacks on the dummy they had stuffed beneath the bed covers were all deep. His stomach tightened. He couldn't help it.

"It's just a scratch, Steel. No worries." She turned to look up at him, her green eyes steady. She winked. "The dummy had it worse. Both of them."

Heaving a breath, he kept his voice even, professional. "You didn't hold position."

She swung farther around to face him, a slight touch of humor in her eyes. "If our positions had been reversed, would you have held your position in the closet after hearing all those shots fired?"

"Obviously not."

"My point exactly, Steel."

He didn't see any concern on her heart-shaped face and her eyes were calm, which further relaxed him. Morris wasn't answering and there was no voice mail. That bothered him. Maybe the general had gone to bed and shut it off. They would have to check on him immediately, which meant a very late visit to the hotel. He hung up. At least they had thwarted Morris' killers. That made him feel good.

"I found this in the killer's pocket." Christie held up a small plastic bag of white powder. "With the machete and coke, they were trying to make it look like MS-13 was hired for a cartel revenge hit from last September. But my guy here has no tattoos and he's very white. Yours?"

Steel lifted his chin. "Same for both. Machetes. Caucasian. No tattoos."

Harry appeared in the doorway, his hood rolled up too. "Same with the guy in the street. Caucasian, no arm, back, or chest tattoos. Got his phone, no ID. He made a call to someone though. Blocked."

Steel nodded. "All pros. Morris was right about the assassinations."

"Why send four men to kill an elderly general?" Christie looked at them.

"They knew he might have protection." Though Steel didn't know how that was possible.

Harry lifted his chin to Christie, his face showing a rare moment of strain. "You okay, sis?"

"I'm good, little brother." Christie looked up from the phone she was holding, her brow furrowed. "You?"

Harry nodded. "I'm okay." His voice lowered. "You got cut?"

"It looks worse than it is." She turned to Steel. "This phone calendar has four dates marked with latitude and longitude. The first date and location are for here tonight."

"We'll turn it all over to General Morris." Steel turned to leave. "Let's get out of here."

The phone in Christie's hand vibrated. Steel frowned and hesitated.

Christie looked up. "The caller's number is blocked."

"Put it on speaker." Steel put a finger over his lips as Christie answered the phone.

Silence.

After three seconds Steel was going to have her cut off the call, but a voice came through. Steel couldn't place the dialect. American, with a hint of Caribbean.

"Given that I am not hearing the agreed protocol response, I have to assume that whoever you are, you have killed my associates. Thus I am informing you of two things. The first is that you have failed. I have General Morris. You can save his life by giving us your names."

Steel became rigid, his hand clenched. He glared at the phone. Christie stared at it too, and Harry moved closer.

Steel had to work to keep his voice calm. He didn't want to admit that Morris was already as good as dead. "Let me talk to the general."

"You will understand that he has a hard time talking now. He lost some teeth and had some other unfortunate things occur so he's not as coherent as he was when you last saw him. He is loyal though. He hasn't given you up."

Steel didn't reply, his eyes glued to the phone. Morris had already been tortured—Steel felt responsible.

Christie bit her lip. Harry squatted, staring at the cell with narrowed eyes.

The man continued, "The best I can do is pass along two approved sentences. Morris said this will verify for you that he's here and alive."

Steel tensed. "Not good enough. I won't know if he's still alive."

The man's voice remained calm. "You don't have a choice, do you? I'm a professional, like you. I have no need to lie."

Steel grimaced. "Give the sentences to me."

The man recited Morris' sentences; "Hey, Buddy, give him your name or you're going to get me killed. Jay would never do that."

Steel winced, his hands fists. He wasn't sure what Morris was trying to tell him, but he decided to verify it as accurate. The message felt too odd for the killers to make it up. "Let's say I believe the general is still alive, now what?"

The man continued. "If I don't have your full name in three seconds—and I have to assume *Buddy* is not your real name—I am going to kill him."

Steel didn't want to give the man his name. They could come after his daughter or Carol—his ex. He also doubted giving his name would keep Morris alive. He kept his voice level, deciding to give them a common surname from Louisiana. "Pete Comeaux. If you set up an exchange for Morris' release, I'll gladly meet you."

"Comeaux is Cajun, correct? You don't sound it."

Steel didn't hesitate. "I was born in Louisiana, but I moved north when I was very young."

"Ah. It sounds plausible, but I don't believe you. I have a very good sense of when someone is lying and I didn't expect to get your name. So General Morris will die as originally intended. You know how. And I'm certain you will not report it, because if you killed four men, without the general to verify your story you are not very credible, are you? And how can you prove a dead man hired you?" The man paused. "Don't bother returning to the hotel. The room is clean. We're elsewhere. We don't leave trails."

Steel stared at the phone. "What else can I give you in exchange for the general's life?"

"Unfortunately I have lost all trust in your words," replied the man.

Steel squatted next to Christie, his hands sweaty. "Look, there has to be a way to resolve this."

"There isn't. It's not personal."

Steel disagreed. It was very personal to him. "Wherever you are, whoever you are, if you kill General Morris, I will find you."

The man replied, "Which brings us to the second thing I wish to inform you of. We will find all of you and kill you. Maybe tomorrow. Or in a few days. Weeks. Months. Whenever. You'll never be safe. Look over your shoulder. We'll be there. The men you killed tonight were amateurs. We're not. Enjoy the rest of your life. You have little of it left to live."

The line went dead.

BUY STEEL JUSTICE ON AMAZON NOW

Read all the Jack Steel and Alex Sight Thrillers.

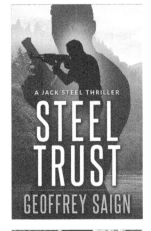
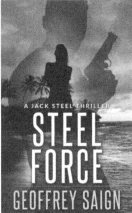
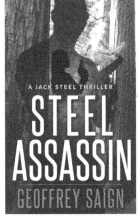
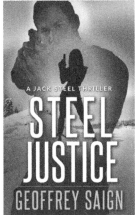
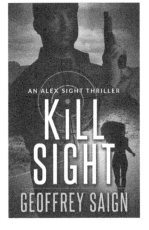

# ACKNOWLEDGMENTS

I WANT TO THANK Stanley Blanchard who used his extensive military background to strengthen the military scenes and give Jack Steel the nuances he needed to play the part. Any mistakes or omissions in anything military is my fault alone. Steve McEllistrem gave the book a read for grammar. I also wish to thank my parents for their critiques—they have always had a sharp sense of what makes a great action thriller. I grew up reading Mom's thrillers, and she's my best critic.

Jack Steel is a character whose discipline gives him advantages over his enemies. As someone who did four-hour workouts nearly daily for five years in kung fu, I thought it would be interesting to create a character who used virtual reality to hone his skills to the nth degree, and then throw him into trouble.

At the time of this writing the cartels run many areas of Mexico. It's not safe to be on the streets in too many places. I've been told that if you see a violent crime in Mexico City, it's best to move on.

The character Jack Steel follows his values above all else. Doing the right thing is something you learn from the adults around you. My parents did a great job of teaching that to me.

Lastly I wish to thank all the men and women who act heroically every day to ensure our safety. We owe you our thanks, gratitude, and support.

A WARD-WINNING AUTHOR GEOFFREY SAIGN has spent many years studying kung fu and sailed all over the South Pacific and Caribbean. He uses that experience and sense of adventure to write the Jack Steel and Alex Sight thriller action series. Geoff loves to sail big boats, hike, and cook—and he infuses all of his writing with his passion for nature. As a swimmer, he considers himself fortunate to live in the Land of 10,000 Lakes, Minnesota.

For email updates from Geoffrey Saign and
your FREE copy of **Steel Trust** go to
www.geoffreysaign.net

Made in the USA
Coppell, TX
02 October 2020

39108485R00218